PRAISE FO

MW01200812

THE TRAITOR BESIDE HER

"Evans's characters are vividly drawn, elevating this story and its revelations about women's little-celebrated contributions to the war effort… Cinematic… Christie-inspired closed-room mystery with vividly drawn characters."

—*Washington Post*

"An exciting read with historical tidbits, a hint of danger, and a touch of romance."

—*Kirkus Reviews*

"World War II and espionage novels are popular, and [Mary Anna Evans] brings both together in a story of young women undercover on the home front."

—*Library Journal*

"*The Traitor Beside Her* is a well-researched wartime spy story, which blends suspense with sharp characterization as Justine Byrne turns code-breaker in the hunt for a ruthless enemy agent."

—Martin Edwards, author of the Rachel Savernake and Lake District Mysteries

"Mary Anna Evans's great talent in *The Traitor Beside Her* is to turn her readers into espionage agents… For Justine Byrne, missing or misinterpreting a clue can be fatal. For the reader, such vicarious mystery and danger are pure enjoyment."

—Larry Baker, author of *Harry and Sue*

THE PHYSICISTS' DAUGHTER
2023—Oklahoma Book Award Winner

"With its smart, Rosie-the-Riveter heroine and intriguing wartime mystery, *The Physicists' Daughter* is a fresh and fascinating glimpse of life on the American home front during WWII. Replete with spies, saboteurs, and save-the-day scientists, the book is a page-turning adventure that sparked my mind and opened my heart. I never wanted the story to end!"

—Amanda Skenandore, author of *The Second Life of Mirielle West*

"A fascinating and intelligent WWII home-front story with a smart heroine who uses her upbringing and knowledge of physics to protect a U.S. factory from a traitor."

—Rhys Bowen, *New York Times* bestselling author of internationally bestselling historical novels, including *The Venice Sketchbook*

The Faye Longchamp Archaeological Mysteries

WRECKED
The Thirteenth Faye Longchamp Archaeological Mystery
2021—Oklahoma Book Award finalist

"Absorbing and erudite, *Wrecked* is a powerful new addition to this long-standing, often awarded series."

—Claire Matturro, *Southern Literary Review*

"The vivid description of post-hurricane events—the misery, the destruction and despair, the hopelessness of losing so much to nature and to looters—all are graphically and realistically portrayed and lend a sense of reality that is incredibly gripping."
—Bill Gresens, Mississippi Valley Archaeological Center

CATACOMBS
The Twelfth Faye Longchamp Archaeological Mystery
2020—Oklahoma Book Award Winner
2020—Will Rogers Medallion Award Winner

"Fast-paced, well-plotted… Those who like richly textured, character-driven mysteries will be rewarded."
—*Publishers Weekly*

"Overall, a solid entry—based in part on an actual Oklahoma bombing—in a popular series."
—*Booklist*

UNDERCURRENTS
The Eleventh Faye Longchamp Archaeological Mystery
2019—Oklahoma Book Award Finalist

"The Longchamp mysteries combine history and mystery in a gritty way that makes them feel different from most amateur-sleuth fare—dark-edged rather than cozy. Faye, too, is not your traditional amateur sleuth; she could just as easily anchor a gritty thriller series and give some of the giants in that genre a run for their money."

—Booklist

"Evans expertly juggles a host of likely suspects, all the while breathing life into the city of Memphis, from its tourist-filled center to its marginal neighborhoods and the spectacular wilderness of the state park."

—Publishers Weekly

BURIALS

The Tenth Faye Longchamp Archaeological Mystery
2018—Willa Literary Award Finalist, Contemporary Fiction
2018—Will Rogers Medallion Award
Bronze Medalist, Western Fiction
2018—Oklahoma Book Award Finalist, Fiction
2017—*Strand* Magazine Top 12 Mystery Novels
2017—*True West* Magazine Best Western Mysteries

"This is a highly successful murder mystery by an author who has mastered the magic and craft of popular genre fiction. Her work embodies the truism that character is destiny."

—Naples Florida Weekly

"Evans's signature archaeological lore adds even more interest to this tale of love, hate, and greed."

—Kirkus Reviews

"Evans sensitively explores the issue of how to balance respecting cultural heritage and gaining knowledge of the past through scientific research."

—Publishers Weekly

ISOLATION
The Ninth Faye Longchamp Archaeological Mystery
2016—Oklahoma Book Award Finalist

"Evans skillfully uses excerpts from the fictional oral history of Cally Stanton, recorded by the Federal Writers' Project in 1935, to dramatize the past."

—Publishers Weekly

"A worthwhile addition to Faye's long-running series that weaves history, mystery, and psychology into a satisfying tale of greed and passion."

—Kirkus Reviews

"Well-drawn characters and setting, and historical and archaeological detail, add to the absorbing story."

—Booklist

"The explosion of the Deepwater Horizon rig in the Gulf of Mexico provides the backdrop for Evans's engaging, character-driven seventh mystery featuring archaeologist Faye Longchamp."

—*Publishers Weekly*

"Details of archaeology, pirate lore, and voodoo complement the strong, sympathetic characters, especially Amande, and the appealing portrait of Faye's family life."

—*Booklist*

STRANGERS
The Sixth Faye Longchamp Archaeological Mystery

"Mary Anna Evans's sixth Faye Longchamp novel continues her string of elegant mysteries that features one of contemporary fiction's most appealing heroines. The author also continues to seek out and to describe settings and locations that would whet the excavating appetite of any practicing or armchair archaeologist. Mary Anna Evans then commences to weave an almost mystical tapestry of mystery throughout her novel."

—Bill Gresens, Mississippi Valley Archaeology Center

"Evans explores themes of protection, love, and loss in her absorbing sixth Faye Longchamp Mystery... Compelling."

—*Publishers Weekly*

"Evans's fifth series mystery...reveals her skill in handling the details of a crime story enhanced by historical facts and scientific discussions on the physical properties of water. Along with further insights into Faye's personal life, the reader ends up with a thoroughly good mystery."

—*Library Journal*

FINDINGS
The Fourth Faye Longchamp Archaeological Mystery

★ "Evans always incorporates detailed research that adds depth and authenticity to her mysteries, and she beautifully conjures up the Micco County, Florida, setting. This is a series that deserves more attention than it garners."

—*Library Journal*, Starred Review

"Faye's capable fourth is a charming mixture of history, mystery, and romance."

—*Kirkus Reviews*

"In Evans's fine fourth archaeological mystery...the story settles into a comfortable pace that allows the reader to savor the characters."

—*Publishers Weekly*

this steadily improving series to female-sleuth fans or those who enjoy archaeology-based thrillers like Beverly Connor's Lindsay Chamberlain novels."

—*Booklist*

"Evans delivers a convincing read… The archaeological adventures are somewhat reminiscent of Tony Hillerman's Jim Chee mysteries. While the story is complex, *Relics* will engage the imagination of readers attracted to unearthing the secrets of lost cultures."

—*School Library Journal*

"A fascinating look at contemporary archaeology but also a twisted story of greed and its effects."

—*Dallas Morning News*

ARTIFACTS

The First Faye Longchamp Archaeological Mystery
2004—Benjamin Franklin Award for Mystery/Suspense
2004—Patrick D. Smith Florida Literature Award

"A haunting, atmospheric story."

—P. J. Parrish, *New York Times* bestselling author

"The shifting little isles along the Florida Panhandle—hurricane-wracked bits of land filled with plenty of human history—serve as the effective backdrop for Evans's debut, a tale of greed, archaeology, romance, and murder."

—*Publishers Weekly*

"First-novelist Evans introduces a strong female sleuth in this extremely promising debut, and she makes excellent use of her archaeological subject matter, weaving past and present together in a multilayered, compelling plot."

—*Booklist*

THE
DARK
LIBRARY

THE

DARK

LIBRARY

MARY ANNA
EVANS

Poisoned Pen
PRESS

Published by Poisoned Pen Press, an imprint of Sourcebooks
P.O. Box 4410, Naperville, Illinois 60567-4410
(630) 961-3900
sourcebooks.com

Cataloging-in-Publication Data is on file with the Library of Congress.

Printed and bound in the United States of America.
VP 10 9 8 7 6 5 4 3 2 1

This book is for our librarians. They keep the flames of our knowledge and our creativity burning.

CHAPTER 1

Bentham-on-Hudson, New York
May 1942

I suppose there are more soul-destroying places to die than at the foot of an ivory tower, but I can't think of many.

Of course, the spires of academia aren't really made out of ivory. The actual tower that killed Dean Jamison was made of rough-hewn rocks, but everything about his death was so grim that I am compelled to give its setting a beauty that was never there. Hawke Hall was a squat, ugly heap of stone and bricks with round towers on all four corners. It looked like a castle designed by an architect who had only seen castles in books.

In 1942, my office was atop of one of Hawke Hall's towers. Behind my desk, a door led out to a balcony big enough for Rapunzel or Juliet, but not for both at the same time. There was barely room for one woman with long golden tresses pining for her star-crossed love, but I wasn't her. I was a woman and I had the golden hair, but I kept it cut to jaw-length.

Hawke Hall was heated by a monstrous boiler, and my tower functioned like a chimney. Thus, I was never cold as I graded papers at a desk too small for my long legs, and I was often hot. The balcony was the only place I could get a gasp of fresh air. Daily, sometimes hourly, I stood there watching the Hudson River flow at my feet, and I could almost hear Manhattan humming, fifty miles downriver. I could almost hear freedom calling.

When you stand so high above the ground, leaning against a frail iron railing, and when you remember that the only person waiting for you at home is paid to do so, it is only natural to tempt your dark side. It is only natural to look down at the slate pavement that has surrounded Hawke Hall since it was built. It is only natural to wonder.

This is how I know what Dean Jamison saw when he stepped onto the balcony of one of Hawke Hall's other towers, swung his legs over the railing, and jumped.

Even after the ambulance took Dean Jamison away, I lingered a few feet from the spot where he fell, kneeling beside his secretary, Marjorie Steed, and our friend Leontine Caldwell.

"But why?" asked Marjorie, hell-bent on making sense of the nonsensical. Wiping her eyes, as dark as her black curls, she said, "Today was just like every day. He came in at eight o'clock sharp." She waved her drenched handkerchief at his office window. "He was wearing his dark gray suit, the same color as the one you're wearing. And the dark gray porkpie hat. You know the one."

Leontine and I both reflexively looked down at our clothes.

I guess we were too rattled to remember what we were wearing. I was the one in a charcoal suit. Leontine's was navy blue.

I already knew the dead man had been wearing gray. Marjorie knew I knew it, because we'd stood over his body moments after it hit the ground. It had still been wrapped in what was left of the gray suit, but the porkpie hat had fluttered away, landing on the far side of the piazza. This fascinated me. I imagined it floating gently down, still moving after Dean Jamison came to a sudden stop. Also, Marjorie knew I'd seen the dean in his dark gray suit hours before it—and he—had been so cruelly torn by the fall.

I too always arrived at eight sharp, just like the late professor. Or, rather, "the late dean." It had only been months since his promotion. Portly, pale Dean Jamison had tipped the porkpie hat at me, and I'd waylaid him with a question that he didn't want to hear.

"May I have a word with you?"

He waved me into his office. When we walked past Marjorie, I said hello while Dean Jamison strolled right on by, like his secretary was no more human than the desk in front of her. His office was as round as mine, but it sat at the base of one of Hawke Hall's towers, so it was far larger. An iron spiral staircase behind his desk led to a room that was a twin of my office. He used it for his collection of rare books, a luxuriously excessive use of space that signaled his elite status as Dean of Arts and Sciences.

I had my own opinions of what the word *elite* meant. During my father's tenure as dean, the shelves in the tower room had held his least-loved books—duplicates and reprints and lesser editions that were now boxed up in my attic. Father had always kept his most precious books at home.

"Yes, Dr. Ecker?" Dean Jamison asked with a toothy smile while he ushered me to an armchair facing his desk with one plump hand flat on my back and the other on my elbow. As I settled into its velvety cushions, he loomed over me.

Dean Jamison was a short man, so he always looked for—and took—opportunities to loom, but he was dealing that day with a woman who had learned to embody the Ice Queen at her mother's knee. I fixed a cool, expressionless gaze on his too-close face and, after a long moment, he backed away. My mother had given me no useful advice for handling men who did not back down from the Ice Queen.

Having lost our staring match, Dean Jamison scuttled to his side of the desk. He had known my mother, but I wondered whether he'd ever been eyeball-to-eyeball with her. She would have left him whimpering.

"When I took this job last September," I began, resuming my campaign to be treated with the deference I'd earned with my doctorate from Yale, "you said that you would look into space on this floor for me. The tower rooms weren't designed to be offices and—"

"Yes, yes. We did speak. I'm sorry to say that there are still no other offices available."

This had made no sense the first time he said it—he knew it and so did I—but he was determined to keep up the charade. On the day that I was hired, there had been an empty office earmarked for the English department next to his. It had remained empty three months later on December 8, 1941, when several of his professors had responded to the declaration of war, a day after the attack on Pearl Harbor, by volunteering for military service and thus vacating their offices. Two of those absent professors had taught English. Added to the already-empty office next to the dean's suite, this yielded a new total of at least three empty rooms where I should have been able to work. All three had stayed empty for months after that, and two were still obviously available.

Nevertheless, on the morning of his death, Dean Jamison had continued to lie. "All of our offices are either assigned to one of our other professors or earmarked for other things."

"Other things?"

"Earmarked," he said with a small nod.

The nod meant that I was to drop the subject. He'd been forced to let me teach when the war stole away the young men on the faculty, and he wasn't over the shock of it yet.

Did their absence mean that he'd given me the title and salary of a professor? It did not. It meant that he'd given me most of the missing professors' work to do, while keeping my title as "research assistant" and leaving my salary alone. I tolerated this, hoping that I'd eventually be placed in one of the vacant professorships.

That hadn't happened. This became a bigger problem every day. I needed a better job, and Bentham-on-Hudson was short on those. Unfortunately for Dean Jamison, I was born persistent.

I wasn't the first woman to teach English literature at Bentham College—that honor had gone to Dr. Cynthia Masters back in the 1920s, and my goodness she must have been lonely for the past twenty years—but I was the second, and Dean Jamison was deeply unhappy about this development.

One woman in the department was an anomaly. Anomalies could be dealt with. Better, they could be ignored.

But two women? Two women in his English department gave him the sense that we were taking over. Since job titles, salaries, and offices were within his control, I was left sitting high in my tower, at the mercy of a petty little man who was desperate to stop his petty little world from changing.

Fortunately for Dean Jamison, a suitable man for one of the war vacancies in the English department had finally been found to occupy one of the offices. Hired after months of searching, too late in the semester to be assigned any classes, he spent his days reading great books and thinking great thoughts while I worked myself to a pulp. His name was Dr. Devan Chase, and he was, by all accounts, charming. Erudite, even. I didn't know for sure, because I was avoiding him.

Dean Jamison had been happy to give Dr. Chase one of the vacant first-floor offices. The ink wasn't even dry on the man's doctorate, and I had seniority at the college. (Only six months' worth, but still.) Nevertheless, I was supposed to labor quietly in my airless cubbyhole and be happy that the men below let me brush elbows with them.

Well, I wasn't feeling quiet.

"Really, Dean Jamison. There's a vacant office right on the other side of that wall." I jabbed my hand at it. "It's insulting to pretend that there's any reason I couldn't work there."

"It would be pointless, my dear." His eyes searched my face. "I wouldn't want you to have to carry your things back upstairs when we hire a permanent faculty member. The men won't be gone forever."

What did he expect? Tears from the Ice Queen?

I held my peace and waited. Professor Jamison knew that it was unfair to give that office...that job...to a man who deserved it less. This made him too agitated to sit in silence, so he prattled on. "I know that you have more than enough shelves for your books at home, but we might be able to make your current office more functional by finding some bookshelves for you."

Oh, yes. I certainly did have bookshelves at home. My father's library had been the talk of the college. No, of the entire state of New York. In literary circles, an invitation to my parents' legendary dinner parties had been a prize to be won, and the parties had been held in my father's stupendous library. Four walls of shelves fourteen feet high had surrounded the banquet table. Each wall had held eight monstrous shelves, and each wall of shelves was served by its own rolling staircase.

(One rolling staircase would have served the entire room—they were, after all, on wheels—but my father always did love wretched excess.)

And now it was all mine.

How many childhood Friday nights had I spent in my nightgown on the landing above our grand entry hall, watching as New York's intelligentsia passed into the library? There, they would vie for Father's favor under four thousand years' worth of books and book-like objects. Cuneiform tablets, even.

From my perch on the stairway landing, beneath a monumental painting and an equally monumental baroque mirror, I'd learned to recognize the faculty by the tops of their heads. Thus, I remembered Dean Jamison from the days when he'd had hair.

Now, I sat in his cushy guest chair, asking to be treated like a colleague. The fact that I held a doctorate from a distinguished university—more distinguished than his—should have been enough. Because it wasn't, and because I needed to be paid like a valued colleague, I chose my words carefully, reminding him that I'd been born to an intellectual giant. Not so long before, he had cowered in my father's presence.

"Since my parents left me, I've been working my way through that huge library, book by book. He never let me touch them when he was alive."

"He never let anybody touch them," Dean Jamison said, arranging his pens, pencils, and letter opener into a neat row.

I knew that, but I wasn't to be dissuaded from my conversational gambit.

"Some of my father's—my parents'—books are handwritten, older than the printing press. Some of them are autographed by scientists I studied in school. I like to read them because knowing the things my parents knew keeps me close to them."

This was a lie. Maybe it was because I was grieving, or maybe a lifetime of being told my hands weren't clean enough to touch Father's books had taken its toll, but I hadn't been able to make myself take a single volume off its shelf, even though he'd been gone eight months.

Dean Jamison didn't seem to doubt me. Lying successfully made me bold, so I followed up my claim with something equally untrue. "I've been thinking it's time to throw dinner parties in that room again."

There was no reality in which I had the money to throw a dinner party, but Dean Jamison didn't need to know that.

"Oh, you should. It would bring back old times." Now he

was rotating each pen, pencil, and letter opener exactly forty-five degrees. "I miss your parents a great deal. We all do. You know, your eyes are almost as blue as his. Hers, too, I suppose."

I rose. "You've talked me into it. It will be good to pull some Bordeaux out of the basement and toast my parents over a good meal. I'll get some invitations out soon, but right now I've got work to do. Thank you for your time."

What was I saying?

Did I think that throwing a party for my pretentious male colleagues and their wives—and one female colleague, mustn't forget her—would get me bookshelves or a better office or respectful treatment or even a reasonable chance of keeping my job when the war was over?

I did not.

Was there a single bottle of wine left in my basement?

There was not.

My salary would barely cover saltines and grape juice for a crowd that size, so I would be having no party. Eventually, Dean Jamison would realize that he'd won this round, but the memory of his hangdog expression would sustain me. It was too bad, because dragging out my mother's beautiful china and digging into her recipe box did sound like fun. Mostly, I would have loved the chance to remind all of them who I was.

After Dean Jamison had finished saying, "No," to me for the twentieth time, I passed through the student lounge at the base of my lonely tower and ascended to my office. I thought nothing more of our conversation for hours. I sat at my desk and typed up research notes for one of my colleagues, a medievalist. At least the work was interesting.

The world outside went about its business, and I paid it no attention, not until I heard a long, piercing shriek. Then there was a short, brittle scream, followed by true pandemonium. I heard the sashes of dozens of windows creak open, followed by the cries of people looking out at Dean Jamison's gruesome corpse.

Rushing out onto my balcony, I stared down at the carnage for a timeless moment, until Marjorie leaned out her open window and wailed, "Dean Jamison! Oh, God, he jumped. Somebody help him!"

I stumbled down my own staircase, thinking with each step, "He fell this far. And this far. And this far," and I hurried to Marjorie's office.

When I reached her, she was standing by the open window with the telephone cord stretched tight between the receiver in her hand and the phone on her desk.

"Please come quickly," she said into the phone, then she dropped it and buried her face in my shoulder. Waving at the window, she said, "He's out there. He's out there lying on the ground, and I can't leave him alone. But I can't go to him by myself. I need you to go with me, Estella."

She hadn't called me by the name on my birth certificate since we were in grade school.

Marjorie pulled back, holding me at arm's length, and said, "Can you do it? Can you go with me?"

My face was cold because the blood had left it. Wherever I turned my eyes, I saw writhing black dots. I wasn't sure I could take a step, but this was no time to be weak. I straightened my back and blurted out the first thing that crossed my mind. I'm not good with people, so I'm pretty sure it was the wrong thing to say, but it's what I said.

"I haven't been Estella since I was a child."

"I know. I'm sorry, E. I just—"

"It's okay. I think we both feel like children right now."

Marjorie was still waiting for an answer.

"Yes," I said. "I can go with you."

We staggered as we left Marjorie's office, but we stayed upright. Leaning hard on each other, we made it through the creaking doors of Hawke Hall's main entrance. I remember the scent of roses on the warm May air.

Across the piazza, Leontine was standing in front of the library where she worked, trying to see what was going on. Hours had passed since she'd slicked her dark hair into its elegant bun, so curls had escaped to frame her oval face. Her gaze met mine and she came running, her perfectly gored navy-blue skirt waving behind her. The piazza would soon be crowded with police officers, the medical examiner, ambulance attendants, and gawkers—many, many gawkers—but Leontine was first. She saw that Marjorie and I needed her and came running, because friends come to you when life smacks you to the ground.

Within seconds, Leontine was beside me, crying out, "What happened? Are you two okay?" with golden-brown eyes that said she cared to hear the answer. In front of us lay a crumpled pile of flesh and splintered bone, all wrapped up in red-stained gray flannel. Marjorie, Leontine, and I walked close enough to see what the hard slate had done, but not close enough to touch what remained of Dean Jamison. That would have been the kind thing to give him, one last human touch, but we couldn't do it. The three of us sank to the ground beside his body.

A moment later, Dr. Bower appeared at Hawke Hall's double-doored main entrance. He was new to the college and new to town, having retired to Bentham after a long career at a university in the Midwest. When the young math professors had marched off to war, he'd been delighted to come out of retirement to help keep the college going. Like a man of his era, he insisted on wearing full scholarly regalia on campus, as my father had. He cut an impressive figure in the doorway, shrouded in black. Then he was moving, the hem of his red-lined robe fluttering as he ran.

Steps behind him, Dr. Chase came running, too, with Dr. Masters right behind him. Dr. Chase was decades younger than Dr. Bower, and it showed in the way he loped past the older man, leaving the sixtyish Dr. Masters to jog doggedly in her knee-length skirt and low heels. Dr. Chase's youth also showed in his casual tweed jacket, khaki pants, and cordovan loafers. No heavy, dramatic academic regalia for him. He reached us first, taking in the sight of poor Dean Jamison at a glance, then turning his eyes on Marjorie, Leontine, and me. "Are you all okay?"

Dr. Bower and Dr. Masters reached us a moment later. They were both breathing hard, but Dr. Bower was still able to ask questions. "What's going on here? Did he—" He paused to rake his eyes over the dead man. Backlit by the sun, his profile was chiseled, aquiline. Shading his face, he looked up at the balcony with its protective iron railing. Then he did what senior faculty always do. He took over, despite the fact that nobody had asked. He also did what senior male faculty had been doing to Dr.

Masters for twenty years. He ignored her. Being a senior male member of the math faculty, he also ignored the possibility of emotion and went straight to logic.

"Nobody accidentally falls over a railing like that one." His booming voice, crisp and firm, echoed off the stone buildings of Bentham College.

Then, as if he realized that "crisp and firm" might not be the right approach to three young women kneeling on the ground beside a dead man, he joined Dr. Chase and Dr. Masters in crouching beside us. Speaking gently, he said, "Do any of you know why Dean Jamison might take his own life?"

Marjorie dissolved into sobs. I felt more inclined to vomit than to weep, but I suppressed both urges and said, "No. Marjorie and I both had perfectly normal conversations with him this morning. Right?"

Marjorie nodded.

"I didn't see him this morning, not before I heard the screams," Leontine said. "He was already on the ground when I came outside."

Dr. Bower scanned the horizon like a soldier looking for his enemy. "You've called for help?"

I remembered the phone receiver in Marjorie's hand and her words: "Please come quickly." She didn't seem able to speak, so I said, "Yes. Help is on the way."

His authoritative presence strengthened Marjorie, as did Dr. Masters's kindness in taking her hand, because I watched the young woman get hold of herself, shaking her head to clear it.

"Was anybody else up there with him?" he asked.

"No," Marjorie said.

"You're sure?"

She cocked her head, thinking. "I suppose somebody could have already gone up to the tower room before I got to work, but I was here early."

Gawkers leaned out most of Hawke Hall's windows, although nobody else had found the gumption to come out onto the piazza yet.

"I presume that anybody who'd been in the tower with him could have left without being seen, once you came out here?"

Marjorie gave him a slow nod. "I suppose so. I guess I really don't know anything about how this happened. Why do I feel so guilty?"

Dr. Chase fastened his calm, hazel-green eyes on her. "You've done nothing wrong. You called for help, and your friends came out to see whether anything could be done for him." He eye-balled the faces in all the windows. "That's more than anybody else has done."

Marjorie blinked back the tears. "Thank you for saying that."

"Then there's nothing for us to do but wait." Dr. Bower's voice visibly settled Marjorie's jitters. He truly had a remarkable presence.

As for myself, I wondered if I were about to faint. My head was so light that it seemed to be rising, higher and higher, taking me with it. Everything grew small, as if I were looking through the wrong end of a telescope from the balcony where the dead man had stood right before he jumped. From that height, I could see for miles. When I looked down, I saw the seven of us—Marjorie, Leontine, Dr. Masters, Dr. Chase, me, the broken Dean Jamison, and the solicitous Dr. Bower. Swirling around us, Dr. Bower's luxuriant black academic robe unfurled around the slight flare of Leontine's skirt.

A gentle hand on my shoulder brought me back to Earth. "Take a few deep breaths," Dr. Chase said. "It will help."

I was still kneeling. When I tried to shift to a seated position, I found that my legs were asleep, and I nearly toppled over. Dr. Chase helped me get comfortable, then he did the same for Leontine and Marjorie.

His solicitude seemed to alert Dr. Bower to the fact that his approach to the crisis was a bit too cerebral. Forcing a note of warmth into his voice, he tried to do better. "I don't believe I've told you, Dr. Ecker, that I knew your father." He couldn't have known that mentioning my father was hardly the way to calm my nerves. "I've been here three weeks. I should already have paid my respects to Malcolm's daughter. I apologize for that."

"But I thought you'd moved here from Ohio to take this job. Did you know him in college?"

"I knew him during the war, the last war. We served together."

Somewhere in the house was a photo of my father in the crisp jacket of a British officer's uniform, high-necked and snugly tailored. He had been well past thirty when the Great War broke out, an American living in England with his wife and a very young me. That's too old for soldiering, but he'd once mumbled something about his language skills coming in handy when enemy telegrams were intercepted. Other than that, I had never heard him speak of his time in the military. I had almost forgotten that he served.

I wanted to ask Dr. Bower what he and my father had done

in the war, but it would have been indecent to satisfy my curiosity with Dean Jamison lying in front of us. I would ask him later.

"If I could be of any help to the daughter of the man I knew all those years ago, I would be very honored." As if realizing that his offer hadn't included all of us, he added quickly, "I would be honored to be of service to any of you."

I murmured, "I'm very grateful," and Leontine nodded. Marjorie said, "Me, too."

Together, we waited for someone—the medical examiner, the police, anybody—to explain why Dean Jamison had done this.

"E, you were the last one to see him," Marjorie said. "And you were the last to talk to him, I guess. He never came out of his office after you left, and nobody else went in. He likes…liked for me to screen his incoming calls, so I know he didn't get any. He made his own outgoing calls, though. The campus operator would know about that. I did ring him several times to ask if he wanted coffee, but he didn't answer. He did that when he was busy, so I didn't think anything about it. I didn't—" She choked a little. "I didn't *go* to him."

I answered without thinking. "If he was even in there."

"I don't understand. He never came out. He—"

I saw it on her face when she grasped what I meant, and I felt it in the tremble of Leontine's hand in mine.

"Oh. You think he might have been on the balcony for a while. He might have been standing on the ledge, thinking."

I swallowed hard. "It's what I would do."

CHAPTER 2

The rest of the day that Dean Jamison died will always be a blur. At some point, the ambulance arrived. Or perhaps it was the hearse. Tiny Bentham-on-Hudson used the same vehicle for both functions. The police, the faculty, and the administrators all asked the same questions.

"Had he been angry or sad?"

"Did he ever give you the impression that he might do this?"

"Do you know why the man might take his own life?"

To every question, I answered no. I hadn't noticed any change in Dean Jamison's demeanor at all. I was no more specific than that. If they'd asked me about his ordinary day-to-day demeanor, I would have been forced to use words like "smug" and "dismissive," and I've never liked speaking ill of the dead, even my father. (And Father deserved it.)

"Are you absolutely certain that your private conversation was cordial?"

To this last question, which was repeated an infuriating number of times, my answer was yes, but that verged on a lie.

I hadn't felt especially cordial toward Dean Jamison. And who knows how he felt about me? But his words had been cordial, yes, and his demeanor, too. Even if the police doubted my word, what leverage did they have to get me to change my story?

They had none. They were simply being cruel because they'd had their fill of me during the months since I'd lost my parents. They'd grown tired of my phone calls demanding to know how they intended to find my mother. If there was a sneering tone of voice known to humankind, the police had used it as they tried to make me accept their view of things.

But they had failed. They would always fail.

The police believed that my mother had jumped to her death. I did not. And they resented me for carrying on my search for her for months after they'd given up.

In my heart, I think they saw her as a nervous, fragile, rich woman who had snapped. And I think they saw me as a younger version of her who would eventually snap, too.

So there I sat at the scene of a grisly death-by-falling, yet nobody in all the hubbub thought to be gentle with me, even after what had happened to my mother. Or, rather, what might have happened to my mother.

Marjorie and Leontine would apologize later, and I'd tell them not to give it another thought. But the others? Did they exert themselves to ask how I was feeling? They did not, and most of them had known me since I was a child.

Their neglect was to be expected. In that town, I wasn't a person in my own right. The people of Bentham-on-Hudson saw me as an inconvenient reminder of two people they had not liked very well, no matter how many times they had kowtowed to them. In time, I think they stopped seeing me at all. I returned their neglect with the supercilious disdain that I had learned at Yale, as surely as I had learned to read Goethe in German and Flaubert in French and Chaucer in Middle English. To be fair to Yale, I'd had years to learn supercilious disdain from masters of the art, my parents.

Eventually the vultures picking over the remains of Dean Jamison's suicide flew away, which meant that we could finally leave. Dr. Bower and Dr. Chase had stayed with us the whole time. Dr. Bower offered to walk us home. Each of us thanked him and said no. Leontine had a car, Marjorie lived just two blocks up the hill, and I had errands to run.

"Really," I said. "I'm fine, and the fresh air will do me good."

Dr. Chase lingered after the others had walked away, asking if I was sure I didn't need an escort.

I was sure.

"I'll telephone to see how you're doing," he said. "You've had a hard day." And then he walked downhill toward the river.

I watched him go. His hair was reddish-gold in the late afternoon sun, and the brown tweed jacket moved with his easy saunter as if it had been designed to make him look relaxed and competent.

He was really interfering with my efforts to hate him for taking my job.

❦

Dean Jamison died on a Friday, so I stopped by the bursar's office for my paycheck, then I walked uphill from the college's riverfront campus to the tiny commercial heart of

Bentham-on-Hudson. Grocery store, laundry, hardware store, diner, bar, doctor, lawyer, dentist... What more could anybody want out of life?

I had lived in Boston for three years after I graduated from Yale, so I wanted a lot of things that Bentham-on-Hudson couldn't give—museums, plays, the ocean, and neighbors who spoke dozens of languages and weren't all white—but I could no longer afford to live anywhere else. I couldn't afford to live in Bentham, either, but these people didn't need to know that.

On that Friday, like all Fridays, I went to my standing appointment with my lawyer...my father's lawyer...oh, even I didn't know what John Wickley was to me. He had been far more than an attorney to my family, smoking cigars on our riverfront veranda as he advised on the complicated financial dealings that went along with my father's penchant for collecting art and rare books. John had taken on that responsibility as a very young man, before he'd even been admitted to the bar.

If I'd ever wondered why my father gave so much responsibility to a man so young, I'd have come to two conclusions: anyone with eyes could see that brilliant, dedicated John was up to the job, and my father was the kind of man who would have wanted to train his legal factotum to do things precisely his way.

And so, on the day that Dean Jamison flew too close to the sun, I sat in front of John Wickley, ready for my weekly humiliation.

"My paycheck," I said, placing the offending slip of paper on his desk.

He hooked his wire-rimmed glasses over his ears, which made him look less like Cary Grant but only a little. The ladies of Bentham-on-Hudson swooned over John, but he preferred women with a certain cosmopolitan elegance. At least, that's who he'd brought to my parents' parties, sophisticated women from New York. They looked very nice on his arm, but we rarely saw them more than once or twice. John saved his passion for his law practice. He was only fully alive with his spectacles on, focused on a knotty legal problem.

John studied the tiny number on my paycheck as if he expected to see a miraculous change from the number that had been on the last one. Every week, he was disappointed.

"This week's cash," he said, taking the check and laying a stack of bills in its place. The stack was thin, as always. I, too, hoped each week to see a miraculous change.

Only John knew how precarious my financial situation was. The house was mortgaged to the hilt. (God, I love that metaphor. It makes me picture myself as Mercutio and the mortgage as an Elizabethan sword buried in my chest to its exquisitely tooled hilt.)

Mother and Father had left debts at the grocery store and at two exclusive haberdashers in Midtown. I would never be able to buy wine from their favorite sommelier again. Even the electric bill had been in arrears when I lost my parents, and the complicated situation of my mother's departure meant that I didn't actually own their estate. Nevertheless, I would be sleeping on the street if I didn't pay their bills.

John's power of attorney for the estate was a godsend. The Manhattan bank holding the mortgage on my house must never know that a woman was responsible for it, so I gave John the money and he paid the notes out of his legal practice's account.

Since the checks carried a man's signature, nobody would ask questions unless I missed a payment. That day was coming.

John had helped me sell the family car at a loss. I didn't need it, I couldn't pay the note, and I couldn't afford the gas. Weekly, he paid the grocer enough to allow me to hold my head up when I shopped. He made sure my utility accounts were current enough to keep my lights burning, my gas on, and my water running. The thin stack of bills on his desk was all I had left for the week.

John did all these things for a pittance, perhaps out of respect for his friend's memory or perhaps out of guilt for failing to halt my father's financial foolishness. He didn't even bill me for that pittance, but my debt to John grew every week.

About every third Friday, he brought up the subject—the single word—that was always on my mind.

"Bankruptcy?"

I shook my head hard.

"Have you really thought about it? You can't keep carrying this load alone."

I shook my head again.

"It's just a house, Estella. I'm sorry. I mean E." He took off the glasses and twiddled with them for a second.

His eyes, gray-blue under heavy black brows, finally met mine. John was a very successful attorney, but he had the guileless eyes of a bookkeeper, with none of the slickness of the fast-talking lawyers who made such good movie villains. When he spoke, this time he didn't say, "Tell your creditors to take a long walk off a short pier." Instead, he said, "You do have one option we've never discussed."

I wasn't stupid. I knew there was no magic way to fix what my parents had done to me.

Instead of magic, he suggested something equally unimaginable. "You could marry."

My laugh was short and harsh, more of a bark. "Men are not exactly throwing themselves at my feet, desperate to take care of me."

"I am."

I do believe that my mouth actually fell open.

"Desperate is a very good word. I've been desperate for you for quite some time. You're a rare individual, not like any woman I've ever met."

John was my father's friend. I'd never thought of him in that way, not ever. How old was he, anyway?

There were a few gray strands in his thick black hair. There were no jowls under his faint five-o'clock shadow. I wasn't sure he had any more lines around his eyes than I did, and I was thirty-one.

I wasn't bad at math, not when you considered that my doctorate was in words and not numbers, but the shocks of the day had ground down my usually sharp mind. I was having trouble adding up the years.

I was born in 1910. We'd moved to Bentham-on-Hudson from England shortly after the war, so I had been eight or nine. John had been just out of law school, which would have made him…twenty-five at the time, maybe? Twenty-four? If math done by someone in complete shock could be trusted, then John was in his mid- to late forties, fifteen years older than me, give or take. It was the precise age difference between my parents, but that didn't mean I wanted my mother's life.

"I—"I swallowed and tried again. "I don't know what to say."

The glasses went back on. "I wouldn't expect you to agree to marry me on the spot. I am capable of wooing a woman, perhaps more than you'd expect. We could blow this one-horse town any time you like. Take a drive to the city. Enjoy dinner at a restaurant that stays open past eight o'clock. Drop the top on the Lincoln. Drive home under the moonlight. Just think about it."

I wasn't sure whether I was more shocked by John's proposal of marriage or his use of slang.

"I'll think about it."

He handed me an envelope to hold my money, as always. Our fingertips barely brushed. Perhaps they'd brushed every Friday, but now I noticed. What would happen if I rejected John and he refused to continue standing between me and unfriendly creditors? I should have long since gotten him to cosign with the bank, so that I could open an account in town.

As I left his office, I cast a glance over my shoulder, sizing up John's looks and bearing. If I'd been a movie producer, I'd have cast him in the role of a reliable, affectionate middle-aged suitor. The words *There could be worse husbands* crawled through my brain, but I squelched them and hurried out onto the streets of Bentham-on-Hudson.

CHAPTER 3

From the village, my walk home was short, which would have been nice if the path hadn't been near-vertical. Bentham-on-Hudson was named after the Hudson's slight bend just downriver from the ferry landing. The town was framed by the river to the east and by majestic stone cliffs in all the other directions. Its houses looked like they were made of gingerbread. Its public buildings were ornate marvels of brick and stone. Its brick-paved streets were charming. Even I had to admit that my hometown was impossibly scenic.

Rockfall House, my aged, turreted Victorian home, sat on a wide ledge halfway up the cliff just upriver from the village. It could be accessed on foot by a narrow path that zigzagged up my own personal cliff, Rockfall Bluff. Every Monday through Thursday evening, I scaled it with the day's groceries and mail. On Fridays, I carried a heavier load, enough food for the weekend. And I was carrying groceries for two, because I had Annie, a fact that was accelerating my nosedive into bankruptcy.

The view across the Hudson from my tower office was

lovely, but it was nothing compared to the view from my home's stony perch. It was a stunning place to live, really, except when you needed to walk up a cliff to get there.

As I trudged up the last switchback on the Friday that Dean Jamison died, Annie hurried to take the shopping bags. Every day, she ran out to help me.

Annie was officially my housekeeper, but she was so much more than that. She was the one who taught me to use a spoon while my parents were busy with their social obligations. She was the one who helped me with my homework. After my parents were gone, she had done everything she could to help me keep things going. Annie was incapable of giving up on me. I never did deserve her.

The meaty smell of Salisbury steaks wafted out the kitchen window, making the last few uphill steps easy.

"I spent some time in the meadow upriver," Annie said, unpacking canned food into the pantry. I stood a head taller than she did, so I took care of loading the top shelf. "You know? That spot where the hickories fell a few years ago?"

"Where the wild onions grow?" I asked, trying not to get my hopes up.

"Yep!" she said, crossing the kitchen to stir a skillet full of savory-smelling gravy. "They're just starting to send up leaves, so I cut a few to flavor the meat."

"Mushrooms?" The thought made my mouth water. "Seems like it's time for morels."

"Not today."

Annie had an idea of how bad things were, no matter how stealthily I stashed the bills in the study. She also knew how bare the shelves were at the market. Even as early as May 1942, the war had reached out its bloody hand and shaken us in tiny Bentham-on-Hudson, a town so isolated that it didn't even have a train station. The war had taken our young men, and that hurt the most, but now it was taking our food. This hurt in a different way. It's hard to forget your loved ones when they're far away, but it's also hard to go for very long without thinking about your next meal. Already, it had reached the point where you didn't make a list. You bought whatever the grocer had.

Sugar had just been rationed. Rumors said that more restrictions were coming, but Annie's foraging skills meant that we'd never starve. Sometimes, I thought she hoped the grocery store would close altogether, giving her the chance to feed us wholly on tubers, berries, and fish fresh-caught in the ponds atop Rockfall Bluff.

I handed her a can of green peas. "This was the last one."

As I watched her put dinner on the table, a yellow-flowered scarf over her short chestnut hair and a matching apron around her stout middle, I thought about bankruptcy and marriage, and I wondered what I was going to do about Annie.

I waited until we'd finished washing dishes to tell Annie about Dean Jamison. The delay meant that I spent the whole meal making idle conversation while trying to not to think about blood and bones and a porkpie hat.

When I told her, we were on the veranda drinking Annie's wild raspberry cordial from my mother's cut-crystal glasses. From there, we could look out over the town, the college, the river, the near hills, the highlands, and the mountains too far away to see from the village. The stars were popping into view when I told Annie what I'd seen that day. She burst into tears, as I'd known she would. Annie was softhearted, but she'd only known Dean Jamison as someone she served at parties. Her tears weren't for him. They were for my mother.

"He jumped, you say?" she asked, her eyes drifting up to the top of Rockfall Bluff. "And he didn't say why?"

"No," I said, knowing what was coming next.

"Neither did your mother. Oh, I should never have gone to town that day. We had enough food right there in the kitchen. Every morning, I wake up and, for a second, I forget that she's gone."

I didn't know what to say. My mother was indeed gone, but I didn't like to talk about her as if she were dead. We didn't know it for sure, and I'd never stopped looking for her. I'd made long-distance calls to every police station and hospital in New York, New Jersey, Pennsylvania, and Connecticut during the eight months she'd been gone. To supplement my long-distance budget, I'd reached out to police and medical workers across the whole country via the postal service. And I'd done more on-the-scene searching than the entire Bentham police department combined. Even I don't know how often I'd walked the waterline below our house, looking for her body but hoping she wasn't there. Despite all my frantic efforts, I'd had no luck.

I was known for my stubbornness, so this lack of luck simply meant that I would be making more calls and typing more letters and walking more rocky paths. Mother couldn't have vanished into thin air.

Somehow, Dean Jamison's suicide, accomplished in the gentle light of May, pushed me to face reality. I had come home the past September and sleepwalked through early 1942, working night and day and worrying about a war that wasn't going well. Meanwhile, my debts grew. My aging house decayed some more.

On the day the dean died, the same day that John Wickley proposed marriage, I said good night to Annie and went to my father's old study—mine, now. As I did every Friday, I sat at my father's desk to do my weekly household accounting, but this time, I was determined—resigned?—to fully take stock of my finances as a whole.

Like all his furniture, my father's desk was an ornate antique worthy of Scrooge, which was appropriate for a renowned Dickens scholar. I'd been using it for more than half a year, but its opulence still made me feel like an impostor. I sometimes caught a whiff of my father's pipe smoke when I sat there.

On that night, I entered my paycheck into the credit column, subtracting the cash that John had given me. I deducted the money for my mortgage and the food bill from the running tally. Wincing, I subtracted the cost of enough coal to get us through the spring. Then I really, truly looked at the amount I owed.

Faced with pencil-and-paper evidence of my insolvency, I allowed myself to voice the words, "This is madness."

I needed to sell the house, but who would buy a leaky Victorian hulk that cost a mint to heat? In wartime, no less.

In my head, John was still saying the word *bankruptcy*, and it didn't even shame me. It terrified me. If I had to walk away from my father's debts, then so be it, but what then? My parents must have had relatives at some time, but the only one I ever met was a distant cousin of my mother's in England, now dead. If Mother and Father had ever had any true friends, they had yet to show their faces…except for their friend, John, who wanted to solve the problems they'd left me by taking my hand in marriage. Did I want this?

I gave myself a full minute to think about it.

No. I didn't want to marry John. I was going to have to solve my problems myself.

I clutched that week's cash for a good long moment, then I put Annie's pay in a cubbyhole set into the kitchen wall just outside the office door. She'd been getting her salary there for as long as I could remember. This kept me from having to put money directly into her hands, allowing me to maintain the fiction that she wasn't really a servant.

I had trembled with rage when I first opened my father's account books and saw that Annie's salary hadn't changed since she was hired. After much arithmetic, I'd found a way to give her a raise, embarrassingly small, but a raise. Because putting a price on Annie would have ruined me, I couldn't speak of it. I just started putting extra money in her envelope, knowing that I needed to find a way to make it more.

It wasn't as if I'd been sitting on my hands and waiting for doom. My efforts to land a better-paying job at Bentham College weren't going well, but I was a realist. When I wasn't carrying on a nationwide letter-writing campaign to find a hospital or police department who could tell me where my mother was,

I'd been mailing out another boatload of letters to high schools all over the Northeast that might need an English teacher. This was why Annie no longer got a look at the mail.

Speaking of the mail and those job-seeking letters, in the drawer of my bedside table was an envelope from a headmistress in Old Saybrook, Connecticut, the first response I'd had. It had been there for two days, because I was afraid. If the answer was no, I wanted to get the bad news when I had some quiet time to lick my wounds.

But what if the answer was yes? That's when I'd talk to Annie. If we had to move, she'd obviously get a say in where we went, but I had to know what our options were. Every year that I'd stayed away, leaving her here with my parents, had been a selfish act. This time, I would do better.

The shock of Dean Jamison's death put my oh-so-familiar account books in a new light. It made me more fully aware of the ways that money charts a life. Looking back through time, I saw the deposits for my father's salary, far larger than mine. It had easily covered the bills I struggled with now, but where were the other expenses? How did my parents afford the food and wine for their famous dinner parties? How did they pay for the exquisite paintings on the walls? How on earth had my father amassed his renowned book collection?

If I'd asked him, he would have murmured something in his it's-crass-to-talk-about-money transatlantic accent. It would have been, "I began trading in books and art as a very young man. As those first purchases appreciated in value, I bought and sold. I traded up."

I would have doubted him, but I would never have been

sure. Once I'd seen his account books, I was willing to call my father a liar.

Too bad he was dead, so I couldn't say it to his face. Too bad he wouldn't be there the next morning, when I would meet with the art dealer John had found, the one who was going to help me turn his exquisite paintings into money.

I had tried to ask Annie, more than once, if she knew anything about the cash that had blizzarded its way through our house, but she had literally squirmed under the question. All I could get out of her was, "I've always thought your mother came from money, what with her fancy talk and delicate ways. I figured his salary paid the day-to-day bills and her money went for all the…" She gestured vaguely. "For all the extras. And I figured her money ran out about the time they started letting servants go. It's been years now since I was the only one."

Maybe Annie was right about my mother having money, but I saw no record of it in my father's accounts. I could do without their high-flying lifestyle, but the house was seventy years old. Its slate roof leaked. Its rubble-lined basement leaked. There were bats in the cupola.

The phone rang. I ignored it.

I slid the account book back into its drawer, defeated. As I drew my hand back, the knuckle of my index finger rapped hard against the bookcase to my right. I instinctively stuck my bruised knuckle in my mouth. As I sucked my finger like a two-year-old, the sound of flesh-clad bone on old wood echoed in my head, and its memory sounded wrong. Why?

I used my other hand to rap on the bookcase, more lightly this time. The vertical board where I'd banged my hand sounded hollow. I ran my hands all over it, hitting pay dirt when my fingernail caught in a crack surrounding a decorative rosette. I pushed the rosette hard, and a hidden drawer, three inches wide, slid out. The drawer held a single envelope.

Inside the envelope, I found a folded letter. I also found five hundred dollars in twenties and fifties. Nobody who has ever struggled with their bills would blame me for being more excited about the money.

Unable to stop myself from fondling the crisp, silky banknotes, I spread them into a green-and-gray fan and just looked at them. I could buy coal. I could do the most urgent house repair, which was probably the roof. I could put a little bit aside for emergencies. And I could do something nice for Annie.

I slid a twenty into an envelope and wrote on its face, "Buy yourself a pretty dress and a new pair of shoes," and I put it into the cubbyhole beside her salary.

I was so busy calculating what I could do with the money that it took me a minute to remember the letter. Snatching it up, I saw that it was a folded sheet of cheap notepaper, rough with wood pulp. Somebody had written on it, "Bring me the rest and you'll get the other half." There was no signature.

I sat there for a long time, wondering what my father had sold for a thousand dollars. Art? Rare books? Antiques?

But what did the note mean by "the rest"? What did my father owe the person who had given him the money in my hand? If I knew, I'd trade it for the other five hundred dollars in a heartbeat. But who would my trading partner be?

Why hadn't somebody come to me after my father died, asking for "the rest," whatever it was? They had wanted it badly enough to promise him a thousand dollars and pay him half up front. Walking away from the deal only made sense if that person had changed their mind or if they didn't want me to know about the transaction. Or if they were suddenly broke. Or if they were suddenly dead.

CHAPTER 4

The terrible news about my parents had come to me in September 1941 in Boston, where I'd spent three years teaching high school and trying not to think of the mother I never saw and the father I never even wrote. I was teaching *Jane Eyre* that day, and I'd gotten to the dramatic appearance of Mr. Rochester midway through the book when the headmistress eased the door open to say, "You have an urgent telephone call from an Annie O'Dell, Dr. Ecker."

And I knew. I knew immediately that my time away from Bentham-on-Hudson was over, because I couldn't imagine Annie picking up the phone and asking Ethel, the town's daytime telephone operator, to place a long-distance call, not if either of my parents were capable of doing it.

Within an hour, I was on a train headed south with no idea why, carrying nothing but the headmistress's promise to ship me all my possessions. I had no idea what was waiting for me at home, because Annie had been crying too hard to say anything but, "Come home. Oh, Miss Estella, you have to come home right now."

When I reached Rockfall House late on that September evening in 1941, I found a bed in the middle of the drawing room. My father was lying in it beneath smooth sheets, the right side of his face drooping and still. His pale hair, always cut long and worn perfectly slicked back, hung lank around his face.

He heard Annie cry out, "Miss Estella!" and his head—his whole body—jerked in my direction. The nurse standing at his bedside reached out to make sure that the sudden motion didn't throw him out of bed.

"Ove…" He struggled with the "r," but I heard it. "Ovuhr de cliv."

I spoke to Annie, but I couldn't take my eyes off my stricken father. "How long has he been like this?"

"Since I got back from buying groceries. I called the doctor, and then I called you."

"Where's the doctor?"

"He's been and gone."

My father groaned out an unintelligible word.

"The doctor left him here like this?" I asked, my voice rising.

"He says that your father had a stroke, but that he's stable. There's nothing they can do for him at the hospital that this lady can't do for him. And he'll have his dignity here."

The nurse's starched cap waggled as she gave a solemn nod. "The drive to the hospital would be hard on him. With rest, there's a chance that he'll recover."

"Gone," he said, and this time his diction was remarkably

distinct. If anybody could will himself back to health, it would have been my father.

"So…" The "s" was strangely sibilant. "So vera sorreeee."

I felt something inside me ice over.

"Why is he sorry?"

"Lily," he said. His partially paralyzed tongue struggled with the *L*'s, but I knew my mother's name when I heard it.

"Ovuh de cliv," he said again.

"Sudge…such a long way down." His words were getting clearer, and I didn't like what I heard.

"Lonnng wayyy." He gestured toward the floor with the hand he could still move.

"Lileeee…" His voice rose as he used that hand and his working leg to try to get out of bed. "Muss get Lily home."

My voice rose, too. "Where is my mother? *Where is she?*"

"Gone." And then, with his usual flair for dramatic exits, my father lost consciousness.

After that, Father spoke rarely, and he spoke no other words that any of us could understand. He just repeated what I heard on the day I left Boston.

"Lily."

"Over the cliff."

"Very sorry."

"Such a long way down."

"Must get Lily home."

"Gone."

He lived two weeks, and the clarity of his speech declined by the day. At the end, he could only whisper, but the words were always the same, and they gave me every reason to believe that my mother had jumped or slipped off Rockfall Bluff into the Hudson or onto the rocks along its bank. Interpreted differently, those words could mean that he pushed her. I could not let myself think of this while he lived, because I didn't want to know whether I was capable of killing a man on his deathbed.

After he died? Yes. I thought it. I parsed the intonation of every raving mumble that I remembered passing his lips, searching for a confession. I never found it, but neither did I find anything that absolved him.

❦

The town police and the county sheriff and all their officers and deputies tried to find my mother. The whole village did. My parents weren't the most popular people in town, but nobody with a heart could turn their back on someone who might be lying injured on the rocks or fighting for life in the water.

Of course, a certain kind of person is drawn to the spectacle of finding a dead body. I was not one of those people, but I knew them when I saw them. They were with us during the days after my mother disappeared.

I remember how the voices of the searchers bounced off the surface of the river, obscuring the location of the shouting people. "You three take that path. Remember, she's wearing blue."

My flaxen-haired mother almost always wore shades of blue, gray, white, black, purple, or silver. She favored floaty fabrics like chiffon and georgette that made her look elfin, almost magical.

I remember the questions that bounced up from below as I stood at the top of Rockfall Bluff. "How far downriver should we look? Do we have people at the village park beach?"

My mother knew how to swim, but she rarely did it. Physical activity seemed…well, not beneath her, precisely, but alien to her. Every movement she made was languid, as if she were swimming in air.

I remember someone shouting "Be sure to stop and listen now and then. If she's calling for help, we want to hear her."

Mother was a quiet woman with a faraway gaze, like someone who was always listening to an internal monologue. I now know that she looked like what she was. My mother was a poet.

Poets can be very hard to know. There were long days while Mother was missing that I wondered whether I had ever known her at all. Was I grieving nothing more than a child's idealized image of the mother I had needed? How terrifying would it be for children to see their parents as the flesh-and-blood people they truly were? It was terrifying enough for me as an adult to come to grips with the hollow emptiness of the man who was my father.

We didn't find her. And, dear God, a lot of people tried during those first days. Every possible agency in the area was alerted. Her photo was in the paper. Signs were nailed to trees. People searched the woods all up and down our side of the river. They dragged the river itself, and that's the worst part. They didn't find my mother, but they did find someone else.

In the cove below our house, a woman's body was lying on the riverbed.

I was there at the waterline when Bentham-on-Hudson's volunteer fire department found the first of her bones. It was a humerus (the left one, I think), and I watched it breach the surface.

The officer beside me said, "It's not her. It can't be. She wouldn't be—" He looked at me as if he'd realized who I was. "Your mother wouldn't be down to bones so soon and, besides, I'm sure she's not in the river. She's still alive somewhere."

God bless him for saying that.

But then he said, "But if we find—" He fidgeted a moment. "If we find someone who might be her, you'll need to go to the morgue and view the body. They'll probably have you view this one."

I managed to hear this without my mouth falling open. I think I should be congratulated for that.

"Just to make sure it's not her," he said, in a hurry to stop me from imagining what those viewings would be like.

Too late.

After the divers finished bringing up the body, I was called to view it, just to be sure, even though all logic said that the dead woman couldn't be my mother. As I stood there, looming like a stork over the delicate bones, I saw that all the woman's pockets—coat, jacket, and skirt—were full of stones. And I saw that those pockets had been sewn tightly shut to make sure the stones did their work.

The stones were more secure in the coat than the woman was. Its caramel-brown wool was torn and several of its daisy-shaped Bakelite buttons were missing, just as her fingers were, but the stitches in her coat pockets had held tight.

When I staggered, the coroner kindly kept me from falling.

He probably thought I was reeling from the shock of seeing a corpse reduced to bones, and he wasn't wrong. It was dreadful to know that nothing else remained of a vital human being, but it wasn't the skeleton that almost took me down. It was the stitches. Tiny, precise, and rendered in fine black thread, every last one of those stitches was a glimpse of doom.

There were four bodies, counting that first skeleton. Four times in the eight months between Mother's disappearance and Dean Jamison's death, I watched someone fold back a stark white sheet so I could stare at a dead woman, praying that she was nobody I knew. This was cowardly, because each of those lifeless corpses had been a human being before she went into the Hudson, coming out somewhere downriver from my house.

Somebody had known them. Somebody had loved them. None of them were my mother.

During the time my father was fading, I was continually torn. When I was with him, I felt that I should be looking for her. When I was looking for her, I felt that I should be with him. Truth be told, Annie was the one who deserved my time.

"It's my fault. It's all my fault." She said it over and over, but that didn't make it true.

It was inconceivable that I would agree with Annie that she could have kept my mother safe by following her around every second of every day. Doing that would have forced me to accept my part of the blame for losing her.

If I hadn't gone away to college, I would have been there for her.

Or if I'd come home after four years instead of staying to get a master's and then to get a doctorate and then to teach high school in the joyous intellectual ferment that was Boston, perhaps I could have saved her. Perhaps my mother would have been spending her evenings with Annie and me on the veranda, her wicker chair next to mine.

I would have closed my eyes and imagined her there, sipping cordial and fretting about a frayed spot on the upholstery, but I didn't dare risk my heart that way.

I preferred to dwell on the point that my father *had* been home that day. Surely, neither Annie nor I could be to blame when he was right there on the spot, could we? But I couldn't wander too far down the path of blaming him, because I didn't know whether he'd had his stroke and collapsed to the drawing room floor before or after she...what?

Jumped?

Fell?

Ran?

And I would almost certainly never know, despite my frenzied typing of letters sent to people I hoped could help me. I wrote doctors, morgues, sheriffs, newspaper editors, so many people that I'd lost count. I couldn't afford the long-distance calls it would take to throw a dragnet over the entire country, so I told myself that the letters were better. They were lasting physical agents of my desperate search. If a woman turned up in some faraway emergency room, blond and middle-aged and delicate and lost, perhaps someone would remember a letter. Perhaps they would find it filed neatly in an administrator's office where they would read the words I'd typed, begging for information on a missing person who fit the description of the woman in front of them.

But was my father the reason she was gone? I might never

know. If the answer to the mystery of my mother turned out to be suicide, then he could have egged her on, for all I knew. I didn't dare close my eyes and imagine him saying, "Why don't you jump, Lily? Why don't you go ahead and get it over with?"

He was capable of it.

I didn't say these things when Annie blamed herself for whatever had happened to my mother. I just said, "I miss her, too."

❦

We were sitting there together when we learned the name of the woman found on the riverbed. It was Helena Frederick, and she had been gone for fifteen years. She had walked away from Bentham College after an uneventful English Lit class, never to be seen again. I remembered her disappearance. I'd been in high school, so who knew whether the rumors I'd heard at the time were any more than the fevered imaginings, some of them contradictory, of girls in their teens?

I'd heard that Helena was distraught because her boyfriend had broken off their relationship. I had also heard that they'd eloped. I'd heard that she was pregnant, but I supposed there wasn't enough left of her for anyone to ever know. I'd even heard that she'd become a Hollywood actress, working under a stage name. One thing that I'd never heard was that she had been found…until the cove was dragged for my mother, and Helena's body appeared instead.

After that, Annie and I sat by Father's bed, wringing our hands over poor Helena. Also, we talked. We reminisced about the picture books Annie had read to me and we remembered the detective novels and romances that I'd read on my own later. For years,

Annie had smuggled them into my room. Father was adamant that such trash be banned from the house, because he was a professor of *literature*. Nancy Drew and Miss Marple were not welcome, and he certainly didn't tolerate the spooky tales that Annie and I devoured about naive but plucky governesses in lonely old houses. We figured that what he didn't know never hurt him.

While he lay murmuring disconnected phrases about my mother and a lonely cliff, Annie and I talked about all the games of hide-and-seek we'd played in the ruins that crowned Rockfall Bluff, especially the rare times that Mother had joined us. (Those days were far more fun, because hide-and-seek isn't the best two-person game in the world.)

I'd learned to swim up there in the series of rock-walled reflecting ponds that had once surrounded a Gilded Age mansion, like diamonds around the neck of a duchess. Now, their unruffled surfaces only reflected crumbling ruins and the faces of white-tailed deer taking a drink, except for when Annie rippled their water with her net. The rich man who had lived atop Rockfall Bluff had stocked his ponds with trout. Decades later, we ate their descendants.

In all the hours we sat with my father, neither Annie nor I said much about him, and he was lying right there in front of us. I'm not sure whether that said more about us or about him.

He lived another fifteen days, and he was never able to tell me what had happened to Mother. He was never able to tell me how to take over his finances. He was never able to tell me he loved me, although this was nothing new.

The day came when my father stopped breathing. He simply went.

CHAPTER 5

I had expected my father's funeral to be attended by Annie, John, and me. (And maybe a sprinkling of people who felt obligated to come because they'd eaten at his table.)

Instead, a large crowd turned out. All the people who would soon become my colleagues in the English department were there, including the two who would join the Army in less than three months, and almost the entire Arts and Sciences faculty. Even the college's chancellor and his wife came.

They filed past me as I stood alone beside his coffin, because Annie had an old-fashioned view of her status in my household. I saw Annie as family. Annie might feel that way at home, but she behaved like a housekeeper in public. I felt her loving eyes on me, but she watched from a discreet distance as I shook one hand after another after another.

Dean Jamison's usual furtiveness was on full display at the funeral. Barely pausing as he moved past me, he mumbled an insincere, "If I can do anything for you…" I loathed him in a way that would have been unbecoming if I'd known he only had months to live.

Marjorie had been just a step behind him. I had known her since we were children, but she was new to being Dean Jamison's secretary. He seemed to be the kind of boss who immediately transformed his employees into extensions of himself. He had hired Marjorie as soon as he stepped into my father's role, after the stroke took him out of the dean's chair but before he was dead. It had only been weeks, but even at a funeral, Marjorie already seemed like Dean Jamison's around-the-clock assistant as she followed solicitously in his wake. However, unlike her boss, she put pure sincerity in her voice when she said, "Call me. No, you don't have to do that. I'll call you tomorrow. If you need anything, I'll be there."

Then the dean turned to her with a "Let's go" nod, and she followed.

Leontine was a good bit behind Marjorie in line. We had played together as children while her mother was fitting my mother with her custom-made dresses, but Leontine had left Bentham for boarding school even before I went away to Yale. She, too, had stayed away for college and graduate school, and I hadn't even heard she was home before I saw her that day. As odd as it sounds, our friendship was rekindled at my father's funeral.

"I lost my own father years ago," she said, "but my mother's death is fresh. Being alone in the world is a new thing for me. When I heard people talking about what happened to you, I wanted you to know that somebody understood."

She had been willing to stand out in an unfriendly crowd,

the only dark face in a sea of pale beige ones, so that she could tell me I wasn't alone. For this, I would walk through fire for Leontine.

Shortly after Leontine shook my hand and walked into the crowd of mourners, I found myself face-to-face with Dr. Masters, the lone woman in the English department. A dignified, stout woman, Dr. Masters usually wore no makeup, but she had applied a dusting of powder and a bit of eye shadow for the occasion. It suited her, or it would have if her powder weren't streaked by tears. It was only when I saw her crying that I realized how very few people at my father's funeral showed any sign of grief.

"Your mother was…is…among my dearest friends," she said, and she seemed to mean it.

The words *Then you must not have any dear friends* crossed my mind, but I managed not to say them. I had seen Dr. Masters at our house at a few dinner parties, but I'd never seen her stop by for a friendly cup of tea with just my mother, because nobody did. Or they hadn't when I'd lived at home.

On and on, the mourners came. Perhaps it was paranoia on my part, but it seemed like they weren't there to pay respects to my father. They were there to see me. But why? They didn't know me, not really.

My parents were too prideful to have true friends. They certainly didn't pretend to have any among Bentham-on-Hudson's rank and file. Well, they tolerated the professors, but nobody else.

Their social set lived in the city. When they entertained, hired cars brought most of their guests from the nearest train stations and the town's ferry landing. Some of the wealthiest guests had drivers who brought them in their own cars up from Manhattan. At least a smattering of faculty members—just enough to make an invitation seem attainable but precious— were present at any gathering, but my parents did not set a place for the grocer or the fireman or the high school history teacher at their table.

Between handshakes, I scanned the room. No, it was not paranoia. All eyes were on me. None of these people had any reason to like me. Even the faces of the classmates I'd known since I still had baby teeth had changed while I'd been away for more than a decade. I hadn't written to them, and they hadn't written to me.

Did they come because they hoped that I'd continue my parents' free-spending ways at their shops and businesses? Or were they simply there out of morbid curiosity? My mother's disappearance was surely the gossip event of the season.

Knowing this, I wanted to turn tail and flee. Instead, I spent the afternoon listening to the sympathetic murmurs of dry-eyed people.

After the funeral, I went home and sat at my father's desk for the first time, ready to take stock of my situation. The shock of this exercise sent me straight to John for advice, and thus began my weekly visits to his office.

"Surely, there's some money somewhere," I said to him during my first appointment, waving Father's bankbook as if I expected dollar bills to fly out of it.

"What you see is all there is," he said. "Or all I know about. I was his lawyer and his financial advisor and his friend, not his accountant. I knew his overall investment strategy, but not the details of his day-to-day financial life."

This was a surprise.

"I know where your father invested and why. I know what his will says. I also know what his favorite cognac was. But that's about all." He gave me a rueful smile, which I found comforting in those days before he proposed a marriage of convenience.

"You were doing quite well as a teacher in Boston, I believe," he said. "Perhaps you could take a job at the local high school."

"Quite" was a strong word. I'd had a salary that paid for a room and not much more, but I'd had Boston and its museums and its beautiful harbor for entertainment, and I'd taught with women who enjoyed exploring the city with me. In that sense, yes, I'd been doing quite well.

"The English teachers here at Bentham High have home-steaded their jobs," I said, "and they're middle-aged, at most. I will starve waiting for any of them to retire."

"Then the college, perhaps?"

The man in charge of hiring at Bentham College, Professor Hanssen, had been a friend of my father's, and he'd known me since I was in grade school. If I'd been my father's son, cronyism would have put me directly into a good job.

But, as I'm sure I have mentioned, I was not, and am still not, a man.

Instead, Professor Hanssen had found me an approved-for-women post as a research assistant doing the English profes-sors' drudge work. Working at the college had allowed me to entertain the illusion (delusion?) that I could eventually be hired as a professor, despite my regrettable lack of a penis. I started work on September 20, 1941.

On December 7, 1941, the world turned upside down. As the year ground to a close, our world in Bentham began to empty. The war hollowed it out.

The emptiness felt bigger than it was. The entire populace was, of course, not all young men of enlistment age, but we missed them bitterly, even those we didn't know. They left man-shaped holes behind them.

The town's homes were missing sons and husbands. Young men were absent from the town's streets. Men's clubs like the Loyal Order of the Moose and the Masonic Lodge felt their absence, and this was before the casualty lists started arriving in earnest. The town grew a little older overnight, a little more female, a little more jaded and bitter. You can mask the kind of bitterness we felt by performing patriotism and pride, but no normal human community has ever been happy to see its young men become soldiers and march away.

As I have said, two English professors marched with them, and every department felt similar losses. Slowly, replacement professors trickled in, not just Dr. Chase in English and Dr. Bower in math, but others whose aura carried a darkness that I couldn't pinpoint.

Even while avoiding Dr. Chase, I could appreciate his youthful, aw-shucks charm, and Dr. Bower was no different from any number of stuffy-but-well-meaning academics I had known, but these other men had a stillness in their eyes and a stiffness in their carriage that was hard to miss. There were two such men working in chemistry, one in math, three in physics, two in military science, one in political science, one in the chancellor's office. The only way to describe them is to say that they looked like people who should have been off to war. They looked like people who were born to be fighting a battle that they might lose against a terrifying enemy. Since they weren't doing that, I sensed that they were somehow bringing the war to us in Bentham.

I presumed that these men who said they were professors but who looked like soldiers were watching something or someone or both. They were probably watching a lot of somethings and someones. What is a college but a place where people know things?

And what are an army's most valuable resources? Arms, ammunition, and soldiers, obviously, but also knowledge.

Through it all, Annie kept me from feeling utterly alone. And Marjorie and Leontine. After my father's funeral, Leontine and I started taking our lunch breaks together, wishing that Dean Jamison would give Marjorie the time off to join us. In her meticulously fitted dresses and precisely hairpinned updo, Leontine brought modern grace to stuffy old Bentham College, but this wasn't why she attracted stares. Almost everybody in Bentham-on-Hudson was white, and people who weren't were not typically met with kindness. I felt that I needed to do something about this, but I didn't know what. For the time being, my pitiful rebellion consisted of returning the stares with the baleful glare that Mother had taught me. My Ice Queen face accomplished little, other than making Leontine laugh, but I deployed it anyway.

Over time, I learned more about Leontine's life before and after we played together as children.

"I was born in the city," she told me once, "but I was a little girl when we moved here. All I remember from Harlem is the shops and the people and the fast cars in the broad streets. Everything was moving."

She was slower to say why they moved to Bentham, because telling the story required her to talk about her dead parents. "My father was a carpenter, the best around. Mama loved living in the city, but he was born here. He said he missed having room to breathe, so where else was she going to take him when he came down with TB?"

Bentham-on-Hudson felt pretty stifling to me. To hear Leontine talk, her mother had felt the same way.

"My mother was as good with her needles as my father was with his hammers and chisels. In the city, she helped dress society ladies. Some of the designers introduced their clients to the woman who did the beading on their fine gowns. She said those designers made her feel like *somebody*, and they were the ones who had the good fortune to work with her again."

I had seen Leontine's mother's work up close, softening the edges of my mother's waifish body, setting her face aglow. My father taught me to recognize artistic genius, and Leontine's mother had possessed it.

"In time, Mama had clients of her own, but she left them behind because Daddy thought the school here was better. Mama let him think she thought so, too. She had to, unless she wanted to let the doctors tell him how sick he was."

Weeks went by before Leontine told me about her father's

long, slow wasting-away. I shared my grief in dribs and drabs, too, afraid that once I started to talk about my parents, the feelings would roar out of me like a river going over a cliff.

I told Leontine about my father's death, but I never once referred to my mother as dead, and neither did she. Every Friday, she handed me a new list of addresses of people who might be able to help me find her, knowing that I would spend hours that weekend typing letters. Librarians are very handy friends to have.

"Mama went back to making dresses when the TB took Daddy. When I got big enough, I helped her," Leontine said.

I remember her eyes as she said it—calm, steady, intent. It's hard to describe the singular gaze of a strong woman, but my female friends have all had it.

"Even here, people knew Mama's work. The rich women across the river are always needing new silk dresses. And velvet. My goodness, they like velvet. They were thrilled that a designer of her reputation was so nearby."

"She was that good," I said. "I saw what she made."

Leontine nodded. "Needles and pins are small things, but they sent me to boarding school. They sent me to college. They put a nice roof over my head, and now it's mine. Free and clear."

But I don't want to be here. She didn't say it, but she said it. I felt the same way, only without the paid-for roof over my head.

In the months after I lost my parents, my time with Leontine (and Marjorie, when her boss and her parents could spare her,),and my dinners with Annie were the only bright, clear spots in a life that was a blur of papers—desperate letters to type, lecture notes to write, professors' papers to edit, students' papers to grade, and my own bills to pay. Time passed.

My mother stayed gone, despite my best efforts, but her body never surfaced. Other women's bodies did, forcing me to go to the morgue for the ritual folding-down of the sheet that divided the quick and the dead. I saw things in the morgue that I do not want to fully describe to you. I saw bloated flesh and muscles shredded by rocks. I saw the work of hungry fish. One body was nearly whole. Helena's, by contrast, was down to bone. The others still bore flesh that was gruesomely incomplete. None of those bodies was my mother's.

"Are you sure?" That was always the question. "Are you absolutely sure?"

My answer was always "Yes." I was sure.

My mother was still out there somewhere.

CHAPTER 6

O
n the night I found five hundred dollars in my father's office, I spent hours searching every nook and cranny in the room. If he had hidden more money, I wanted it.

The telephone rang three times while I searched. After the third call, I lifted the receiver off the hook and laid it on the desktop. Then I went back to running my hands over bookcases, cabinets, and desk, knowing that I had a big house full of fancy furniture. I was going to need to search it all for more hidden treasure.

This was the strategy of a fairy-tale princess. I was no such thing, but I'd been reduced to hoping that magic would save me.

❦

At some point, I was too weary to keep searching for more secret compartments filled with cash. Most people never found a single one, so why did I think I'd find more? It was time for bed.

I slid the money back into its hiding place. It had been safe there since my father died. Maybe it had been there for years and years.

Once in my room, I pulled on my pajamas and hoped that they would make me sleepy. They did not. If I wanted to rest, I needed something to read, something comforting.

For the first time since I'd come home, I let myself reach for the box under the bed. Why had it taken me so long? Yes, my father disapproved of the books I'd hidden from him, but he wasn't going to reach out from the grave and snatch them out of my hands. He'd already snatched them once, when I was fifteen. And then he'd set them on fire.

"No daughter of mine will read such trash!" he'd bellowed as he hefted the crate full of books Annie had given me, one book a month bought out of her tiny salary for years and years. I'd been foolish enough to leave the crate in the reading alcove. He'd found it and hauled it downstairs to the east parlor, where there was a fireplace so massive that he could throw every last one of my books into its flames.

"Agatha Christie. Edna Ferber. L. M. Montgomery. Anna Katharine Green. Louisa May Alcott." He said their names like they tasted bad. Overhanding a copy of *The Murder of Roger Ackroyd* directly into the flames, he looked around for my mother, so that he could bellow at her, too. "What were you thinking when you bought these?"

She extended a graceful palm toward Annie that asked for silence. Then she slid that hand around my waist and clapped her other hand over my mouth. At age thirty-one, I finally understood that she had been keeping me from incriminating Annie.

She leveled a glare on him, as intense as an X-ray. Incredibly, my father backed away from her and from my books.

She gave me a gentle push toward the stairs and took a step toward him. "You've told me so many times that I'm incapable of rational thought. And yet now you contradict yourself. Am I intelligent enough to choose suitable books for our daughter? You flatter me."

Her English accent was still strong. It never faded, not as long as I lived with her.

She advanced on him as he backed into the entry hall, and Annie made her own advance on the fireplace with a tremendous pair of brass tongs.

I lingered on the landing.

"To bed with you," Annie said, and I fled.

The next morning, I woke to the faint smell of smoke. Under my bed was the crate. It was still full of books, some of them blackened around the edges. Neither my mother nor Annie ever spoke of them. It was impossible that my father would find them, as this would have required him to take an interest in sweeping and mopping. Since he couldn't acknowledge any conflict unless he emerged the winner, he too never mentioned the incident again.

(Nor did he ever bestir himself to make sure I had books that he did consider worthwhile. My mother did that for him, supplementing Annie's supposedly lowbrow reading materials with the classics and teaching me French and Italian. I entered Yale quite well-prepared, no thanks to him.)

I had been too sad since I lost my parents to look at the books under my bed. Their charred edges incriminated my dead father, and I was already angry enough with him. Tonight, though, I didn't want to think about how the books came to be scorched. I just wanted to commune with them in the way that you might write a long, newsy letter to an old love.

I opened the box, fumbling around for *The Secret Adversary*, when an unfamiliar cover caught my eye. It was mustard yellow, and the black outline of a calla lily adorned the dust jacket. Its title, printed in black block letters, was simply *Portent*, but its subtitle wasn't simple, not to me. The book in my hand was called *Portent: Poems by Lily Ecker*.

How had I never known that my mother wrote a book? And that it was dedicated to me:

> *For my daughter Estella Emily Ecker, because*
> *children are portents of a future that we will not see.*

I had hated my name for so long. Seeing it in my mother's book changed everything.

Oh, I still hated being named Estella. The girls in my classes had carried crisp, modern names—Hazel, Alice, Irene, Evelyn, Grace—but my father had wanted to brand me as the daughter of a Dickens scholar. He could have called me Nancy or Nell, presuming he was willing to ignore their sad ends. He could have called me Clara. He could even have called me Pip, instead of giving me the name of the coldhearted deceiver who entraps him. Who names his only child after someone like that?

This is why I prefer to be called E.

But reading my mother's poems shed a new light on my middle name. I knew why she chose it as soon as I read the first stanza of the first untitled poem in *Portents*.

(Of course, it was untitled. They were all untitled. By the time I had read the first few pages of my mother's book, I knew that every poem, all thirty-two of them, would be built of quatrains in common meter—eight-syllable lines alternating with six-syllable lines. Or, as we literary scholars say, iambic tetrameter alternating with iambic trimeter. From the first page, I was certain that no poet had ever more devoutly wished to be Emily Dickinson, the queen of titleless common meter, than my mother.)

The poem's literary value was debatable, but it struck me to the heart.

> *Because the ocean lay so wide*
> *Along the shifting dunes*
> *Because its salt left both eyes blind*
> *I could but reach for you*
>
> *And once my hands curled round your wrists*
> *My heart said yes—yes—this*
> *Now yet my hands curl round your wrists*
> *I still want this—just this*

This was the work of a woman in love with a man who had come to her across an ocean. My English mother loved my American father, or at least she had when she wrote these undated lines.

I flipped back to the dedication page. My own name stared back at me.

Emily. I'd always hated my first name fully, but not my

middle name. Emily Brontë was one of the goddesses of my existence. The windswept cliffs of Rockfall House were, in their way, wuthering heights, and I'd somehow become convinced that my parents saw that similarity and named me after Brontë. Until I saw my mother's book, I'd never realized that my middle name was given to me by a poet who had another literary goddess in mind.

I didn't mind being named after Emily Dickinson. I didn't mind it at all. Fortunately, this revelation wasn't going to force me to rethink my preferred name, because E suited an Emily just as well as it did an Estella.

How was it possible for me to live thirty-one years and not know that my mother was a poet? And that she had insisted, for I knew in my heart that she'd had to insist, that I be named for Emily Dickinson?

If I'd known my parents better, I would have known all this. Hardly a day passed when I wasn't forced to admit that they were strangers to me. But, oh, how I wanted to know my mother. With her book in my hands, I wanted it more than ever. She just couldn't be dead, not before she'd explained herself to me. I wouldn't allow it.

It had been days since I'd shed tears for her (for them?), but Mother's book brought them back. Damp-eyed, I read the first poem again. As with all poetry, it had saved some meaning for the second reading. There, under the word "both" was a faint pencil mark. I didn't know why it was underlined, but poets had their reasons for every mark on the page. Even after this book was published, my mother had wanted to emphasize that word.

She had left me this book, this poem, that barely readable pencil line, and a host of random marks on every page that I had no idea how to interpret. In the end, those silvery-gray pencil marks reduced me to sobs.

CHAPTER 7

I t is an odd thing to try to sell your patrimony immediately after rising from the breakfast table, but John had only found one art dealer willing to take the long train-to-ferry-to-car trip from Manhattan to my house, and he was only willing to come at nine o'clock on a Saturday morning. The fact that he would come at all told me that he had filled the rest of his weekend with appointments across the river with various Vanderbilts and Roosevelts. Since nine a.m. was an hour too inhumane for people with real money, Oscar Glenby was graciously willing to come then and take a look at what I had to sell.

Mr. Glenby was wan and thin, but his handshake was firm. He said, "Hello, Dr. Ecker," in an oddly musical voice for a man with such flinty blue eyes. Then, for the second time in two days, I heard an older man say, "I knew your father."

Of course, this man knew my father, who had spent many a weekend in New York at auctions and in galleries. I smiled at him, because that's what you do when you're trying to sell something. You smile at strangers.

"Well, then, perhaps you recognize some of the paintings on my walls, Mr. Glenby. Come take a look. Then you can tell me whether you might have buyers for them."

"Oh, surely you're not planning to sell them all," he said. "This is a grand house. She deserves paintings on her walls, like a lovely woman deserves an elaborate hairstyle."

He had all the charm of an undertaker, but I forced another saleswoman's smile. "This grand old lady deserves a lot of things. One of them is a fresh coat of paint. She may need to part with her jewelry to make that happen. Please, come look at the collection."

Annie and I had spent hours making the place ready for him. Since my father's death, we had confined our lives to the kitchen, the study, the drawing room, our bedrooms, and one bathroom. In anticipation of Mr. Glenby's visit, we'd lifted the yards of cloth keeping dust off the furniture and paintings in the house's formal rooms. The library, the smoking room, the twin parlors, the fabulous marble-floored entry hall—we unveiled them, and then we swept them clean.

The vibrant colors of the undraped paintings lit the dark before we even opened the drapes. It had made sense to close off most of the house to cut costs but, my goodness, how I felt my spirits lift when the light streamed into those unused rooms.

Mr. Glenby had a poker face, so the tour was mostly a monologue. My burblings about the fine brushstrokes of this portrait and the delicate coloring of that landscape were accurate, I think. I'd certainly heard my father show off his art often enough. I think I was wise to resist the urge to use his wooden pointer, like a pool cue only longer and stouter. Father had used it to point out details on his paintings or to call attention to a rare book on a top shelf. I couldn't force myself to step that fully into his persona, so I had left the pointer in its usual spot in the library, leaning against the bookcase nearest his chair at the head of the table.

Glenby punctuated my narration with a word here and there. Once, he said "Lovely."

I thought that was encouraging.

Another time, he said, "Almost figurative…interesting…" while looking at a Cubist nude in the library, but he honestly seemed more interested in the library itself and its floor-to-ceiling array of colorful leather and gilt.

As we passed from the library into the entry hall, he paused below the floor-to-ceiling Expressionist painting hanging at the landing. It was the first things guests saw as they entered the huge leaded-glass front doors. At right angles to the painting, a massive mirror hung, so that a woman—namely, my mother—could check her appearance before turning at the landing and making her entrance.

When one stood in the doorway, only the painting showed. But if one stood at the right spot, and I absolutely placed Mr. Glenby at the right spot, the mirror reflected an oblique view of the huge abstract work, giving a double dose of its writhing tertiary colors. It was a stunning effect, really.

After contemplating the painting and its reflection for a while, he murmured, "Your father always did appreciate scale." I had no idea what to make of that comment.

As we left the entry hall, I kept an eye on the mirror, as if I expected my mother to appear in it. It struck me that there were no pictures of her in the house. No photos. No paintings. It seemed odd to me that an art collector with a beautiful wife wouldn't want to show off her image.

Come to think of it, there were no images of me or my father in the house, not even a run-of-the-mill "happy family" portrait in his study. Not that this mattered when I was trying to sell paintings, because who would want to buy a portrait of somebody else's not-famous family? But surely somewhere in the house was an album of photos that they had turned to during the years I was gone. I wanted to think that they missed my face when it was far away. Annie had sent me photos of them, and there had been days when I'd looked at my parents far more than was good for me.

When Oscar Glenby and I returned to the drawing room, Annie was waiting. She poured our tea and served slices of crumb cake on tiny dessert plates. Then she evaporated, as my parents had required. We would only see her again when she mysteriously intuited that we needed more tea.

"No one had an eye like your father," Mr. Glenby said, taking a sip of the scalding brew.

What did this mean? Did he think he could sell the collection? I would be sad to see the autumnal riverscape go, and also the rather astonishing tertiary-hued whatever-it-was on the landing, but not sad enough to skip meals so that I could keep them.

"It would help me in my assessment if I knew the provenance of the paintings—who he bought them from, where the previous owners got them, when he bought them. Things like that."

Yes, I had those records, but should I really show them to him?

"Any purchaser is going to want to see a piece's provenance. If I knew your father, he recorded information on pricing in separate files."

"I'll see if I can find the information."

Annie's eyes asked me a question as I passed through the kitchen to the study. I could only shrug. I couldn't read Mr. Glenby at all.

Flipping through my father's filing cabinet, I could see that Glenby was right. Each painting had two files, one labeled "Provenance" and one labeled "Price." I loaded my arms with files I was willing to let him see.

He flipped through them, opening a few to rake his eyes over their contents. He never took anything out of the stack to set aside. Did this mean that he found none of them interesting? Or that he found all of them interesting? I needed so desperately for him to buy something. Anything.

He set the entire stack on the table beside him and picked up his dessert plate. "Have you shown me everything? I didn't see the Hopper. Or the Moran. And I don't see them in these files."

He lifted a tiny silver fork full of crumb cake.

"My father was…um…not able to tell me much about the collection by the time I got here, but…"

My father was essentially unable to speak when I came home.

I turned my attention to my own tea and cake while he waited for me to finish my sentence.

I regained control of my breath. "…but he traded paintings like some people trade stock. I presume that he traded the Hopper and the Moran—"

"And the Cole."

"And the Cole. I imagine that he traded them for some of the paintings you see."

I didn't say "I hope he traded well and that the current collection is worth even more," but I was thinking it.

He set his teacup on its saucer gently, but I could still hear its faint porcelain-on-porcelain clank. "I'm sorry, my dear, but I can't do much for you. Only the wealthiest art lovers are blasé enough about world events to add to their collections during a war. The ones who are bold enough and rich enough to do so enjoy fire sale prices." He inclined his head toward the river framed in the drawing room windows and, I presumed, in the general direction of the Roosevelts, the Vanderbilts, and their ilk. "This is not good news for people with art to sell."

His words were a body blow. For all these months, the art collection had been my last hope.

He blotted his lips with a tiny, delicate napkin that I had ironed myself. "I cannot in good conscience advise you to sell anything I've seen today. You would lose your shirt." He gave a thin smile at the indelicate metaphor. "If I were you, I'd hold all of it until things get better. When the war is over, perhaps their prices will even appreciate. Your father had the best eye I've ever seen."

I tried to be deliberate with my answer, as if I were considering my options…as if I had any real options to consider. "I might be willing to take a small loss to sell now."

I would be extremely willing.

He shook his head. "You misunderstand me. Your father had a gift for finding a young artist, buying several canvases, inviting him to dine with his influential friends, and then kaboom. His friends made the young artist famous, and your father's just-bought paintings were easily turned into enough cash to do it again."

And, I felt sure, to fund more fine wine and hand-tailored clothes. It was funny how my father's influential friends had vanished when he died and the parties stopped.

"Sometimes," Mr. Glenby went on, "he used the money from his star-making ventures to buy a piece by an established artist, something less speculative."

"Like the Moran."

"Yes. And the Cole. And sometimes he was fond enough of a newer painting to keep it."

"Like the Hopper."

"Yes. But he seems to have sold those. Everything I see here today shows excellent taste, but—"

"But they have no market value."

"Not on a bet, my dear." For an instant, I saw the gambler hiding behind the art connoisseur. "You don't have to show me what your father paid for these paintings. I know that it wasn't much, and the war has knocked the stuffing out of the little value they had. At the moment, they are decorative, but no more."

He allowed himself a nibble of cake.

"There was a time when your father owned true treasures, but this is not that time. I watched him sell his valuables through the thirties, presumably to keep your family afloat in bad times.

The Depression was hard on everybody, and you remember that Europe was at war long before Pearl Harbor dragged us into it."

"So you're telling me that the art is worthless."

He emitted a slight "Hmm," that was a mannerly man's way of agreeing that I had nothing to offer him.

"The books?" he asked. "Would you mind if I took a closer look at them?"

Something about his tone sounded dishonest. Something about his tone sounded like my father.

"Do you deal in books?"

"No, not really—"

My suspicious side, also reminiscent of my father, was fully triggered. "Then I think perhaps I will contact a book dealer directly."

I had considered the paintings my ace in the hole, but they weren't. Selling the books had been unthinkable, but now I had thought it. I had to at least try turning them into money. But I didn't have to let Oscar Glenby profit when I did it. I had decided that I didn't like this man.

Since I wasn't giving him what he wanted, he was ready to leave. I could see it. But he was sitting there drinking my tea and eating my cake, so he had to make conversation until he could find a polite way to go.

"Your father collected and traded paintings for money, but he collected books for love. As far as I know, he never sold a one, and I can't think of a book dealer who would come this far up the Hudson to look at them."

"Even the cuneiform tablets? And the scrolls?"

"Even those. I know that they seem priceless, but they're

more curiosities than objects of value. The most likely purchaser for your father's collection would be another English professor, but first you'd have to find an English professor with your father's particular tastes who had money to spare. I may not be a book dealer, but I have connections that you don't."

"Oh, I know plenty of professors." Any fool would hear my tone and know that the conversation was at an end.

He drained his cup and downed the cake, and then he moved on to people whose valuables were actually valuable. I was left to beat back encroaching despair before I let Annie see my face.

Fortunately, I'm good at that. You don't spend eleven years convincing the lions of literature at Yale that you deserve a doctorate, despite your unfortunate femininity, without being dogged. And now I had amused myself by smashing together the images of literary lions and a yappy dog into one sentence, so I was ready to face Annie with a smile.

She'd gone outside to work while I finished failing to sell Mr. Glenby my treasures, so I changed into my gardening clothes and joined her. Even there, my father's follies slapped me in the face. In the rear garden, between the house and the face of Rockfall Bluff, he had hired a team of gardeners and stonemasons to construct a semicircular reflecting pool fed by a narrow man-made waterfall rushing down the cliff. To accomplish this, he had cannibalized a few of the old ponds, creating an oval cliffside pool up top to feed the waterfall. When I thought about the cost of all that labor, it took my breath away, but I had to admit that the effect was lovely.

Surrounding the semicircular pool were terraces planted with rhododendrons, roses, and peonies, all of them blooming white, because Mother chose them with my eventual wedding in mind. They were flanked by Japanese maples that flamed red in the fall and hollies that held their red berries all winter. Surrounding it all were the deep green hemlocks that had always grown there.

The terraces had been spectacular until Annie and I gave up on keeping it all weeded. Like all my father's accomplishments, his fantastical garden had started to decay as soon as he wasn't around to prop it up with money and megalomania.

Annie leaned on her rake among the radishes as I approached. She used her eyes to ask me how things went with Mr. Glenby, but all I could do was shake my head and pretend to be carefree, as if his disinterest in my paintings made no difference to our lives at all.

CHAPTER 8

My experience of romance had been confined to one ago-nizing heartbreak dealt to me in Boston by a fiancé named Bradley, preceded by a long series of men who…well, they weren't *enough*. These flirtations had typically ended when I decided the man was boring, and he decided I was strange. I was not so desperate for companionship that I was willing to figure out how to be less strange, so I had decided that my own company was more than sufficient. Friends like Annie, Leontine, and Marjorie were icing on the cake.

Given this checkered romantic past, it was only to be expected that I would be wearing my father's Bermuda shorts and carrying a garden rake when confronted by my first suitor in years. (Other than John, and I'm not sure that a man who proposes marriage with no preliminary wooing whatsoever counts as a suitor.) Annie's instincts in this arena are better than mine, which is alarming when you consider that she is sixty and never-married.

She tried to help me. Unfortunately, I was beyond help. I

would have thought that passing into my thirties would have put an end to opportunities to embarrass myself in front of men, but I would have been wrong.

We'd just begun cleaning up the asparagus bed when she hissed, "There's a car turning in the driveway," flapping her hands in a shooing motion. "I don't know who might be calling on you, but go freshen up. I'll bring whoever it is into the drawing room."

She was pink with excitement. I wondered what she would think about John's offer to solve my problems by marrying me.

"Don't be silly, Annie. It might just as easily be someone coming to see you."

"That's unlikely. There's a young gentleman behind the wheel." Annie flung a glance over her shoulder as the car climbed the steep, curving drive. "Go! Really, Miss Estella—"

My glare made her remember how I felt about my name, and also that she was not to call me "Miss."

"Really, E." The car negotiated another curve. "Go!"

And then it was too late.

A black car, old but waxed to a high shine, pulled up beside us. I recognized the man at the wheel by his strawberry blond hair and freckled skin. It was Dr. Chase, who had crouched beside Dean Jamison's broken body with me just the day before. He had been kind, and this was bothersome, because I had been carefully nurturing my righteous anger against him for taking the job that should have been mine. My doctorate was from the Ivy League and his was from…someplace lesser. I didn't actually remember where. I had arrived at Bentham College with teaching experience, and he was as green as grass in the classroom. I had a book under consideration at a respectable press, and he had nothing but an unpublished dissertation.

Why was he here? To rub my face in the fact that he made enough money to own a car?

"You're home!" he said. "I told you yesterday that I'd call to check on you, but I couldn't get through. Your phone was busy for a long time last night and again this morning, but the weekend operator said your line was never tied up that long."

I remembered the phone ringing the night before while I ransacked my father's office for more hidden money, and I remembered taking it off the hook so I could focus on my ransacking. However, so much had happened since Dr. Chase had made his promise to call—John's proposal, the magical appearance of five hundred dollars, and the odious Oscar Glenby's visit—that I had forgotten,

Dr. Chase and his shiny car had caught me so off guard that I showed my usual social grace by saying something awkward.

"How kind of you to come check on our phone service."

Ouch. That was definitely graceless.

"Happy to be of help." He nodded respectfully to Annie and said, "Excuse me, ma'am. I should have introduced myself. I'm Devan Chase."

"I'm Annie O'Dell. I'm—"

"She's my oldest friend," I blurted, unwilling to hear Annie call herself a housekeeper.

"Well, then, you must be a longtime citizen of Bentham, just as E is."

Hmm. He'd heard Marjorie call me E, and he'd remembered. My other colleagues hadn't managed to do that.

"I wouldn't ordinarily just show up on your doorstep," he said, "but yesterday was hard on everybody who knew Dean Jamison. I just wanted to make sure you were okay, E. Also, I had the chance to borrow my buddy's sailboat. I can sail her alone—I've done it lots of time—but it's more fun to have company. Can I steal you away for the day?"

Oh.

Annie had been right when she said that this man was calling on me, wielding the old-fashioned phrase as if he were a Victorian swain arriving in top hat and gloves, calling card in hand. Why couldn't I manage to remember that Annie was always right? She was also frequently Victorian.

I should have realized that the man was angling for a date when he admitted to phoning me an unhealthy number of times. I'd heard the phone ring two times—no, three—while I was in my father's office and, based on what he'd just said, he'd tried to reach me at least twice more since he got up. That was a lot of calls. Selma, the weekend operator, did a pretty good job of keeping the town's secrets, but she must be ready to burst over this bit of gossip.

What was my answer going to be? Did I want to go sailing with this man?

I could think of no reason to say no, and the way his hazel-green eyes squinted when he flashed his brilliant smile gave me a more-than-good reason to say, "I'd like that."

I hated to leave Annie with the interminable yard work to do, but her face said that she was determined to do it alone. She had an arm around my waist, ushering me into the house and beckoning for Dr. Chase—Devan, I supposed—to join us.

"I'm sure there's a breeze on the river, a nice and brisk spring breeze." Annie was prattling. She never prattled. "So you'll need a wrap. Your light blue cardigan will be just the thing. It's on a shelf in your closet, just above your espadrilles."

And now Annie was trying to dress me, as if I had no sense of style at all. I do have style. It's just my own, and it leans toward tailored black suits and snowy white blouses, which even I know are not suitable for sailing. Annie leaned more toward frills, florals, and pastels.

She seated Devan in the drawing room while I went upstairs to change. The room—indeed, the entire house—was newly swept and dusted for the disappointing visit of Mr. Oscar Glenby. This was fortunate for dating purposes, as Annie was patting the sofa cushion and inviting Devan to sit. It was fascinating to watch her demeanor shift from "doting mother" to "servant" and back again.

She aimed a maternal nod at me. "Take your time getting ready for your outing, dear." Then she catered to Devan. "Make yourself comfortable right here, Dr. Chase. This sofa accommodates tall men and their long legs so very well."

Not only did Annie have different postures and expressions when she was acting like a servant and when she was being her regular self, I had long since noticed that she talked to men and women differently. For Devan, she used a sweet, chirpy voice.

Perhaps this had been my problem with men. I didn't have a special voice for them.

Devan made himself comfortable on the sofa, flashing me a smile that had just enough devil in it for me to think, "Well, this one's not boring." I stopped feeling like Annie was pushing me to accept a date with a man—any man—and started feeling like a sailing excursion with this particular man might be fun.

I wondered how our house looked to him. There was no way for him to know that it had been mothballed for months. He could just barely glimpse the library from the delicately frayed chesterfield sofa where he sat, but he had a good view of the bay window and its panoramic river vista, as well as the many-windowed veranda door and the finely carved back staircase. To my eye, the house still looked grand, worn but grand. Somehow, I thought that a man who was comfortable enough in a sailboat to take it out on a big river alone might know a little bit about grand houses.

I flicked my eyes in his direction as I headed upstairs. Yes, the perfectly barbered tawny hair, the elegant wire-rimmed glasses, and the exquisite drape of the chocolate brown polo shirt over his broad angular shoulders all said, "Old money." So did his firm jaw and its determined angle. His plummy accent said, "Probably from one of the richer enclaves in New England."

I didn't know what my clothes said. I supposed it would depend on whether he realized that my well-made Bermuda shorts were hand-me-downs from my dead father. I knew that my speech said, "She doesn't come from generations of wealth, but her parents had aspirations and she's read a lot of books."

Shutting myself up in my bedroom, I grabbed at the powder-blue cardigan like a life buoy. It had been my mother's, and so had the crimson blouse I was wearing. I wrapped myself in the soft cotton cardigan and saw that Annie was right. The sweater and blouse looked nice with my father's tan shorts. Matched with my multicolored espadrilles, the outfit seemed right for sailing. It looked intentional—polished, even—in the full-length mirror that my mother had thought was so crucial to my future. Nevertheless, in some way that I couldn't define, I didn't look *right*.

When I looked at the shorts, I saw the way my father had worn them, with his long legs and elegant slouch. The cardigan had set off my mother's pale, knife-sharp features and otherworldly glamour. I had my father's legs and my mother's face, and I had both their blue eyes, but I had none of their charisma. I looked like a gangly child playing dress-up, if you ignored the fine lines across my forehead. The only indisputably beautiful traits that I'd inherited from them were their blue eyes and fine, wavy, golden hair—angel hair, Annie called it—but I'd chopped mine off in anger when I was seventeen years old, and I still refused to let it grow past my jaw.

In my mother's closet, I found a straw hat to clap over my short yellow hair. It had a strap to hold it on in the wind and a narrow brim to shade my face, so it was the closest thing to a boating hat in the house. I cinched the strap and headed downstairs, ready for a day with a man I barely knew.

❦

The road between my house and Bentham-on-Hudson went the long way round. On foot, I walked a direct path up Rockfall Bluff, but no car could manage such a steep, twisting climb. To get to town by automobile, you had to drive the completely wrong way for miles, then loop around and drive several miles more. Devan had traveled all those miles without even knowing whether I was home. As we reversed his course, I worried that I would run out of things to say, but he was easy to talk to, as easy as Leontine or Marjorie. We had books in common, obviously, but he had a sense of humor that I suspected could be wicked when he wasn't performing first-date decorum. He did let his hair down long enough to do a spot-on imitation of the self-important Dr. Bower.

"Stand back, everybody!" he barked, brushing aside the imaginary tassel hanging from his imaginary mortarboard. "Only I, a math professor, can be in charge of this poor man's death scene."

"Maybe he thought the police would need some help with their calculus," I offered.

"Chief D'Amato didn't seem like the calculus type to me."

This was true. It also reminded me of my struggles to get D'Amato to keep looking for my mother, so I changed the subject. "It seems like a perfect day for sailing."

"On this matter, E, you are absolutely correct."

As we waited for an attendant to take us to the moored sailboat, the calm river's dappled light made me want to be on the water, moving with it.

"Nice wind. Sunny sky. Smooth waters. And good company," Devan said as he helped me into the boat. I was glad for my flat-heeled, rubber-soled espadrilles and their ankle straps. Maybe Annie knew enough about sailing to know that they'd be just right. And here I'd thought she was only recommending them because they were cute.

Devan set a canvas rucksack by my feet. "You sit by the tiller and point it where I tell you to point it."

"You want me to—"

"Yes, indeed. I brought you out sailing. You, my esteemed colleague, Dr. Ecker, are going to sail."

I grasped the tiller's sun-warmed wooden handle and said, "At your service, Dr. Chase."

"But you need to sit on the other side of the tiller."

Obediently for me, I shifted to the other side of the boat, but I did ask why it was necessary.

"Because the wind's coming from that direction." He pointed to my left. "When it catches the mainsail, we're going to heel over. We want our weight to work against any chance that we might capsize."

"Not capsizing. That sounds like the thing we want to do."

He waggled his eyebrows, which I presumed meant "Yes."

He scrambled around the small sailboat, maneuvering the sails and pushing us away from the mooring. The boat began to turn as he said, "I should probably handle the tiller while we get underway. Afterward, it will be all yours."

He steered us into a diagonal course aimed at the far side of the river, tightened the mainsail, and put my hand back on the tiller, placing his lightly atop it.

"Remember this. Tiny motions. Even a small boat like this isn't going to turn on a dime, so you can't give it big, fast commands. Not like a car. You drive?"

I nodded, enjoying the way the river spoke to my hand via the faintly vibrating tiller. "I've got my license, but I haven't had much practice."

"I'll take you out to practice, if you like. You're smart, and you seem levelheaded. That's all you need to be a good driver.

And a good sailor. Honestly, I think it's all you need to do a lot of things."

In my head, I knew that the sailboat couldn't possibly be going as fast as a speeding car, but the wind and spray in my face made it feel that way.

"Now try out the tiller. A little movement to the right will turn us to the left. And vice versa." He laughed at my surprise. "It's just the opposite of a car."

Gingerly at first, I experimented with guiding the boat in one direction and then another. Devan watched me closely, but he didn't hover like a man who expected a woman to be inept. It had never occurred to me how universal the men in my life had been in their belief that I was, at rock bottom, not a capable person. By contrast, Devan sat back and gave me time to test out the tiller, giving me a chance to get a feel for how moving it made the boat behave. I was confident that I could figure things out, and he seemed to feel the same way.

No, this man was certainly not boring. It remained to be seen whether he might think I was strange.

The late morning sun cast a column of light on the water ahead of us. "It's a wide river," he said, "but we'll run into the far bank if we keep going this direction. So we're going to make a forty-five-degree turn and head that way." He pointed with one hand, but he kept a tight hold on the boom with the other. "In this wind, we'll do that by tacking. When I say go, give the tiller a gentle shift to the right and I'll deal with the sails."

I nodded, gripping the tiller harder than I probably needed to.

"Oh, and you'll need to move to the other side, because we're going to heel over in the other direction."

It looks so simple and smooth when you stand on the shore and watch a sailboat change direction. On the water, it's exhilarating. The inexorable motion of the bow turning in response to the tiller, the noise of the flapping sails as they seek a new equilibrium, the startling reversal of the deck's slant—it all feels dangerous and out-of-control, and I loved it.

I loved it, at least, until the boat wheeled around and gave me a full-on view of my home and the cliff where it sat. Right at that moment, Devan got the sails in order and turned to me.

I must have looked frightful, because he said, "You don't look well. I should have realized that you might get seasick. The water's calm in that cove straight ahead. We won't need to be heeling this way and that to get there, so I think you'll be okay until then. Just sit back and relax."

It bothered me that he thought I was seasick. I was made of sterner stuff than that, but it was better to let him think me weak than to tell him about the cove. He hadn't been in town long enough to realize the history of it. So I did what he said. I relaxed, and I focused on the feel of the boat knifing through the water.

Soon enough, Devan loosened the sails and steered us to a halt by turning the bow into the wind. In minutes, he had us anchored. He had no way to know that it was the jagged rocks surrounding us, the ones that guarded the cove and kept the water so still, making me want to faint, vomit, run.

"I packed a picnic, but I don't know whether it will make you feel better or worse. Seems to me like tuna salad sandwiches could go either way," he said, opening his rucksack and handing me a sandwich wrapped in a blue-striped napkin. Reaching back into the bag, he pulled out a bag of peanuts, a bottle of apple cider, and two tin cups. "The cider is hard, so go slow until you see how it makes you feel. But maybe it'll fix you right up."

"I feel fine. I just... I can't explain it. Have you ever felt like somebody was walking over your grave?"

Have you ever felt like you might be sailing over your mother's grave?

He pointed at the bluff. "I was going to say that the house up there looks a little spooky, what with the tower and Gothic arches and all, but then I realized that it was your house. I imagine it just looks like home to you."

"Whatever 'home' means," I muttered, taking a big bite of the sandwich.

He used a hand to shade his eyes as he looked up. "Your house's setting is rather magnificent, halfway up the bluff. It dominates the landscape."

"It didn't when it was built. There was a true mansion at the very top, Stenen Klif Manor, owned by a man called William Van der Waal. If you look through the trees, you can see some of the ruins up there." I pointed at the crest of the bluff. "There's not much left but heaps of stone and a chain of ponds. Well, there's also a pond full of waste from the coal gasification plant, but it stinks, and I don't recommend it."

"Coal gasification? Wow. I guess if you wanted to have gas-lights in the mid-1800s while living way out here, you had to run a pretty self-sufficient operation."

"I imagine so. There are also miles and miles of overgrown carriage roads and bridle paths where guests could be self-sufficient in the entertainment department. You can see them there"—I pointed at a thin line threading through a grassy gap in the trees—"and there. He owned quarries up and down the river—"

"Judging by your house alone, that's not surprising. Somebody hauled a lot of rocks up there."

"He didn't have to haul them far. Those were some of his quarries." I pointed to rocky scars in the landscape downriver from the cove and the village. "Van der Waal built both houses out of stones from his quarries, and he named his house to suit its location. 'Stenen Klif' is Dutch for 'stone cliff.' My guess is that the stones of Van der Waal's house were the finest to be had in his time. My house is probably built of the rocks that weren't quite good enough for a robber baron."

He laughed out loud, and I was startled. No man had ever found me funny before, not even Bradley. I have never understood why he seemed to love me for a time.

"I'm not kidding," I said. "You can see the scars in several of my house's stones where somebody's chisel slipped."

"Looks pretty good from this distance."

I gave him a thank-you smile. "Our house was built for van der Waal's estate manager, so it was an extremely fine home for a lucky middle-class man who stumbled into an excellent job. That's why it's just called Rockfall House, instead of something grander like Rockfall Manor or Rockfall Hall. Robber barons like to make sure that everybody knows their place."

"Have you ever seen your house from this angle, sitting on the water?"

I shook my head. It was true that I'd seen it from almost this exact angle on the worst day of my life, but I hadn't been sitting on the water. I'd been clambering from rock to rock, searching for someone I didn't find that day. I hadn't found her yet.

I took a swig of cider. The alcohol burned all the way down, in a good way. It distracted me from the possibility that my mother lay in the deep waters below. It distracted me from the stones that had filled the pockets of Helena Frederick. Leontine had told me that her mother sewed for the Fredericks, so she had probably made the girl's skirt and its nightmarish pockets.

I pushed Helena Frederick out of my head because Devan was speaking.

"Pardon me if this is a foolish question, but is that the rockfall?"

He waved his cup of cider at the upriver side of the cove. There, an enormous pile of rocks rose halfway up the cliff to roughly the same height as my house, which stood a goodly distance—a safe distance, I hoped—away. A scar above the pile of rocks showed where a slice of the cliff had sheared off, crashing to the riverbank and breaking into a tremendous pile of locomotive-sized boulders.

"Yes, that's the rockfall. When I was a child, I thought it looked like an ossified waterfall. You can see rockfalls all up and down this part of the Hudson."

He nodded without flinching at the fancy word "ossified," which marked him as somebody who wouldn't make fun of me for being bookish. With this, he passed his first test. Belatedly, I realized that testing him meant that I cared whether he passed or failed. This made me become suddenly fascinated by my bag of peanuts.

"You're very impressive, you know?"

Was he saying this because I'd used the word *ossified*?

"Am I?"

Did I think I was impressive? Probably. But one doesn't admit to thinking such things, certainly not while one is on a date with a man whom she might possibly upstage. "You're the one who knows how to handle a sailboat and a car. You're the one who landed a professor job at what I think must be a pretty young age."

Watch it, E. If you like him, you cannot let him know that you felt cheated when Dean Jamison gave him that job. If he has an iota of self-awareness, he already suspects it.

"You're the one who wrote the definitive response to McIntyre," he responded.

"You mean my piece questioning her twenty-year-old essay on whether Gothic literature is really Gothic? Everybody in my field has an opinion on that one. People love to poke fun at critics who make everything—everything!—about Shakespeare."

And then I blushed, because he was a Shakespearean scholar.

He refused to take the bait. "You're the one who stirred up enough interest to get a publisher interested in your book. I have to say that I love the title."

"Gothic Literature as Social Criticism?"

"That's fine, if a bit dry. It's the subtitle that I love."

"Unhappy People in Big Houses?"

"That's the one! You could file a healthy fraction of all literature under 'Unhappy People in Big Houses.' *Hamlet* and *Macbeth* certainly fit the description. But listen to me making everything about Shakespeare."

I felt myself smiling, despite the fact that I was floating atop that cursed cove. "Well, Shakespeare certainly didn't invent stories of unhappy people in big houses. Snow White's stepmother comes to mind. So do King David and his wandering eye."

He laughed again. Then he asked why I thought so many Gothic novels were written by women, and I stopped worrying about sounding awkward. I just started talking to a man who cared what I had to say.

After an hour, he said, "Is it time to go back? Annie strikes me as someone who would skin me alive for bringing you back sunburned."

"No, she wouldn't. She'd say that I should have had the good sense to wear a hat with a wider brim. But we should go back. Your nose is getting pink."

"It does that. The sun reflects off these glasses, the ones that have so far kept me out of the army." His mouth had the tight look that I often saw on men who wanted me to know why they hadn't volunteered before the wreckage at Pearl Harbor had cooled.

"There are other ways to serve." It was a cliché, but I couldn't think of anything better to say.

"Well, I don't think teaching Shakespeare is a particularly valuable occupation right now," he said with a grin. "Never fear. I'll find a way to do my share. I've already emptied my apartment of anything the folks running the scrap drive would take."

He bagged up our trash and took my empty cup. "Except for these tin cups. Shhhh. Don't tell anybody."

Devan gestured at the tiller as he raised the anchor. "The helm is yours, Captain Doctor Ecker. The breeze has shifted, so you're going to see what it's like to run before the wind. Sometimes, speed is the only cure for a world gone mad."

He had to help me as we maneuvered out of the cove, but he left the tiller to me while he adjusted the sails. And then—I don't know how to explain what it was like. Riding with the wind means that you're moving with the air. To you, it seems like the wind has calmed, but the boat is more alive as it cuts through waves that slap hard against its hull. The river is more alive. *You* are more alive. You are, for the moment, free.

I laughed out loud, and that made Devan laugh. "I can see that I won't have any trouble getting you to go sailing with me again."

Too soon, it was over, and the attendant was returning us to the creaking dock.

"I can help you take care of the boat."

"No, it's a quick drive to your house and back, and the sails need to dry before I stow them. I'll put you to work another time." He gave me a hopeful glance. "Not that I can borrow the boat all that often. Can I interest you in a different kind of outing?"

"If you'd like to see the ruins of Stenen Klif Manor, we could take a hike up there. The gardens are overgrown, but they're full of rare plants, and the reflecting pools are beautiful."

This would be about as interesting to most people as watching paint dry, so I tried to sweeten the offer. "I could pack the picnic this time."

And then I worried that this was forward of me. I honestly wasn't very good at being a woman, or so everybody wanted me to believe.

"Bridle paths, rare plants, abandoned ponds, piles of first-class stones, a spectacular view, and a picnic. And good company. What could be better? Next Saturday?"

"Next Saturday."

He leaned close, and I thought he was going to kiss me right there in public, but all he did was meet my gaze. His eyes were murky behind those lifesaving glasses, shifting between brown and green as easily as the wind changed direction. I couldn't read what those eyes were saying, so I took a guess. I rose up on my toes and kissed him long enough to let him know I meant it, then I pulled away.

After a moment of eye contact that felt long but was still (probably) short enough for decorum in a public place, he put his arm around me and escorted me down the dock. I was both glad and regretful to reach solid ground. Even so, it shifted underfoot as if I were still in a boat on the river.

CHAPTER 9

When I got home, I came in through the kitchen door. Annie was there, her hands deep in the biscuit bowl. "How was your date? He seems very nice." She patted out a pale round of dough and set it gently on a cookie sheet.

Something was wrong. Annie wasn't excited enough about my sailing expedition. She had anguished for years that I seemed headed for spinsterhood. She should be pumping me for the details of every minute I'd been gone.

I tried to get her to look at me, but she had both eyes fastened on her biscuits, needlessly so. Annie could make perfect biscuits blindfolded.

I took the bowl and clutched it to my chest. "Tell me what's wrong."

"I thought—" She reached for her biscuit bowl, but I lifted it overhead where she couldn't reach it. "I thought the art dealer was going to solve our problems, but he didn't. And he doesn't think that selling the books will solve them, either."

I raised an eyebrow.

"Yes, I listen at the door. I was trained to give perfect service. How am I supposed to know when to bring in the teapot if I can't listen to how the china clinks when it hits the saucer?"

"Fair enough," I said, wondering what else happened just out of my sight.

"Thank you for your approval, but I don't need it. I know I'm good at my work. As for Mr. Glenby, I could tell by the sound of your voice that you wanted him gone, so I let his empty cup clink so you could get him out of the house."

I wanted to say, "For that, you get a raise." Instead, I offered her a thank-you gift that I could afford. "For that, I'll cook dinner for a week."

"No, you won't. You work too hard for that ungrateful college to come home and do my cooking. Speaking of which, it seems like I need to find another house to work in. A good cook can always get a place somewhere."

Maybe with one of the rich families across the river, but not in Bentham.

"We'll figure things out, Annie."

It will kill me if you go.

"Estella…E… Surely you hear what I'm saying. If I found another place, you could go back to Boston, where you were happy."

How did she know? I'd only told her the bare story of my time away—teaching job, low pay, spartan boardinghouse room. I'd never mentioned my joy at being on my own, because it would have hurt her to hear it.

"Let's not talk about Boston, Annie. I'm not going anywhere."

"I see the way you hide the mail. You've got to be looking for work, because I know you. You're not your mother and father. They were more than willing to drown in debt instead of seeing that change must come. But not you. And not me."

She leaned against the pantry door and wiped her floury hands on her apron.

"If somebody offers you a job, you need to take it. I'll get by. I have skills. Trying to keep this house going will bleed you dry. And for what?"

For you. I have to keep this house going for you. Or else I have to find a way to support us both somewhere else.

"That's for me to worry about, Annie. You have your job, and I have mine. It's my job to run the household. It's your job to make sublime biscuits. You're doing great. I'm—well, I'll figure it out eventually. If, in the end, it all comes apart, I hope you'll go where I go."

She wrung the apron between her strong hands. "I'm done, Miss Estella."

"What do you mean you're done? If you're tired, I'll do more of the chores. If you need more pay, I'll find the money."

Annie had been the buoyant constant in my life, the single solitary spot of undying cheer for a lonely girl whose classmates had thought she was snooty, when she was just awkward and shy.

My parents had been too wrapped up in themselves to consider whether their only child needed something besides the things they bought her. (And, in my mother's case, weekly French and Italian lessons and the rare game of hide-and-seek.) Annie was the one who'd told me fairy stories when she tucked me in at night. Annie, with her mildly lurid detective novels and romances, was the one who had taught me that reading wasn't just for cultivating my mind. Annie had known that stories could be *fun*.

Running away from my parents had been the best thing I ever did for myself and the worst thing I ever did to Annie. Now I was back home, ready to do right by her, and she was saying she was done with me? This couldn't be.

I repeated myself. "What do you mean when you say that you're done?"

"I'm done protecting him. Well, I guess I was protecting you, too. I'm just protecting his memory now, but I'm done doing that."

"What are you saying?"

"I saw the money that ran through your father's hands. How could that man have left you in this state, wondering how you're going to buy coal, for goodness' sake? Didn't he care whether you were warm? Didn't he care about you at all?"

I lowered the biscuit bowl to the kitchen table.

"Some people are so scared of dying that they don't think about the mess they'll leave behind," I said. "I learned today from Mr. Glenby just how bad my father was with money, which I honestly should have known as soon as I saw his account books."

"All those years, the money flowed through this house like water. But that's not the worst of it."

There was something worse than leaving your daughter bankrupt and cold?

She stood on her tiptoes to get her lips to my ear. "I saw the bruises on her, Miss Estella. I mean E. I heard the names he called her."

I imagined my mother, slender and frail, trying to defend herself against my father, equally thin and no taller, but made of nothing but muscle. When his fist struck my image of her, she shattered like porcelain.

"Always, Annie? Did he always treat her like that?"

"The name-calling? Now and then, but he couldn't shout when you were little, for fear you'd hear. He never dared strike her where you might see the mark. After you left? He never cared what I heard or saw, so he got much worse when it was just the three of us."

I had left my mother and Annie alone with…that…for four years of undergraduate schooling and seven years of graduate school, but perhaps a seventeen-year-old can be forgiven for seeking an education with no thought for anyone else. The three years in Boston after I graduated, though, when I lived from paycheck to paycheck, but I was so very carefree and happy… The guilt for those years was a heavy thing. I was as selfish as my father.

"But that last day—oh, that last day." Annie's voice had lowered to a moan.

"Did he hit her that day? *Did he hurt her?*"

The words *Did he kill her?* echoed in the kitchen, but I couldn't say them. I wasn't at all sure that Annie would be able to answer me, even if the answer was "Yes."

Annie cowered at my raised voice, and I wondered if I sounded like him. I calmed myself, so that I could modulate my tone. "Have you been protecting me from anything else? Is there anything else I should know about that last day?"

She raised a hand, still covered in flour and dough, to wipe her teary eyes. "Yes. They were fighting. They'd been fighting all day."

"All day? You said he left early that morning, before you went to town."

"I was protecting him, more fool me. I never went to town."

If Chief D'Amato had done even a smidgen of investigation, he could have asked around town and torn a hole in Annie's story. But he hadn't. He thought my mother was unstable and suicidal. Why would he check stories?

"They fought all morning, but she finally got done with it after lunch. She tried to run out through the kitchen, but he blocked her way, so she ran out onto the porch and down the steps."

Down the steps. Annie was talking about the veranda steps that led to a path running between the house and the cliff, only a few feet from the edge. We'd always called it the Precipice Path.

"He chased her, E."

"Did he catch up to her?"

Did he grab her there, on the edge of the bluff?

"Not for a long time. She ran and ran, and he only caught up with her when she got to that marshy meadow above the upriver side of the house. I ran to the bedroom window on that end of the house, and I saw. The tall grass caught on her dress and the muddy ground slowed her down. That's when he grabbed hold of her."

"I don't remember a single pair of her shoes that would have stayed on her feet in that mud."

She always wore such dainty, impractical shoes on her slender feet.

"Oh, she was barefoot, Miss E."

She was barefoot. I'd forgotten. That was part of the description Annie gave the police. Blond, blue eyes, thin, fifty years old, blue silk shirtwaist dress, sapphire-and-platinum bracelet, bare feet.

She was barefoot, and he was chasing her.

I had no choice but to ask the worst question of all. "Did she go over the bluff?"

No, that wasn't the worst question I could have asked. The worst would have been, "Did she jump, or did he throw her over the edge?"

"No, I never saw her go over. I wouldn't have kept that secret. Never."

"I believe you."

"But she did throw something over, right after she ran down the veranda steps. I don't know what. It slowed him down, because he stopped to see where it fell. She would never have got as far as the meadow if he hadn't stopped."

I couldn't think of anything she could have thrown that would have made my father stop in his tracks when he was that angry. Maybe a fistful of cash. I remembered him saying "Ovuh de cliv." Maybe it was never my mother's body he was talking about. Maybe he was talking about the thing that she threw over the cliff.

"He caught up with her there in the meadow and grabbed her by both shoulders. He slapped her to the ground, then he picked her up and shook her. He just kept shaking her. He was shouting, but I couldn't hear the words. And then she pulled back her arm and rammed her elbow right into his throat. I'd never known her to fight back, not once. I don't think he was hurt, but he was surely surprised. It made him lose his grip. She shook his hands off her and took off running again."

"Did she go up the carriage road on the far side of the meadow, like you told the police? The one she called the Meadow Path?" It led nearly straight up, ending near the ruins of Stenen Klif Manor.

"Yes. That part was true. I just didn't tell anybody that he was chasing her. She ran up out of my sight, and I never saw her again. I went up in the belfry then, so I could keep an eye on the meadow. And the Meadow Trail, at least as far up as I could see. It seemed like I was in that belfry so long, watching for either one of them to come back down."

"What about my father? Did you see him come back?"

"He must've come down another way, probably the bridle trail that starts out back of the house and goes up to the ruins."

"The Garden Path?"

"Yes, probably that one. I don't know for sure, because I didn't see him. So I don't know if she was with him. Maybe she was, and that's why her body didn't turn up in the river. All I know is that I heard the engine start. I looked back at the driveway to see the car tearing out of here. That was when I called you."

When Annie had called me that awful day, she'd been weeping too hard to say anything more than "Come home." It had never occurred to me that he hadn't had his stroke yet when she called.

"I did all my watching on the upriver side. If she went over the edge, it was probably downriver, unless she was a goodly distance away. If she didn't, then…she has to be somewhere, doesn't she?"

"When did he get home?"

"About dark, or not long before. When I saw that he was by himself, I about lost my mind. I'd been so sure he was going to bring her home. I'd made dinner, chicken in a mushroom sauce and a big pot of rice."

I had been on the train by that time, somewhere in Connecticut.

"Why did you tell everybody that he left after breakfast, long before she disappeared?"

"The officers were asking me questions right in front of you. I just couldn't tell the truth about what he did to her, not with you listening. And not with your father lying in his bed, babbling nonsense. Part of me hated him, but the other part couldn't bear to think of him in jail in that condition. Or worse, locked up in an asylum."

I was staring at her, open-mouthed.

"I was trained my whole life to be a good servant, Miss E. I will bring no shame to this house."

The tears were running down Annie's face, dripping off her jaw.

"Did anything happen when he came home that I don't know about?"

"He came in from the car like I've been telling you all along, right through the kitchen. He was red-faced when he found me pacing a hole in the drawing room carpet, and he was raving about nonsense. I ran to him and asked where your mother was, but all he could do was say my words back to me."

I leaned back against the pantry door to keep myself from falling.

"I said to your father, 'Where is she?' and he said it back, just like I said it. Then I asked him, "Where is Mrs. Ecker? Do you know where she is?' and those words came right back out of his mouth. Then he started shaking and dropped to the floor. I called the ambulance, and I called the police. I had already called you."

"Did it take them long to get here?"

"Oh, they came right quick. The doctor examined him while the nurse and I brought his bed down. After I got through talking to the police chief, the doctor said he'd done all he could do and left the nurse to do for your father. Not so very long after that, you came in the door."

"And that's all you know?"

"That's all I know."

I was pulling away from Annie, and there was nothing I could do to stop myself. I had to find my mother, so I was following her trail.

I left Annie in the kitchen with her biscuit bowl, and I fled through the house and out the back door. Down the veranda steps I ran, along the Precipice Path, out to the meadow, and up the Meadow Path to the top of Rockfall Bluff. Piles of perfect stones waited for me up there, and I needed to search my way through them again.

I'd spent days and weeks among those stones after Mother disappeared. I'd lost track of how much time I'd spent on the highest rim of Rockfall Bluff, afraid I'd see her body down below, but afraid not to look. From my perch, I'd searched everything below me for blue fabric, pale skin, yellow hair. And red blood. I'd found none of those things.

And all the while, the cove had waited at the base of the bluff. Under ideal atmospheric conditions, its water could take on a strange blue tinge. How many times did I let that odd color convince me that I'd seen her dress among the rocks? How many times had that otherworldly blue led me to make the long walk into Bentham and then to the river?

I never found anything on the riverbank but water, rocks, muck, trash, and—once—a dead fish. I cannot tell you how unsettling the foul smell of rotten fish is when you fear that you are looking for a dead body.

On the day that Annie finally told me the truth, the Hudson was an unremarkable gray-brown. I don't know how long I watched the unremarkable water that day. I don't know how long I wandered among the stones looking for a sign that my mother had been there. I just know that, at some point, my foot slipped in a puddle that had collected around the rock dam that held one of Stenen Klif Manor's reflecting ponds in place. I went down hard, my face inches from the wet clay. That's where I saw it.

My mother's bracelet had been stomped into the ground, perhaps by her or by my father as they continued their fight. Or perhaps by the feet of the people who looked for her. Perhaps I had trampled it into the muck myself.

I couldn't remember ever seeing her arm without this bracelet, crafted of platinum filigree links set with diamonds and sapphires. Did finding it in the mud prove that she was dead?

It did not. But it undid me, anyway.

You see, I had held on to the hope that the bracelet held my answer. You must remember that the condition of the bodies the coroner had asked me to view had been so very poor. This was to be expected of any human body that fell from such a height. You must also remember that the Hudson's palisade-like cliffs have stones at their feet. I cannot even say the name of my home, Rockfall House, without remembering the rocks where my mother would have fallen, if she fell.

Except for Helena Frederick and her remarkably preserved coat, the bodies I'd seen were naked. I couldn't trust that I'd be able to identify Mother by her blue shirtwaist dress. Worst of all, the bodies were… Only Helena's and one other were even close to complete. By looking at the length and girth of their surviving thigh bones, I had judged that they were all shorter and stockier than my willowy mother. This is how I'd been able to say that none of them was her.

The next corpse might not be so obviously someone else. Part of me had hoped that a body would be found with this bracelet around its wrist, because then I would know for sure. Yet there it was, dangling from my palm.

Without the bracelet to mark my mother with certainty, I could see no end to the mutilated corpses I must view. This was the moment that I fully grasped the truth. I might never know what had happened to my mother.

I was fooling myself when I blamed money—or the lack of it—for the paralysis keeping me in Bentham-on-Hudson. I wasn't being held there by fear of losing Annie. Annie and I might have to pinch pennies, but we were resourceful and we would manage. We weren't bound to Rockfall House because we had no place to go.

We were trapped there by my mother. Or, rather, by the lack of her. Something at my core kept saying, "If you go, you will never find her." The part of me that had longed to pierce her impenetrable nature kept saying, "If you go, you will never know her."

I barely heard myself begin to moan. There, on my knees in the mud, clutching a bracelet that I could sell to cover several mortgage payments, I felt my grief emerge as sound. A high keening wail left me, and it went on and on until I had no breath left. After the echo of it died, I knelt there until the stars came out, like cut diamonds set in a sapphire sky.

CHAPTER 10

The full moon rose before I left the ruins atop Rockfall
Bluff. It shone so brightly on the Precipice Path that I
had no worries about slipping over the edge. As I hurried,
because Annie was surely worried sick, I caught a view of the
cove below, its smooth waters reflecting the round moon. There
was something floating on the water, and it wasn't supposed to
be there.

I dropped to all fours and crawled to the rim. Why was a
boat sitting in the cove, right where Devan and I had enjoyed
our floating picnic? It was directly above the spot where Helena
Frederick had rested for fifteen years.

I couldn't see details, but I knew that I wasn't looking at a
sailboat. The watercraft had no mast, and it was small, probably
a rowboat. This would explain why I hadn't heard it approach.

Did people fish at that hour? I didn't know.

As I watched, the shadow of a human being stood up. I
couldn't have said whether I saw a man or a woman, old or young,
but a double-flash of reflected moonlight moved between the

person's face and chest, as the shadowy person held field glasses, looked through them, and lowered them again.

There was nothing to see at night on Rockfall Bluff but my house. In the daytime, yes, maybe a nature lover might stare through the field glasses at the bluff's rocks and trees. A bird-watcher might be looking at something as benign as a robin. But the only thing visible through those lenses at night would be the lit rooms of my house.

This was where Annie was waiting for me. I had to get back to her.

When I got home, I held the bracelet out for Annie to see. Her face crumpled.

"The police should know," I said. "I'll leave a message with the dispatcher, but I can't imagine that I'll hear from Chief D'Amato until Monday. Finding Mother's bracelet doesn't mean much, not to him. It doesn't change anything. She's still missing, and the bracelet doesn't give us any new ideas about where to find her. It also doesn't make it any more or less likely that she's dead. And they think she's dead."

I stepped into the study to use the phone, and Annie said, "When you finish with the dispatcher, you have two calls to return."

My heart gave a little skip. It had only been a few hours since I'd said good-bye to Devan, so surely he hadn't called already, but the little skip said that he mattered to me.

"No, not him," said Annie, who knew me very well.

"Marjorie and Leontine?"

"Yes. Your father may not have left you anything but this

leaky heap of rocks, but you do have good friends." She swatted at me with a dish towel. "Go. Call the dispatcher, so that you can call Marjorie and Leontine. What you need is some girl talk that will make you forget your troubles. I'm going to bed."

Selma put me through to the police department's night dispatcher, who listened to the news about my mother's bracelet but didn't say much. She did promise that somebody would get back to me on Monday. I supposed I believed her. I almost told her about the boat in the dark cove, but I stopped myself. There was no law against taking a boat out on the river, and I would sound paranoid if I told the police that somebody taking an evening pleasure cruise was watching me. Chief D'Amato and his men already thought I was histrionic. There was no sense in making it worse.

After I spoke to the bored dispatcher, I didn't call Marjorie or Leontine right away. Instead, I went up the main staircase and then up a ladder into the cupola. Trying not to think about the bats hanging overhead or the guano beneath the soles of my shoes, I groped toward the far wall. In a few steps, I reached the cupboard where my father's handheld telescope waited beside one of his cameras.

My mother had bought him the telescope when I was small. The camera was older than I was. Father had adored the storybook landscape of the Hudson Valley, and the telescope had let him explore it for miles around. The camera had brought the view from our cupola indoors. He had developed his landscape photos in the basement, and they still lined the walls of the second-floor hallway.

As I lifted his telescope from its velvet-lined case, it struck me that his photos and his telescope were the only things in the house that made me feel warm toward my father. Touching the telescope's wood tube felt like touching him again. It made him palpably alive.

I pointed the telescope at the cove and got the rowboat squarely in my field of sight. Yes, it was still floating there. I had been right to avoid turning on the cupola light and giving the person in the boat a handy silhouette to focus on. Depending on the quality of those field glasses, I might even have been visible looking back at him in the dark. Or her. Unfortunately, even the telescope couldn't show me anything that might help me identify the person spying on me.

I saw no link between the boat, Dean Jamison's death, and my mother's disappearance, other than me, but I could be wrong. Watching the boat wouldn't tell me anything except when it left. I resolved to go about my business, checking on it from time to time. At the moment, my business was in the study.

I perched on the desk chair, wishing the telephone were anywhere in the house that wasn't my father's desk. Was that his aftershave I smelled?

Marjorie's voice was as timid and sweet coming out of the phone as it was in person. "I just called to see how you were feeling after…after yesterday."

"I'm doing pretty well," I said. "What about you? Did you get any sleep last night?"

Marjorie said, "Yeah, sure, a little," and I knew this was her mannerly way of telling me she hadn't slept a wink.

"You?"

Me? I had been too wound up to go to bed at a reasonable hour because I'd found five hundred dollars that my father had hidden from me. I was ashamed that I'd pushed Dean Jamison's suicide so far from my mind, but I just said, "I'm okay. I got a little sleep."

"I'm glad," Marjorie said. "I was wondering if you wanted to do something tomorrow? I mean, we usually do something with Leontine on the weekends, but would it be unseemly when Dean Jamison isn't even cold?"

I wasn't sure if there were rules for how we were supposed to act after something like that.

"Even just a cup of coffee?" she asked. "My parents are always hard to take, but yesterday was awful, and it's got me so rattled. If I don't get out of the house, I'm going to start yelling at them and never stop. And I'm no yeller."

She really wasn't. I worried about Marjorie. She was so sweet-natured that I could imagine her spending her whole life with people who took advantage of her. I knew for a fact that she paid her parents rent, but her mother still made her do all the housework. She could have afforded an apartment—a little one, at least—but her parents said that living alone would make her look like a loose woman. Personally, I thought they didn't want to lose Marjorie's rent checks and her free labor.

Did I have time to sit down for a cup of coffee? No, not really. I'd planned to walk to the cove to see if the mysterious person in the mysterious boat had left any signs, but there was no reason Marjorie and Leontine couldn't come, too. The shoreline path was lovely, painfully so, and they didn't have to know why I wanted to go there. The only reason we hadn't already spent a Saturday morning on the shoreline path was that the sight of it hurt me so much.

"I was going to go for a walk," I said, "but we could do that together. Why don't you meet me at the park down the street from your house?"

Why didn't I want to tell Marjorie about the stranger in the boat? I guess I wanted to protect her. Marjorie always seemed so vulnerable. And so young. I had enjoyed spending time with her when we were small, in the way that older children see younger children as fascinating toys. Our six-year age difference had put us in two different worlds when I was twelve and she was six, so we'd only become really close since I came home from Boston. As adults, our age difference only mattered at times like this, when Dean Jamison's death brought out the fragility she tried to hide. My response was a desire to take care of her.

"A walk sounds perfect," she said. "It will tire me out, so I won't have the energy to yell at Mother when I get back."

"Shall we meet at nine, while it's still cool out? We could follow the shoreline to the far side of my house, then hike up Rockfall Bluff. We should be able to do it in time for lunch with Annie. I'll call Leontine and let her know."

"We've never done that walk. I bet it's glorious. Since I'm the one who mentioned coffee, I'll bring a vacuum bottle of it and a bite to eat. We can have our breakfast on the hoof."

We'd hung up before I thought to tell her to wear shoes she didn't mind getting wet. I thought about calling her back, but I reminded myself that Marjorie was too nice for her own good, but she wasn't stupid. She'd figure it out.

I picked up the receiver again and asked Selma to put me through to Leontine.

"Do you want to take a walk with Marjorie and me tomorrow morning? She's bringing coffee and breakfast, and we'll have lunch at my house."

"Name the time and place, and I'll be there."

"We're meeting at the park at nine." Remembering the head-to-toe elegance of Leontine's workwear, I added, "Do you even own ugly shoes? And clothes? Because we'll probably get pretty dirty."

"Don't worry about me. I like dirt. I grow the best tomatoes in town."

It was only after I hung up the phone that I realized that I hadn't told Marjorie and Leontine about my date with Devan. I hadn't told anybody, not even Annie, about John's proposal, but that made its own kind of sense. The idea that I might consider marrying my father's lawyer—Or was that my father's best friend? What was John to my father, anyway?—was embarrassing. Disturbing, even. But a date with a new man was the kind of thing I'd ordinarily want to share with my friends.

Why did our time together feel like something private that should stay just between Devan and me, even if only for another day or two? I didn't know, so I fled the office and the telephone that invited me to tell people things that I might not want to admit.

On my way to bed, I took a detour, turning out every light in the house and climbing to the belfry in utter darkness. I trained my father's telescope on the cove to see what was there.

The water was smooth and the boat was still floating on it.

The urge to stay at the window and watch was strong, but the longer I did, the more likely it was that the watcher would see me, even in the dark. Reluctantly, I backed into the hall.

Besides, I didn't have time to watch someone who was watching me back. I had a letter to read and more letters to write.

CHAPTER 11

Once in my room, I closed the blinds tightly while the room was still dark. Light escaped around their edges, but the interloper in the cove would see nothing but thin bright shards. Satisfied, I got to work, laying out stacks of stationery and envelopes around my typewriter. I needed to find my mother, and I needed to make my own way in the world. I was going to do whatever it took.

But maybe I'd already taken my first step toward that second goal. I reached into the drawer in my bedside table for the letter from Old Saybrook, the one I'd been afraid to open.

Using the silver letter opener my mother had given me, I sliced the envelope open and peeked at the first sentences:

We are pleased to make you an offer of employment as a teacher of English literature. Your fine credentials will be an asset in our pursuit of education for the young women of Connecticut.

I slid it back into the envelope quickly and allowed myself to dream.

I had been to Old Saybrook one time, while I was in college. A friend had invited me to spend Thanksgiving with her family. I'd been charmed by its historic downtown. The town was on the Connecticut River, so perhaps I wouldn't miss the Hudson too much, and Long Island Sound would remind me of the Boston waterfront.

The problem of finding my mother shadowed my excitement over Old Saybrook, but it was only May. Surely, I could find her before school started in September.

She'd gone missing in September. I could not make myself think that she could be gone for all four seasons of a year.

Holding the letter, I imagined a classroom with rows of students listening as I tried to sell them on the wonders of *Villette*. I pictured Annie and me in a tiny cottage where ocean breezes freshened every room. Then I finished reading the letter, and the ocean breezes blew my hopes away.

The salary was too low. It was horrifyingly, infuriatingly too low. I didn't know how much it cost to live in Old Saybrook, but it couldn't be less than living in a backwater like Bentham-on-Hudson.

I knew what it had been like to live on a salary that was just barely adequate for Boston, counting every cent spent on my food and room. My carefully balanced budget would have disintegrated within a month if I'd tried to carry both Annie and me. My Victorian novels might bandy about the term "genteel poverty," but there was no such thing.

I needed more than I was being offered. I deserved more. And so did Annie.

I wasn't even disappointed. I was livid. If a school had a rule, as this one did, that a teacher could not marry, then it couldn't even use the asinine excuse for poor pay used elsewhere: "It is presumed that the women who work here have husbands to pay their bills."

I stared at the letter for too long, defeated. At last, I found the anger I needed to crumple it, mashing it into a ball with both hands until my knuckles went white. I would hang on to hope for a high school to make me a better offer, but this one felt like a harbinger. No matter where I went, it was unlikely that I'd be able to force the numbers to add up to a comfortable life for Annie and me.

With a professor's salary, it was possible that I could escape that conundrum, but I couldn't get Bentham College to give it to me. If I was too female to be considered for a professorship at a college desperate to fill its wartime openings, then I was probably too female for other coeducational institutions. (The idea that a men's college might hire me was laughable.)

But there were women's college in the world, and they were about to hear from me. A library trip, and Leontine's help, had put about a thousand deans' names in my address book. (Or so it had seemed to my right hand when I was copying them all down.) She had given it to me along with a new list of people to write about my mother. (As she did every week, God bless her.) I would be typing letters to deans for weeks, and I would be writing morgues until I found Mother, but it would give me something to do while I waited for answers to scores of letters I'd already mailed.

Tossing the wadded-up Old Saybrook letter into the drawer,

I pounded the keyboard until I fell asleep face down on my cold metal typewriter. When I finally woke, the glow-in-the-dark hands on my alarm clock said it was four in the morning.

I staggered to my cupola vantage point. When I pointed the telescope at the cove, the boat was gone.

Getting up at four makes it easy to be on time for a nine o'clock appointment. I was rarely awake before Annie, so the early hour gave me a chance to putter around in the kitchen unsupervised.

I'd promised Marjorie and Leontine lunch, so what would it be? A large can of chicken and a loaf of bread sitting on a pantry shelf gave me ideas, especially when I remembered that there were apples and walnuts in the cellar. Chopped apples and walnuts, stirred into the chicken with a big spoon of Annie's homemade mayonnaise, seemed like a very nice sandwich spread to me. We had crumb cake left from Mr. Glenby's ill-fated visit, so I felt prepared to be a hostess.

Even with all the time I spent in the kitchen, I still left home early, and it was a good thing. In a small town, it's impossible to take a walk without seeing somebody you know. The thing that had changed was that those people suddenly wanted to talk to me.

I bumped into Dr. Masters exiting the laundry with five of the brown and beige skirted suits she liked to teach in.

"Dr. Ecker," she said, and I knew that she used my title because of the years she'd spent struggling to be respected for hers. "I've been thinking of you constantly since the…loss…of our dear Lily. Dean Jamison's sad end reminded me of everything you've been through. I should have arranged to check on you ages ago. Could you join me this afternoon for tea? Say, about four? Your mother gave me her recipe for jelly rolls, and I'd love to make some for you."

It might have been my mother's recipe, but Annie had always made the jelly rolls at our house.

Did I want to say yes? I supposed I did, even if only to find out why this woman seemed to believe she was so close to my mother.

"I'd love to come," I said, and I was astonished to hear myself say it in my mother's voice, higher and flutier than my own.

Dr. Masters flinched and said, "If I were to close my eyes when you speak, I could believe that Lily was right here."

"It's kind of you to ask me to tea, Dr. Masters."

"Please call me Cynthia."

"Okay. I'll see you at four, Cynthia."

I have never seen anyone look so distressed by the sound of their own name. Upon reflection, I realize that the problem was not her name. It was the fact that I sounded like Mother when I said it.

Cynthia Masters rose above her distress. She waved good-bye and said, "Jelly rolls at four!" in a cheery voice that broke my heart.

I'd hardly taken six steps when I bumped into John unlocking the door to his law office. He took a step back, probably because my face was speaking for me. It was saying, "This man asked me to marry him, and he never got an answer. What do I say?"

I was pretty sure that the proper way to turn him down wasn't an airy, "Good morning, John. Thank you, but no."

He saved me from the awkwardness of it all (and perhaps this was a point in his favor as a potential life partner) by opting for a casual greeting with a dollop of business on the side. "It's nice to see you. I'll have the income analysis we discussed at our next Friday meeting."

This was a graceful, fit-for-eavesdroppers way to say, "I'm willing to keep things businesslike while you mull over my offer to keep you solvent via romance."

I said, "Yes, we can talk about that on Friday," in a voice that sounded vague even to me.

"I'll have some ideas for you then." I wondered whether this meant I really intended to give his proposal more thought. He could certainly jump to that conclusion, if he were so inclined.

In response he took my hand and held it in both of his. It was a gesture that could reflect the friendly warmth of his words, which were, "I'm happy to help. Your family has been important to me for a long time." But it was also a gesture that could say, "I want to hold you. All of you." It could say, "I never want to let you go."

But he did let me go, with one last gentle squeeze of my hand. "Until Friday."

At the end of the next block, I saw Dr. Bower across First Avenue, but he hurried to greet me. He was dressed for hurrying, or at least for serious walking, in his black knickerbocker pants, high-laced brown boots, and sturdy tweed coat. On his back was a pack so worn that I would have believed him if he'd told me he carried it while scaling the Alps.

I make him sound ridiculous, but he wasn't. The practical clothing and backpack hung from a trim, broad-shouldered torso and his well-developed thigh muscles strained at the knickerbockers. His hiking gear made him look ten years younger. Or perhaps his academic regalia made him look ten years older. I'd heard that he was a retiree who had only returned to the classroom to fill in for young men gone to war, but he hardly looked fifty.

"How are you, Dr. Ecker? You were put under a tremendous strain on Friday when poor Dean Jamison died."

"I'm sad for him, but I'm doing well enough."

He peered into my eyes as if assessing whether I was truthful. Somehow, I believed Dr. Bower could see through any lie. I wondered if he made his math students quake in their boots.

"Well, if it would help to chat over a cup of coffee—hell, after what you've been through over the past year, it should be a beer—I'd be happy to buy the beverage of your choice."

Oddly, having a beer with my father's army buddy didn't sound excruciating.

"I'd love to hear about what you and Father did during the war."

He pulled the brim of his cloth cap lower and gave me a lopsided grin. "I can tell you some of it, but I can't tell you everything. Oath of secrecy, and all that."

I don't know why I was surprised. "After all these years?"

"Yes, after all these years. Same enemy, y'know. You could almost say that it's the same war." His tone was conspiratorial.

"Coffee, then. Or beer. This afternoon?" He stopped to consider. "Nobody's going to sell us beer on a Sunday.

"I'll be having tea with Dr. Masters anyway. Tomorrow, after work?"

"Tomorrow, it is. Koval's? Their beer's middling, but so is everybody else's. And the jukebox selection at Koval's is choice."

I wondered what music a middle-aged World War I veteran would consider "choice." My father had been a World War I veteran, but his musical taste had leaned toward opera. I was certain that Lenny Koval wouldn't have wasted any of the twenty-four record slots in his Wurlitzer on arias.

"Koval's. Beer. Jukebox. Five-thirty tomorrow?"

"See you there." He tipped his cap and walked away, as jaunty as an untried doughboy marching off to a war that would still be raging more than twenty years later.

By the time I got to the park, it was just past nine. Marjorie was waiting at the gazebo, wearing a pair of thick-soled brown brogans that were almost as hideous as my black ones. Leontine was walking toward us, looking stylish in a pair of fitted dungarees, a crisp chambray blouse, and a pair of oxblood oxfords buffed to a gleaming shine.

"These are your gardening clothes?"

"My mother set certain standards, and it doesn't make sense to spend money on ugly duds just for working in the yard. These pants wore through at the knee and the collar of the blouse started to fray, so a little darning and a few overcast stitches and abracadabra! Gardening clothes."

Marjorie waved away our apologies for being late. "I've lived in Bentham-on-Hudson all my life, so I know how hard it is to walk straight through town without being waylaid by a half-dozen people you know."

"Dr. Masters, John Wickley, and Dr. Bower for me," I said.

"Three of the chattiest people in town. You deserve a cup of coffee."

There was a vacuum bottle on the picnic table in front of Marjorie, with three stoneware cups beside it. She smiled as she poured, and her dimples showed.

Handing the cups around, she asked, "Do either of you take sugar? I didn't risk bringing cream or milk. It would spoil if we didn't use it."

Leontine took a cube of sugar, but I shook my head.

"Thank you, but I drink my coffee black. I save my sugar ration for my tea."

"Leontine and I are sugar spendthrifts," Marjorie said, as they both dropped cubes in their cups. "We're treating ourselves nice this morning."

Then she pulled a paper sack out of her tote bag. "Our breakfast. Just some bread and butter, but it'll keep us going."

Leontine opened her bag to show us three rosy apples. "We can save these to fuel us up when we get tired. I've never walked the route we're going, but that last leg has got to be steep. You must think Marjorie and I are finally ready for the kind of mountain goat walks you take every day."

"This path's got its challenges," I said, not willing to talk about why our weekend walks had never taken this route. We were going to be walking right past the cove where Helena

Frederick had rested…where my mother might still rest. I needed to stop thinking about these things, so I rose from the picnic bench and said, "We should go. We have lots of rocks to climb over and some creeks to jump."

We raised our cups to toast the morning, and we were off.

The path was easy at the beginning, with just a few small rocks to keep things interesting. Marjorie led the way. I nearly choked on my coffee when she tossed a sly question over her shoulder.

"So how was your date with Devan Chase?"

"But how did you—I didn't tell anybody. How—"

Leontine's snicker said that she knew, too. "Everybody knows he likes you. You're not supposed to talk in a library, but people do. And did you really think you two could drive through town and sashay through the marina without being seen?"

"Devan's been asking me about you since he came to town," Marjorie said, stepping over a big mossy rock. "Just a question here and there. One day, it might be, 'That blond woman, what's her name? You know, the research assistant?' Another day, it might be, 'Has she been working here long?'"

"He's been to the library a lot," Leontine said. "Always comes in right after you leave."

"Sounds sneaky," I said. "Maybe I don't want to go out with a man who checks up on me."

"Devan's not… He's not one of the people who…" Leontine stopped talking, clearly trying to figure how to say what she wanted to say. "It's not Devan who makes a shiver run up my back when I see him come in the library. He comes straight to the circulation desk and tells me hello. He turns in his books before they're due—"

"Sounds like a real Boy Scout." Marjorie said with her habitual giggle.

"That's actually a really good description of him." Leontine said. "When he needs help finding a book, he asks for it politely. When he talks to me, it feels like a real conversation, even when it's just about the weather or"—She flung me a mischievous look—"when he just wants to talk about you."

I blushed so hard that even my hands turned pink. God knows what my face looked like.

"The other new professors, though... A lot of them trouble me. I joke about Devan looking to see what you've checked out, but the men I'm talking about pay a different kind of attention to the books other people have been reading. For one thing, they never talk to the people they're snooping on. They don't say much to anybody, really, and they don't do much. We librarians might laugh about professors sitting around and thinking for a living, but we're not serious. Most of them *do* work on their research, because they're passionate about it. These new guys just sit in carrels and watch other people work."

I'd noticed the strange, silent substitute professors, but I hadn't spent any time with them. It was interesting that Leontine had noticed them, too. "Who are they snooping on?"

"One of them's real interested in Professor Bower's work on number theory. Two of them are snooping on the whole physics department. The physics profs can't even use the card catalog or the *Readers' Guide to Periodical Literature* without somebody watching. It's like somebody thinks the physicists are all going to pack up their research and go give it to the Axis."

"Devan's a new professor. You're saying he's not like that?"

"Only when it comes to you." A smile lit Leontine's face. "He doesn't waste much time trying to figure you out by the books you leave in the return cart, though. He talks to me, and mostly he talks about you. He's pretty smooth about it, but I can see what's going on. One thing he likes to do is to make point-less conversation about his colleagues' literary research...which everybody knows you help with. He's on a Dickens-reading jag, which is something every English literature professor eventually does, but in his case, reading Dickens means he's reading books your father wrote on the subject. Every now and then, he stops pretending that he's not smitten with you. That's when he asks his *real* questions."

I looked at Marjorie, who said, "Yeah, I get those ques-tions, too."

"And you two answer him?"

"Sure," Marjorie said. "But only when the answers are in your favor."

"We girls have to stick together," Leontine said, leaping puddles in the mucky path.

We were headed downhill, directly for the river's edge. I had to watch where I put my brogans to keep from slipping.

"What kind of not-in-my-favor answers did you avoid?"

No answer.

"Marjorie? What did Devan ask you?

"Well...hmm. He didn't always come right out with his questions. He'd just say, 'I bet she's got a sweetheart.' He did his best to get me to tell him everything I knew, but I don't ever tell *everything* I know."

"What *did* you tell him?"

Marjorie walked a fallen tree like a tightrope, holding her coffee cup at arm's length for balance. "Don't sound so worried. I just said, 'She doesn't have a steady date that I know of, but I bet there's a man waiting for her in Boston. If you want your chance, you better ask her while she's still here.' Then I asked him if he did want that chance, and he said, 'Yes,' before he could stop himself."

Leontine was laughing so hard that I thought she might have to sit down. "The army should put you in charge of interrogation."

"They should," Marjorie said to Leontine, but she wasn't finished interrogating me. Fixing her dark eyes on mine, she said, "Is there?"

"Is there what?"

"Is there a man in Boston? You never say much about the years you were away."

"There was, but there isn't. It ended badly about a year before I left."

She jumped off the fallen log and held up a hand to help me down. "You loved him."

It wasn't a question. I needed to work on being harder to read.

Leontine jumped off the log, too.

There was no help for it. I was going to have to tell them the unvarnished truth. "Bradley decided he was better off with a girl whose family had owned a second house in Newport since 1885. One day, we were planning our wedding. The next day, he was squiring her to a debutante ball. I literally found out about it when his name turned up in the society pages."

"Oh, honey," Marjorie said.

"Did he marry her?" Leontine asked.

"He did. Just as soon as her debutante season was over. I guess she didn't want to miss out on all those parties. Bradley looks good in a tuxedo, so there were pictures of them in the paper for months. I know this because everybody in my life made sure I saw them."

"I hope he's miserable," Leontine declared, showing that she had the same petty, vengeful streak I did. I loved her for it. "How did you bear up under all that?"

"I got through it. Well, my friends and my books got me through it. About the time I was starting to feel like myself again, my parents... Well, you know what happened."

Marjorie squeezed my hands and let them go. "I've always thought it was brave of you to leave home. But coming back was brave, too."

All I could manage was a strangled "Thank you," because none of it was true. I'd been thrilled to leave this place behind. It had taken death and insolvency to bring me home. I would leave in an instant if I could. These women were my friends, but I had one foot out the door. This was what Bradley had done to me. I was no better than he was.

We went back to walking. Another log offered another tightrope walk, and that distracted us. Then Marjorie made another of her lightning-fast conversational shifts. It took us right back to Devan.

"He almost gave up, you know. Devan, I mean. When your phone was tied up all evening on Friday, and he couldn't get through, he called me and said, 'I think you're right that Estella has a boyfriend. She's been on the phone for hours.'"

Marjorie spun on one foot, walking backward down the log

to watch my response. She clearly wanted me to ask what she'd said to Devan to keep him from giving up.

I wanted to know, so I did. "Don't keep me waiting. What did you say to him?"

"I said, 'Maybe she does have a boyfriend. But if she does, he's there and you're here. And also, she likes to be called E, not Estella. If you get that right, she'll like you better.'"

I stumbled and nearly fell off the log.

"Remind me to stay on your good side, Marjorie," Leontine said.

Like a bloodhound trailing the smell of fear, Marjorie persisted. "So how was your date? You never said."

How did I answer that? How *was* my date?

"It was good. It was—I had a really good time. He took me sailing."

We jumped off the log.

"Ooh! Sailing! I bet he's even more handsome when he's not wearing a coat and tie. Short sleeves? Muscles?" Leontine asked.

"Short-sleeved polo shirt. Bermuda shorts."

"Arm muscles *and* leg muscles?" Marjorie looked over her shoulder, so she could watch me blush.

"Yes, and yes."

"Did he hold your hand?" Marjorie said, crawling over the boulder in front of me.

I took the boulder at a run. When I cleared the top, she was on the other side, waiting for an answer. Leontine was behind me, preparing her own assault on the big, slippery rock.

"Did he? Hold your hand?" Marjorie's grin was as irrepressible as the curls escaping her hairpins.

"Sort of. When I was holding the tiller, he put his hand over mine to help me."

Marjorie hooted. "'Helping you' was just an excuse. It was a sneaky way to put his hands on you, but it counts."

The next boulder was flat-topped and tree-shaded. We sat on it, and Leontine handed around the apples. I took a big juicy bite. Our rock overlooked the cove, but I was trying not to look down at it. Craning my neck, I could barely see the stone foundation of my home, high above us.

Now Leontine asked her own embarrassing question. "Did he kiss you?"

"No. I kissed him."

Marjorie waved her apple in joy. "You're my hero! He'll kiss you next time. Did he ask for a next time?"

I nodded.

"Perfect. Now you owe me a boyfriend."

Still chewing, I tried to protest, but Marjorie said, "Oh, I know you've just had one date, but he likes you. I can tell. So when you go looking for somebody to take me out, do me one favor?"

Afraid of what the favor might be, I said, "Sure."

"Just don't set me up with Mr. Kingston at the post office. He flirts with me every day, but I like my men under seventy-five."

I thought Leontine was going to choke on her apple.

"What about Dr. Bower?" I asked. "If my math is right, he's about fifty."

Leontine waved her hands as if shooing an old man away. "Not for me!"

"Me, neither." Marjorie said. "You owe me a boyfriend as good as the one I got for you."

We sat there on the rim of that damnable cove, and our laughter bounced so lightly off the rocks ringing its shoreline that I could almost forget where we were. I could almost stop imagining my mother under the water, her blue silk dress moving in its lovely ripples.

The conversation lulled, each of us thinking her own thoughts. Mine were about Mother, so you'll understand why I didn't immediately know what Leontine meant when she said, "I wonder if we'll ever know what happened to her."

"My mother?"

"Oh, no. No. I'm so sorry. I was talking about Helena."

Of course, she was. We were sitting so very near the spot where her body had been since I was sixteen.

"I should have thought before I spoke," Leontine said. "You'll get good news about your mother soon. I just know it."

"Do you remember the day that Helena disappeared?" Marjorie's voice had that dreamy tone that I associate with "Once upon a time," or "Do you want to hear a ghost story?"

"Vaguely," I said. "High school seniors are self-centered, so I remember the way people competed to come up with lurid rumors. And I remember being scared. I'd never thought of Bentham-on-Hudson as part of the real world. You know? The real world where murderers and kidnappers lived? That was the first day when I thought monsters might be real."

"I remember it clearly, but not because of Helena," Leontine said. "At least, not directly because of her. My mother took me out of school, not just for the day but forever. She'd gotten wind that a young woman had gone missing before the rumors circulated at school, and that was the final straw for her. She taught me at home for the rest of the school year, then she sent me to boarding school in North Carolina. When I finished there, she sent me to study at Howard, and she kept me there for my master's degree. She never said so, but I knew she hoped I'd marry and never come back here."

"I don't think my parents know that there's a world outside this little town," Marjorie said. "They've certainly never tried to show it to me, but I've always had my books. I give them credit for sending me to college, though, even if it was tiny little Bentham College in tiny little Bentham. They didn't understand why I wanted to stay in school for a master's degree in literature, which they considered completely useless, but they didn't try to talk me out of it."

"You're talking to two people who know books aren't useless," Leontine said.

"I know, and I love you both for it." Marjorie's customary high spirits resurfaced, and she spread her arms wide to take in...everything, I guess. "Books will take you anywhere," she declared to the world. "To Mars, even." Then she looked into her empty coffee cup as if it there was an image of the red planet at its bottom, and her face fell again. "I can't believe it took this long to find out what happened to Helena."

"After I came back home for good, I asked Mama about Helena," Leontine said, "and she was willing to say more since I was grown up and she was so sick. She spent a lot of time telling me things she wanted me to know before she...was gone. It seemed like a bad movie when she took sick before I'd been home two weeks."

"Leontine," I said. "I'm so sorry. I would have come if I'd known."

"There was no time." She stopped to clear her throat and dab at her eyes. "To her dying day, Mama was sure that Helena was gone...dead...and the man who killed her was still roaming the town. She wanted me out of here, even if she had to send me away from her." She kept her eyes on the water as the words spilled out. "Maybe it wasn't a man. Maybe it was a woman who threw Helena in the water. But the person who put her in that river, whoever it was, cost me fourteen years with my mother."

She jumped to her feet. "I'm too mad about it to sit still. Let's walk."

It took us a few minutes to put away our apple cores and soiled napkins. I used that time to give the shoreline a good look. If the boater from the night before had come ashore, I wanted to know it. I saw no footprints, no sign of a beached boat, nothing.

At some point, though, I looked up. If I hadn't, I'd never have seen the faded splash of mustard yellow beneath a stone fifteen feet above my head.

It didn't belong there, and I had an idea what it was. Standing on the rock where we ate our picnic, I brushed my hands over the face of the steep slope. At knee level, I found a projecting root that would hold my weight. I stepped onto it, then I found a narrow ledge for my other foot.

Root by stone by root, I scaled the face of Rockfall Bluff as Marjorie called out, "Where are you going?"

I was too focused on not falling to say much, so I grunted out, "Tell you in a minute," and I hauled myself higher.

"E!" Leontine called out. "Do you need me to help?"

I was too breathless to answer, so I shook my head as I stood with my toes jammed into an inch-deep ledge. Leaning my head back to look up the cliff face, I reached up and stuck my hand into a hollow under a flat stone that had been knocked out of place by…something. A falling object had jostled the rock loose, I was pretty sure. And then the rock had slammed down and protected the fallen object from the weather.

The yellow thing was battered but familiar in its sheltered hollow. As I think about it now, I'm grateful that the hollow didn't also hide a venomous snake.

After all those months, the mustard-yellow book didn't look like much more than a piece of garbage, a weathered mass of paper that had been wet, dry, and wet again. I stashed the gluey paper inside my shirt and climbed down to safety.

"What is it?" Marjorie asked. "It must be something you wanted pretty bad."

I pulled the wad of wood pulp and ink out of my shirt. Leontine and Marjorie came closer to get a look. "I just…I just had a hunch that it would be interesting. That bright yellow cover called out to me."

First, I pried the damaged cover open, then I peeled the first few pages apart until I got to the title page. And there it was.

"Lily Ecker" was still legible below the title.

Marjorie jabbed a finger at it and cried out, "Your mother—it's her name!"

I heard the pride in my voice when I said, "It seems that my mother wrote a book. I just found out about it last night."

The dust jacket had gouges in it, made by sharp rocks as the book bounced down the bluff's face. Dampness had left brown stains on its pages, but the book had been amazingly protected beneath the dislodged rock. With some coaxing, the first few pages could still be separated and turned, although the rest of it was a total loss.

Leontine peered over my shoulder. "Your mother wrote a book?"

"So it seems. There's no mention of a publishing house on the copyright page, so my guess is that she had it printed herself."

Marjorie brushed a finger over the battered cover. "What's it doing here?"

"Annie said that Mother threw...something...over the edge. You know. On that last day."

Marjorie and Leontine watched me squint up at the ledge where my house sat, then trace an imaginary line down to the water's edge with my eyes.

"If she fell where the book fell, we would have found her," I said.

"That's good. It means that she didn't fall, and she's still out there somewhere," Marjorie, said. "Right, E?"

"Yes, if she fell from a place right above us. But that's not true if she went over the cliff there."

I pointed at an inlet a stone's throw upriver, near where Annie said my parents fought. There, the bluff face was essentially vertical, and the water looked deep. If she fell there, her body would have gone straight into the water. It might even have been carried into the main channel of the river. She could have washed to Staten Island since then, and this is why I could count on being asked to view a continual stream of corpses fished out of the entire lower Hudson. It would never end unless I found her.

Despite all this, finding her book gave me a solid reason to ask the police to drag the cove again.

"I need to make sure I can find this spot."

I hadn't finished speaking before Leontine began gathering rocks to make a cairn. Marjorie quickly joined her. As they piled up the stones, Leontine pointed to the top of the cliff.

"See that big cedar up there? If you imagine a line from these rocks to that tree, the book was on that line." She pointed above my head. "That's how you can show the police where you found it."

Satisfied with the pile of rocks, Marjorie hefted her bag and said, "We should get to your house. You need to call the police about that book."

CHAPTER 12

Annie looked at the damaged book on the kitchen table and shook her head. "I don't know, E."

"You don't know what?"

"I don't know if this is the thing your mother threw over the cliff. It may be. It's the right size, but I don't know for sure. She must have been hiding it in her skirts, because I didn't see anything in her hand when she left the house."

She touched the yellow dust jacket with a tentative finger. "I didn't know there were any of her books left."

"Why wouldn't there be?"

"She had them printed herself—not many, just a few boxes—and he was so angry. 'You shouldn't have spent so much money on nothing,' he said. 'You're too stupid to be trusted with money.'"

Marjorie's hand went to her mouth in shock. I wondered if my father had approved every dress and every pair of shoes that my mother ever bought. And all my toys.

"She said to him, 'My poems aren't nothing. You wouldn't

let me send them out to publishers, so I took them to the print shop in town. They deserve to be read. I deserve it.'"

She did deserve it. Anyone who could find poetry in a life with my father deserved to be heard.

"He called them doggerel, Miss Estella. I didn't always understand his fancy words, although I did learn a good many just from working for them, but I caught his meaning well enough. And so did she. If you could have seen her face, you would have wept. Then he fed her books to the furnace, one by one."

"Not all of them."

"No, I guess not. She saved this one somehow. She must have hidden it from him." Annie stroked the ruined book.

She saved the one she hid under my bed, too, but I didn't tell Annie and Leontine and Marjorie that my mother had made sure I would have her book for always. It was something that was between Mother and me.

Marjorie and Leontine knew they should go home and let me absorb what I'd learned about Mother's book, but Annie wouldn't hear of it until they'd eaten. Maybe she was right. Sitting around the kitchen table with my friends did help my nerves. Or maybe the tea that washed it down was what calmed me enough to call the police. I never understood why Annie's tea was better than anybody else's. I suspect her of hoarding a bottle of something ancient, illegal, and happy-making, like laudanum, to drizzle into it.

The police department's weekend dispatcher, who knew my voice by now, said, "You found Mrs. Ecker's bracelet yesterday, after five months of searching, and now you've found a book that she may have had in her possession that last day." Why did I hear a question mark in her voice? She probably thought I was pretending to find clues, so the police would put more effort into finding Mother. D'Amato would no doubt agree.

Heck. In their shoes, I probably wouldn't believe me. I'd been present for Dean Jamison's suicide and when Helena Frederick was found. Maybe the number of people falling to their deaths in my vicinity—presumably, in my mother's case—had put the mark of Cain on my forehead.

Did the dispatcher think I'd been preparing the book for months—wetting it, gouging it, letting it dry, over and over? Why would I do that? So I could create a story that didn't end with my mother dead?

That's what D'Amato had accused me of doing.

"She's gone," he had bellowed after we'd been looking for weeks. "What evidence do you have that she isn't dead? What do you think we should be doing that we haven't done?"

I didn't bellow back. I made my voice calm, because I'd spent the first seventeen years of my life with an angry man. Quietly, evenly, I said, "It's not my job to know that. It's yours."

I honestly thought he was going to hit me. I flinched and he saw it. If he was angry before, that flinch made him incandescent. He had stalked out of my house, pausing just long enough to shout, "Never...*never*...accuse me of not doing my job, Miss Ecker."

"That's '*Dr.* Ecker' to you."

He acted like he didn't hear me, but I said it before the door slammed. He'd heard.

My instincts told me not to tell the dispatcher about the boat in the cove. I had no proof that it had been there, and this woman sounded doubtful even about things I could prove with physical evidence.

The quickest way to get myself dismissed as hysterical was to say, "Somebody's watching me. I don't know who, but they are. You have to believe me!" Women were locked up for less than that. I didn't feel good about this decision, not when the boat had been floating in the cove where we'd found Helena Frederick...where we might yet find my mother.

After Leontine and Marjorie left, I retreated to my bedroom, where I paged through the remnants of my mother's book. It was the same as the copy I'd found under my bed.

Of course, it was the same as the other copy. That was how printing presses worked.

The weatherbeaten book did not, however, have the copious pencil marks that littered the pages of the book my mother had hidden for me. In that copy, letters were underlined, words were circled, dots and dashes and arrows and letters filled the margins. The more I looked at the marked-up pages, the more they looked like monochrome versions of my father's Expressionist paintings. The markings held the seeds of madness, like Munch's *The Scream* or van Gogh's bristling *Sunflowers*.

Was my mother mad? She'd never seemed so to me, but I'd been gone a long while. Maybe nobody ever truly knows their mother, and I'd left at seventeen. The odds that a seventeen-year-old just out of high school could know and understand a complex middle-aged adult were infinitesimal.

The poems themselves were unadorned, eight-line sequences of plain words. The slim book was laid out to highlight them, each brief poem set, jewellike, on the right page in an expanse of white space, with the left page blank. Despite their simplicity, Mother's poems captured the confined beauty of life lived in a gorgeous prison. She had this in common with her idol, Emily Dickinson. I had never realized how rarely my mother left the house. She walked into town every now and then, but Annie ran most of the errands. Several times a year, my father took her to New York to shop and go to the opera, but those luxurious trips seemed less delightful when I was confronted by her poems. They showed how small her world truly was.

She wrote of longing and lack. She wrote about the view from her bedroom window and the winding path to town. She wrote about the mad joy she felt as my father drove her to the city. He had kept his appealingly ornamental wife on a very short leash. Despite this, her luminous love for him showed on the first page and it recurred throughout the collection.

Mother's poems returned again and again to the ruins atop Rockfall Bluff and to the Hudson River below. These images made me imagine the arc of her body diving from the cliff.

Her book oozed pain like blood. I laid my flat palm across each page after I read it, trying to trap the rage. My own rage at my father threatened to consume me. There was no need to give it more fuel.

An hour passed. Two. The sun passed its maximum and began its slow journey down. I let the poems sink in, parsing each line, dreading the final one.

When I reached it, she was waiting there for me in electric blue ink and perfect penmanship. Her familiar handwriting overwrote the printed poem, crossing the page from edge to edge.

He is going to put me away.
He said it and he meant it.
I don't know where.
You have to find me, Estella.
I'm so sorry. I mean E.
(Honestly, dear, I have always
thought of you as my own Emily,
but I want you to be who you are.)
I need you to find me, E.
Mother

CHAPTER 13

Are you okay? You don't sound okay." Leontine's voice came out of the telephone receiver, comforting but firm. That's exactly what you crave when you're spiraling into panic. "What do you need?"

"I need you to get me into the library."

"You have a library emergency? As far as I know, there has never been a library emergency in the history of Bentham College."

"That's where they keep the phone books."

"I'll meet you there."

I ran straight to the college, and she was waiting when I arrived breathless at the library door.

"Why do you need phone books? The one you have at home won't do?"

"I need phone books for the whole state. I need to call insane asylums, maybe a lot of them, and we don't have any in Bentham-on-Hudson. I think my father had my mother locked away."

"I'll look up the numbers. All you have to do is make the calls."

She unlocked the library door and shooed me through. Then she patted the seat of her own chair at the circulation desk. "Sit here by the phone."

I dropped into the chair so hard that it hurt. "I don't know how I'll pay the college back for these long-distance calls."

Leontine laid a sheet of paper with a list of department codes on it. One of them was circled. "The library has a code we use when we're helping professors with their academic research. We know that they also use it for cheating on their wives and calling their bookies. We don't tell anybody their secrets and they don't question any calls we charge to their account."

Knowing my father, he'd used it to communicate with his haberdasher and his sommelier.

Leontine cleared the area around the phone—papers, books, note cards—so that I'd have all the workspace I needed. "I had a feeling that you would need a lot of help. Help with the phone books and…just plain help. An extra pair of hands. An extra pair of shoulders to cry on. Marjorie's on her way."

God bless her. I did need my friends.

Leontine plunked a notebook and a pen in front of me, setting up two more workstations at a table nearby. Then she looked at me like a battle-hardened commander looking to a general for orders. When your battlefield is a library, paper and ink are your weapons.

Leontine and Marjorie were busy compiling lists of telephone numbers of New York asylums, and I was hell-bent on calling them until I got the right result. This was going to work. I felt it.

My mother had been missing for eight months. As those months passed, I'd been forced to face the fact that she'd had time to hop on a bus or a plane or a boat that would take her literally anywhere. She could have been halfway around the world, for all I knew. This would have taken her into the teeth of the war, but was that worse than living with my father? The worldwide scope of my search had made a telephone campaign impossible, and that was why I had typed countless letters, hoping to get lucky.

But calling every insane asylum in New York? This was an achievable goal. I could do that.

The library had a direct line, so I didn't have to go through an operator. I could bypass the university's version of Ethel and Selma, avoiding gossip over the humiliating thing I was doing. Nervously spinning the numbered dial, I called asylums all over New York—Haverstraw, Nyack, Poughkeepsie, Dover, one after another—and asked, "Is Lily Ecker in residence?" as if I were calling fashionable resorts looking for a socialite. Every time, the answer was no.

Somewhere, my mother was being held against her will. I couldn't let that go on, not for another second.

Finally, Leontine took my shoulders and gently shook some sense into me. "This is an information problem, E. Information is what I do. Let me help you organize what you know."

I closed my eyes and pictured a map in my mind. "Annie

said my father was gone for hours, from the middle of the day to about sunset. Let's call it six hours. Buffalo has a famous mental hospital, and Long Island has several, but they're too far away. So are the ones on Staten Island. There's no way that my father could have taken her to any of those places and gotten back home, not in the time Annie said he was gone."

Leontine struck them from our list. "There are a lot of other places he could have taken her in that time, and they're not all in New York."

The three of us huddled over a map to define the area where my father could have reasonably made a round trip in six hours or less. I redirected my increasingly frantic calls to sites in New Jersey. She wasn't in the Trenton Psychiatric Hospital nor the one in Glen Gardner, but this did not deter me. The Garden State is bigger than it looks, and I called a lot of its asylums and hospitals.

Marjorie placed a list of Connecticut facilities in front of me, an eyebrow raised to say, "Any luck yet?"

I answered with a little shake of my head. Saying the words, "I can't find her," would have brought the tears, and I couldn't afford them.

I called all over Connecticut—the Fairfield Hills State Hospital in Newtown, the Norwich State Hospital in Preston, the Cedar Crest Hospital in Newington, and others I can no longer recall. None of the people who answered those phones had heard of my mother.

Too late, it occurred to me that she might not be registered under her own name. I obviously wasn't thinking clearly, because this was precisely the kind of thing my father would do, either to cover his tracks or to avoid the embarrassment of having an unstable wife. I was going to have to do the whole thing all over, calling the same asylums with her physical description, instead of her name. It was the same description that I'd given the authorities on the day she disappeared, but surely she still looked the same?

Blond, blue eyes, thin, fifty years old, blue silk shirtwaist dress, sapphire-and-platinum bracelet, bare feet.

No. Scratch the sapphire-and-platinum bracelet.

I couldn't fail to find her, not after reading her plea for help. The thought made the pen fall from my shaking hands, but it was their trembling that gave me the answer.

Why was I shaking? Because I was emotionally overwrought.

My father had never been overcome by emotion in his life. Even when angry, he was cold. Before any action, he calculated precisely how it would affect him, his reputation, his wealth, his social status. He probably did that calculation every time he struck my mother. I needed to ask myself how a man like that would go about putting his wife in a madhouse.

"I'm a fool."

"Hardly," Marjorie answered.

"I've been acting out of emotion. I'm afraid that my mother's been hurt. I'm afraid I'll never find her. My father didn't feel emotions like that."

Marjorie was saying, "Oh, surely he loved you and your mother," at the same time that Leontine was saying, "You knew the man. If you tell me he was evil, who am I to argue?"

The word "evil" caromed off my eardrums. I hated the sound of it, but Leontine wasn't wrong.

The man who had burned my books and destroyed my mother's poems was perfectly capable of locking a woman away against her will. But the prideful man who had been a darling of the New York intelligentsia would not have checked his wife into Hollywood's idea of an asylum. There would be no brick-and-stone Gothic monstrosity with straitjackets and glum-faced orderlies for Lily Ecker. He most certainly would not have chosen a state hospital, where her elegant elbows might have brushed the elbows of people who owned nothing in the world. Nothing at all.

That man would never have used her real name.

I asked Leontine and Marjorie to look up private rest homes. I called sanitariums. I called hydrotherapy spas. I called every place I could imagine where a husband might cage his wife in a genteel way. Each time, I patiently described my mother.

At a homeopathic hospital in remote Dutchess County, New York, the receptionist put the facility's weekend director on the phone. She said, "We've been wondering when someone would call for her." Frustration put an edge on her voice.

The people who had my mother didn't even want her. I collapsed forward, my forehead to the tabletop, the phone's receiver still clutched to my ear and lips.

I heard myself say, "You were wondering when someone would call for her because she's not ill and doesn't need to be there?"

The woman's voice was chilly. "We were wondering when someone would call for her because the man who brought her hasn't paid her bills, he didn't leave a working telephone number, and she won't give us one. She had some money on her person, but it's going fast. Come get her, please."

I called John, whose marriage proposal I hadn't even answered. He didn't pick up the phone, and I couldn't wait.

I only knew one other person with a car whom I liked and probably trusted. Devan answered on the fourth ring. Words tumbled out of my mouth.

"My mother…Dutchess County…mental hospital…can I borrow your car?"

"I'll pick you up in fifteen minutes." His voice was calm and steady. I needed that.

It would have been nice to let someone else take the wheel, but this was not the time.

"Nobody else should see her this way. I can't do that to her."

"Of course. Take the car." He said this in the same steady voice, despite the fact that he was handing over an expensive machine to someone whose expertise was hardly more than theoretical. "Keep it as long as you need it. I can walk to work until you get it back to me."

"I'll be careful with it. I'll—" My voice threatened to break, so I had to stop. I couldn't let anybody hear me be so vulnerable.

"Whatever you need, E." His voice was so gentle, gentler than either of my parents could have managed. "I'll be here when you come back."

Once I got through Poughkeepsie, the roads narrowed, and the green tree boughs interlaced over the speeding car. I saw few cars and fewer houses. I was not calm, but I was growing more confident in my ability to race along in Devan's car without perishing in flames. There was nothing in the car but me and some random items I flung into a bag. They were probably useless, but I needed to take something, anything, to my mother. Things had always been so very important to her.

I had to hand it to my father. When he put my mother in a private facility, he took the word "private" to extremes. The farther I drove, the worse the roads became. I let the potholes jostle me while I mentally apologized to Devan for anything that the jostling might do to his car.

The Dutchess Rest Home and Spa was invisible from the road, marked only by a black iron light post. The voice on the phone had warned me not to miss the post, as the road wouldn't be wide enough to make a U-turn for another five miles. Even so, I almost passed it by. I was forced to swing wide and brush the nose of Devan's car through a hedge to make the turn.

I found myself on a gravel lane with a small gatehouse. A uniformed man swung the iron gate open and waved me through.

After a half mile, the trees opened up to reveal a Victorian mansion painted in shades of russet, pumpkin, and cobalt blue. Its impeccably mown grounds were crisscrossed with slate footpaths. Signs pointed toward the hydrospa, the greenhouse, and the swimming pool.

The sun was setting, so the lawn was deserted. I parked near the front door, snatched up the bag I'd brought from home, and ran up the porch steps to ring the bell.

A woman in a maid's uniform answered. "You are expected," she said, gesturing to a reception area on my right. "The director will be out soon."

I sank down on a damask sofa. The wood beneath my feet shone golden. So did the brass chandelier above my head. I didn't have a long wait, but I felt every minute of it.

The director appeared in the arched door, wearing a dark suit, dark tie, and horn-rimmed glasses. The weekend director on the phone had been a woman, so perhaps he was her boss. Was my mother such a problem that the director of the whole hospital felt the need to intervene, even on a Sunday? He beckoned, leading me deeper into the old house.

At every turn, I felt less like I was in a home and more like I was in an institution. Light fixtures stopped being brass and started being black-painted metal. The air began to carry the odor of isopropyl alcohol and bathroom cleaner. The wood floors under my feet, no longer buffed to a golden sheen, carried the marks of many nurses' rubber heels. We followed those marks like breadcrumbs until, at last, we reached a closed door.

The director paused without putting his hand on the doorknob. "We are glad that Mrs. Decker is going home."

He hesitated.

"Excuse me. I mean 'Mrs. Ecker.' It appears that the man who checked her in—her husband?—did so under an assumed name and left a false telephone number. We have been at a loss as to how to proceed. Her course of treatment was prepaid, but she completed it two weeks ago. We are obviously interested in reaching the person who guaranteed payment."

Had my father intended to leave her here for months on end? My mouth tasted like ash.

The director reached in his breast pocket and pulled out something that looked like an invoice.

Did this dour man intend to hold my mother hostage until I paid her bill? I thought of the five hundred dollars I'd found in my father's study—four-hundred-and-eighty dollars now, since I'd given Annie a pittance for clothes. I should have brought it with me.

I had no idea whether it would even put a dent in the cost of two weeks in a place like this. The whole humiliating story spilled out of me.

"I didn't know. I didn't know where she was. My father put her here and died before he could tell me. It's taken me this long to find her. I don't—"

I tried to gulp down the rising panic.

"I don't have the money to pay her bill, but I'm here to take her home. I need to take her home." This did not seem like the kind of charitable establishment that would absorb a financial loss.

The director of the Dutchess Rest Home and Spa didn't go so far as to smile, but his cheeks flushed. They were the only spot of warmth in the institutional hallway.

"There is no need. She had funds on her person that we applied to her account. You reached us before there was any arrearage."

What did he mean by "on her person?" It made no sense to think that she was carrying her purse when my father chased her out of the house barefoot. If she'd grabbed it on her way out the door, Annie would have mentioned it. Besides, if she'd had a purse downstairs that day, it would have been in the kitchen closet with her walking shoes. She could only have had money on her person if it was stuffed in her bra.

In my mind, I walked through Annie's description of my mother's last moments in the house. She and my father had been arguing all day. She reached her limit and ran to the kitchen door, but my father stood in her way, so she ran out the back.

It was so clear to me now. She had been trying to leave him when she went running for her purse and shoes with a wad of bills—probably two wads—stashed in her lingerie. Oh, and a precious surviving copy of her book hidden in the folds of her skirt.

The kitchen door led to the path into town, the only escape for a woman who didn't know how to drive. So little cash had passed through her hands that it must have taken her months to amass enough money to make her think that escape was possible. Now it was gone, spent to imprison her.

The director of the Dutchess Rest Home and Spa handed me the invoice, stamped "Paid in Full," but he handed me no check or cash to go with it. Either I had arrived on the precise day her last dollar was spent, or this man had decided his facility was entitled to keep my mother's money. It was possible that he had made this decision because she was troublesome. I had a spiteful hope that she'd been very troublesome, indeed.

Well, let him have it. I wasn't going to negotiate her release. My mother wasn't spending an extra second in that place.

His flushed cheeks were fading, now that the financial niceties had been tidied up. "I'm glad to finally know her story," he said. "She hasn't spoken since he checked her in. It is our doctors' opinion that she is able to speak but has been unwilling."

Of course, she hadn't spoken. I'd been too distraught to make sense of the barrage of information that had battered me since I found her note. If she'd been willing to speak a word to the people running this place, she could have told them who she was. Even if they didn't believe her when she said that her husband had given them a false name—she had, after all, been involuntarily committed for psychiatric care—they would have been motivated to listen when her money threatened to run out.

But why hadn't she spoken? She was certainly obstinate enough to maintain her silence for months, but what if she'd been silent because she couldn't speak. What if she'd been drugged?

My jaw clenched when I allowed myself to consider the worst explanation for her silence.

What if my father had been right? What if she truly were mad?

"We've never had a resident quite like your mother," the director said, still making no move to take me to her, "and I can assure you that we have a long history of female patients who are accustomed to ruling their households. None of them adjust well to our program, but your mother is a special case. She is quite regal in her silence. And in her refusal to participate in a single therapeutic activity. We call her the Duchess of Dutchess County."

And with that, he opened the door and took me to her.

My mother was waiting in a room that was as drab as the hallway outside. She sat on the worn sofa, wearing the blue shirtwaist dress that we'd been trying to find for so long. It had been ruined, of course, by a trip through an institutional washer and wringer, probably with lye soap. Even so, stains remained around its calf-length hem, evidence of her flight through a muddy meadow. The dress was wrinkled all over, with deep creases from neckline to hem and across the waist. From the looks of it, someone had taken it from her, washed it, folded it, then stored it in a bag for eight months until she was ready to go home.

What had she been wearing all this time? A plain cotton uniform, skimpy and tight, like the ones I'd seen in movies about women whose husbands had put them away? Surely, she hadn't been strapped into a straitjacket.

If she had been, she would never tell me. My mother was a mystery to me, one that I wanted desperately to solve, but I knew her well enough to know that she would keep her confinement locked inside herself forever.

Because she had arrived barefoot, she had no shoes of her own. Instead, she wore cheap black canvas shoes, crepe-soled and secured by a short, buttoned strap. I think it was the hideous shoes that hurt me the most.

Even in ruined silk and plebeian shoes, my mother was still herself. The blue skirt unfurled around her like the petals of an iris. Her right elbow was propped on the sofa's armrest. It supported a hand that hung in the air near her face, as if it held a cigarette. My goodness, she must have missed her cigarettes.

Her hair was combed away from her brow and tied back, revealing her bare face in a way that I'd never seen. She had always worn makeup, and she had always hidden behind a curtain of rippling gold. While I was living in Boston, I saw a film called *I Wanted Wings*. Veronica Lake became a star when her hair fell across her eyes in that movie, just as Mother's had always done.

Without her hair hiding one eye, I hardly recognized her. But, oh, I knew her. Or at least I knew her face.

She had aged in the years since I left home, but only slightly. I, on the other hand, could see every one of those years when I looked in the mirror. On that blood-red sofa, her chin upturned and her blue eyes focused on mine, I didn't see the face of the mother I remembered. I saw my own.

Her eyes were steady and sane, and they bored into me as if I should intuitively know what she wanted. And I did. Those eyes said, "Take me home."

The bag I'd brought dangled by my side. I'd packed her a dress, underwear, a pair of shoes, a toothbrush, toothpaste, and a hairbrush. I'd imagined her as a character in a melodrama, her hair matted and her clothes filthy. Yet here she was, clothed in her own dress, clean and well-groomed, ready to walk out the door.

Still, those shoes. They simply wouldn't do.

I reached into the bag for the kid pumps I'd brought, flat-heeled and handcrafted in a luxe shade of bone. Kneeling, I unbuttoned the institutional shoes, threw them aside, and slid the pumps onto her feet. Then I stood, held out a hand, and helped her up.

Now she looked like my mother, but was there anyone at home inside the silk dress? I couldn't know, because she maintained her refusal (inability?) to speak while I said good-bye to the director. As I ushered the Duchess of Dutchess County out of his building, he looked unutterably glad to see her go.

While I stowed the bag and my purse on the back seat, I saw her glance around the unfamiliar car, as if wondering where my father's larger one had gone. Still, she was silent.

Only after I had steered Devan's car down the long drive, pulled out onto the narrow road, and pointed us toward Poughkeepsie did she speak.

"It's good to see you, dear. Didn't your father come with you?"

CHAPTER 14

I had been in motion since I'd learned where my mother was being held. I'd had no time—or ability—to think. After I'd arranged to borrow Devan's car, I'd run headlong out of the library, calling out to Marjorie, "Please call Dr. Masters and tell her that I won't be coming to tea. And Dr. Bower. We're supposed to have a beer tomorrow, but I'm going to have my hands full." Then I'd sprinted up Rockfall Bluff to the house, so that I could gather some things to take to Mother.

Devan was there in minutes. After making sure I was familiar with the car's controls, he'd left on foot while I was accelerating down my driveway at a speed that was well beyond safe.

The need to watch the road had given me no chance to think. Certainly, I'd given no thought to how I would tell my mother that her husband was dead. But now she was asking, "Your father didn't come with you?" and I needed to think of something to say.

I started strong with a simple "Mother." Then my brain froze solid.

Her hands fumbled at the nape of her neck where an elastic band bound her hair. "I know he was angry with me. And he still is. That much is obvious."

You were leaving him. Why are you speaking like a woman planning to spend the rest of her life with the man who did this to you?

She gestured behind us in the general direction of the Dutchess Rest Home and Spa. "He left me there for so long, and now he doesn't come with you to get me? And he doesn't even let you use our car to do it?"

I should have been relieved by this long string of sensible words. They indicated that nothing was seriously wrong with her mind. Instead, I was more concerned with forming sensible words of my own.

"Why didn't you give them his number? Or why didn't you call him yourself? Surely they would have allowed it at some point."

Surely they would have allowed it when the money started to run out.

I also could have asked her why she didn't give them his name or even her own name, but those questions tiptoed up to the one I couldn't ask: Are you mad? Has living with my father for so long done that to you?

"E," she said. Her tone was condescending, but that was nothing new for Mother. "You don't understand our marriage. How could you when I protected you from it? Your father will do anything to win. I, on the other hand, can never win, but I can stand between him and victory. I would have stayed there forever before I would grovel to him. My silence insured that my jailers had nothing to tell him. If he wanted to know what I was thinking, he had to drive to my prison and ask me. But now it seems that he has found a way to avoid losing. He has sent you to avoid coming to me himself."

I had to tell her about Father. She needed to know. But what would the news do to her mental state? Was she mad? She didn't seem mad.

"Father…fell ill on that very first day you were gone. His condition was serious."

"And that's why you've finally come home from Boston? Because Malcolm is ill." Then, more faintly, "Not for me?"

Her hair was free now, curling around her face. Meticulously, she used her fingers to separate the curls into ringlets, spreading her golden tresses over her shoulders the way she always wore it…the way my father liked it. After everything he had done, she was still trying to be pretty for him, and it was killing me.

"I came home for both of you. Annie called to tell me that he was ill. And that you were missing."

"Missing? The bastard has known exactly where I was the whole time."

There it was, the anger that made me hope she would be all right again. But could she hold on to it? It had always evaporated in the face of his scorn. I realized that I had no mental image of my mother in the absence of my father. He had sculpted her with that scorn.

"He did know where you were, and he tried to tell us. But he couldn't." I worked hard to put some gentleness in my voice. This was not the time to say how I felt about him. "I could tell that there was something very important that he wanted me to know, but he had a stroke before I got home. It took his speech."

She paled. "It's hard to imagine your father unable to wield language like a scalpel. But now he's recovered enough to tell you where to find me. That's encouraging, yes?"

"No, Mother. I'm sorry to tell you this, but he had several more strokes. He only lived two weeks after the first one."

Her gaze never wavered. It was as if she didn't under-stand or she didn't choose to understand. Or perhaps she was relieved.

"It's taken me this long to find you. I might never have managed it, if you hadn't left me that message on the last page of your book."

"My book. You found the note I hid for you. I knew you'd come home if he put me away, and you'd need your books for comfort. So I knew that you'd find it. Well done, E."

My mother was sparing with praise, so those words put a flutter in my chest.

"Keep that book safe," she said, putting a hand over mine where it rested on the stick shift. "Your father did his best to destroy them all. Are you working on your own book?"

"The one based on my doctoral research? I wrote you last summer that it was under consideration. The publisher still has it. I think it has a good shot," I said, knowing that this wasn't the book she meant.

"Don't play dumb. It never works with me. Are you working on your suspense novel?"

I stopped myself from blurting out, "Do you mean the man-uscript that Father threw into the garbage on the day I left for college? The day I chopped off all my hair, just because he insisted that I wear it long?"

Instead, I said, "I would have had to start over, and I just couldn't make myself do it. I went to graduate school and wrote a dissertation instead."

He had paid my tuition all through my undergraduate years, and all that time I wrote letters to her, the long chatty letters of an adolescent, but not to him. I never wrote him once. Perhaps I should have been grateful to him for funding my education, but I knew why he did it. It was his last weapon in the battle to get me to come home.

Oh, let me call it what it was. Paying my tuition was his last chance to get me back under his thumb. When I got the fellowship that paid for my graduate work, he knew I was lost to him, because I started returning his checks uncashed.

Once I was fully self-sufficient, I let myself feel my anger toward her for letting him treat us so terribly, but I never stopped writing her. And of course I wrote Annie. I addressed their letters in care of the postmistress, who held them until they picked them up. Annie lived her own life, the only person left in the echoing servants' quarters that consumed a wing of the third floor, but I knew that Mother had no place of her own. She had nowhere to keep my letters where she could be sure my father wouldn't find them, so I don't know what she did with them.

Maybe she answered them and then burned them. She had spent her life twisting herself in knots to please him, but there is no rope stronger than the umbilical cord. Its shadow binds us to our mothers for life. Over time, my chatty letters shifted to terse updates that said little more than, "I graduated," or "I live in Boston now," or "My dissertation might be published." But I always wrote, and she always wrote back.

Now we were face-to-face, and Mother was tugging hard on my umbilical cord.

"Yes, I do mean the manuscript your father tried to destroy, but there's no need to start it over. You'll find it in the basement behind the onion bin. You can imagine how terrible it smelled after hours in the kitchen garbage. With chicken bones. And fish heads."

She gave an elegant shudder and waited for me to respond. I didn't, so she burbled on. I guess she had eight months of words pent up inside.

"You must admit that it was a stroke of genius to hide it with the onions. They did a magnificent job of covering the odor, and so did the photographic chemicals in your father's darkroom. He never suspected your manuscript was there. I meant to return it to you when you came to visit, but you never came. So I never did."

She had hidden the books he tried to burn under my bed. She had hidden one copy of her own book with it and thrown a second copy over Rockfall Bluff. She had hidden my manuscript behind the onions. My father had hidden five hundred dollars in his study. What else did my home conceal? Other than, of course, the fact that the man of the house had treated the women of the house despicably?

"Well, I'm home now. I've taken a job at the college as a research assistant, and I've begun teaching classes, too."

I didn't say, "My salary is holding things together for Annie and me," but perhaps she would understand. Or perhaps my father had excluded her from their financial life so thoroughly that it wouldn't occur to her to wonder how we were managing.

"That's very nice, dear, but really. I encourage you to finish that book."

I mumbled something about not having any time to write.

She shifted her weight on the car seat. "I wish you'd brought the Packard. It's more commodious, much more suited for long rides."

"No doubt," I said, feeling a strange need to defend Devan's Chrysler. Seizing on the only superiority that I'd noticed, I said, "Look at your door. There's a place to rest your arm."

It was dark, her eyes were fifty years old, and there would never be a day when my mother agreed to be seen in glasses. She peered at the car door, groped around, and found the armrest. Sliding her elbow onto it, she murmured, "This *is* very nice. Quite luxurious."

Mother might be unflappable, but she'd just been released from an eight-month stint in a mental hospital, only to be told that her husband was dead. There was no need to tell her that we would be without a car, even an unimpressive one like Devan's, for the foreseeable future.

Her head began to nod, its curls glinting in the moonlight. Slowly, she leaned to the right, her arm supported by the armrest and her cheek resting against the window.

"I never thought there could be an improvement over the Packard." Her voice drifted off, but my mother would be rendering judgment as long as she had an audience and was conscious. "So luxurious…this car is very luxurious, after all…"

The reunion with Annie was as emotional as anyone would expect—many tears from Annie and even a few from my mother.

Mother was asleep on her feet, but Annie force-fed her a chicken salad sandwich, a slice of crumb cake, and a cup of tea, weeping over the pounds she'd lost to the rest home's inferior meals. She led Mother upstairs and drew her a bath, then retreated with the creased and stained dress. Charging right through the kitchen and out the back door, Annie stuffed the offending dress in the garbage and slammed the lid hard, as if it might try to escape. Then she hurried back upstairs and waited to help my mother into a soft mauve negligée and matching peignoir.

While Annie was helping Mother, I called the police department's night dispatcher. When I told her my mother was home, she was gracious enough to mumble, "That's good news," but it apparently wasn't good enough news to disturb D'Amato late on a Sunday night. She said that he'd call me in the morning.

When I went up to tell Mother good night, she looked a thousand times better than she had on that execrable red sofa in her wadded-up dress. Her hair was slightly damp. A cigarette from her eight-month-old stash was in her hand, and two butts were in the Lalique ashtray on her bedside table. Her body had achieved the considerable feat of relaxing into her lingerie as if it were made to wear nothing else, while maintaining a ramrod-straight spine. She sat imperiously erect, despite being supported by about a million cushions in icy shades of pink and blue. Annie tended to go overboard when making sure my mother was comfortable.

"Thank you, dear," she said, extending an arm that invited me to lean down for a kiss on the cheek. "Thank you for finding me. Thank you for saving me."

I gave her the kiss she wanted. "You pretty much drew me a road map. You saved yourself."

She put her hand to her mouth as if stifling a silent laugh. "I suppose you're right. I did save myself. How very unlike me!"

"Sleep well, Mother," I said, backing away from the troubling sight of her fragility. Her thin legs barely rippled the bedcovers.

She inhaled the tobacco smoke and held it in her lungs for a long, long time. "Sleep well, my darling E. Tomorrow, I will learn what this new life of mine will look like."

When I came down from Mother's room, I found Annie rifling through the pantry.

"Whatever am I going to cook for her breakfast? We're down to one egg. Maybe some French toast? But we don't have a drop of maple syrup."

"Annie."

She kept shuffling cans and canisters.

"Annie, we have oatmeal. Mother likes oatmeal."

"It hardly seems right for a homecoming breakfast. Not after what she's been through."

"She hasn't tasted your cooking in months. You could serve her dry toast, and it would be better than what she's been eating."

I couldn't know for sure that the food Mother was offered had been terrible, but I saw how thin she was. I wondered how long she'd held on to hope that my father would come back. Had she thought she could outlast him, waiting for him to come to her without being called? Had the day come when she gave up? I tried to imagine looking around and thinking, "This is my life now. I live in a mental institution, and I always will."

I squeezed past Annie and pulled something off the top shelf, the one she couldn't reach. "We still have pear preserves."

She seized the jar like a lifeline. "Thank you! This will make her oatmeal special."

"Don't forget the walnuts in the basement."

"Walnuts and pear preserves! That will be perfect, E."

I was about to add, "It'll be quite a feast for wartime," when I realized that my father had locked my mother up weeks before Pearl Harbor. Did she know about the war? Would she understand when we told her that some of her favorite foods just couldn't be had, not for any amount of money?

Annie pulled away from me like she meant to run to the basement and start cracking nuts, but she staggered as she went. I grabbed her shoulder.

"Annie. Go to bed. You've been through a lot today, too. I'll bring up the walnuts. They'll be shelled and waiting for you in the morning. And if you oversleep, I know how to make oatmeal."

She shook her head at the very idea that I should shell my mother's walnuts, but she did go to bed. As she left, she called back, "You've got messages, a lot of them. They're on your desk."

All of them but one were telephone messages taken in Annie's handwriting. John had left his own note. "Annie called and told me what was happening. I came right over to see if I could help, but all I managed to do was keep Annie company. I left when she started to yawn, hoping she might get a little rest. I hope all is well. Call me when you can."

His unanswered proposal echoed in my ears. I needed to let him know about Mother, but I wasn't ready to talk about anything personal. I needed some sleep before I was ready to talk to him at all. Surely, he would understand.

Annie had taken down a phone message from Devan: "I hope you found your mother and that everything is okay now. Call me if I can help. I'm here whenever you need me."

I would wait until it was a decent hour of the morning to arrange for returning his car. Still, I held on to those two messages for a while, studying them. In three short sentences, Devan had said he wanted good things for me and that he wanted to help me, but I had to ask. He wasn't going to just rush in and fix things unless that was what I wanted. I liked that.

But there was plenty to appreciate about John's message, too. He had come as soon as he knew I was in trouble. He had been kind to Annie. He wanted to know how I was doing, but he, too, was willing to wait for me to call.

There were five messages from Marjorie, all of them variations on a theme: "Call me. I can't stand the suspense. Are you okay? Did you find her? Call me." The last one said, "My parents are going to bed. Go ahead and wake them up if you need to call. Otherwise, I want to hear your news first thing in the morning."

There was only one message from Leontine: "I'm hoping against hope that you find her. Call me any time of the day or night and let me know. I'll be waiting by the phone."

I wouldn't call a brand-new beau at midnight. I didn't want to call John at all. I wouldn't disturb Marjorie's parents unless it was an emergency. But Leontine lived alone, and she seemed to sincerely want to hear from me. I fetched a bowl of walnuts and a nutcracker to my study, picked up the phone, and asked the operator to put through a call to Leontine.

She answered with, "E? How *are* you?" because who else would be calling at that hour? "Did you find her? Did you find your mother? How is she?"

"I did. She's okay. She's sleeping in her own bed."

"I'm so happy for you. I wish my mother was in hers."

And then we were both crying.

While we got ourselves together, I nestled the phone receiver between my shoulder and my ear, freeing both hands to crush a walnut shell with the nutcracker.

"What was *that*?" Leontine yelped.

"I'm cracking nuts for my mother's welcome-home breakfast. Mind if I work on them while we talk?"

"Oh, sweetheart. If I could still do a single thing for my mother, nothing would stop me. You crack away."

"Thanks," I said, using a pick to get each half of the nutmeat out in one piece.

"Your mother was Mama's favorite client," Leontine said. "She brought big-city style to this stick-in-the-mud town. All she had to do was wear a dress to one of her dinner parties and everybody would come ask for one like it. Not that Mama ever copied a design, but she dressed your mother's friends in clothes that were right for them. Your mother brought mine her biggest clients."

"Were they friends? Our mothers, I mean?" I asked, and then I wanted to rip my tongue out. There was no way on this earth that my mother would be bosom buddies with her dressmaker. Leontine was taking some time to think about her answer, so I let the nutcracker make its loudest noise to fill the troubled silence.

"Friends?" Her tone was careful. "No, I wouldn't say they were friends, but your mother respected mine. I remember her dress fittings so distinctly, even when I was a little girl. She came here for them, instead of insisting that Mama pack up her scissors, pins, fabric, and chalk, just to carry them across town. And she brought you to play with me. Or maybe to babysit me, since you were too old to be interested in paper dolls, but I didn't see it that way at the time. I remember thinking you were so grown-up and sophisticated."

"And now you know the sad truth about how unsophisticated I still am." I used both hands to ease the cracked walnut open. "My mother isn't a very practical woman in most ways, but she is when it comes to fashion. It only makes sense that your mother could do her best work in her own studio with her own tools."

"Exactly. You understand that, and your mother understood it. She treated Mama like a successful businesswoman. She treated her like an artist whose work she admired, the way people say your father treated his favorite painters. She never questioned Mama's bills, and she always paid them on time. I can't say that about everybody, not even those rich folks on the other side of the river. Especially them. Those things speak well of your mother, don't you think?"

I actually thought that the behavior Leontine described represented the bare minimum of polite human interaction, but I kept quiet. Tonight, Leontine and I were celebrating our mothers. Or perhaps we were celebrating our love for them. Maybe we didn't know our mothers at all.

"Next time you come for lunch," I said, "Mother will be here. I know she'll enjoy seeing you again. It will be like old times. If you could have seen her sitting alone in that place where he left her…"

"I know it broke your whole heart."

"It did. It really did."

CHAPTER 15

Annie carried the pear-and-walnut oatmeal upstairs on a tray at seven-thirty sharp, along with a cup of tea made exactly the way Mother liked it—milk and sugar, but no lemon. (The war had made lemons impossible to find, so it was a good thing Mother didn't care for them.) Annie always kept the china and silver in perfect condition, but they gleamed a little more on that morning. Maybe they gleamed a little too much for my taste, as I would have liked it if my mother had come down to have breakfast with me on plain, ordinary plates at the plain, ordinary kitchen table.

While Mother lingered upstairs, I was on the phone with Marjorie, filling her in on my rescue mission to the Dutchess Rest Home and Spa.

"Obviously," I said, "I won't be able to come to work today. It may take all week to make sure she's really okay and to get her settled and comfortable. Would you tell—" I stopped to think. Who was there to tell? Dean Jamison had just died on Friday, so Marjorie didn't technically have a boss, and neither did I.

"Things are going to be in turmoil at the office today. The entire College of Arts and Sciences will be unsupervised, and nature abhors a vacuum," Marjorie said. "My guess is that Dr. Bower will think he's in charge. Dr. Masters will sincerely doubt that, since he's been at Bentham College for a few weeks, and she's been here since you and I were in grade school, but nobody's going to put a woman in the dean's chair. She'll be out of luck."

Marjorie paused and made a "poor thing" noise of sympathy for Dr. Masters.

Dr. Masters had been kind at my father's funeral, so I'd prefer her as dean to Dr. Bower, but I'd prefer him to any of the other new professors lurking around Hawke Hall. They seemed nothing like scholars and everything like surveillance officers. They made me feel rebellious enough to sign up for courses to brush up my German and learn some Japanese. That would give them a good reason for their surveillance, but I couldn't risk being thrown into a military prison. My mother needed me.

"There are a few old-timers who'll never be called into active duty," Marjorie continued, "so my guess is that it will be one of them. Maybe Dr. Yeats or Professor Schmidt. It would be Professor Schmidt for sure, if he didn't have that German name. That's just silly, because he's got the heaviest Virginia accent I've ever heard, and he brought home medals from the last war, but it's the way things are. Dr. Dumont is young, but his eyesight's too terrible for the army, so it could be him."

"You're the one who's tapped into all the office politics at Hawke Hall. I just work there."

Marjorie didn't deny that she was a political savant. She just laughed. "Chancellor Hampstead will be underfoot all day, handling the crisis. Nobody but your students will even notice you're gone. I'll have to cancel your classes today, but after that I can get people to teach them until you're back. I know where you keep your lesson plans."

"Thank you. Truly."

"A week's not very much, not after what your mother's been through. Why don't you take some more time?"

"I can't afford to let the college think I'm dispensable."

"When you put it that way, I wouldn't risk it, either. Do you want me to tell anybody what's happening at your house?"

I thought about it. "Only if there's a pressing need."

"What about Leontine?"

"Leontine knows, but maybe you could call her at the library and ask her to keep the news to herself for a while?"

"Sure thing. Devan?"

"I just called him, and he didn't pick up. He's probably walking to work, because I've got his car. When you get there, can you ask him to call me?"

"I will very much enjoy the chance to talk to your handsome man."

"He's not mine."

"You can say that. But I don't believe it."

"Your mother was where?"

The police chief's voice was loud, really loud. His tone was incredulous. Honestly, Chief D'Amato always sounded like he thought I was lying, but this was a different kind of incredulous. He literally could not believe what my father had done.

"Say that again. Your father left her where?"

I hadn't factored the police into my plan to keep my mother's time in an institution quiet. I had no faith that D'Amato's people would behave with even a hint of professionalism. Everybody for miles around was going to know about the Dutchess Rest Home and Spa before the day was done. If I hoped to have any control over the stories being spread about my family, I had to be very clear with this man.

"My mother needed rest. My father took her to a place where she could get it, but he had his stroke before he could tell anybody where she was."

"Say that again?"

I said it again, word for identical word. Then I told him about my mother's bracelet and about the book I found on Rockfall Bluff. I couldn't tell if he already knew about them or not, but he should, since I'd told the dispatcher. I considered telling him about the boat lurking below my house in the dark, but I was now the daughter of a woman who had suffered a nervous breakdown. He had even less incentive to believe me. So I hung up and called Marjorie back.

She picked up, out of breath. "I was heading out the door. If you'd called a minute later, I'd have been on my way to work. What's up?"

"Here's what's up. I've changed my mind. You're going to tell people what happened to my mother, anybody who wants to know. Especially the people in the English department. And the entire College of Arts and Sciences."

"I am?"

"You're going to say she was overtired. My father was

worried about her, so he took her someplace where she could get some rest, but then he had his stroke, and he couldn't let us know where she was. And that's all you're going to say. It may not be the whole truth, but it's the truth. If I don't circulate a nonsensational story, the whole town will think she was shackled in a cell on Blackwell's Island."

"That place has been closed for years."

This didn't keep me from imagining my mother locked away in a Victorian madhouse.

"I know it's closed. But that won't keep the busybodies in Bentham-on-Hudson from spreading lies."

"That's very true. Okay, I'll take care of the problem. I know exactly which busybodies to tell."

On cue, I heard a pair of leather-soled heels tapping their way down the upstairs hall. When they paused at the top of the stairs, I knew I was expected. Mother had a passion for making an entrance.

"I may not have time to talk to Devan if he calls, and I need to get his car back to him. What does his schedule look like? Is he free at lunch?"

"He has an eleven o'clock meeting that finishes up at one. I imagine he'll eat after that."

"Tell him that he's very welcome to walk up and get it then. I'd drive it down now and walk home, but I can't leave at the moment. If Annie says I'm not available when he comes, tell him to just take the car and I'll talk to him when I can. I have the kind of mother who can take up a lot of a person's time when she's in the mood."

Annie and I hurried to greet Mother. As she descended the first flight of stairs and came into sight, I saw her eyes flick toward the mirror at the landing, checking to make sure every last curl was in place as she slowly approached us.

Too slowly, perhaps. Her time at the hospital—asylum? rest home? What was it, anyway?—had taken something out of her. Not her beauty, surely, but a thin woman doesn't lose twenty pounds without also losing something vital. Muscle. Energy. Youthful reflexes. A springy stride. To become smaller, a person has to lose something.

She had chosen a simple frock for her first day home, a black crepe Kitty Foyle dress with a white collar, white cuffs, and mother-of-pearl buttons from neck to hem. The black-and-white spectator pumps on her feet pulled the whole outfit together, because Lily Ecker was not constitutionally capable of ignoring that kind of detail. My mother might have lost a bit of vitality, but she was still wholly herself.

When she was sure we were looking, she turned to descend the last flight of stairs, still moving slowly. Perhaps she hadn't walked down a staircase since she left home. She certainly hadn't walked in heels since she ran barefoot away from my father.

"Breakfast was just lovely, Annie," she said, trailing a hand along the banister. Her voice was as shiny as her shoes. "I've missed your pear preserves desperately."

I didn't even have to look at Annie. I could feel her preen.

"Miss Estella—E—she shelled the walnuts."

And now Mother stood in front of us, at our level. "Thank you, E, for the walnuts. I suppose Malcolm's...absence...means

that there will be nobody to stop us from calling my daughter
by the name she prefers."

She walked through the library to the drawing room window
and looked down at the river. "I feel certain that there are things
I need to know about Malcolm's passing and about his estate.
And, I suppose, about the events of the past two hundred and
fifty-one days."

Of course, she had counted the days. Who wouldn't?

She looked at my face as if the cool shadow that I felt crossing it was real. "You mustn't feel bad, dear. Neither of you should
feel bad for something that my husband did two hundred and
fifty-one days ago."

A sob escaped Annie. Mother gave her shoulder a gentle
squeeze.

"It's a lovely morning, and the three of us need to talk,"
Mother said. "Perhaps you could bring some tea out on the
veranda?"

So Annie was part of the family when it came to discussing
our most personal business, but she still had to serve the tea? I
felt myself become sixteen again, livid and rebellious.

But I said nothing, because Annie was so happy to be able
to bring my mother something she wanted.

Mother made a slow circuit of the drawing room, running
her hand along the wainscoting. She grazed her eyes over the
rug, and I knew she was looking for spots. Finding none, she
gave the davenport the same treatment. With a small nod, she
walked out onto the veranda. I followed, painfully aware that
my father had been chasing her the last time she walked out
that door.

Leaning forward slightly, she rested her forearms atop the railing, calling my attention to its intricately carved sheaf-of-wheat design. So much human labor had gone into the building of our house.

"While I was gone, I closed my eyes every morning and imagined the sunrise from this spot," she said. "I slept through it today, but I saw the last few pink clouds from my bedroom window. Well, there's always tomorrow."

She looked so calm, but her clasped hands squeezed and relaxed, over and over, like a heart pumping arterial blood. "Then, in the evenings, I pictured us sitting out here while the sun set behind us and turned the clouds rosy again." The hands squeezed and relaxed again. "A thousand colors of pink." Her voice, always low, was barely audible.

The door opened and closed behind us.

"Sit! Drink!" Annie sang the words as she swept past us with a fully loaded tray. She set it on the low table in front of the white wicker settee and picked up the teapot, but Mother flapped her hand at a chair sitting at right angles to the settee. Annie sat and poured us all some tea.

I took mine black, and I noticed that Annie did, too. It was as if we'd decided through mental telepathy not to tell Mother that sugar was rationed. Not yet. If we ran out before the week was out, I would have to tell her then.

Did she even know about the war? She couldn't possibly know that the corpse of Helena Frederick had been found. She seemed too fragile for much truth-telling, but she was going to leave the house or look at a newspaper sometime. I needed to get her alone and tell her how things were.

"I don't know…" Mother's voice trailed off, and she filled the gap with a sip of tea. "I don't know how to plan my day. Your father took up so much…"

She took another sip before finishing her thought. "So much space. And time."

How had my mother spent her days while my father was alive? I had no idea, but Annie must know. I turned to her, but her eyes were on her shaking teacup.

Annie set the cup down hard enough to slosh tea into her saucer, and said, "You kept yourself busy trying to keep peace in the house. That's what you did."

"And failing, usually."

"None of it was your—" Annie's voice failed her. She tried again. "It wasn't your fault."

"You're right. I had no control over my life, none at all. I was such a coward."

Annie erupted in a string of monosyllables. "No no *no no no no. NO.* You were no coward. You stood up to him. I saw you. And not just on that last day."

"Did I?"

I didn't know the answer, so I focused on the lovely view from our balcony. Fluffy clouds. Gentle sunshine. Green mountains in the distance and the wide river below.

"Annie. E. Tell me something."

I looked away from the river, into my mother's face.

"What?" I asked, and Annie echoed me.

"Am I supposed to miss him?"

CHAPTER 16

We were silent on the porch, Annie, my mother, and me. It was impossible to speak while my mother's words echoed.

Am I supposed to miss him?

It should have been a terrible moment, but I was happy in our companionable silence, now that my father wasn't spreading poison over my entire world like a cloud of mustard gas.

When the truth sank in—that I was now happier than I'd ever been at that house—the resentment that I'd felt toward my mother and her cool, remote essence slipped away. For a moment, I thought, "We could be happy here at Rockfall House, just the three of us." And then I remembered that I couldn't possibly pay for our beautiful life there.

My mother would wilt like a month-old violet if she had to live without a car, her cigarettes, her silk stockings. Hell. The cost of a single tube of her favorite fuchsia lipstick would buy a bag of groceries that would feed the three of us for days.

At least she liked oatmeal. Thank God for small blessings.

"Hello?"

It was a woman's voice echoing through the house, and it was coming from the vicinity of the front door.

"I knocked," the voice said, "but nobody came, and the door was unlocked."

The voice was familiar, but I couldn't place it. Mother could, though. She was instantly on her feet, calling out, "Cynthia!"

Annie scurried toward the entry hall, her face dripping with guilt. She had left the front door unlocked and untended, a cardinal sin in her mind. Under her breath, she muttered, "I should have locked up after I went out to check the radishes." Then, in a voice like a trumpet, she called out, "I'm so sorry I missed your knock. I'll be right there."

She returned with Dr. Masters, who wrapped my mother in a hug and didn't let go. It took me a moment to realize why I was so stunned. The emotional display seemed out of character for Dr. Masters, but I didn't really know her. Maybe she was a weepy bag of mush when she wasn't at work. No, it was my mother's behavior that stunned me. She simply didn't show emotion physically.

I remembered occasional kisses brushed across the top of my head as I left for grade school. I remembered cool hands on my cheek when I had a fever, but they were quickly withdrawn when Annie arrived with cold water and aspirin. I remembered a single arm slipped around my waist as I left for college.

But this? This bear hug, rocking to and fro as two women said, "I missed you," in a dozen different ways? I didn't know my mother was capable of anything resembling it.

I helped Annie pile the tray with our dirty dishes and left

my mother to visit with the friend we hadn't known she had. At least, I hadn't known, and Annie looked as confused as I was.

I murmured, "I have some phone calls to make, so I'll leave you two to catch up." I got no answer from either of them.

As the door closed, I heard Dr. Masters whisper, "Tell me everything."

I didn't actually have any urgent calls to make. It was hard for Leontine to use the phone in the silence of a library, so I didn't want to bother her. I'd told Marjorie to ask Devan to call me, and even my out-of-practice womanly wiles were good enough to tell me, "Don't pester the man. He knows where you are, and he knows where his car is."

There was a good chance, though, that Marjorie was alone in her office at that time of the morning, so I listened to Annie bumping around in the kitchen as the campus operator put me through. Marjorie's professional, "Dean's suite. May I help you?" shifted immediately to "How *are* you?" when she heard my voice.

"I'm fine, but you're better. In fact, you're miraculous. How on earth did you spread the news about my mother so fast?"

She made modest noises about how she hadn't done that much, but when I said, "Dr. Masters is already here," I heard the springs in her desk chair creak as she sat up straighter.

"I just told her. I mean…I just told her, not half an hour ago. It would take her almost that long to get to your house, whether she walked or drove. She must have made tracks as soon as she left me." I heard a rustling of paper and a low whistle.

"I'm looking at the teaching schedule right now. She must have canceled her morning class."

"She did look very anxious to see my mother."

"So it would seem."

"I take it that everything at Hawke Hall is going fine without me?"

"We miss you dreadfully, but we're limping along. I taped 'Class Canceled Today' signs on the doors of your classrooms. Also, I've informed the professors in no uncertain terms that they were not to bother you at home."

"Dr. Masters ignored you."

"Evidently, despite the fact that I was very clear. When people were around, I said you had a confidential family emergency, but when I was alone with the biggest busybodies, I told them what it was. Dr. Masters is no gossip, so I just told her that your mother was home resting after some time away."

"You're a good friend."

"Anything for you. Is there anything else I can do? I could show up after dinner tonight with a jigsaw puzzle to prevent any uncomfortable silences. It works at my house, especially if you keep the radio playing. I've seen some awkward family situations, but yours takes the cake."

I pictured a table set up in the drawing room, covered with puzzle pieces and with four heads bent over it—Marjorie's, Mother's, mine, and Annie's. Make that five, because I would want Leontine there. And maybe six, because I had the feeling we'd be seeing a lot of Cynthia Masters. I was surprised at how much I liked the idea. Was this how households that didn't involve my father spent their time?

"That sounds great. Maybe next week, after she's had some time to rest up?"

"Certainly. Name the day."

Since I was indoors instead of out on the veranda, I heard the knock this time, long, insistent, and woodpecker-like.

"I have to go, Marjorie. Somebody else has come to visit. I knew the news would spread fast, but I didn't expect so many people to want to see Mother with their own eyes."

"That just shows how much you don't understand people. Go help your mother greet her public. Call me if you need me."

The line went dead.

Annie beat me to the door. She opened it to reveal Chief D'Amato. Any competent law officer would have come as soon as possible, yet he'd waited half the morning before showing up unannounced.

I knew that the man didn't like me personally, but I'd found a missing person his people had failed to find for months. A little respect would have been nice. Some good manners, at least.

Instead, he slouched at my front door, his gaunt frame fully uniformed and one clawlike hand clutching a notepad.

"Can I help you?"

"I'm here to talk to your mother."

"She's with a guest."

He stuck his foot in the door like a door-to-door salesman. (It would've been fun to slam it on that foot, but I was better brought up than that.) "She's been gone under mysterious cir-cumstances for the better part of a year. An interview with law enforcement is her first priority. I need to hear her story from her lips, and I need to make sure she gets any necessary medical care."

I pointedly looked at the dainty gold watch on my wrist, an impractical high school graduation gift from my impractical parents. Its spindly hands told me that it was after ten o'clock. He and I both knew that it was too late in the day for him to pretend that my family was his first priority.

Having made my point, I ushered him to the veranda. Mother must have complained of a chill, because Annie had wrapped her in a lacy blue shawl. Dr. Masters leapt to her feet at the sight of D'Amato, stammering as she said her good-byes. I wondered if he enjoyed spreading discomfort everywhere he went.

He dropped uninvited into the chair that she had vacated, then flicked a dismissive glance at me. "I need some time alone with the witness."

"Do you mean victim?"

"That remains to be seen. Couldn't she be both?"

In this, he was correct. I left them on the veranda and went inside to perch on a chair beside the open window directly behind D'Amato. He couldn't see me on the other side of the wall. Mother couldn't see me. But I could hear every word. I was damned if another arrogant man took advantage of her vulnerability.

"Tell me what happened to you, Mrs. Ecker."

I heard her shake a stale cigarette out of the monogrammed silver case where she kept them. Annie or I needed to go restock her supply. I heard the flick of a lighter, and I knew it was his. My mother never lit her own cigarette when a man was handy. I didn't hear her long inhale and exhale, because audible breathing was a suggestive sound that a real lady never made.

"It seemed like any other day. My husband took me for a

ride, a long ride. He said he'd booked me a week at a luxury spa as a surprise, and I was stupid enough to believe him."

So she wasn't going to tell D'Amato that they'd been fighting. I didn't blame her.

"The place he took me looked like a spa from the outside, very luxurious, very elegant. Even the interior looked posh when you first stepped in the door. He was gone before I realized that he'd checked me into a mental hospital. Can you imagine? He drove away, and he never came back. I don't want to tell you about the indignities."

I imagined the scene as they took her clothes and a roll of cash fell from her bra. I imagined her face when they handed her a cotton smock and those cheap buttoned shoes.

"Does my story confirm what my daughter told you?"

"It seems to," he said in a voice that insinuated that we might have agreed on a fake story. Also, he was lying when he suggested that I had told him anything. We'd barely spoken. All he knew was what I'd told the dispatcher.

"She tells me that my husband is dead. I presume this is also your understanding."

"I attended his funeral."

Mother was silent for a moment, absorbing the fact that she'd missed her husband's funeral. But she rebounded. She always does. "Is it true that he was stricken as soon as he returned from imprisoning me? Or has my daughter told me this to make me think he would have driven back that very night to get me, once he'd had time to think about what he'd done?"

The lighter flicked again as he paused to light something of his own—a cigarette? A cigar? A pipe?

Sharp-smelling smoke wafting in the window answered my question. D'Amato smoked a cigar.

"Your housekeeper said that he collapsed as soon as he came home, without telling her where you were, just as your daughter said. The doctor came quickly. His opinion was that your husband's symptoms looked like he had just had a stroke."

"What are you saying? Are you implying that it wasn't a stroke? Or that Annie and my daughter are lying about when he was stricken?"

"I've known Dr. Brown for a long time. He's good at what he does. When he says 'stroke,' then that's what I write down in the file."

"Then why are we having this conversation? I'm sure the hospital has a record of the time he checked me in, and you know where I've been since then. You know where my daughter was teaching, so you know which train brought her home and the time it arrived. What else can I tell you?"

He emitted a grunt.

She had been so weary when she got home that I couldn't have said for sure that she was listening when Annie and I explained the timing of that terrible day. I should have known not to underestimate the sharp mind behind her sleepy blue eyes.

"My husband's death, and the months of imprisonment it cost me, are a family tragedy, not a crime." I heard her shawl rustle as she gathered it around her. "Annie will show you out."

Brava, Mother.

"No, Annie won't show me out, because I'm not here just to

talk about your husband's death. We need to talk about the other
dead body that showed up that week."

Oh, no. Annie and I should have told her about Helena.

"Other?"

"Do you recall the young woman who disappeared fifteen
years ago?"

"Helena Frederick." Her voice was thin, choked. "Who
could forget her? Nobody who ever saw her parents' faces after
she was gone. Those poor people. That poor girl. Are you saying
she's been found dead?"

"A literal stone's throw from where we sit."

I knew the view from that veranda so well—the rocky cliff
tumbling down to the calm cove below.

"You found her near here?"

"We dragged the cove looking for you."

A breathless, "Oh," escaped her.

"We thought perhaps you fell. Or you jumped. Perhaps you
were pushed. Maybe your dead body was thrown in the river.
Any of these things might have taken you to the bottom of that
cove. You weren't there."

I heard him take a drag on his cigar, hold the smoke in his
mouth, and let it go in a whoosh before she answered him.

"Evidently."

There was another pause that gave him a chance to wave
the cigar at her or perhaps to point at the water and force my
mother to look. It would make sense for an interrogator to force
his target to think about the bones of Helena Frederick, picked
nearly clean by fish and decay. This didn't keep it from being a
cruel thing to do.

"It's awful to think about her being so close to us for so long. Do you have any idea what happened to her?"

"The same things we thought might have happened to you. What do you remember about the day she went missing? And the days after?"

"I remember what everybody else remembers. The word spread fast when she didn't come home. My husband and I were playing cribbage after a quiet evening. Our daughter was upstairs in her room, probably asleep. The phone rang, and Annie took the call, as she always did. She came to us, white-faced, and said, 'The housekeeper at the Frederick house called to see if we'd seen their daughter Helena. She hasn't been seen since she left Hawke Hall at two this afternoon. Her friends, her boyfriend, her professors—they've called everybody, and nobody knows where she is.'"

"Did their housekeeper tell yours anything else?"

"No, nothing. I remember that my husband and I looked at our watches and saw that it was after ten. And I remember that Annie said the exact same thing I was thinking, 'It's horrible. Horrible. It could be our Miss Estella out there, missing.'"

This part of her story had to be the God's honest truth, because I remembered frantic conversations with all three of them late that night. First Mother, then Father, then Annie came to my room, desperate to see me and to hear my voice. They made me promise to be careful. No talking to strangers. No car rides with people (and by "people," they meant men) that I didn't know well. No careless meandering around town without a friend to look after me. (And by "friend to look after me," they also meant a man, but it's unfair to expect frightened parents to be consistent.)

"Were you questioned by anyone from my office?"

"Surely, you remember. You questioned me once. You questioned my husband several times. It bordered on harassment."

This was news to me.

"Your husband was the Dean of Arts and Sciences, and his office was in Hawke Hall. He was in a position to know if anyone in the building, student or employee, could have been a risk to the missing girl."

"Nobody was ever arrested, unless you did it while I was gone, so it seems that you harassed my husband and his colleagues for no reason. If the killer was associated with Hawke Hall, nobody knew it. Not even Cynthia Masters, and the girl was last seen in her class. She didn't know a thing about where Helena went afterward. And I know Cynthia wouldn't lie about a thing like that."

"That may be." Cigar smoke trailed into the window. "But your husband did lie to you that day."

"What?"

"He was one of the professors that Helena's parents called at work when they first realized she was missing. He already knew she was gone when your housekeeper came to tell you. For whatever reason, he let you think it was news to him."

Mother said, "Well. Hmm," in an uncharacteristically flustered tone. She rallied by changing the subject.

"All you've said is that she was in the water. Is there any reason to think that she...took her own life?"

"I can't rule it out. We don't have all of her body. We don't even have all of her bones."

I thought of the stones carefully sewn into Helena Frederick's pockets. I'd never heard any gossip about them, so D'Amato had kept that information quiet.

If Helena was the one who sewed those tiny, tight stitches, then she sincerely wanted to die. But if somebody else made them, then they sincerely hoped that her body would never be found. And it might never have been, if my father hadn't locked my mother up and walked away. I remembered that they dragged the cove the day after Helena went missing, so either they'd missed her body that time or it hadn't been there yet. If Mother's disappearance hadn't triggered another search, Helena might have lain on the riverbed forever.

A disloyal part of me wondered if my father's lies meant that he had done the killing. Why would he do that? Eighteen-year-old girls don't tend to pose a huge risk to powerful older men—not unless there's been an affair and she's threatening to tell the world. Or she's pregnant.

For all his flaws, I would have sworn that my father was besotted with my mother, but some people are going to cheat, no matter what. So maybe he had. I hadn't lived with them for years. Annie had described his atrocious behavior toward my mother while I was gone, and I'd seen for myself that he'd locked her away against her will.

But could he sew?

I couldn't visualize my father doing something as messy as beating someone to death. I could, however, imagine him strangling her, then wrapping her body in her coat and slipping stones into her pockets. The only argument against this scenario was that I couldn't imagine him threading a needle and sewing them shut. Sewing was one of the reasons one kept wives and housekeepers around.

"Are you planning to question everyone again, or just me?" Mother asked.

"I'll question the ones who survive. Your husband and Dean Jamison aren't around to answer me now."

"Dean Jamison? Harry Jamison took Malcolm's place as dean? He's dead?"

I imagined my mother's Ice Queen face, immobile, beautiful, and completely unreadable. She'd tried to teach me how to fend off importunate men with that face, but I was never as good at it as she was. I was only now realizing that she'd been keeping my father and his temper at bay (mostly) with nothing but her face since she was just a girl. She was only seventeen when she married him.

My mother's life had been harder than I'd ever imagined, and I'd never known, because the Ice Queen revealed nothing. The quaver in her voice when she said, "Harry Jamison?" was more revealing than a torrent of tears in another woman. I should have told her he was dead. I should have told her everything, but good God, she'd been free less than a day. How much emotional battering could she take?

My father. Dean Jamison. Helena Frederick and her bones. Our desperate financial situation. The war. I had wanted her to wake up to her new reality slowly.

"Dean Jamison took his own life last Friday."

At least he had the decency not to tell her how he did it. I had seen the aftermath. I didn't want her to imagine it.

"I'm sorry, but I'm suddenly very weary. Do you need

anything else from me? I—I need some time to take everything in."

I expected him to find one last way to wound her, but I was wrong. He said, "Not at this time," and passed from the veranda into the house before I'd had time to move away from the window. From the way he looked at me, I guessed that he'd known I was listening. Maybe he'd wanted me to hear. Maybe he was more dangerous than he seemed.

He stood and looked down at me. "You heard what we said?"

"I heard enough."

"If I were your mother, I'd be angry that you'd been keeping things from me."

"I was planning to dribble out the information. It's a lot to take in."

"Sorry to interfere with the way you run your family life."

No. You're not.

"I'm going to need to take the bracelet. And the book."

"What could you hope to learn from them? They've been out in the rain and wind for months."

"For starters, maybe it's not your mother's bracelet. Maybe it belonged to Helena Frederick."

"I have photos of her wearing it."

"Was it custom-made? The only one in the world?"

"No. Take it, if you must, but I have a lawyer. It's valuable, and I want it back."

"And the book."

I opened my mouth to say that it was irreplaceable, the only one left in the world, then I closed it again. I was so upset that I'd forgotten I had two of them, and I'd never told him about the one hidden under my bed. He didn't know about the note she'd written in it, and I felt sick inside at the thought of him reading her call for help. He couldn't have that book, but he could have the one I found on the cliff.

I fetched the bracelet and book and reminded him that I had a lawyer and I wanted them back.

Could John get them back for me? I had no idea, but I pretended that he could as I handed my mother's things over.

Was this another secret for me to keep from her? Probably not. The past hour had shown that keeping secrets from her was a risky proposition.

CHAPTER 17

Once I was rid of D'Amato, I hurried back to the veranda. Mother didn't move at the creak of the hinges, so I stood in the open doorway a moment, staring at her back as her shoulders vibrated with silent sobs. I needed to stop this barrage of visitors and give her time to get her bearings.

Before I could get started doing that, we both heard another knock at the door, less insistent than Chief D'Amato's had been, just a few sharp raps.

Mother's head whipped around as if she'd heard a rifle shot. She half-rose, but I motioned for her to stay where she was.

"I'll get the door," I said. "And I'll get rid of whoever it is."

But I was too late. Annie was already ushering Dr. Bower through the door. "You say you're an old friend of the Eckers? From England? My word, that was a long time ago, long before I came to work for them. I know you're happy she's home. She's on the veranda. It's right this way."

There I stood, between my mother, who was in the midst of a breakdown, and a man from her past who was moving at an unseemly speed. He was actually leading fleet-footed Annie, now that she'd pointed out where he needed to go.

I couldn't think of any way to stop him. I should have screamed, "Fire! Run for your life!" But I didn't think of that.

"I heard about your mother," he said as he passed me to get to her. "Are you quite all right? And is she?"

"I'm fine," I said. "Happy to have her home, obviously. She's doing as well as could be expected. You just missed Dr. Masters." *And the police chief, but never mind him.* "Maybe I should have called a faculty meeting on our veranda."

This made me think of Dean Jamison's death scene, where Devan, Dr. Masters, and Dr. Bower were practically a faculty meeting quorum, particularly if you counted the dead dean.

I'd expected my mother to be surprised to see Dr. Bower, but I hadn't expected her obvious confusion. As he took her hand, he was saying, "I felt a duty to my dear friend Malcolm to see after you. It has been so many years since we were all together in England," but my mother's eyes were saying that she didn't know this man.

Her eyes also said that she felt fear, or something like it. Foreboding, perhaps. I had left her on the porch alone with D'Amato, because his official lawman's aura had caused me to take leave of my senses. It wouldn't happen again. I would be babysitting her for the entire time Dr. Bower was present.

"It has been so many years." Dr. Bower's tone was warm, his brown eyes respectful behind old-fashioned round horn-rimmed glasses. "I was barely out of high school and far from home. You have no idea what a simple invitation to dinner meant to me."

Was he speaking of one dinner or did he mean he had been a frequent guest in their home? When he said, "when we were together in England," was he speaking of working with my father? Of spending time with my parents together? Of spending time with just my mother? Every sentence from his mouth was an enigma.

My mother, the most socially astute human being I have ever met, was wearing her perfect mask. It was cordial, but it gave away nothing to the casual bystander. I, however, could see behind it.

Was it more likely that this man would pretend to know her or that the pressures of the past months had taken her grip on reality or affected her memory? I didn't want to think about it.

As they spoke—actually, Dr. Bower did most of the talking—Annie gathered the dirty cups and brought out another steaming pot. It struck me that she must get very tired of brewing tea leaves. It also struck me that our supply of tea was not infinite, and I hadn't bought groceries in days. Even in small ways, my mother's return was going to have its costs.

All the while, Dr. Bower talked and talked. He spoke of playing three-handed euchre with my parents for hours. He praised my mother's cottage pie and her Dorset apple cake.

She thanked him delicately, saying that her cooking had never been anything to write home about, but that people had always liked her apple cake and her cottage pie. When he called her a cutthroat euchre player, she simply laughed, but I'd played euchre with her. I knew it was true.

I knew that my mother never lost at euchre, so maybe this man did know her. I could see that she was doing the same calculus, so she obviously didn't remember him. Only she knew whether she could make cottage pie or apple cake or whether she could even cook at all. I couldn't imagine Annie letting her muck about in the kitchen, but there had been a time in Mother's life before Annie. Before me. Even before my father. If she couldn't remember it, then nobody could, except maybe this man. How much had her stay in the asylum cost her?

For an excruciating half-hour, Dr. Bower talked. Mother mostly nodded. He never stopped reminding her of a past she didn't remember, and she never stopped pretending that she did.

Eventually, he said, "I must go. Don't bother calling your housekeeper. I can let myself out."

After Dr. Bower left, my mother murmured something that sounded like "Very tired," and disappeared into her bedroom.

Annie hurried upstairs behind her, carrying a tray of sandwiches. When she returned, none of the three sandwiches had left the tray. Annie, with her pile of bread thinly spread with the last of the chicken salad, looked defeated.

Since there was no reality in which my mother ate three sandwiches at a sitting, or even in one day, I presumed that two of them were for Annie and me. I grabbed one and said, "This will make a nice picnic. If she needs me, I'll be on the Garden Path."

Annie filled a bright red vacuum flask with cold water from the tap and handed it to me. Then she took the sandwich out of my hand, wrapped it in a white napkin and handed it back. "I know it hurts, E."

I remained expressionless and didn't meet her eyes, which I knew made me look just like Mother. "I'm fine. I'm just a little hungry and I'm feeling cooped-up. A walk will fix me right up."

"You stayed home from work to spend time with her and what did she do? She spent the morning talking to other people. Now she's nowhere in sight."

Annie never did mince words.

I decided that Mother deserved some grace. "It wasn't her fault those people came to see her."

"That's right," Annie said. "Give her time. She's so glad you're here. I can see it."

Oddly enough, I could see it, too. This didn't mean that I wanted to sit around twiddling my thumbs until she reappeared.

"I just need a distraction," I said. "I'll be back before she wakes up from her nap."

❀

Vacuum bottle in one hand and sandwich in the other, I headed for the Garden Path. It was an old bridle trail that started in my father's terraced garden and climbed the downriver hillside overlooking our house. It went all the way up to the ruins of Stenen Klif Manor.

I was headed for a particular spot that I'd loved since Annie first let me go outside alone. The path's first two switchbacks stayed within sight of the house. Trees blocked the view after it switched back again, but there was a sunny spot with a lovely view nestled in that second hairpin curve. The grass was scattered with flat-topped rocks at just the right height for sitting. I knew they'd be sun-warmed and ready for me.

But it appeared that I was never destined to get there. Before I'd gone three steps, I heard a sound coming from the driveway behind me, gravel crunching under a pair of feet. Who else had decided to pay my mother a visit? Did I dare let her manage this encounter by herself?

I did not dare. I turned around with a sigh.

"You don't sound—or look—glad to see me."

It was Devan, and I was mortified.

"I didn't mean—I thought—"

He laughed and said, "I wasn't serious. If I'd been through what you have, I'd be flat on my back in bed, not trying to greet guests with a smile."

"I tried to call you—"

"I know. Marjorie told me. She said I should come after my meeting broke up, but I should have called to confirm."

"No, it's what I meant for her to do. And for you to do. I'm just—is it really that late? If your meeting got out at one and then you walked up here…well, I guess time flies when there's a family crisis. I wouldn't have thought it was past eleven." Also, I'd forgotten he was coming, but that seemed understandable, given the morning I'd had.

"It really is nearly one-thirty. So will you tell me something?"

I felt a suspicious stillness wash over me. It was the icy aura I associated with my mother, the one that kept people at a distance, and I willed it away. Giving Devan the most scintillating smile I could manage, I put a flirty edge on my voice. "That depends on what you want to know."

My voice didn't sound flirtatious to me, much less

scintillating. It sounded fake. There were kinder words that I could use to describe my mother—both my parents, really—but "fake" actually suited them quite well.

Devan didn't seem to notice the family quarrel going on in my head.

"Okay, here's my question. Who *were* you planning to meet with that glare?"

"I don't know. Just another one of the people who can't seem to leave my mother alone."

"I don't have to stay. I'll just ask how you are, and then I'll go."

"I'll tell you, but you just got out of a meeting that went straight through lunch, then you walked all the way up here. You can't possibly have had a chance to eat. The least you can do is let me feed you. I seem to remember promising you a walk and a picnic."

I was able to maintain the flirty tone for that long, but then I drifted into my usual clumsiness. "I mean, unless you need to get back to work. I don't know if you have other appointments or—"

"I have plenty of time. Let's take a walk."

"We can split this sandwich and bottle of water." That sounded like starvation rations, but the pantry was getting pretty bare. Racking my brain for portable food, I fumbled in my pocket.

Did I have my keys? I did. I also had his.

"Come down to the basement with me," I said, handing him his car keys and sliding a key of my own into the padlock holding a heavy metal door shut. "I'll pack us a bag of apples and walnuts. I'm sorry if that sounds like something you'd feed livestock."

He laughed and whinnied like a horse, then he helped me lift the Bilco door.

The basement was only half underground. The upper half of its masonry walls was pierced with small windows all the way round. They gave the place a watery light but left dark shadows in the corners.

Once in the cool dimness, I lifted my hand to pull the light chain, but Devan closed his over it. With one hand on my waist, he lifted my face to his.

"How *are* you, E?"

Faintly, I said, "That's what Marjorie said. And Leontine. They said it just that way."

"I don't know Leontine, but Marjorie's your friend. It sounds like Leontine is, too. I'm your friend. I haven't talked to you since you found your mother. All I know is what Marjorie told me. I want to hear it from you."

There, in a basement smelling of onions, apples, and dampness, I stood with his arms wrapped around me, and I let it all tumble out. The barely disguised madhouse. The barely stable mother. The duplicitous father. The doomed Helena Frederick. The strangely ominous visits of Dr. Masters, Sheriff D'Amato, and Dr. Bower. The words came out as fast as my lips could shape them. Faster, some of them. I'm sure I sounded like I was the one who was barely stable.

When it came to the point of admitting to impending bankruptcy, my natural reticence reasserted itself, so I limited that confession to a brief, "It's going to cost a lot to have Mother home. She's an expensive individual." I think he knew what I was saying. And then the flood of words petered out.

"You're carrying a heavy load," he said, and he pressed his lips to the top of my head.

It was just the right thing for him to do. He seemed to really see me in a way that Bradley never had, which was funny in a way that wasn't funny at all, because Bradley had seen me naked. Somehow, Bradley could always use my vulnerability to his own ends, without ever seeing me at all.

I'm not saying that I didn't want passion from Devan. I did, just not then. A man who took advantage of a moment like that one wasn't someone to be trusted.

After a time that was just long enough, Devan let me go. Taking a bag hanging from a wall hook, he looked around the dim room. "Point me at the apples and walnuts. You promised me a picnic and a walk. I think that's exactly what we both need."

CHAPTER 18

Devan seemed to enjoy our picnic. The grassy spot at the trail's second switchback still had warm rocks to sit on, just as it did when I was a child. We had a perfect view of my father's terraces and the waterfall cascading through them to the pond below. The rhododendrons and roses were just coming into bloom beneath the shaggy red leaves of overhanging Japanese maples.

The ground at our feet was scattered with nut shells. I'd forgotten to pack a nutcracker, but it had been great fun to smash open our walnuts with rocks.

"Your garden is magnificent. It suits the house."

"My father had it built. He hired Frederick Law Olmsted, Jr.'s firm to create exactly what he wanted."

"Olmsted? The man who built Central Park?"

"You're thinking of his famous father. He designed the gardens at Stenen Klif Manor." I pointed to the top of Rockfall Bluff. "They're still beautiful, even after decades of neglect. My father wanted to restore them, but there was always another project that caught his interest."

Devan was still studying the terraced garden. "I'd say that your father managed some impressive things."

I wasn't in the mood to praise my father, so I didn't answer.

It made me uncomfortable to talk about the garden that my parents had planted with my wedding in mind. Jumping to my feet, I said, "I promised to show you the Stenen Klif ruins as part of our picnic. Let's do that now, while we still have some get-up-and-go." And I started walking up the hill, so that he'd know I meant business.

"Wait," he said. "Slow down. We can do that another time. You've got to be exhausted."

And then he bumped into me as I stopped in my tracks, and not because I was exhausted. There were two footprints in the soft soil of the path's shoulder.

The path itself was paved with weathered gray gravel. Turning around, I could see that it hid our tracks well. The only explanation for these two footprints—medium-sized, so not obviously made by a man or woman, and pointing downhill toward my house—was that somebody had climbed this trail in the week since it had last rained. If they hadn't stepped off the path on the way back down, I never would have known.

The person who left those prints wasn't me, and it wasn't Annie. She didn't take walks for the fun of it, and this wasn't the path she took to gather wild onions.

I sincerely doubted that my mother had been traipsing around between midnight and seven-thirty a.m. And she completed the list of people who had a right to be on our property.

"These aren't yours?"

I shook my head.

"Who else has access to this trail?"

It was fascinating to watch an affable academic transform into a fierce protector.

"Nobody outside my family," I said. "This is all our land—from the park's river trail up to the top of the bluff, including the land around the ruins and all the old paths and trails. Basically, all of Rockfall Bluff came with the house. You can get to this spot without being seen from the house, but you'd have to cross a property boundary marked with 'No Trespassing' signs, and you'd still have to walk a long way on bridle trails that are really overgrown."

"Are there maps that would tell someone how to do that?"

"Leontine's library has old drawings of Stenen Klif Manor and its grounds. A lot of libraries might. It was pretty famous in its day. My question is *why* somebody would want to do that."

"I guess people like to explore." Devan's mouth said it, but his face looked unconvinced.

The sound of voices below us drew me away from the footprints, back to the grassy spot where I could see my house. Mother and Annie were talking outside the kitchen door.

"She's up from her nap," I said. "I should go spend some time with her."

Even as he agreed, my mother flung a black cardigan around her shoulders, adjusted the brim of her black straw hat with a black-gloved hand, and set off on the trail to town. She was moving at an impressive clip for a woman in Cuban-heeled spectator pumps, and she carried her handbag like a woman with purpose.

"She appears to be well-rested," he said.

She did. And it appeared that she had priorities higher than spending time with me.

"Looks like I have time for a walk to Stenen Klif Manor after all. Would you care to escort me? I might need protection from whoever's been prowling around my property." Remembering that my mother's return meant that the property wasn't strictly mine, I corrected myself. "My family's property."

Bowing at the waist and holding out a bent arm for me to hold, like a fairy-tale prince, Devan said, "Let us ascend to the heights, lovely lady." He managed not to look silly doing it and, to be honest, it was probably the best possible way to woo a scholar of Gothic literature.

❦

It was almost always windy at the top of Rockfall Bluff. The heights there were truly wuthering, and the purple cloud lurking to the north on that afternoon only added to the effect. The standing stones that remained of Stenen Klif Manor had never looked so foreboding. My, how I loved them.

"You can see that most of the mansion's facade has survived, but the rest is basically rubble. The driveway that ended here was more than a mile long. It brought guests and supplies from the old road that came up from Manhattan and the ferry at Nyack. That road is still the main north-south highway around here."

"Is the driveway still usable?" he asked, and I knew he was thinking about the footprints.

"It's washed out in several places. Maybe you could walk it, but it would be hard." I pointed to the far side of the ruins. "The pleasure gardens were north of the house, and they've more or less gone wild." The old flowers made a pink-and-crimson carpet beneath the green trees.

I pointed away from the bluff, "In that direction, there were some cleverly disguised privies, the stables, the apple orchard, and the drinking water reservoir. Beyond that, up the hill, was the coal gasification plant that kept the lights on. Robber barons did like their gaslight."

"Shady business dealings aren't so ugly when they're committed in a golden glow."

"Exactly," I said, unable to ignore the sun on his golden-red hair. "Anyway, there were no ugly necessities here, near the cliff's edge. This meant that his guests could look down at… everything."

The soaring mountain-and-river view from the ruins of Stenen Klif Manor looked like one of my father's most expensive oil paintings.

Devan took it all in. "I'm guessing he didn't waste money on stained glass for this wing."

I shook my head. "Nope. Why would he hide a view like this? The wall was all windows, as close to uninterrupted glass as you could get back then. They say you could see sunshine sparkling off Van der Waal's windowpanes for miles around."

"And the ponds?"

"I'm sure they sparkled, but not from that distance. Come see."

The rock-lined ponds were clear and fresh. This may have been an accidental benefit of the work Father did to build his waterfall. Water moved quicker through the ponds than it had when I was a child, so there was a lot less green muck floating on top.

"Van der Waal diverted a brook into the reservoir," I pointed up the hill, "letting gravity feed water from pond to pond, and eventually back to the brook. Father changed the design when he added this," I pointed to a modern oval pond hugging the edge of the cliff, out-of-place but beautiful in its own way.

"It feeds the waterfall in your back garden?"

I nodded.

Devan dipped his fingers into a pond, ruffling its still surface. "I see scorch marks on the ruins. The house burned?"

"Yes, sometime during the last war. Gaslight is pretty, but it'll set your curtains on fire in a heartbeat. Van der Waal moved to Newburgh, but he didn't live long. It takes the heart out of a person to watch a dream die."

The wind turned cool and blew the purple cloud closer. I felt a chill of recognition, as if I'd seen this moment in my sleep. Did I still have any dreams?

"Good thing you're not old enough to believe that all your dreams are dead," Devan said, pulling me close. This time, I wanted him close.

Oh, I was as vulnerable as I'd been in the basement, and he knew it, but he was the only bright spot I could see, and I wanted him. He was as warm and golden as gaslight, and I was a moth. I knew the heartache he could cause, but nothing could have made me fly away.

He leaned me against a tilting rock and kissed me like he'd never stop. The sooty stain from that scorched stone will never wash out of my mother's powder-blue cardigan, but it will hang in the back of my closet until my last day. If the storm hadn't come to drench us and aim thunderbolts at us, both of our clothes would have been ground into the dirt beneath us. Part of me wishes that we'd braved the lightning, even if it struck us down. Part of me wishes that we were both there still.

CHAPTER 19

My return home was awkward. Devan and I were so wet that we might as well have slid down my father's waterfall. The rain was diluvial. The thunderclaps were worthy of Zeus as we ran up to the kitchen door.

Annie threw it open and yelled, "Get in, both of you. You'll catch your death."

She dragged me inside with both hands, but Devan stayed out on the stoop. Its tiny roof did nothing to protect him from the horizontal rain.

"There's no reason for me to track even more water into your beautiful home." He looked ruefully at the puddle under my feet. "It will just take me a few minutes to drive home, where I have some dry clothes and a great lot of hot water."

"But Dr. Chase…"

"I'll be fine, Miss O'Dell. You make sure E gets warm and dry."

He turned to leave, but a low voice behind me said, "Dr. Chase. Please do go get comfortable at home, but I hope we see you again under less drippy circumstances."

Framed in the drawing room doorway and wrapped in a sky-blue housedress with a vermilion belt, my mother looked like a Gainsborough portrait.

"You can be sure of that, Mrs. Ecker."

Devan gave her a respectful nod, turned back to me, and said, "I'll see you soon, E," then he dashed to his car.

☙❦❧

After my bath, I folded a towel, put it on my bedroom floor, and laid the soot-stained cardigan out to dry. I'd soaked it in hot soapy water the whole time I was in the tub, then I'd rubbed it until the yarn started to pill. The stain was there to stay, but I was keeping the sweater. Mother would never miss it.

Pink all over from the hot soak, I slipped on an old pair of pajamas made of a fussy yellow-and-blue flowered flannel that Annie had found adorable. With a red bathrobe over them, knitted green house slippers on my feet (also courtesy of Annie), and a snowy white towel on my head, I shuffled down the staircase, determined to make an entrance that matched my mother's. Or, at least, one that was more colorful. The mirror at the top of the landing said I was doing okay on the colorful front. I sashayed into the drawing room, toweled head held high.

Annie was putting coal on the fire, unruffled by the fact that she had spent my bath time mopping up about a hundred gallons of rainwater that I'd dripped on her polished wood floors.

"I smell bean soup," I said, dropping a kiss on the crown of her head.

"I know how much you like it. That soup and your hot bath will keep you from catching your death of pneumonia. There's some beautiful dinner rolls for you, too. Your mother got them at the bakery."

Hesitating, I decided to plunge into the unknown. I dropped an identical kiss on my mother's curly head to see what would happen. She looked surprised but pleased, kissing the air while I did it, so I considered my experiment a success.

The phone rang, and Annie hurried to take it.

"I liked the look of your young man," Mother said. "Redheaded men always seem so roguish, even when they're perfectly respectable. Is he respectable?"

"Devan? I think so. He has a PhD in English literature."

"Like you and your father." The question of whether the word "respectable" could be applied to either of us hung in the air. "And so many of your father's friends and colleagues. Doctorates in English literature lie thick on the ground around here, and some of them belong to reprobates."

"Don't hold it against him that he's an academic. He knows how to sail a boat, and he's handy enough in the kitchen to pack a picnic. You'll love the fact that he has very nice manners and good posture."

"Clothes make the man, but it's unfair to judge him on that count when he was drenched to the skin. Even so, he was very handsome under all that water."

I wanted to be angry at her shallow judgment of a man I rather liked, but I also wanted her to pass judgment in his favor. I will never be consistent where my mother is concerned.

"We have Devan to thank for the car that brought you home. John wasn't home, and I don't know who else I would have asked. You might have had to spend another night away."

She lowered her eyelids, and I realized that I'd been cruel to remind her of her confinement. I also realized that I'd done it on purpose to get back at her for being shallow about Devan. Why is it so easy for our parents to make us act like children?

"Madam?" Annie's voice arrived before she did, and it was shaky. Something was wrong, because she never called out from room to room when Mother was in the house. Mother found it unseemly.

"What is it, Annie? Who was on the telephone?"

"It was Mrs. Jamison, ma'am. She called to respond to the RSVP. She says she's coming."

"RSVP? What is she coming *to*?" I asked, and I could hear my father's angry bark of frustration at the preposition I'd just ended a sentence with.

"Our dinner party!" Mother said, folding her hands in her lap and flashing the smile of a movie star.

I collapsed into a faded plaid armchair that clashed with my motley nightclothes. "What dinner party?"

"After the parade of guests we entertained this morning, I thought, 'There are so many kind people who want to welcome me home. Why not invite them over so we can become reacquainted all at once?' So I went upstairs after Dr. Bower left and wrote up the invitations. Then I walked them to the post office. It wasn't long after lunch, so I imagine most of them were delivered in the afternoon post."

I had been in Boston too long. I had forgotten the simple mechanics of small-town life. Local mail was handed to the postmaster, who put it straight in the post office boxes of people who got their mail that way. The rest went straight in the bag of the man who carried letters from house to house twice a day. In a matter of hours, my mother had reassumed the reins of our household—which had been my household for a time—and I was now the passenger of a carriage driver who was egging on a runaway horse.

I pulled the towel off my head and let wet hair fall around my face. "When is this party?"

My mother was near to giggling. Her irresponsibility was familiar, but this giddiness was new. I was glad she was happy, but I wasn't sure she was sane.

"Our party is on Friday."

"This coming Friday?"

She gave me a happy nod.

It was Monday. She'd had a fleet of servants to throw her parties when I was a child. Did she think Annie could do it alone in four days?

"Mother, Friday is a terrible day for this kind of thing. People will have to come home from work and hurry to get dressed for a formal dinner. It's inconsiderate not to take that into consideration."

"I prefer to think that I'm giving working people something to look forward to while they're drudging through the week."

So spoke a woman who had never been paid for drudgery in her life.

"I don't have the money on hand to buy food for a crowd by Friday. And wine. I can't afford wine."

"It's not a party without wine. We will have wine."

Mother was big on enunciation, so I thought she might see reason if I spoke deliberately. "There. Cannot. Be. A. Party."

She wore a disbelieving smile. "Of course, there will be a party. The invitations have gone out. Guests have responded in the affirmative. It's impossible to cancel it now."

This was, of course, why she had sent out the invitations in secret.

"You're not listening. Things are different now. We can't get all the food we need, much less enough food to entertain a crowd. To spend money on wine now, when the world is—"

"No. You're not listening to me." She rose and left the room.

It appeared that I was never going to get a chance to utter the word "war" in her presence.

Not knowing what else to do, Annie and I followed her through the library and into the short passageway that led to the basement stairs. At the bottom of the stairs, Mother fumbled around for the light switch, but Annie found it for her. This enabled Mother to make a suitably sweeping progression past the onion and potato bins, past the furnace and its coal bins, and between boxes of old paperwork. My parents truly threw nothing away.

She stopped in front of an unassuming wall built of bricks and reinforced with wooden beams. Leaning close, because she needed those glasses she wouldn't wear, she brushed away the moss and mold, finally locating a metal button hidden beneath a prominent timber. Using her knuckle to avoid any risk of breaking a nail, she pressed it hard. Like something out of "Ali Baba and the Forty Thieves," a section of the wall swung open and revealed a hidden cave dug into the soil of Rockfall Bluff.

A hidden wine cave.

CHAPTER 20

Mother beckoned us into the wine cave. "During Prohibition, we had to be creative about where we kept our liquor."

She strolled among the bottles, lifting one and then another, blowing off the dust, grazing a finger over their old, old labels.

"We have wine," she said. "And wine makes a party. I've invited nine. That's eleven with the two of us, which leaves three seats at the table for your friends, E. I imagine one of them will be that handsome Dr. Chase."

Her tone was arch. I hated that tone, but I'd seen her keep four men mesmerized by it simultaneously.

She turned her mesmerizing voice on Annie. "Surely you can put together a menu for a small group of fourteen. We won't even have to put a leaf in the table."

A small group of fourteen. I could hear the cashier ringing up my grocery bill. I could also see Annie's face, overjoyed but also distracted. She was already calculating ingredients and portion sizes.

"I could make something like trout amandine," she said, "only with walnuts, because that's what we have. I doubt I can get lemon juice for the sauce, but I could substitute wine. We do have lots of wine." She looked around the fully stocked wine cave, mouth agape.

"That's the spirit," Mother said.

"You're not planning to fish the ponds up at Stenen Klif for enough trout to feed fourteen? You can't do that between now and Saturday, not when you're busy getting ready for a party like that." My eyes pleaded with both of them to see reason. "And Annie, how could you possibly cook for so many people and serve at the table? There's only one of you."

I could not imagine Mother agreeing to serve a dinner party smorgasbord-style, laying out the food and letting guests serve themselves while her lone servant labored in the kitchen out of sight.

"I know how to get the help, E. Mrs. Bakker across the river—you know her?—she's hired a new cook who's not working out. Word is that Mrs. Bakker's desperate for somebody to come help. With your permission, Madam, I'll offer to come for a week and train the poor woman. In exchange, I'll ask for all the help we need for your party. She'll send people all this week to catch the fish and help me in the kitchen. They can serve at the party and help with the cleanup. Once the party's behind us, I'll go train Mrs. Bakker's cook."

I was horrified at the idea of trading people's services like... well, it wasn't slavery, but it felt something like it. People are not stocks and bonds.

Annie mistook my expression to mean that I was horrified

by the thought of looking after myself. "Don't worry, Miss E. I'll leave plenty of things in the refrigerator for the two of you to eat while I'm gone."

Mother was captivated by the thought of a week with so many servants. "It will be like old times."

I still hadn't even told her about the war.

Annie was in heaven. For years, she'd run a money-is-no-object kitchen, but the idea of entertaining grandly on a shoestring clearly inspired her. "I don't think we should try to manage every single one of the usual courses. Scaling back is the right thing to do these days. It wouldn't feel cheap. It would feel patriotic."

Let Mother make of that what she would.

Annie's eyes darted toward the rear wall of the basement, and I knew she was picturing the kitchen garden on the other side of it. "For a first course, I could make a nice asparagus soup. There will be plenty of shoots for that by Friday." She glanced at me. "I'll need to buy some cream, but pureed asparagus will stretch it nicely."

Mother clapped her hands. "Asparagus soup. Served with sherry. Sherry doesn't age particularly well, so we should use it."

Annie nodded. "For the second course, I could make noodles the way Mrs. Ajello's cook taught me. She called it *spaghetti alla chitarra*, because you cut the noodles with a frame made with wires like guitar strings. They come out—not round, but square. Long and square. Very elegant."

"Square in cross-section," I said to Mother, who nodded.

"If you say so," Annie said. "I thought I could toss spinach from the garden with the hot noodles to wilt it a little. And I could brown some fiddleheads and wild onions in butter and stir them in."

"Some mushrooms, maybe?" I asked, momentarily excited by the thought of feeding a crowd with as little money as possible.

"Oh, no, not mushrooms," Annie said.

"No morels?" I asked. "That's too bad. I thought I saw some this afternoon."

"No. But some cream stirred into the buttery fiddleheads and a light grating of hard cheese on top would taste very good and look very elegant, I'd say."

"I'd say so, too," said Mother. "You could probably splash some white wine in the sauce."

Annie nodded at her and spoke to me. "For that course, I'd need to buy some butter and a little cream and a little cheese, but I promise I can make them go a long way."

"And then we'll serve the fish?" Mother asked.

"Yes. I'll dip them in flour and egg, roll them in the walnuts, and fry them up in butter for a thin crust. And a little wine, too, to deglaze the pan for the sauce—"

If Annie and Mother had their way, our guests would be sloshed by dessert. Perhaps that wasn't a bad thing.

"The flour, egg, and butter will cost, but the trout will be free. And the wine. And the walnuts."

"You'll slice the nuts really thin?" Mother asked. "You're so good with a knife."

"Very thin. Yes, Madam."

"And then dessert?" I asked, hoping we could get to the last course before the grocery list got any longer.

"Of course," Annie said, "but first a green salad. We have

lettuce and radishes and green onions, and I can slice the radishes and onions very thin." She beamed at my mother. "I'll toss the salad with herbs, oil, and vinegar. I can do something with the apples for dessert."

"Apple tarts?" Mother asked.

"They take a lot of butter. I'm thinking an apple cake, with pear preserves in the batter to take the place of sugar. And raspberry cordial for richness. I'll need some eggs, though. No getting around that. If need be, I can swap some more of my time for eggs. The Bakkers' gardener keeps chickens. But remember that we can make the salads without buying anything at the store, Miss E."

Never mind that we could have eaten the vegetables, the apples, the herbs, the walnuts, the preserves, and the fish ourselves. And we could have drunk the wine. If we had planned well and were disciplined about it—fancy Mother being disciplined or Annie letting her be!—we could have eaten well for weeks on food we already owned or could grow or forage. This party was going to reverberate over time. I hoped it didn't leave us hungry by July.

"Well, that's sorted," Mother said, tucking a bottle of Bordeaux under her arm and shooing us out of the wine cave, so that she could pull the hidden door shut. "E, when you were up at Stenen Klif with that red-haired young man, what was in bloom?"

"The peonies are almost at their peak."

"The pink ones?"

"Yes. The daffodils are playing out, but the apple trees are magnificent."

"And our own rhododendrons are blossoming. I saw that when I walked to town today. Annie, don't you think the Spode will look well with tall vases of pink peonies and branches of apple blossoms and white rhododendrons?"

"The china with the peacocks and flowers? Oh, yes. And with a few daffodils tucked in, if there are any left."

"Lovely." Mother scaled the basement stairs. Her steps were fast and light, as if she weren't fifty years old and one day out of involuntary confinement. "I'll pour us some wine to celebrate this grand venture."

Annie, whose excitement over the party was keeping her sixty-year-old steps light, was right behind her until she stopped stock-still.

"Ma'am, did you open this window?"

She was pointing to a double-hung window in an unobtrusive spot near the top of the stairs. There was no need for anybody to pass it unless they were going to the basement. Devan and I had come into the basement from outside, but I'd passed it when I went downstairs the night before—Sunday—to get walnuts for Mother's breakfast. I'd also been down those stairs the morning before that—Saturday—to get apples and walnuts for the lunch I made for Leontine and Marjorie.

I couldn't have sworn that the window had been shut, but it seemed like I would have noticed an open window.

"I never raise this window, Madam, and I'm sure you didn't?"

My mother shook her head. "No."

For a moment, Annie looked at the offending window as if it had bit her. Then she closed it, locked it, and went to fetch three etched crystal goblets for our Bordeaux.

Mother poured our glasses full, too full for polite society. On Friday, we would drink sedately, but nobody was watching that night, and Mother didn't hold back. She held up her glass, and we toasted our incredibly ill-advised party.

I thought we'd sit then, drinking our wine and talking about…I didn't know…our lives? How much Annie and I had missed her? I'd had no chance to talk to Mother about anything except crises—and her party was a crisis—since she got home. But I could see that the conversation I wanted would not be happening that night.

Mother recorked the bottle of Bordeaux and tucked it under her arm. Carefully balancing her still-full goblet, she moved quickly through the library, into the entry hall, and up the stairs. Halfway up, she paused, and her curls bounced as she turned to call back a few final words.

"I know about the war, dear. Cynthia told me."

"But why—"

"Why the party? I remember the last war. If they're rationing sugar now, there are more hardships coming. Let's put them off as long as we can."

Cradling the Bordeaux like a baby, she drifted up out of sight.

"Miss E," Annie said, sympathy spread over her face.

"It's okay, Annie. I know how she is."

"I'll spoon you up some soup," she said, and I let her fill a bowl with the dark, beany stew. As she handed it to me, she plopped a pillowy roll onto its rim. It was unbuttered, since we were entering a week when we would be hoarding butter for the party. After that there would be a month…probably two months…when we would skip butter to make up for what the party had cost.

"Your mother and I ate while you were in the tub, but I'll sit with you while you eat."

I wanted nothing more at that moment than to be alone. I needed time to decipher what it meant to have my mother home. I was pretty sure it meant that I was financially responsible for a household over which I had no control. Maybe, if I meditated over my bean soup, I would decide that this was not a fact, but I doubted it.

"No need to sit with me, Annie, not when you're dying to curl up in bed with pencil and paper. Go cipher out how much butter, flour, cream, and sugar we're going to need, and I'll figure out how we'll get it."

"I know you will. I won't pretend I'm not excited to entertain again. I want the people of Bentham to remember who this family is—who you are."

I realized that I had no idea whom Mother had invited. She and I would be at the table, obviously. Mrs. Jamison had called to accept her invitation. Based on what I'd seen that morning, Cynthia Masters would be coming. I supposed the identities of the other dinner guests would be my breakfast surprise.

"Go on, Annie. Make me a shopping list, and I'll do my best to find it all. I have some cash that I think will cover it."

I thought of my father's five-hundred-dollar stash. This party would take a huge bite out of it, but now I had a wine cave to search. If my father had hidden his alcohol there, maybe I could find something more spendable, too. First, though, I had some bean soup to enjoy.

There were no envelopes of money hidden in the wine cave, alas. I climbed back upstairs and realized that the party was an excellent excuse to call Devan.

"Are you warm and dry?" This was the first thing he said after "Hello."

"I never stopped feeling warm."

"It did seem to me that the raindrops sizzled when they struck you."

Never date a man who is good with words. They say things like that, and your wits simply fly away.

"What about you? Are you warm and dry?"

"I have a garage apartment behind Chancellor Hampstead's house. It only has three rooms, but I get to enjoy his stupendous river view. I can even drag a lawn chair down to his boat launch and sit by the water. You should come sometime. When I've been out in the rain, though, the important thing about my apartment is that one of my three rooms is a bath with endless hot water and a deep, deep tub. I'm very cozy at the moment, but I'm alone. Regrettably."

"Very regrettably. I called to ask you a question. Are you free Friday evening? My mother is throwing an 'I'm-home!' dinner party."

"A dinner party at Rockfall House? I may have to read up on etiquette. I do my best reading in the tub, but I have"—he mumbled *one two three four*—"four nights to study in the bath before the big party. I should be able to brush up on the fine details."

The idea of him reading Emily Post, glasses perched on his nose and long, bare legs propped on the rim of the tub, made me wish I were there. It also made me laugh, especially because he gave the impression of being on the posh side. He would undoubtedly meet and exceed my mother's high behavioral standards.

"I'd be honored to come. Black tie?"

"If you have it. Most men will be in black tie, but there's no need to go out and buy something. You're not being received by the queen."

"I've seen your mother, and there's not a lot of difference. But never fear. I have a tux."

Of course he had a tux. With his rangy height and broad shoulders, he would look as imposing in his tux as Dr. Bower looked in his academic regalia. It occurred to me that I had no idea what I was going to wear.

"Mother will want your address for the invitation. Is it the same as the Chancellor's? I know Mother's got his address in her book."

"She doesn't have to go to all that trouble. Not unless she's going to have Annie checking for invitations at the door."

"That would be very déclassé, so no, but Mother will still want to send you an invitation. She's a stickler about that kind of thing."

"Then tell her that if you add Apartment 1A to the end of the Chancellor's address, you've got mine."

"Consider it done. Oh, and come hungry. Annie's going to be cooking all week."

John's calm reliability was capable of traveling over telephone wires. A day with my mother had left my heart racing. John knew she had that effect on me, so he had called to purposefully, consciously soothe my nerves.

"Lily looks well," he said.

"You've seen my mother?"

"Oh, yes. She passed through Bentham-on-Hudson like a royal procession of one. She stopped at the bank, the post office, the bakery, the bookstore. Everybody saw her. My law practice will probably get a boost from the fact that she stopped at my office."

"I've always had the impression that you got all the business you needed. That's why you can afford charity cases like me."

And my mother, but that wasn't how she would ever see herself.

"She asked me some pointed questions."

I felt nervous prickles on the back of my neck. "What did you tell her?"

"The truth, Estella. I had to tell her. She was your father's heir, not you. You and I had the power of attorney that let you take charge of the estate while your father was ill—"

I couldn't push the image of John and my father and a pen and a piece of paper out of my mind. Heaven knows how I would have managed without that power of attorney, but it had left a mark on me to watch my father, a renowned man of letters, struggling to wield a pen.

"—and I don't mind saying that I didn't feel good about getting him to sign that paper when I couldn't be sure what he understood. Now that he's dead, and we know that your mother's not, there's no question about who's in charge. She is."

The yeasty taste of the roll was still in my mouth. What had my mother bought it with? The Dutchess Rest Home and Spa had left her penniless. How had she even bought the stamps for the infernal party invitations?

"John. How much money did you give her? How much did she take out of the bank?"

"She's my client, Estella. I can't tell you."

"Can you tell me whether to be terrified?"

"She's an adult. She's his sole heir. Her name is on the bank account. She may have emptied it after she left me. I wouldn't know, and I couldn't tell you if I did."

"The bank was *bothered* by the fact that I was a woman. She's a woman. How is this different?"

"You are correct." His voice was warm. He was using it to soothe me, but I resisted. "Yes, there are legal constraints on your mother's financial life, because she is a woman. But they know her at the bank, and sometimes that smooths things out. Like you, she has someone to help her navigate those waters, if that makes you feel better."

"You."

"Yes. And as your father's friend, I take the responsibility seriously. Your mother is less…"

"Rational?"

"She's less pragmatic than you. I'll guide her as best I can, but she is an adult. Her mistakes are hers to make."

The people who made the laws didn't seem to think either Mother or I should be able to make our own mistakes.

"But she'll take Annie and me down with her."

"You and Annie have salable skills."

Being on my own, free of any responsibilities but teaching

for my keep, sounded like heaven. The offer from the school in Old Saybrook beckoned. I had wadded it up, but I hadn't turned it down. But whatever I did, my mother would be a millstone around my neck unless and until she married again.

She was beautiful and charming. It could happen.

"Estella, I know that I would have heard from you by now if you were anxious to say yes to my marriage proposal, but I'm not an especially proud man. And I am a lonely one. I realize that you are a package deal. If you were to say yes, we wouldn't be living in my little townhouse, and you wouldn't have to stay in that ancient pile your parents have been propping up for years. I would build you a modern house with a kitchen worthy of Annie. I would also do my best to keep Lily from spending herself into penury. When I inevitably failed to do that, there would be a room—no, a suite—for her in our home."

I made a wordless noise that he mistook for disbelief.

"I assure you, dear, that I advised your father prudently."

"John, I never doubted that."

"Your father might not have listened to my investment advice, but I took it. I can look after you and the people you love."

I thought of his patient eyes and his kind—no, handsome—face. Devan was younger, but John had a face that grew older without growing old. Also, was I so shallow that this mattered more than his kindness? I admitted to myself that I'd been cruel, and I quite possibly had been foolish. It made no sense to push away someone who certainly cared for me, just because my head was turned by someone I barely knew. "I shouldn't be taking so long to answer you."

"You haven't had a moment this week to think about your-self and what you want."

I thought about the time I'd spent with Devan, and I knew that this wasn't true.

"Take the time you need, Estella. I imagine that you'll be busy during our regular Friday meeting. Everybody in Lily's orbit will be dressing for dinner then."

"You're not wrong. She told you about the party?"

"Indeed. If I don't see you before the party, I'll see you then. I am the lucky recipient of one of your mother's invitations. I'll break out my dinner jacket, and maybe you'll find time to share a glass of wine with me in the garden. I remember how sweet the roses smell out there this time of year."

I should have known that Mother would invite John. And now I'd invited Devan.

Annie's menu might say "trout," but my goose was cooked.

CHAPTER 21

I poured my woes about Mother's stupid party over the telephone lines and into Marjorie's ear. She was excruciatingly sympathetic. Good friends never say things like, "It's her house. I guess she can have a party if she wants to."

At the same time, she was excruciatingly excited to be invited. "I've never been to a party so elegant. Tell me about the menu again. And about the china. Did you say it had peacocks on it? Tell me about the crystal and everything! My parents will think I've really come up in the world. My mother, especially. That's way more important to her than it is to me."

"I can't say that my mother is an especially good friend to have, but I'll introduce them."

She fretted for a minute about whether she had anything to wear, other than a several-years-out-of-date gown she'd worn to a high school dance. I know how friendship works, too, so I said, "I'm sure it still fits beautifully."

"My mother has evening gloves I can borrow. Gloves are right for this kind of thing, aren't they?"

I assured her they were, but I also told her that I'd heard that even the wealthiest women were wearing dresses they already had and going without gloves, so that the soldiers would have silk for their parachutes. "If it were up to me, we'd call it a victory party and tell people to come in their gardening clothes, but that's not how my mother does things."

"This is going to sound ignorant, but what do you do with your gloves while you're eating?"

"You take them off when drinks are served and carry them in your other hand. Then you keep them in your lap at the table, which is a nuisance when you're wearing a slippery dress. I tuck them under my legs, so that I don't risk having to get somebody to crawl under the table and fetch them."

"You'll have no problems, because you're going to give yours to Devan to keep in his breast pocket."

When I hung up the phone, I was still absorbing the last thing she said to me:

"I can't wait to see Devan in a tuxedo."

Neither could I. But I had failed to answer John's invitation to step away from Mother's party for a drink alone, so he had probably interpreted my silence as a yes. I had already invited Devan to the party. Why didn't I speak up?

There was a spark, more than a spark, between Devan and me, and this would be obvious to John from twenty paces. I was wrong for not turning John down cold, but I'd known him all my life, and I cared for him. I didn't want to hurt him. And I would be lying if I said that the security he represented wasn't attractive in its way.

These are the things that I confided to Leontine when I called to invite her to Bentham-on-Hudson's biggest dinner party of 1942. She said, "I've seen John around town for years when I was home from school, and I've seen him with women. A successful man who looks like John has had his share of romantic ups and downs. Also, he seems like a man who will understand that you're at your absolute wits' end. Honestly, I don't know how you're still standing. How can he expect you to think straight at a time like this? If he's smart, and he is, he'll give you some time to figure things out."

She followed that with a chuckle and cut to the chase. "So what are you going to wear to this event where two men will be watching your every move?"

"My closet looks like it belongs to a schoolmarm."

"This is a crisis. I'll be at your house tomorrow after work, and I'll be carrying my mother's sewing box."

❦

The route from my study to my bed took me through the kitchen and the drawing room, then up the back staircase. There was no reason to take a flashlight through the darkened library and walk down the passage toward the basement stairs, but I did it anyway.

I couldn't stop myself. I wanted another look at the window. I wanted to know why it was open.

I trained the flashlight's beam on the windowsill, where I

saw nothing out of the ordinary. If it had been forced open from the inside, I would have seen scarring on the wood, but I didn't.

Running the light over the window frame, I looked for marks there, and also on the sash. Nothing.

The panes, with their wavy surfaces of old, old window glass, were held firmly by their muntins. They didn't rattle when I raised the sash a few inches and slammed it. The only thing notable about the window was the fact that I *could* raise it and lower it. I had seen Annie lock it.

Something about the lock mechanism wasn't right.

I held the flashlight close to it. Even the window locks of the house had a certain ostentation. This one was cast in bronze, now weathered to a brassy black, and it had the deeply engraved ornamentation of the Eastlake style.

I pushed the lever that operated the lock and watched it pivot. The other piece of the lock, designed to catch the hooked end of the lever, wasn't doing its job.

No, that wasn't quite right. It wasn't that the end of the lever wasn't hooking properly. It was missing. It could have broken off any time during the past forty years due to simple wear-and-tear. Or somebody could have broken it off within the past twenty-four hours.

If you spun the lock into place but didn't check to see if it caught, then you would never know. This is what Annie had done.

Was somebody trying to get in my house? Had somebody already *been* in my house?

I considered the possibilities. Someone could have crept around outside at night, trying windows until one opened. Then they could have come inside, done what they came to do, and slipped out. But why would they leave it open? Perhaps to be sure nobody heard it close?

If somebody had done that, they hadn't taken anything obvious. We had silver and antiques on open display. (Not to mention art and rare books that I had, until recently, thought were valuable.) None of us had noticed anything missing. If anything had been missing, it was something I didn't know we had, like Father's five hundred dollars and Mother's cave full of wine.

But what if they hadn't come inside yet?

Or what if someone had opened the window—maybe even breaking the lock—planning to come back later?

This idea upset me so much that I went to the basement for a hammer and two nails. I drove them into the wood of the sash, just above the part that lifted. As long as those nails stayed where they were, the window would be closed.

Once I'd secured the window, I made a tally of people who had been in the house recently.

Mother, Annie, and me, obviously, but who else? ·

Dr. Masters.

Chief D'Amato.

Dr. Bower.

Oscar Glenby.

I hardly knew any of these people. If any of them had been hoping to sneak into my house, I would be angry, but I wouldn't be hurt. Mr. Glenby had come invited, but Dr. Masters, Chief D'Amato, and Dr. Bower had just shown up on my doorstep.

Had any of them been left alone for even a few minutes?

Yes. D'Amato had been alone when I went to get Mother's

bracelet and book. Dr. Masters had let herself in. Dr. Bower had let himself out. Mr. Glenby had asked me to go get my father's files on the artwork.

But other names belonged on the list, and I would be very hurt if any of them had planned to steal from me.

Leontine.

Marjorie.

Devan.

Devan had arrived unannounced that first day on a pretty slender pretext. Well, it was only slender if he was pretending that he found me attractive, but that idea felt slimy. I wanted to ignore it, but I couldn't deny that I'd left him alone in the drawing room while I dressed to go sailing and Annie made his tea.

I had invited Leontine and Marjorie, and they'd been to the house many times before, but that meant nothing. Either of them had the opportunity to open the window. They'd both excused themselves to the powder room to wash up before lunch.

One last name on my list of visitors caught me up short—John. He had volunteered to come sit with Annie on the night I went to get Mother. She would never have thought twice if he excused himself to the bathroom. Also, it was entirely possible that she had dozed off while he was there. He could have had the run of the house.

I had to presume they'd all had the opportunity to sabotage the lock on an out-of-the-way window.

My mind strayed to the footprints along the trail above the house and to the boat lurking in the cove. Had they belonged to the same person, and had that person been trying to get in the house? Or were the open window, the footprints, and the boat evidence of two, even three, people with an unhealthy interest in my house?

For a while, I stood by the nailed-shut window and watched the rain. It had been coming down in sheets since Devan left.

Maybe Annie had opened the window and forgotten. Maybe the lock had been broken for years. Maybe I was imagining things.

I turned off my flashlight. In darkness, I crept upstairs and up the cupola's ladder. There, with the bats, I looked out at a dark and empty cove, only visible through the storm when lit by lightning bolts. Above it stood Rockfall Bluff, also dark and empty.

Well, it was empty of everyone but Annie, Mother, and me.

CHAPTER 22

On Tuesday, three days before the party, I came downstairs to find Mother already stirring. She'd had her breakfast in bed, because that was where she and Annie thought she should have it, but she'd done it in the pink of dawn.

She sat at the kitchen table surrounded by sheets of paper, all covered with her neat-as-copperplate handwriting. In her right hand, she brandished a gold-nibbed tortoiseshell fountain pen. Her address book was at her elbow.

"I need the names and addresses of your guests, so I can mail their invitations. I presume you're inviting young Dr. Chase?"

"Yes. He lives at the Chancellor's address, Apartment 1A."

"Ah, the garage apartment. It's very nice." She added his name to the guest list and copied the Chancellor's address next to it. I noticed that using good penmanship made writing very slow as Mother etched a precise "Apt. 1A" onto the page.

"And your other two guests. Will they be another young couple?"

"No, two of my woman friends. They're both single. Leontine Caldwell and Marjorie Steed."

"There was a girl named Marjorie who was a few years behind you in school, so she must be around twenty-five now. Leontine is Marie's daughter, and she's Marjorie's age or a little older. I remember her from when she was just a girl, but she's been away a long time. Is she home from college?"

"Yes. I think she got home not long before your…absence."

"I imagine she came back last summer when her mother fell ill. Marie was gone before I'd even heard she was sick. I missed the chance to say good-bye. Poor Leontine." Mother wrote her name on the guest list. "If she's grown up to be like her mother, then I'm sure she's a good friend to you. Is she living in Marie's house?"

"Yes."

Mother paged through her book, found the address, and put it on the guest list. Then she did some more paging.

"You said Marjorie's last name was Steed. I presume she still lives in town. With her parents?"

"Yes."

More pages turned as Mother said, "Steed…Steed…Annie, do we know the Steeds?"

"Yes, Madam. Well, I do. They'll be in the telephone book. Her father's name is Edgar."

Once Marjorie's address was duly copied, Mother turned to the finished guest list.

"I have the names in my head, but I forget who I've written down." She pushed the list back to arm's length, so that her middle-aged eyes could read it. "Help me count to make sure

I've got everybody. You, Devan, Marjorie, Leontine, and me. That's five. The other nine are Cynthia Masters—"

I'd guessed that one right.

"Dr. Bower."

I wouldn't necessarily have guessed him, but Mother seemed determined to remember who he was to her.

"Chancellor Hampstead—Tom—and his wife Clarissa."

Not many people called Dr. Thomas Aquinas Hampstead "Tom." I wasn't surprised to hear that they were on the list. Together, he and his wife wielded more social power in town than anybody but Mother.

"John, of course."

Of course.

"Dr. Homer Hanssen. His wife Eloise left him a year or two ago, so I only invited him. Homer isn't officially the provost, but he took over faculty hiring long ago, because Provost Johnson is regrettably senile. I've also asked Professor Schmidt and his wife—" She tapped her forehead with the base of her pen. "Lester and Beatrice. Yes, Lester and Beatrice. Now that poor Harry Jamison is gone, I feel sure that Lester Schmidt will be the one who takes over as dean. It would be good for you to have some social time with Homer Hanssen and the Schmidts. And the Chancellor, of course."

I had always seen my mother as so utterly self-focused that I wouldn't have expected her to intuit my career predicament, but perhaps I was wrong about her. Perhaps I'd always been wrong about her. Or was it that, as her child, she saw me as somehow subsumed into her? My well-being was her well-being?

She looked back at her list. "Oscar Glenby?"

I locked eyes with Annie and tried to send a message to her via brain-radio. *We are never going to tell Mother that I tried to sell our things...her things.*

"Why Oscar Glenby?" I asked.

"He is our conduit to the New York art world. Your father had personal connections. I do not, other than Oscar. Since Cynthia had the good manners to tell me about the war"—she shot me a meaningful look—"I know that our social life may be constrained for a while, but wars don't last forever. I can be a patron of the arts without your father. I just need connections."

And money she didn't have, but part of me believed that Mother would always find a way to shape the world to her liking.

"That's thirteen," Annie said. "We can't have thirteen at the table. It's bad luck."

"Of course, we won't have thirteen at the table. You remember that Eva Jamison called. I've invited her and she's accepted."

I should have kept my mouth shut, but I couldn't stop myself. "She just buried her husband on Sunday."

"That's exactly why we must invite her. I too am a recent widow. You've lost your father. Leontine's mother is hardly cold. We all need our friends to comfort us."

I tried to imagine Mother, a walking icicle, as an object of comfort. I failed.

The weather on Tuesday established a pattern that would hold all week. The rain eased up in the early morning hours, just as Annie's troop of borrowed servants arrived. The overcast sky promised more rain, so she sent the footmen out to work while the weather held. It was too early for them to fish and forage, but it was just the right time to clean up the grounds. The terraced gardens began to emerge from months of decline like princesses rising from a long refreshing sleep.

The young men cleared out the saplings that were choking the blooming shrubs. They cleaned the roses of fading blossoms, so that the buds could have all the bushes' energy. They spread weathered manure around everything, ready for the afternoon rains to take nutrients into the soil. Anything can be beautiful, really, given time and attention.

Mother, Annie, and I busied ourselves with detailed lists. How many of our silver soup tureens would need polishing? How many pounds of butter should we buy or barter? How many eggs would Mrs. Bakker be willing to part with? It was cozy work, especially when the rain tapped on the slate roof and sent me to the basement for coal to warm the vast kitchen, which only felt cozy because Annie was there. It had been built to feed a large family, their guests, and their servants. There were two extra cookstoves and two extra ovens that Annie hadn't used in years, but she would be using them this week.

On my way to get the coal, I absently patted the nailed-shut window as I passed. This prompted me to walk the whole house, checking windows. All of the others were locked tight.

The question of why someone might want to get into my house still bothered me, but my rational side hung onto the plausible theory that nobody did. The window latch was simply broken, and one of us had forgotten that we opened the window. This did not explain the boat in the cove or the footprints beside the trail, but there was no law against going boating. There was a law against trespassing, but people did it. Perhaps all was well.

True to her word, Leontine drove into our driveway at the end of the day, her back seat full of dressmaker's tools. I held an umbrella over her as she unloaded them, then we carried it all upstairs where Mother waited in her dressing room with an armful of diaphanous lavender silk.

"It's good to see you, Leontine, and it's so sweet of you to make a house call."

"It's a busy week for everybody in your household. I'm glad I can help make your party special."

Mother held out the lavender dress. "This is the last one your mother made for me. It was the latest thing last spring. People would notice that it wasn't new if I wore it in New York, but it will be perfectly fine here. The problem is that it simply hangs on me now. Can you help?"

The reason for her thinness was unstated, but I heard it, and Leontine surely did, too. *They didn't feed me enough at the rest home.* Or, more likely, *I refused to eat in silent protest.*

"Of course I can help, Mrs. Ecker. Do you have foundation garments for it, and do they still fit?"

"They fit well enough. I may need some padding to fill out the cups."

"That's easily done. E and I will step out while you put those on."

While we stood on the other side of the dressing room door, Leontine whispered, "Under no circumstances will you let her pay me for this. I'm a librarian. That's what I do for my profession, but I am happy to sew for my friends and their families. Understand?"

I did.

When Mother called us in, I was unprepared to see her so vulnerable. She wore a one-piece strapless garment, heavily boned to lift what was left of her breasts and to whittle her waist even smaller. Its rubberized fabric stopped at mid-thigh, where stocking clips secured the tops of her sheer hose. In places where her body peeked through—her collarbones, shoulders, neck, and arms, and a narrow band of her upper thighs—her skin was paper-white with light tracings of blue veins, and it was beginning to sag, either from age or poor nutrition or both.

Carefully, we gathered the skirt so that she could slither in arms first, like a diver swimming through a tunnel. When she straightened up, we let the bias-cut skirt fall rippling around her. After Leontine and her buttonhook made quick work of the tiny, fabric-covered buttons running up her bony spine, Mother stood in front of the full-length mirror, twisting this way and that to examine the dress's fit.

"This is the real problem," she said, pinching at the excess fabric around the set-in waist.

Those rumples simply wouldn't do, but the rest of the dress was divine. The wide, structured portrait neckline framed her face, and the lavender silk brought out the violet in her blue eyes. Her face was bare, because even my vain mother wouldn't risk makeup stains on her dress three days before a party. Even so, there was color in her cheeks that I hadn't seen in a long time. Mother loved dresses and she loved parties.

Leontine made reassuring noises as she pinned the dress to fit Mother's new shape. "A dart here. A tuck there. I'll rework that set-in waist. It'll be beautiful." She stepped back and studied her work. "You'll be beautiful."

"Thank you, dear. Let me get my—"

"It's my welcome-home gift." Leontine's voice was firm. My mother was gifted at reading social cues, when she wanted to be.

"That's lovely of you. Thank you."

Mother had spent enough time with couturiers to know the work involved in altering three layers of chiffon over a charmeuse lining. Her thanks sounded sincere, especially when she followed it with, "I'll think of your dear mother whenever I wear it—whenever I wear anything she made me, really."

She smoothed her sheer sleeves and turned to study her reflection. "Now. What about E?"

After studying the contents of my closet, Leontine and Mother both took a literal step away from it.

Leontine cringed visibly. "You did say that you had the closet of a schoolmarm."

"You've seen me at work. You've seen me gardening and hiking. I have clothes for those things. How many formal events do you think I go to?"

My wardrobe was heavy on sober-colored skirted suits, poplin for warm days and wool for cold ones. The skirts' sedate hemlines hit me just below the knee. My high-necked blouses were all in shades of white and cream. They'd been silk when my father paid my bills, but now they were rayon. Behind the suits were cotton shirtdresses for my days off. Folded on my shelves were dungarees, Bermuda shorts, polo shirts, and cardigans, most of them my parents' castoffs.

"I might call it the closet of a maiden aunt." Mother's expression was pained.

"I don't want the men at work to see me as a woman. I want them to take me seriously."

"You've certainly got the 'sexless' look down pat," Leontine muttered.

Bradley and I had gone on bohemians' dates—lots of art galleries and free outdoor concerts and street fairs and romantic dinners in hole-in-the-wall restaurants with fabulous food. My clothes had been perfectly fine for those things. I only learned that he owned a tux when he left me for a debutante. I had no evening dresses but the ones I'd worn before I left home as a teenager, and it hadn't been 1927 for a long time. Loose-fitting with dropped waists and knee-length skirts, my formal dresses were the very definition of "dowdy."

Leontine handled a sash tied in a big bow around the hips of a celery-green satin shift. She drew back her hand as if she'd touched an eel and said "No."

"I'm taking suggestions," I said.

"We're going to my closet," Mother said.

Which was worse? Wearing my prom dress at age thirty-one or wearing my mother's clothes? I couldn't decide.

As it turned out, the better answer was "wearing my mother's clothes."

Leontine oohed and ahhhed over the chic gowns her mother had made for mine. She pulled out several that I quickly rejected—a white crepe de chine strapless that was way too bare for my taste, a green organza number that made me look like a houseplant, and a tomato red ballgown, also strapless, that made me look like a fireplug.

She patiently explained why she'd suggested them. "You and your mother are almost the same size and height, but your shoulders are broader than your mother's. That doesn't matter with a strapless gown—"

"I'm still not wearing one."

"—and it doesn't matter for the green one, because the organza just floats over your shoulders and turns into a train."

I didn't answer her, because my head was in the closet. "What about this one?"

I pulled out a bias-cut slip dress made out of silver-gray faille, with a matching jacket that was tailored within an inch of its life. Neither my mother nor Leontine bleated out an immediate, "That's awful." I saw this as a good sign.

Slipping on the jacket, I said, "You're right about the shoulders, which is too bad. Otherwise, it fits beautifully."

"Give it to me," Leontine said. Turning the jacket wrong-side-out, her shears snicked as she made tiny snips like a surgeon excising a tumor. Victorious, she pulled a little fabric package out of each shoulder of the jacket. "With shoulders like yours, you don't need pads."

"You're going to use those to fill out my bra, aren't you?" Mother said.

"I might."

Leontine handed the jacket back to me. "Try it on now. With the dress and all the appropriate underwear under it."

The ensemble fit perfectly. The crisp faille jacket with its dull sheen hugged my torso, ending at the fullest part of my hips. Its ornamental buttons were made of faceted jet.

Leontine had dropped to the floor and was sitting cross-legged, straight pins between her teeth.

"What are you doing down there? The dress fits fine."

"This flared skirt and circular train is right for your mother, but not for you." Moving the fabric this way and that, she pinned it into the shape she wanted. "For you, this gown wants to have a hobble skirt with a slit up to here," she chopped at my knee with the blade of her hand, "and just the slightest sweep of a train. I'm having a vision of the most elegant riding habit of all time."

"And the most revealing," Mother said, and I couldn't tell whether she approved.

"Only when her leg peeks out, which won't be all the time. It will be an occasional beautiful surprise."

"I have some fabulous shoulder-duster earrings," Mother said, rushing to her jewelry box.

"No," Leontine said. "Small. Simple. Platinum, if you have them."

I was pretty sure Mother had them.

"A necklace?" Mother dangled something sparkly.

"No. I have some black Alençon lace, and she's going to tie it around her throat. Like an ascot."

I was intrigued. I also felt like we were playing paper dolls again, but I was the doll.

Leontine stood and circled me. "You're going to use the tiniest bit of pomade to comb your hair straight back." She looked at my mother. "Do you have something pretty she can use to hold it in place? A barrette?"

"But her beautiful curls…"

"There will be a knot of golden curls at her nape that will only show when she turns her head and shows off that long neck."

Mother pulled a jeweled barrette out of the box, and Leontine nodded.

"Keep your makeup light. Play up your eyes, but only use a little color on the lip and cheek."

This wasn't what other women were wearing in 1942, but I trusted Leontine. Also, I'd never dressed like other women, so why should I start now?

Leontine started packing up her tools. "Do you have some garment bags? I have to get home and get started on these, and it's still raining cats and dogs."

Mother hurried down the hall and tapped on Annie's door. "Garment bags?"

"Yes, Madam. I'll fetch them."

Shrugging off the evening jacket, I handed it to Leontine. "Enough about us. What are you wearing?"

"Deep crimson shantung, beaded, off the shoulder, sequin trim. Peau de soie heels, dyed to match. Tried it on last night and it hugs every curve I've got. I've got time to fix you two up."

I shed the dress and put my boring everyday clothes back on, Annie brought the garment bags, and we took everything to Leontine's car.

She was still talking about dresses. "I'm calling in sick in the morning. If I work on these tonight and tomorrow, I can get them done in time to make a house call at Marjorie's tomorrow after work. She told me about her prom dress. It sounds truly unfortunate, but I can make it right for her."

As she drove away, a thunderclap scared us back into the house, where we built yet another coal fire to dry ourselves before dinner. There was no help for it—the house was cold—but it felt like I was burning dollar bills while we ignored the folly of it all.

Mother and Annie were bathed and in bed before the sun had fully set. (Mother may have absconded with another bottle from the wine cellar. I couldn't say for sure, and it was her wine.)

As soon as I was alone, I headed for the cupola. The rain continued, but it is a rare storm that rages without ceasing. This one had its ebbs and flows, and I was patient enough to bide my time.

I waited thirty minutes, maybe an hour, and I was rewarded with a momentary break in the weather. There, in precisely the place that it had been before, was a small boat with a single passenger. The fog and rain closed in, so I saw no more than that, but I still had my patience.

I waited another hour for the weather to clear again. This time, I could see the repetitive double-glints from a pair of field glasses being raised and lowered. Someone was so interested in sitting on the water beneath my house that they were willing to do it in the rain.

CHAPTER 23

T he rain cleared for a few hours on Wednesday morning, two days before Mother's dinner party, and I was restless. The sky was blue, but an electricity in the air said the thunderstorms would be back. Mother stayed in bed, complaining of a sick headache. She had always suffered from aches and pains during bad weather. My own head tingled, as if it might start hurting any minute. I needed distraction.

It was too early to cut asparagus or bake cakes or gather fiddleheads or fish for trout. Dusting the furniture should wait until the last minute, and so should the flower-gathering. It probably wasn't too early to crack walnuts or polish silver, but Annie shooed me away from both chores.

"I traded Mrs. Bakker for people to do those things, and they're going to do them. Go...find something to do with yourself. I don't know what ladies do to make themselves beautiful before parties, but I'm sure your mother can tell you. Put on some cold cream or give your hair an oil treatment or something."

The idea of making myself greasy and then sitting quietly

in that condition sounded abhorrent. Days had passed since I'd found a wad of money in my father's office. It seemed like a good time to search the house for more of his hidey-holes.

He and my mother hadn't shared a room since before I left home. I eased his bedroom door open, so that I didn't disturb her across the hall. His space was as different from hers as it could be. Mother's room was all 1930s glamour—sheer white drapes, royal blue carpet, white walls, and a low-slung bed spread with an ice-blue comforter and piled with pastel pillows. Her room smelled as cool and fresh as it looked, like violets.

Father's room was furnished like a Victorian men's club. Its heavy mahogany furniture sucked every last ray of light from the room, despite its large windows. The green plush carpeting and brown leather upholstery were suffocating, but maybe that tight feeling in my chest was triggered by the remnants of his pipe smoke. Or the pervasive smell of old paper. Like everything in his life, his bedroom was dominated by books. Every wall had at least one shelf that reached from floor to ceiling.

I decided to search his furniture by starting at the top and working down, pulling his desk chair from bookshelf to bookshelf, so I could reach the top shelf. The chair swiveled, which seemed somehow appropriate. It was as unsafe as he had been.

I tapped the bookshelves carefully from top to bottom and across each shelf. Any of them could hide a secret compartment like the one in his office, right? Maybe they all did, and the eight bookshelves would yield a cool four thousand dollars.

They didn't.

I poked my hand into all the crevices in his chairs' upholstery. I looked under his mattress and under his bed. I rolled back the emerald-green carpet, one side at a time. I found nothing, so I moved to his desk.

Sitting on the swivel chair, I lifted the desk's rolltop. Surely, he wouldn't hide anything in an obvious place like the pigeon-holes. I looked in all of them anyway. The window behind me, opening onto the water garden, made me uncomfortable. If I turned around, I might see someone standing on the hillside where Devan and I had found footprints, snooping on me as I snooped.

But my father was dead. It wasn't his desk any longer, so was I really snooping? I supposed it was Mother's desk and not mine, so I was.

Finally, I heard it again, that hollow sound of a piece of wood hiding an empty compartment. Shoving my hand deep into the rightmost pigeonhole, I triggered a spring-operated drawer like the one in the bookshelf.

Oh, please. Let it hold five hundred dollars.

The open-topped wooden box was just big enough to hold a roll of cash or a bag of precious stones, but that's not what I found. The only thing hidden in my father's pigeonhole desk was a Bakelite button in the shape of a six-petaled daisy, its color dappled to look like tortoiseshell. It was a dead ringer for the ones I'd seen on the coat wrapping Helena Frederick's body.

I was staring at the button, trying to forget the way Helena had looked in the morgue, when the door to my father's office banged open.

I dropped the drawer and its hidden button in my lap, cov-ered it with my hands, and screamed. A nearly identical scream came from the figure in the doorframe. It was Mother.

Her hands flew to her mouth, holding in another scream. They muffled her voice, but I understood her words perfectly.

"I thought he had come home. I thought he was back."

The scream had hardly left my mother's mouth before I heard Annie clomping up the stairs. Tenderly, she wrapped an arm around my mother, who still had both hands clamped over her mouth, and she ushered her back to bed. Once they were out of sight, I crammed the spring-loaded drawer back into its pigeonhole.

I slammed the desk's rolltop closed, but that wasn't enough to make me forget the shape of the Bakelite button behind it, resting on the drawer's red felt lining. Helena Frederick's button had seared a scar on my retina, as if I'd looked at a daisy-shaped sun.

I couldn't make myself think about why my father would have the button of a dead woman. I had to get away from it. I had to get out of the house.

I remember noticing dappled shadows on my hands as they rested on the desk's tamboured cover. I found those few weak sunbeams electrifying in a way that's hard to describe. I guess I was just grateful—grateful that the thunderstorms had retreated enough for me to leave Rockfall House. Helena Frederick's Bakelite button made me realize that I should be grateful for every sight, every sound, every minute. Blue-black clouds clung to the northern horizon, so the rain and lightning would be back, but not yet. I could safely go outside and be a part of the world.

I ran to the kitchen, threw an apple and a waxed-paper-wrapped hunk of cheese in my handbag, pulled on a trench coat, and hustled out the door before Annie knew I was leaving. I didn't want her to ask where I was going, because I didn't know yet. In the pale, temporary sunshine, I stood in the driveway and considered my options.

I could walk out onto the Precipice Path, where my father had hounded my mother on the day he hid her away. I couldn't think of any place on Earth worse than that, so no.

I could walk up the Garden Path to the ruins of Stenen Klif Manor, but this would take me past the worrisome footprints. Or, rather, it would take me past where they'd been. They must have washed away by now. I wasn't sure my nerves could take it if there were footprints in the new mud. If somebody had been up there again, I didn't want to know.

There was only one direction I wanted to go and that was down, away from the ruins, away from the footprints, away from the house, and away from the button in my father's desk. This meant that I was going to town. And if I was going to town, then I was going to work, because what else was there for me, really, in Bentham-on-Hudson? I could hide in the public library there. I could browse the grocer's half-empty shelves. I could shop for clothes I couldn't afford. I could, heaven help me, stop by John's office and contemplate strategic marriage. Instead of doing any of these things, I would let my feet take me where they usually did. I would let them take me to Hawke Hall.

As much as I didn't want to go back into the house, I did. There was something in the basement that needed to go with me to work. I hurried back through the kitchen door, hoping that Annie was still upstairs with my mother. After pausing in the study to grab my briefcase, I ran downstairs. Reaching behind the onion bin, I groped around for a pile of loose paper.

And I found it. I found my long-lost manuscript, right where my mother had left it. The sheets were crumpled and stained from their trip through the garbage, and they smelled like old onions. I didn't care.

I knelt, putting the sheets in order by page number. When I was sure that they were all there, I tapped the stack against the stone floor to square up the edges. Then I laid the manuscript lovingly in my briefcase, like a mother tucking her baby into a crib.

I wasn't supposed to be at work until Monday, so I had no responsibilities at the college. I could spend the rest of the morning and all afternoon in my office reading. After so many years away from it, I would be able to tell whether the novel I wrote when I was in my teens was any good. I owed this to the girl I'd been. I owed it to myself.

The path to Bentham was slick. I had to look at my sturdy shoes to keep from slipping, but this was good. It kept my eyes from drifting to the cove where Helena Frederick had rested. I didn't know how she'd gotten into the water, but it was likely sometime after she lost the button hidden in my father's bedroom, the one he'd kept hidden since I was sixteen.

Fifteen years. He'd kept that button for fifteen years,

The manuscript made my briefcase feel heavier than it was. Two hundred pages of cheap typing paper weighed almost nothing, but these particular pages carried the weight of my father's disapproval. They also carried the weight of responsibility, because my mother had risked his anger when she saved them for me.

❦

I felt quivery as I walked across the travertine piazza where Dean Jamison met his death, staying as far as possible from the spot where he fell. I was dizzy when I reached Hawke Hall, but I was still on my feet and still clutching the handle of my briefcase.

I stuck my head in Marjorie's door. She was so surprised to see me that she knocked her pencil cup over as she jumped to her feet.

"E! I thought you were going to be out all week."

"I am." This wasn't a very smart thing to say, since I was standing right in front of her. "I mean, I'm not here to teach or to do any research for the professors. I just…"

I just what?

"I just can't stand it in my house a minute longer."

"I understand. It's hard to live with your parents. I imagine it's even harder when you've been away, but I wouldn't know about that."

"Mother is… I've told you enough that you can guess what she's like, but that's not really why I'm here."

As soon as I said it, I knew it wasn't true. I had come to work because it was a place that was fully outside my mother's domain. My office was a quiet place where I could think thoughts that had nothing to do with anybody but me.

Not so long ago, all of Hawke Hall had been my father's

domain, but he was gone, and now one little part of it—one tiny tower office—was mine. And, for a few hours each week, a couple of lecture halls were mine, too. Maybe one reason I'd come to work that day was that I was feeling a little territorial about my teaching.

I looked at my watch. One of my classes met in five minutes.

"I'm not here to lecture," I said, as much to convince myself as to convince Marjorie. "I'm not prepared."

I wasn't even dressed to teach. I was wearing a shirtdress and cardigan under the trench coat. Undergraduates dressed better than that.

"But could I sit in on my class? Maybe I could learn something from whichever old codger you've got teaching it."

"I'm sure you could teach them all a thing or two about up-to-date scholarship, if they'd listen." Marjorie checked her desk calendar. "Dr. Bower's giving your sophomore American Lit lecture. Hurry, and you can catch his opening remarks."

"But...he's a math professor."

"Math professors think they can do anything. He's apparently a big fan of nineteenth-century American prose. Nobody else was willing to fistfight him for the chance to talk to your sophomores, so I couldn't tell him no. I gave him your lecture notes."

Okey-dokey. I guessed I was going to have the privilege of hearing what a mathematician thought about Edgar Allan Poe.

Dr. Bower cut a fine figure standing behind my podium. He was wearing his dark academic robes and a black velvet tam with a golden tassel. Bands of gold-trimmed black velvet adorned his drooping sleeves. His back was turned to the gathering students as he wrote his class notes on the chalkboard, and this showed off the red-and-gold satin hood hanging down his back. Those medieval guys who designed academic regalia really know how to make a person look smart, and I mean regally, ceremonially, inarguably smart.

Dr. Bower showed his instinct for drama when he wheeled around to begin talking, but I ruined the effect. His eyes caught mine as he opened his mouth to speak, and he was so surprised to see me that he stuttered.

"Wa—Washington Irving. Today, we will be talking about a man who lived in and wrote about our own Hudson Valley. Irving was a master of the short story and the essay, but he was also a true Renaissance man. He wrote biographies. He wrote histories. He was America's ambassador to Spain. But he always came home to New York."

Washington Irving? I'd already covered him thoroughly—thoroughly enough for an introductory course, anyway—so the students sitting around me had heard everything Dr. Bower was likely to say. Marjorie had given him my notes, so Dr. Bower knew that Washington Irving was in our rearview mirrors. He also knew that my plans for the week had been to lecture on Edgar Allan Poe.

After a pregnant pause, he resumed lecturing. "Irving founded the literary magazine *Salmagundi* while still a young man, and it was in this magazine that he gave New York City its nickname 'Gotham,' which meant 'Goat's Town' to the Anglo-Saxons. He is also responsible for use of the term 'Knickerbocker' as a nickname for Manhattanites."

As Dr. Bower rattled on, I realized that this kind of thing would be happening in my classes all week, but I also realized that I should have seen it coming. I'd known that Marjorie would have to cajole every old blowhard in the English department to each take one of my classes. (Plus a stray math professor.) Whatever made me think that any of them would bother to teach anything except what they already knew?

Dr. Yeats specialized in the Transcendentalists, so he was going to lecture on Emerson, who had dismissed Poe as a "jingle man." Poe, a more talented insult artist, had considered Transcendentalism to be "Taste on her death-bed." My dear Edgar was not going to get his due from Dr. Yeats.

Dr. Dumont specialized in French literature, so he was going to drone on about *Madame Bovary*, and never mind that it was a great book by a French author who had no business being taught in an American Lit class.

My students deserved to learn about the subject they'd paid to study. They deserved Poe, and quirky old Poe deserved the attention of their bright minds. So did Emily Dickinson. I needed to get back into the classroom as soon as Mother's party was behind me.

After class, I stopped by Marjorie's office and found her talking to a friendly man with a round face, thick gray hair, and dimples like hers.

"I hear you're a new friend of my daughter's. I'll leave you two to your girl talk," he said, patting Marjorie on the shoulder. "I just stopped by because I was at the bakery, and they had those cinnamon rolls she likes." As he left, he called back to her, "Don't forget Bible study tonight."

"I'm going to get fat if Daddy doesn't stop this," Marjorie said. "Please take some of this and help me save my waistline." She tore the pastry in two, paper wrapping and all, and held half out to me. "He's here nearly every day, usually with some kind of treat. Some people just aren't meant to be retired. I think my mother keeps her job as the receptionist at the elementary school so that she doesn't have to be home alone with him all day. He's so—"

She stopped as if she'd heard herself and was embarrassed. "Don't get me wrong. He's a great guy. I came along late in life for both of them, and they just can't… I mean, everybody gets tired of the people they love sometime, right?"

I'd gotten so tired of my parents that I'd stayed away for years, but maybe that meant that I didn't actually love them. I was pretty sure that it was just my father that I hadn't loved, though. I still had hope for Mother.

As far as married love went, my parents had seemed completely enmeshed, together every minute that my father wasn't at work, and yet I was appalled by what Annie had told me about their relationship. What was a normal marriage like? Or a normal family? I certainly wasn't the person to ask.

I dodged the question. "If you want to skip Bible study, come eat dinner with us."

"Thanks, but it makes him happy when I go. I enjoy it sometimes."

I took my half of the cinnamon roll with me to my office, balancing it on one hand and holding my briefcase with the other as I scaled the spiral staircase. The round office at the top was as tiny and airless as ever, but it was mine. I was surprised to realize that I'd missed it. I pulled my old manuscript out of my briefcase and immediately opened the balcony door to let the onion-y stench escape.

Ignoring the smell, I munched on my cheese, apple, and cinnamon roll, turning the pages with my other hand. My seventeen-year-old self had stuffed every spooky trick offered by Gothic literature into that book. It had doppelgängers and mirrors and masks and subterranean caverns and a foreboding castle and a heroine who underestimated herself and a handsome-but-possibly-dangerous love interest. The younger me had created a preposterous fantasy world, but it was full of believable human beings. I was proud of her.

There was a tap at the door, and that was odd. Nobody ever visited me in my office.

"Yes?"

Marjorie opened the door. "It's almost time for your British Lit class. I thought you might want to sit in."

I wasn't sure I wanted to watch somebody else trample all over my lesson plans. I know it showed on my face, but she just said, "Devan is standing in for you. Maybe it might be worth going?"

"To see how he teaches my class?"

"Why else would you want to go? Of course, it's also an excuse to stare at him for an hour."

Devan's brown herringbone jacket, ecru dress shirt, and chocolate-brown tie suited his russet hair. They also made him look like a whole different breed of professor from Dr. Bower.

Which I guess he was, because he didn't hurl my lesson plans into the garbage, not exactly. What he did do was even more embarrassing, because he sidestepped my plans to teach about the Brontë sisters in favor of teaching about me. Or rather he used my own scholarship to teach about the Brontës.

Somehow, almost certainly by finding a copy that Leontine had shelved at the library; he had gotten his hands on a four-year-old essay I'd written for an obscure Scottish journal. In it, I had laid out a logical case that the Brontës' entire body of work consisted of the three unmarried sisters railing at a society that considered unmarried daughters to be useless burdens. (Not to mention the fact that even the married women in their books— maybe especially the married women—could end up locked away, if they became inconvenient. This part of *Jane Eyre*'s plot had always made me queasy. By the time I heard Devan speak on my essay, my mother's experience had made me fear that nothing had changed in a hundred years.)

Things got really weird when Devan started talking about things I hadn't published yet. "This paper was a precursor to Dr. Ecker's upcoming book."

Unless he knew something I didn't, that book was far from a sure thing.

"And the subtitle for her book, 'Unhappy People in Big Houses,' lays out the entire foundation of Gothic literature and, if I may summarize her bolder claim, of many of the greatest works of literature ever put to paper." He gave no citation for this information. Decorum precluded it, because he'd gotten it while on a sailing date with the author.

Devan had looked sheepish for about a second when I

walked in. After that, he had clearly decided that his best bet for delivering this lecture with me in the room, while avoiding the embarrassed stammering of Dr. Bower, was to pretend like I wasn't there. Somehow, he managed to rake his eyes over the assembled students without ever meeting mine.

"Dr. Ecker's thesis certainly holds true when you consider the work of the Brontës and, of course, Mary Shelley. Her creation, Victor Frankenstein, is so unable to be happy in his carefree, wealthy existence that he feels compelled to create life. And then he treats that living being so poorly. Why on earth couldn't Victor Frankenstein just settle down and enjoy being rich?"

Everybody laughed, and he said, "If you can answer that question, you'll understand Victorian literature as well as Dr. Ecker does. And you might even understand why people keep taking things that they don't need and that don't belong to them. If Hitler had been able to leave other people's things alone, we might not be in yet another war."

There were a few titters, as if the students felt like they were supposed to laugh again, but they didn't think this joke was very funny.

"I guess that's enough politics," Devan said, turning to write on the board. "I've excerpted some important quotes from Dr. Ecker's paper. Let's dig into her ideas more deeply."

This may have been cowardly of me, but I took the opportunity to flee while his back was turned. I spent the rest of the afternoon in my office with a red pencil, editing my smelly manuscript. When another knock came at my door, it was Devan this time.

"It's past five, and I thought you might want a ride home. It's raining like there's no tomorrow."

Other than my desk lamp, there wasn't much light in my tower room. I hoped the dimness hid my blush. He moved closer, into the cone of light around that one lonely lamp, and he said, "I wish you'd stayed to hear what the students said about your essay. They think the world of you. One of them said you've made her love books."

He might as well have said I had hair as black as ebony and lips as red as drops of blood on unmarred linen. If my heart wasn't already his, he took it then.

CHAPTER 24

D evan was correct that the storm was back in earnest. Or was it a new storm? When I remember the time leading up to the party, it seems that the wind and rain toyed with us all week, lulling us with sunshine and battering us again once our guard was down. The thing I remember about that ride home from work was the way the water rushed over the roadway and the car shook with each gust of wind. I also remember the warmth of Devan's hand covering mine. It might not have been wise to drive with one hand in weather like that, but I've done things that were far less wise. Who was I to tell him to play things safe?

When we reached the house, the storm and its sideways rain made Devan's umbrella pointless, but he insisted on holding it over my head as he walked me to the door. Once again, he used his wet shoes and dripping clothes as an excuse to slosh into the night without coming inside to meet Mother.

"I suppose we'll get to know him Friday night," Mother said.

Annie said, "Hmm." What else could she say? She would

be busy in the kitchen, ordering her borrowed staff around. If Devan stayed in my life, and he seemed to want to do that (at least for a time), Annie would get to know him, but not on Friday night. Then, she would be firmly in her role as a servant.

She and Mother were sitting together at the kitchen table. They looked like friends as they studied the seating chart for the upcoming party. I didn't want to hear my mother give Annie any imperious orders, so I made an excuse to leave that was more than plausible.

"I've got to get out of these wet clothes."

My mother was distracted by the seating chart problem— algebraic in its constraints and complexity—of who could be allowed to sit beside whom. All I got was an airy, "You do that, dear."

Annie said, "There's plenty of leftover bean soup. Come get some when you're clean and dry."

As I left, Mother was saying, "Let's break up the married couples or the conversation will simply drag. Put the chancellor to my left and seat dear Marie's daughter Leontine on his other side. It will be good for her to have plenty of time to impress him. The director of libraries has one foot in the grave, and we should line Leontine up for his job. Put Professor Schmidt to my right with Marjorie Steed on his other side. He'll need a secretary, and we can't have her thrown out on her ear just because her boss did away with himself."

Somehow, I thought the Allies could finish up the war in a few weeks, if only someone had the good sense to put my mother in charge.

I disappeared upstairs and into the bath, and I saw no sign that she noticed I was leaving.

❦

On Thursday, one day before Mother's big party, Annie's operation shifted into high gear. It was no longer too early to begin making the food.

Annie went to town for one last butter-egg-and-cream purchase. I wasn't clear on the details, but she seemed to have sources beyond the grocery store. I imagined a shadowy black market of housekeepers desperate for dairy goods, and other housekeepers who needed to trade theirs before they went bad. I asked no questions, because I didn't want to know.

The borrowed footmen were dispatched to the Stenen Klif ponds to fish. Annie didn't like the idea of holding their catch in the refrigerator for a day, but the weather was too iffy to wait. What if it rained for forty-eight solid hours and she was left without an entrée? Or, worse, what if my mother had to attend her party without jewelry, because I'd hocked it all to pay for lamb chops?

What were we doing? What was *I* doing? Apparently, I was giving my mother one last chance to pretend she was rich.

The borrowed kitchen staff were assigned to crack walnuts and peel apples, because Thursday was cake-baking day. When Annie returned from town laden with possibly illicit bottles of cream and blocks of butter, she took charge of the trickiest parts of the cake-baking. She was determined to macerate the chopped apples in raspberry cordial herself, while keeping a close eye on the toasting walnuts. She used a very, very generous hand with the cordial. If there were any cakes left over after the party, they would keep longer than a Christmas fruitcake.

Annie tasked me with supervising the gardening, which was a polite way to get me out of the house. While the borrowed staff raked, trimmed, and weeded, I walked the terraced flower gardens. The morning sun coaxed out the flowers' scents—the roses' honeyed musk would have been cloying if the peonies' light citrus fragrance hadn't cut through all that sweetness.

In the kitchen garden, the spinach and lettuce were lush. The red shoulders of radishes cresting through the soil made my mouth water at the thought of their peppery bite. The asparagus bed bristled with plump green spears. In the herb garden, the odor of chives and thyme overpowered even the roses.

I wandered up to the bluff, where men carried heavy stringers of fish. The surge of fresh water from the week's rains had left the ponds so ice-clear that fishing was a matter of plunging in a dip net and snatching up silvery trout that were too fat to hide.

In the estate's overgrown gardens, the curled ends of new fiddlehead ferns were as plentiful as the asparagus and trout. Mother's guests would be eating well. This might be the last time my table groaned under the weight of a feast, but she, Annie, and Mother Nature had made sure that we'd be going out with a bang.

❦

Leontine arrived that evening after work, bearing an armload of lavender silk chiffon and silver-gray faille. We hung my mother's gown in her dressing room and mine in my closet.

I lifted the dress bag to peek at the creative way Leontine

had reworked the skirt of my dress, then I pulled something out of my pocket and held it out to her on my palm.

"This is for you. It's a thank-you gift, but it's also just something I want you to have."

It was a slender golden bangle bracelet, unadorned but elegant. My parents had given it to me for my sixteenth birthday.

"You don't have to wear it to the party if it doesn't suit your dress."

"Of course, it suits my dress. It suits everything. Thank you, E."

She slipped it on and held out her hand to admire it. Then she reached into her bag and took out an exquisite bit of black lace wrapped in tissue paper. "Tie it around your throat and it will frame your face just right. Devan won't be able to see anything but those blue eyes."

As she left, the storms began again. Rain and wind battered the house all night long.

Annie spent the evening supervising the two most talented kitchen maids as they made the chitarra noodles. Meanwhile, the rest of her bartered staff polished the silver and removed every speck of dust from the first floor.

By then Annie had stopped pretending I wasn't useless, so I retreated to the library and flipped on the gaslights. The floor had been buffed until it glowed. Carpet sweepers had raised the nap of the jewel-toned rug, so massive that it extended for the length and width of the banquet table plus enough room for all fourteen chairs.

Place cards inscribed in Mother's beautiful penmanship were already set out. Mother had placed me between Devan and Dr. Bower, with the bereaved Mrs. Jamison on Devan's other side. The chancellor's wife was seated on the far side of Dr. Bower. (Leave it to Mother to make sure no woman within twenty years of my age was seated near the man I had my eye on.)

Maids wielding feather dusters had made sure the gilded leather spines of my father's books gleamed. His thirty-two bookshelves, eight per wall and each of them eight shelves high, called to me. For the first time in my life, I pulled a book off the shelf. I half-expected to hear Father's voice yowling from the great beyond, but the only sound was the shushing of the book's cover as it slid past its neighbors.

The book fell open to reveal a photograph, a sepia-toned print like the ones my father made in his basement darkroom. It showed a cluster of three people in deep conversation, and I recognized none of them. It looked like they were at an indoor sporting event, perhaps a boxing match. Why was it in my father's book?

Curiosity took hold of me, and I pulled more books off that shelf, one at a time. In the first eight books, I found more photos, all of them of strangers who didn't appear to be doing anything interesting. Some of them showed small groups of people at an indoor event, possibly the same one as in the first photo. Another photo showed people standing around outdoors, drinks and sandwiches in hand. They were the kind of pictures you'd take at a family reunion or a church picnic. Judging by the clothing, most of the photos were many years old. If I had to guess, the oldest were taken in the 1920s.

Not sure why I thought it mattered, I carefully replaced each photo right where it had been and returned each book to its place on the shelf. After the eighth book, I found no more hidden photos on that shelf.

But what about the shelf below it? Being me, I was too curious to leave it alone.

One, two, three, four, five, six—the first six books yielded more photos of people I didn't know. (This made the fact that he didn't take photos of my mother and me even odder.) These photos were also shot outdoors, but the people were in a city setting, probably New York. In one of them, a tall brunette man and a short blond woman were embracing behind a pile of boxes in an alley, deep in a passionate kiss and clearly unaware that anyone could see them. Another photo caught two light-haired men in a similarly compromising position, hiding in a copse of trees and rock outcroppings that I thought might be in Central Park.

I worked methodically down that shelf, but I found no photos after the sixth book.

Why did my father have these pictures?

The whole business made the books feel disgusting in my hands. I didn't want Annie or my mother to see me searching them, but my curiosity was insatiable.

I decided I could risk searching one more shelf, because Annie was doing a great job of keeping everybody in the house busy but me. (And my mother. But Mother was upstairs, probably soaking in lavender bath salts with cucumber slices on her eyes. This was irksome, because we could have eaten those cucumbers.)

The next shelf turned up photos in the first eight books, and the first seven weren't much different from those I'd already seen. They were just people living their lives, and some of them were doing so with…hmmm…great passion. I diligently replaced each photo in its book and reshelved it, feeling like a voyeuristic librarian. But then I got a good look at the last photo.

The shock of it made me drop the book, which made a tremendous slapping sound that was horrifying in two ways. First, my father would never have let me live down dropping a Dickens first edition, but second, the noise was going to bring people running.

I pressed the photo flat against my thigh, covering it with my hand as I stooped to pick up the book.

Annie came from the kitchen at a sprint. She heaved a sigh and said, "You made all that noise with just a book? I'm nothing but a barrel of nerves, getting so worked up over something like that."

"It's nothing to get worked up over, Annie." Mother's quiet voice came from the staircase. I walked out of the library to see her. She stood at the landing, where the mirror seemed to echo her words as much as it did her form. I had no idea how long she'd been standing there.

Annie was still collapsed against the library wall, panting. This party was too much for her. This week had been too much for her. The past year had been too much for any of us.

"You should be resting, E," Mother said. "The party is just a day away and I think you underestimate the strain of being a hostess." She drifted back up the stairs, presumably to resume her pre-party resting regimen.

I retreated to the basement, so rattled by what I'd found that I checked the nailed-shut window as I passed. It was still closed.

I passed through the open part of the basement and into my father's darkroom, glad that I'd hired a locksmith to replace the basement's antiquated interior locks with modern ones opened by a single key. I kept a copy of the key beneath a loose brick. Fitting it to the darkroom lock, I entered my father's private domain. He'd never once let me in, no matter how much I begged him to show me how the magic of photography worked.

The darkroom looked like I 'd expected—the developing trays on his worktable, the red light bulb overhead, the shelf of chemicals, the wires where he'd hung developing pictures like clothes on a line, the shelf filled with photographic film, the cameras and flash apparatuses. I had always liked it that he enjoyed photography. It seemed like a harmless hobby, and he wasn't browbeating the rest of us when he was doing it. I should have realized that he'd find a way to pervert any art form he touched.

Placing the photo I'd been hiding in my hand on the work table, I closed the door to the darkroom and flipped on its red light. This made the sepia-toned photograph look bloody. I hardly wanted to touch it, but I did.

Helena Frederick looked out of the paper at me, wearing the coat with its daisy-shaped tortoiseshell buttons. Seeing it— and her—untouched by rot made me sway on my feet. She was whole and beautiful, wavy hair framing her narrow face, and she was terrified.

The photo was taken on campus, in the parklike area that separated the academic buildings from the river. I recognized the spot because one of Hawke Hall's towers could be seen above the trees.

Helena held a hand in front of her as if reaching through time, but someone was holding her back. One of his hands encircled her wrist tightly enough to break it, and the other gripped her buttocks. Was my father the man restraining her? The man had his back to the camera, so all I could see was his suit and hat. He could be almost anyone.

I studied his posture and the angle of his shoulders. I examined the length of his legs and the way he held his head.

I didn't think that this man was my father. More likely, my father was holding the camera.

Did the two people know that their photo was being taken? Neither of them was looking at the camera, which was several paces away, far enough to presume that the photographer might have been hiding. If my father took the photo, why was he skulking in the bushes? Why was he taking it in the first place?

Helena Frederick was still alive when the photo was taken, so it didn't necessarily show that she'd been murdered by anybody, much less by the man in the photo. Or by my father. It did, however, show the faceless man behaving terribly with a very young woman. This photo would have made excellent blackmail material even before she disappeared.

After she was gone? This photo was worth everything the man groping Helena Frederick owned. And I could tell by the cut of his jacket that he was not a poor man.

I thought of the other photos I'd seen hidden in the library. There were twenty-one of them, and I'd only searched a fraction of it. I didn't know who those people were, but my father had.

If every one of those photos, plus the hundreds more that could still be hiding anywhere in the house, represented a secret that somebody would pay to hide, then I had answered the question that had bothered me ever since I took over my father's estate: Where did all his money come from?

I was certain that it came from blackmail. Nothing that I knew about my father argued against him doing something so odious.

I remembered the note I'd found hidden with five hundred dollars in my father's study. The person who wrote it had promised more money when my father brought him "the rest." This made plenty of sense if "the rest" was the negative of a compromising photo. And his darkroom was crammed full of negatives.

Should I call Chief D'Amato about my suspicions? Under ordinary circumstances, yes, but I had no reason to think he'd take me seriously. Also, and this was more disturbing, I couldn't swear that the man photographed holding Helena Frederick by the wrist and buttocks wasn't him.

I didn't know how tall Helena had been, so I couldn't gauge the man's height. He had been wearing a suit with a slouchy cut that didn't reveal much. Fifteen years had passed, so I couldn't have identified him by his body shape, not for sure. His posture could be different by now, more stooped and bent. If my sense that the man was substantially older than Helena was accurate, I guessed that he was currently in his forties at the youngest.

If my father was documenting violence committed during an ongoing affair and not an assault by a stranger—and I didn't think the people in the photo were strangers to each other—then any man over forty who had spent time in Bentham-on-Hudson in the late 1920s could be the one in the picture. There were a lot of people in town whom I couldn't afford to trust.

I needed to gather my evidence and make a careful decision about how to share it. Considering that my house was full of guest workers, with another twelve guests arriving in twenty-four hours, this was going to take me some time.

I slipped out of the darkroom and locked it, returning the key to its hiding place. In the kitchen, Annie gave me two slices of bread and butter, a glass of wine that was really quite good, and a dire warning to leave her to her work or suffer the consequences. I heard her tell some of the staff to go to the basement to fetch the seldom-used cookware that she'd need for the big day, so I knew that I couldn't count on any more time alone down there. I retreated to my bedroom with my bread and wine.

I was too nervous to read and too nervous to sleep. The sound of the driving rain made it impossible to think. Throwing caution to the wind, I stood at my window and peered through the blinds, knowing that anybody watching from a boat in the cove could see my silhouette. I could see nothing.

CHAPTER 25

On the morning of the party, my mother and I planned our bath times over breakfast. Our house's three bathrooms—a private bath for my parents on the second floor, another on the second-floor hall for me and our guests, and a Spartan one on the third floor for the help—were considered unnecessary frippery by most people, but we did have them. What we didn't have was sufficient hot water.

We decided that Mother would bathe early in the morning, so that she could put her hair in curlers and give it all day to dry. Leontine had told me to slick mine back and let my curls do what they liked, so I could safely wait until the water warmed up again to begin the process.

I stood in the drawing room and listened to Annie clang pots in the kitchen. Her workers were outside, setting up a garden party tent between the driveway and the front door. Our guests might get damp, but maybe they could get out of their cars and hurry inside before their clothes were ruined. Upstairs, I heard water in the pipes as Mother ran her bathtub full. I figured I had half an hour before somebody missed me, so I ran for the basement.

In my father's darkroom, I found the lighted viewer that he'd used to look at negatives. I settled in to see how many I could view in thirty minutes.

❦

Photographic negatives are odd things. Up stays up, down stays down, and left and right keep their positions. Black is white, and white is black, but gray is still gray.

A huge number of my father's negatives showed people in the throes of passion. Some of them were simply kissing or gazing into each other's eyes, but others were…doing a lot more than that. I didn't recognize anyone, but that didn't mean a lot. For one thing, their faces were a lot less obvious than their other body parts, and for another thing, these pictures, like the ones in the library, were quite old. Just because I didn't recognize this bare-breasted young flapper or that young dandy in a raccoon coat with his hand up a woman's skirt, didn't mean that I didn't know them now as staid bastions of society.

I did recognize one thing. My father's darkroom belonged to a blackmailer. Or, I supposed, a pornographer. Or a man who took risqué photos for couples who liked to look at themselves, but my money was on blackmail. Granted, there were also regular ordinary photos of people in conversation, but regular ordinary people had things to hide. At rock bottom, everybody had something to hide.

It was time to go, but as I stood in the darkroom door, my eye lighted on the wall that hid the entrance to Mother's wine cave, and it made me wonder. It made me turn around and go back into a blackmailer's lair.

A darkroom is dim by design, so I turned on the overhead white light and the red light that lit the developing trays. I even turned on the little light in the negative viewer. Then I slid my hands over every square inch of exposed wall within reach. In the darkest corner, I found a button like the one on the wine cave's door.

I pressed it hard, and the wall moved away from my hand. The hidden room was even more poorly lit than the darkroom, but I saw shelves, lots of them, all loaded down with old, yellowed folders stuffed with old, yellowed paper. And, unsurprisingly, I saw stacks of old photographs.

How many dirty pictures would it take to empty the pockets of the Hudson Valley's philanderers? Bentham-on-Hudson and the other river towns just weren't that big. My father must have been blackmailing all of Manhattan, too. By the looks of the yellowed papers, he had been doing it for a long, long time, since we'd arrived in the early twenties. It was going to take time to figure everything out, and I didn't have it. I had to go.

On the way back upstairs, I paused by the window with a faulty lock. Now that I knew what my father was, it made sense that somebody was trying to get into the basement. Probably, they wanted to retrieve an incriminating photo. Based on what I'd just seen, I wished them good luck in finding it.

Still, I would love to know who it was. It might be Helena Frederick's lover—rapist, more likely, considering the look on her face—trying to get the photo I'd found in the library. Or it could be her murderer (who could be the same person) in search of the Bakelite button my father had hidden away. Or, and this thought made me draw a ragged breath, my father might have had the button because he *was* her murderer. It was the first thing I'd thought when I found it, and I had no reason to think he wasn't capable.

The window could have been opened by the person who had been watching my house from the cove or by the person who left footprints at a spot overlooking the house. Was this person among the twelve people invited to join us for dinner that very night?

It was possible. Everybody who had been in my house during the time the window was probably opened—Dr. Bower, Dr. Masters, Oscar Glenby, John, Devan, Marjorie, and Leontine—would be there. They were the ones who'd had the opportunity to break the lock.

Wait. I was forgetting Sheriff D'Amato, who had been in the house, but wouldn't be at the party. And I was forgetting that Devan, Marjorie, and Leontine were too young to have killed Helena Frederick or to be pictured as adults in any of the photos I'd found. If any of them had opened the window, it had been for a different reason. It was all very confusing.

Once at the house for the party, would one of the guests try to sneak downstairs and search Father's darkroom? I judged that it would be risky to let anyone be out of sight for that long.

To guard against that, I would station a footman to lurk in the basement passage. If he saw somebody make a move to go downstairs or open the window, I'd call Chief D'Amato on them before dessert was served. But if nobody did, then the odds that the chief himself was the culprit increased significantly.

Did I want to leave the prowler any clue I was suspicious? That seemed unwise.

I ran downstairs and got a claw hammer. It made quick work of ripping out the nails holding the window shut. Let the prowler think that we'd found it open and closed it. If they'd come back in the meantime and found it impossible to open, let them think that the old paint had stuck to the frame.

The person might try to raise it again, ready for a late-night visit, but I didn't need—or want—the prowler to actually lift the window. I just wanted a witness to see someone walk close to it, either from inside the house or outside the house. I needed to know who my opponent was.

"Come on. Try to use this window to get in my house," I muttered out loud. "I'm ready for you." And then I took the photo of Helena and her attacker back to the library. It had been safe there for years, so I presumed that it would be safe to leave it in a Dickens first edition for a little while longer.

Mother was out of the bath, and I was waiting for the water heater to catch up. This always took a while, because she used a lot of water. I stood in the library watching a full roster of servants do the kind of work I hadn't seen done since I was in my teens. I called one of the young men over, a boy named Matthew who couldn't have been eighteen.

Of course, he wasn't eighteen. If he were, he'd be on the other side of the world, fighting a war.

"I have a special assignment for you, Matthew. I need you to wait in the corridor to the basement in case one of the guests gets lost. But don't embarrass them. Just come get me, and I'll make sure they get safely back to the party. Tell Annie I said so."

If any of the guests came down the corridor to leave the window open, Matthew would tell me. And if anybody tried to come through it from the outside during the party, Matthew would see.

Annie would be full of questions, but she'd have no chance to ask them until the evening was done.

While I watched, Matthew and the other servants began laying out the fourteen place settings. Hand-painted porcelain. Whisper-thin crystal. Sterling flatware rubbed over a period of decades to a warm, shining patina. Towering over them were thirty-two shelves of my father's books, some of them hiding dangerous secrets.

Leontine was a magician with a needle. There's no other way to describe what she had done to my dress.

She'd added boning to the silvery faille jacket, so it fit even more smoothly over my curves, and she'd completely remade the bottom half of the slip dress I wore beneath it. Its silhouette was the reverse of an A-line, tapering from the width of my hips down to a tiny span that struck me just at the ankles. It would have hobbled me, if not for the daring slit up my left leg. I've worn silk hose that revealed less of the shape of my legs than that skirt.

Since Leontine knew everything about style and I knew nothing, I followed her directions to the letter. Black lace jabot knotted at my throat. Hair slicked back and secured with a jeweled clip that released a knot of curls at the nape of my neck. Barely there earrings. Dramatic-for-me eye makeup, but just a little pink on the lip. I looked nothing like myself, but I looked like a woman about to hostess one hell of a party.

I recognized Mother's tap at my door. When I opened it, I heard the hum of voices and the tapping of hard-soled shoes on the marble floor of the entry hall. So many voices—twelve guests and about as many servants. The festive scent of burning candles rose up the stairs, and the excited hum of all those people vibrated the floor beneath the soles of my black satin shoes.

Mother stepped through the door, afloat in the lavender of her dress. "I brought some joy," she said, squeezing the bulb of a crystal atomizer and letting a cloud of perfume rain on us. Of course, she wore Joy. It was notoriously the most expensive perfume in the world.

She slid her slender hand into the crook of my arm and squeezed. "I'm so glad you're home."

I thought back to the months when I'd thought she might be dead. "I could say the same to you."

"Thank you for finding me. And thank you for this." She waved her hand around, presumably encompassing the dresses, the perfume, and the humming excitement of the coming party.

"It was your idea."

"And you thought it was a terrible one, but you made it happen anyway. I am not unaware of the obstacles you faced."

I thought of the borrowed servants, the remade dresses, the foraged food, and the bartered eggs, and I wondered how aware she really was.

"I have a plan. Well, not really a plan, but a philosophy. You and I—we get knocked down, but we always get back on our feet. Always. You're a great deal like me, you know."

All I could say was, "What?"

"I know what scares you. You're afraid that you're like him."

How could she know that? How could she know something buried so deep inside me that I couldn't say it out loud? I had always been silently terrified that I'd never be free of him, because the terrifying part of me *was* him. I was his daughter. It had to be true.

"Your father was cold, self-centered, dishonest. You're not like him in the least. Annie and I made sure of it. We protected you." She guided me out the door. "Come. People are waiting for us."

As we made our way down the hallway, I teetered a bit in the satin pumps I'd borrowed from Mother. I had done my best to live my life so that I'd never need to wear foolish shoes, yet here I was, balanced on heels shaped like ice picks.

Mother, on the other hand, was gliding along in her glittery sandals like a woman who had spent her life in shoes designed to hobble her. Because she had.

She brushed her hand over my brow, smoothing my already slicked-back hair. "I know why you had to go, E. I knew it when you left. That's why I never came to Boston and brought you home, though I wanted to. I wanted it desperately, but not as much as I wanted you to be far away from him."

I teetered again, and this time it wasn't because of the shoes. It was because my legs were shaking. All of me was shaking.

Mother steadied me with her grip on my elbow. "Are you ready, dear? It's time to make our entrance."

As we descended the staircase, I could hear the slight metallic rattle of crystal goblets being carried on silver trays, so I knew that the wine was already flowing. My mother carried herself like she was weightless. I knew it was a trick of good posture and smooth motion, but I'd never mastered it. All I could do was try to move more like Mother and less like a horse.

One stair at a time, we neared the landing and its tremendous mirror. To our right, Father's disturbingly oversized tertiary-hued abstract painting came into view. Its clashing colors looked the way I felt. Just a few stairs below us was the landing where we would turn left and descend the final flight of stairs. Our guests would be waiting at the bottom, with the giddy smiles that come when the alcohol has just begun to course through their veins. They would be waiting to move with us through the massive doors into the library, still closed. Behind those doors, the real party waited.

I'd seen my parents go through this ceremony before, many times, but this…this party was mine. This glorious house belonged to Mother and me, and so did all the beautiful things in it. For one triumphant instant, I thought that maybe Mother was right. Maybe we should spend what was left of our money pursuing shimmering moments like this one.

And then I saw the two of us in the mirror, full-length, and I felt my heart turn to lead. No, it turned to something heavier than lead.

We stepped onto the landing and pivoted left, and I could see that our guests, too, saw what I saw.

My hair was combed straight back like his. My tailored gray

jacket hugged my broad shoulders, so much like his. The black lace at my neck looked, from a distance, like a man's tie. My hobble skirt had the narrow-bottomed silhouette of a pair of trousers. I looked exactly like my father, returned from the dead to repossess his place in the world...to repossess my mother.

With Mother clutching my arm, I stepped off the last stair and into the crowded entry hall. Every single person who had known my father took a step back, leaving Devan, Leontine, Marjorie, and the servants looking around, confused.

Mother was saying something that was probably "Welcome," but her voice was distorted in my ears, as if she were speaking from deep in the basement. My head swiveled from left to right, taking in all the guests' faces. They, too, were distorted. Fear can do that. It can take over your senses and make everything monstrous.

Somebody—possibly someone in my home at that moment—was being blackmailed over the death of Helena Frederick. At least I presumed that was my father's purpose in keeping the hidden photograph and button. At last, I had come up with a reason to absolve him of *something*. If he had killed her, he would have disposed of the button immediately, probably in the same way that he'd disposed of the body.

If one of my guests was her killer, that person would have to have been terrified of being exposed. That kind of terror should be obvious to anyone with eyes, right?

In the moment when I escorted my mother down the stairs, looking uncomfortably like my father, I realized the difficulty at the heart of this presumption. Nobody stood out in the crowd as particularly afraid, because a lot of people were terrified of my father.

CHAPTER 26

One of our borrowed servants threw open the massive double doors, so that Mother and I could lead everyone into the library. Silver candelabras lit the banquet table, and massive cut-crystal vases held whole branches of roses and rhododendrons and apple blossoms. Cocktail tables, set with white candles and small arrangements of white peonies, had been set up in the four corners of the room, well away from the precious books. They provided comfortable places for guests to stand and talk and sip their wine. A cocktail hour would have been more fashionable, but we did not have a secret cave full of liquor. We did, however, have a stupendous formal space for drinking wine and dining.

Father had insisted that the gas chandeliers and sconces in the library be spared when the house was electrified. I'd been gone for a long time, so I had forgotten the magic of warm lighting that flickers and glows. Everyone is beautiful in gaslight. My father's library had never looked better. Its shelves and rolling ladders extended into the darkness above the reach of the gasoliers' tiny flames.

The gaslight kissed away the last haggard traces that Mother's imprisonment had left on her face. Looking at my parents' longtime friends—Dr. Masters, Chancellor and Mrs. Hampstead, John, Professor and Mrs. Schmidt, Dr. Hanssen, Mrs. Jamison—was like time-traveling to the days when they were in their prime and I was a child. Everyone looked young and happy, and I don't think this was a product of the glass of wine I tossed down as soon as it was handed to me. I looked around for Annie, because I wanted to see her rejuvenated, but she was hidden away in the kitchen.

Marjorie took three excited steps in my direction until she remembered that she was trying to be sophisticated. She shifted so abruptly to a dignified stroll that it made me laugh. Her dress was certainly sophisticated, a white, one-shouldered frock that harked back to ancient Greece. I suspected that Leontine had surgically removed one sleeve from her senior prom dress.

"E, you look stunning," Marjorie said. "And your mother, my goodness. I want to be her when I grow up."

Mother was standing at a table across the room, chatting with Chancellor Hampstead and his wife.

"Where's Leontine?" I glanced around the room and spotted her chitchatting with Mrs. Jamison and Dr. Masters. She hadn't been lying about her curve-hugging crimson dress. She looked like she had stepped off a Paris runway.

She saw us looking her way and excused herself to hurry over.

"You two look like a million dollars. Each." She ran a critical eye over us to make sure we were wearing her designs properly. When she smiled, I presumed we were.

"How is Mrs. Jamison holding up?" Marjorie asked. "I need to go speak to her, but I've been working up the courage. You know she thinks of him when she sees me and remembers that I was there when...you know..."

"She's doing okay, I guess," Leontine said, peeking at the woman through the wavy curtain of hair that she had strategically placed to set off her exquisite cheekbones. "She's nervous as a cat, but wouldn't you be?"

I wasn't so sure that it was Marjorie who was making Mrs. Jamison uncomfortable, although Marjorie might think so. The woman spent most of her time staring at me.

"Mother thought it was a good idea to invite her. My mother's not always the most practical person, but she does know a lot about social things."

"Mrs. Jamison has always been a little twitchy," Leontine said. "I think Dr. Masters sees that she's not doing well, so she's staying close by. It's very sweet of her."

It took me a moment to remember that, until recently, Leontine had lived away from home for many years. "Always? Have you known Mrs. Jamison a long time?"

"She used to help my mother sometimes, so I remember her from when I was little."

"Don't look," Marjorie hissed, "but Devan's staring at you."

"He's probably looking at that long stretch of leg." Leontine murmured. "I left it uncovered just for him."

I felt my face go as red as her dress, which was apparently

what she'd intended, because she gave a satisfied laugh. I needed to put my eyes somewhere, anywhere, that wasn't Devan's face. I swung my face away from him...

...and locked eyes with John.

"Hell." I whispered it under my breath, but Marjorie and Leontine heard me.

"So this is what happens when she drinks? She curses?" Leontine spoke to Marjorie as if I weren't standing there suffering. "Let's get her another glass of wine and see what happens."

I pasted on a smile and turned away from John. "Don't leave me," I said without moving my lips.

"Why?" Marjorie asked.

"After knowing me for—I don't know, maybe a quarter century—John has developed romantic intentions, and I don't know what to do about it."

Leontine, who already knew about John's unexpected proposal, looked at him out of the corner of her eye. "He's good-looking. I'll say that for him. Is the problem that you haven't decided whether you like him? Or is it that you don't know how to let him down easy?"

"I don't know anything."

"I know John from church." Marjorie said. "He's very good with numbers, especially when they have a dollar sign in front of them. I can distract him with a question about the building fund." She glided off to rescue me.

"Devan's still looking at you," Leontine said. "Everybody is."

Yes, they were. Everywhere I turned my eyes, somebody was giving me that look, the one they'd all worn when I appeared on the stairs, looking like my father. There was hatred in that look.

Whether it was for me or for him, I couldn't tell. But what could I possibly have done to them?

Leontine saw their stares differently. "You're the belle of the ball. If it weren't for Devan, I'd say it was too bad that most of the male guests are old enough to be your father. But who cares that they're not for you? Devan is, and he seems to really like you." She positioned herself in my line of sight. "Don't look at him. Look at me. Give him time to come to you."

He was deep in conversation with Dr. Bower and Oscar Glenby, so that might take a while. Fortunately, my mother was there to make sure I didn't look like a wallflower. She approached with Chancellor Hampstead at her right elbow and Dr. Hanssen on the other. Leave it to Mother to make sure I spoke to the two people most able to give me a professorship within the first ten minutes of her party.

"Your mother's been telling us about your research, Dr. Ecker," the chancellor said. "She says that your book on Gothic fiction is due to be published any minute now."

"It's under consideration—"

"*Serious* consideration," Mother purred.

"It's under serious consideration by an editor who contacted me after I had essays in *PMLA* and *Modern Language Quarterly*—"

"Both?" Professor Hanssen asked.

"Both," said Mother, who wouldn't have been able to explain the difference between *PMLA* and *Ladies' Home Journal* on a bet. *Vogue*, however, she would have known.

"I'd like to hear more," the chancellor said. "You should call my assistant and set up an appointment."

This was a signal for Dr. Hanssen to say. "I'd like to hear more, too. I've been thinking it was time to find you a better office."

"And now I must find my wife, so we can pay our respects to Dean Jamison's poor widow," Chancellor Hampstead said, and it wasn't lost on me that they'd spent the minimum necessary time with the daughter of their hostess. I didn't get the sense that they were brushing me off as unimportant, though. They just wanted to get away from me.

"Yes, dear Eva. She has been so brave." Professor Hanssen's eyes shifted from my face to the bookshelf behind me and back again. He was ready to move on.

It was as if my resemblance to Father was a scarlet letter on my chest. I wondered if it would help if I disappeared into the bathroom and came out with my hair freed into its usual mass of curls. Maybe I could get rid of the menswear silhouette of my gown by taking off the black jabot and unbuttoning the jacket.

I would have done almost anything to make people stop looking at me in fear. How did my father stand it?

I knew the answer. He loved it. He loved their fear.

There were books behind me, in front of me, and to both sides. I'd opened just a small sampling of them, but I'd found several compromising photos, one of which might point to a murderer. I surveyed the room from right to left, a slow pan that took in everyone. All the male faculty members were surreptitiously eyeing the books. So were their spouses. So was Oscar Glenby. Dr. Masters was openly looking at my mother. And Mrs. Jamison was staring at me.

Were there pictures of them hidden in those books? Was my father blackmailing them all?

I had no chance to think about it, because Devan had decided it was time to make his move. He was at my elbow in a few long-legged strides. The satin stripe down the side of his tuxedo pants made his legs look even longer.

He took my hand, and I forgot everything. My father. My mother. Helena Frederick. Even Annie. I forgot the room full of people who were staring at me. I had thought that I loved Bradley, but I'd been wrong. I didn't know if this was love, but it was the strongest thing I'd ever felt. If I'd married Bradley, I would have lived my whole life without it.

I could have sworn that the room grew quiet, and maybe it did. Maybe the gaslights even flickered.

It fell to John to break the spell, not with a word, but with the sound of his footsteps on the hard floor and the bang of the front door slamming shut behind him. It was impossible to be in the same room with Devan and me without seeing how things were. I was sorry to hurt a good man, but nobody can create love out of thin air. It either is or it isn't.

Every head had turned to watch John go, which was the only time that evening when I was sure that nobody was looking at me. And what were the words running through my mind at that moment?

Now we will be thirteen at dinner. Annie will be horrified.

CHAPTER 27

J ohn's departure extinguished every conversation. Part of me was surprised that it didn't extinguish the candles and the gaslights, too.

It is very difficult to restart small talk in a room that has been shocked to silence. It is rather like trying to restart a flooded engine. Sometimes there's nothing to do but give the situation a little time, even if you'd rather not.

I stood there beside Professor Schmidt and Chancellor Hampstead, Devan's hand in mine. Now the men who could hire me had some justification for filing me under "Woman in Search of a Husband." Or, if they grasped why John had just stalked out of the room, they could file me under, "Manipulative Woman with Multiple Lovers." If I'd ever had a chance at a real job at Bentham College, it was now gone.

I scanned the room again, looking for faces I recognized from my father's blackmail photos. I saw nothing. If I had seen these people, in black-and-white or in the inverse white-and-black of a negative, I didn't recognize them.

Leontine hurried over to join Marjorie, whom John had left in the dust. My mother had moved away from me when Devan took my hand, and she was now standing with Dr. Masters and Eva Jamison. Mrs. Jamison had passed beyond merely looking nervous. She was now trembling visibly. Mrs. Schmidt and Mrs. Hampstead had noticed, so they joined in forming a protective circle around the recent widow.

This support did not seem to be helping, because Eva Jamison began to pace. Well, I guess you would call it pacing. It was more like an aimless walk around the perimeter of the room, with her knot of protective women following along. I was reminded of the scene in *Pride and Prejudice* when Miss Bingley invites Elizabeth to join her in taking a turn around the room, and Mr. Darcy skewers them by suggesting that they just want everyone to see their figures from a nice angle.

My mother was the only woman over forty in the room with any figure fashionable enough to write home about, and even she was on the too-thin side, having spent a lot of recent time in a madhouse. Dr. Masters wore a shapeless black satin sack that gave no clue as to what was beneath it. The professors' wives wore girlish pastels, with Mrs. Hampstead and Mrs. Schmidt in matronly shapes that suited their softly padded frames. Mrs. Jamison was, by contrast, terrifyingly gaunt in her well-made magenta frock. This made her look like a flamingo.

The flamingo and her flock had made almost a full turn around the room before they neared me. Eva Jamison glided past Marjorie with a withering glare, and then I was in her sights. She was steering a collision course for me, and she was speeding up.

"You," she fumed, coming closer with every long stride. "You. You're just standing there enjoying it all."

It was my party. Wasn't I supposed to enjoy it?

"How can you look us all in the face? It was cruel to invite us here, knowing that we couldn't say no."

My mother was the one who had done the inviting. I looked at Mother, trying to see whether she knew what this woman was talking about.

Mother, as I have said, is expert at disguising her feelings, donning her Ice Queen face and sailing through every storm. At that moment, though, she wore no mask. She was truly confused, and that is how I knew that she was innocent.

Whatever it was that was upsetting Mrs. Jamison, Mother didn't do it. I knew that I didn't do it. That left only one possible guilty party, and never mind that Father was dead.

"He called me, you know," she raved, running her fingers through her brunette updo and pulling out the hairpins, one by one.

Who? Father? Was she talking about a phone call sometime in the past? Right before he died? Or back in 1923, maybe? I couldn't pin her accusation down in time.

"On the day he died, he called me, and he told me what you said."

On the day he died, my father had forgotten how to talk. Also, I hadn't had a conversation with him since I was seventeen. He couldn't have told her anything I'd said since then.

"Why would you treat my husband that way?"

Oh. We were talking about Dean Jamison. I did speak to him on the day he died, but what could I have possibly said to trigger this woman's breakdown?

I had simply asked him for a bigger office. He had said no, but I saw nothing wrong with my asking the question.

"He said you told him you'd been reading your father's books. Spending a lot of time in the library, you said. *In the library*." Her face was red and blotchy. "You conniving bitch."

In the dead silence that followed her words, I remembered. I heard again exactly what I'd said to Dean Jamison and the superior tone I'd used to say it.

I've been working my way through that huge library, book by book, page by page.

Somewhere in the room where we stood, hidden in one of the thousands of books, was something that Dean Jamison was desperate to keep secret. When I told him that I was looking through all my father's books, I had been trying to impress him with my intellectual ancestry, but he had heard a threat.

When I went on to say, "I've been thinking it was time to throw dinner parties in that room again," I had been whistling in the dark, pretending that I still had the money to carry on my family's legacy. But what Dean Jamison had heard was, "I'm going to invite you to a party in the room where my father hid your shame, and you're going to come. Because I say so. You're going to stand in a crowd of your friends and take anything I dish out, because I own you. Just like my father did."

He had thought my faux invitation was a threat, because my father had done it to him before. Judging by the horror on their faces, Dean Jamison wasn't the only person my father had invited to see his library. I imagined each of them standing alone with him as he explained that, somewhere in the room, he had hidden evidence of a sin that could end life as they knew it.

It struck me that Dean Jamison's sin had been so horrendous that he'd literally ended his life. On the day he died, this poor woman in front of me had taken one last telephone call from her terrified husband. The next time her phone rang, the person on the other end of the line had told her she was a widow.

I don't know whether she saw on my face that I finally understood what she was talking about. It may have been that she had simply come to the end of pretending that she would ever be okay again. For whatever reason, Mrs. Jamison erupted.

She whirled away from me. In a blur of hot pink rayon, she ran down the length of the room, plucking random books off random shelves and hurling them at the banquet table. China shattered. Crystal splintered. Only Marjorie's lightning reflexes kept the tablecloth from going up in flames when a book overturned a candelabra and sent lit candles flying.

By the time she reached the last shelf on that wall, Mrs. Jamison had worked up some speed. She thrust out her hand and used her momentum to rake an armload of books onto the floor. One of them landed on its spine and splayed open. The thing that fell out of it made the poor woman shrink back, mouth wide open and arms crossed over her belly.

Humans are voyeurs at the heart, all of us. Everybody unthinkingly took a few steps nearer, fascinated by the black-and-white thing on the floor. It was a photo, but it wasn't just a photo. It was the front page of a copy of *The Bentham Herald* from 1939, folded in quarters, and a photographic image filled the entire quarter-page that we could see.

It was a wide-angle shot taken from a high seat at Madison Square Garden, which explained all the photos I'd thought were taken at a sporting event. Behind the stage, a huge German swastika hung between two American flags. I'd heard of a 1939 Nazi rally in New York City, and now here it was, attended by throngs of regular everyday U.S. citizens. My father had taken or purchased photos of people at the rally, surmising correctly that all these proud American Nazis would eventually wish they'd kept their fascist politics quiet. Once that swastika became the symbol of the enemy, Father could wave this article at, say, the boss of a federal employee whose paycheck would immediately be history. Or he could make it very hard for the mayor to win the next election. The citizens of Bentham might have tacitly agreed to forget this event had ever happened, but Father had made sure they couldn't do that.

Teetering from shock and alcohol and the effort to balance on my sky-high heels, I bent and picked up the paper. Opening it to get a look at everything above the fold, I saw that the reporter had done the thing that small-town reporters always do, and it had made the article ten times worse. He had listed the local residents who had attended the news-making event, so even people who had evaded the camera's lens were implicated.

The Schmidts.

The Chancellor and his wife.

The Jamisons.

Dr. Hanssen and the wife who had recently left him.

It was unlikely that these people had suddenly decided they were Nazis in 1939. If I knew my father, there were stacks of photographs in my basement of people attending smaller meetings like this one over a period of years when fascism and eugenicism were appallingly acceptable. It wasn't like the war had changed the minds of people with those views, but they kept them quiet now. When the U.S. declared war on Germany, the blackmail value of those photos had skyrocketed, because proof of sympathy for our enemy would be a career-ending, life-altering thing.

Father had foreseen this. He hadn't lived long enough to capitalize on this photo, but I'd seen others in the basement that were just as damning for the people unlucky enough to sin in front of my father's camera.

It hit me in the gut to think that Nazis were drinking my wine at that very moment.

Everybody in the room took a step back from the picture and from me, but the guilty parties kept going.

Dr. and Mrs. Schmidt, Dr. Bower, Chancellor and Mrs. Hampstead, Professor Hanssen, and Mrs. Jamison backed out of the room, mumbling inane things like, "Must go!" and "I'm suddenly not feeling well," and "We must get home to check on the dog." They pillaged the coat closet, ran under the tent that led to the driveway, and they were gone.

There was a moment of silence while those of us who remained tried to take in what had just happened. Then thunder boomed, and Devan jerked like a man waking from sleep.

"Mrs. Jamison," he said. "I gave her a ride from town. She's out there alone. Despite…this…" He waved a disgusted hand at the clipping. "I can't let her be out on foot in this weather."

Everybody was still mesmerized by the photo, so we all just mumbled, "You're right. Go."

Marjorie took the newspaper from me, so that I could follow Devan and help him find his coat. The others had left in such a stampede that they'd knocked other people's things to the floor. Half-buried in that pile was a familiar tweed coat. Dr. Bower hadn't even bothered to dig around for it before he ran out into the rain.

With a quick kiss and an "I'm so sorry. I'll call you," Devan was out of the house. He was already driving away as I fought the wind for control of the heavy front door.

CHAPTER 28

When I came back into the library, there were more people in the room than when I left. Four footmen stood awkwardly at the head of the table, bearing trays laden with bowls of cream of asparagus soup. The rest of the servants were in the drawing room, peeking at us through the open door.

Annie was pushing her way through my guests to reach me, asking, "What has happened here, Miss E? We've made a lovely formal dinner for fourteen. I think formality has gone out the window, but somebody needs to eat this food right now. It'll only taste good for about five more minutes."

I didn't know how to tell her that I might never want to eat again. Before I could spit out words to that effect, Marjorie opened and flattened the paper to read the text below the fold, gave a short, brittle scream, and dropped it.

"I have to go."

Why was she acting like all those middle-aged people who fled when they saw their own faces in the paper?

I picked up the paper and scanned the list of Bentham

residents, who grew progressively less socially prominent as I read. I only understood Marjorie's scream when I reached the names printed below the fold. Two of those names were Edgar and Vonnie Steed.

Marjorie was backing into the entry hall, and I was calling for her to stop. "It's not your fault. Nobody blames you for something your parents did."

She paused long enough to answer me. "No, I didn't do the things they did. But I knew. I knew what they were like—what they *are* like—and I stayed. I'm not brave like you, Estella. I'm not brave enough to be alone." Then she was running.

She was faster than the older people had been, and she didn't pause at the coat closet, but Leontine and I were young, too. We caught her on the front doorstep, each of us grasping a wrist.

"We're your friends," Leontine said. "Please stay."

Marjorie couldn't look at her. "I can't make it right. I have to go. Don't come after me."

She yanked her arms so hard that we had no choice but to let her go. Holding on would only have hurt her. She ran out into the storm wearing a wisp of white silk and a matching pair of pumps with vertiginous heels.

Marjorie had asked me not to come after her, but she hadn't said anything about sending other people. The footmen had surged into the entry hall, painfully young and overflowing with chivalry. In other words, they were itching for an excuse to rescue a fair maiden. I gave the word, and they bolted out the door and down the footpath to town.

Not knowing what else to do, I went to Annie. She was in the kitchen, and she was in her element. While we waited for the footmen to return, she administered her own brand of medicine—food and wine. And also steaming hot tea.

She cast a dark look at the wreckage of the banquet table. To the kitchen maids, she said, "Gather up the flowers, mop up the spilled water, and leave the rest. We may be able to get some of the tableware repaired, and that's for me to decide."

Annie settled Mother and Dr. Masters in the drawing room and laid their dinner out on tea tables. She wanted to put tea tables in there for Leontine and me, too, but I said, "We have things to talk about. We'll eat at one of the cocktail tables in the library."

"You'll pick one that's not too near the broken glass?"

"I'm not stupid, Annie."

She laughed. "That you're not. Neither of you."

Leontine and I nibbled at the succulent trout and the still-steaming *spaghetti alla chitarra*, coated in a creamy sauce studded with fiddleheads. We sipped the cream of asparagus soup, and it tasted like springtime. So did our crisp salads. We avoided the liquor-soaked apple cake, which seemed too heavy to bear, and both of us drank water instead of wine. I believe we sensed that we would need our wits about us that night.

I moved the flower arrangement off our cocktail table, so that we could study the newspaper clipping. As I ate, I read every word of the article, which celebrated isolationism and bigotry, searching the whole time for my parents' names. I didn't find them. Whatever their other sins, and my father's included profiting from the shame of the people at Madison Square Garden that day, I saw no evidence that my parents had been Nazis.

"This is awful," Leontine said gesturing at the article, "but would Dean Jamison have killed himself over it? People might play dumb about it, but deep down, don't you think there are still plenty of people around here who agree with the things that were said in this article?"

"No. I don't think this article would have been enough to make a man kill himself. But I think this might have done it."

I walked to the three shelves I had explored, studied them for a second, and found the book I wanted, the Dickens first edition. Opening it, I showed Leontine the photo of Helena Frederick being groped by an unidentifiable man. "Could this be Dean Jamison?"

As she studied it, I remembered the familiar way he had touched me with both hands on that last morning, one hand on my elbow, the other flat on my back. I remembered the way he ignored Marjorie at work while she followed him like a shadow. I remembered how he'd pulled her away from me at my father's funeral in a controlling way that sharply contrasted with the dismissiveness he showed her at the office.

Two questions were fighting in my head, and they were both making me ill.

What did Dean Jamison do to Helena Frederick before she died? And did he do the same thing to Marjorie?

Leontine and I stared at the photo lying on the table, our hands in our laps as if we were afraid to touch it.

"We need to talk to Mother."

"Oh, my word," Mother said when I showed her the photo. "Who is the man terrorizing that poor girl?"

"We don't know. Could it have been Dean Jamison?"

She peered at the photo. "I can't tell. But I do know that the women at our parties gave him a wide berth. Women who were new to town were warned. I would never have thought him a murderer, but he was known to be a lecher."

Dr. Masters said, "I never heard any gossip about Dean Jamison and Miss Frederick." She paused. "But I do know that the students always made it a point to tell freshman girls to avoid being alone with him."

"Oh, God." The words left me in a breath. Marjorie's work had put her alone with him on a daily basis.

This shed some light on the withering glare that I'd seen Mrs. Jamison direct her way.

I backed into the library and Leontine followed.

"People knew," I said. "They knew what he was like."

"The women tried to warn each other."

"Was that enough?"

Leontine closed her eyes. "It wasn't enough to help Helena. And maybe Marjorie. Also, we still don't know whether that's him in the picture with Helena, and we don't know for sure whether he did anything to them. Maybe he had nothing to do with Helena's death. Or maybe he terrorized her until she killed herself."

"There's evidence of that. There were stones sewn into her pockets, and maybe she did it. I can't imagine Dean Jamison making stitches that small and neat."

Leontine's eyes opened wide. "She did what?"

"She sewed her pockets shut. I don't think the police made it public, but they showed me the body."

"They couldn't hide those pockets and their rocks from you," she said.

"No, they couldn't. But wait. Did you tell me that Mrs. Jamison worked for your mother?"

"She did. And if you mean it when you say that the stitches were small and neat, Dean Jamison didn't sew them and neither did an eighteen-year-old who came from a family with money. My mother did all the sewing for the Fredericks. I doubt Helena could thread a needle."

I thought through the possibilities. "Maybe he killed her—maybe out of anger or by accident or to keep her quiet—and he got his wife to help him sink the body. Or maybe Mrs. Jamison got so jealous that she killed Helena and sank the body herself. She doesn't seem like a strong woman, so I'd guess that he did the killing and sinking. She just did the sewing."

"But she knew about it. She was part of it. Anybody could see tonight that she was terrified. And the rest of them?"

"I think the newspaper article was enough to send them scuttling out of here. But who knows what else my father had on them? He hid enough evidence to blackmail this town dry. You should see all the photos and papers in the basement."

I thought of the daisy-shaped button hidden in his desk. "Father may have seen Helena's murder. Maybe it happened when he was hiding, taking photos to use for blackmail. This photo could have been taken that very day. I know that my father kept a button from her coat. I bet there was a struggle and it fell off. He could have picked it up after the killer hauled her body away. Imagine how much it would be worth to a blackmailer."

"No wonder Mrs. Jamison is terrified of what you might know."

I heard the kitchen door open, followed by the sound of excited young male voices. Leontine and I ran to meet the footmen.

"Did you find Marjorie?"

Matthew was the one who spoke up. "No. We went all the way down the path to town. We weren't sure what to do at first, then we decided to go in a restaurant—"

"The one on Main and Second," interjected one of the other men.

"Yeah, that one," Matthew said. "We went in and asked the owner if he knew somebody named Marjorie—black hair, nice smile—"

"And pretty," said another one, who then blushed to his hairline. They were so very young.

"I told him we didn't know her last name, but the man said he knew who I was talking about, because Bentham is such a little town. So we went to her house."

"Was she at home?" Annie asked, moving among the dripping young men and throwing a blanket around each of them. "Did you find Marjorie?"

She nodded at one of the kitchen maids, who took a steaming teapot and filled a row of teacups waiting on the kitchen counter. After asking each one how he took his tea, she handed out the cups.

"No, ma'am," Matthew said. "We didn't find any sign of her at all. Now her parents are worried and for good reason. They've called Chief D'Amato, and he's sent people out to look for her."

I slipped into the study and asked the operator to ring Devan's number. I was so relieved when he picked up the phone. At least he wasn't out wandering in the storm.

"Did you find Mrs. Jamison? Is she okay? Are you okay?"

"I did and I am," he said. "I took her home, and she's as okay as she can be under the circumstances. She's not over whatever it is that caused her to fall apart at your party. I know that for sure."

"She shouldn't be. I've still got a house full of people, but I'll fill you in later."

"What about you? A woman just cursed you out in front of the leading lights of Bentham-on-Hudson."

I didn't need to stop and think about whether Eva Jamison's words had hurt me. They hadn't. "When I tell you what I've learned, you'll know that I'm sincere when I say that I couldn't care less what those people think of me."

"If it matters, I think a lot of you. And I think of you a lot. I have a feeling that little Bentham-on-Hudson is about to turn into a powder keg, but I can't say just how. I would ask you to lay low. I'd ask you to lock yourself in that stone fortress of a house you live in and let the storm pass, but that's not the kind of person you are."

"You've only known me a week, but you seem pretty sure you know what kind of person I am."

"Sometimes, you just know. You're a rare person, E. I can see that. Please stay safe so I can have a chance to know you better."

"I've never taken a physical risk in my life, so you can feel pretty confident that you'll have that chance. I sense that you're pretty rare, too. And I can't abide boring men."

The warm sound of his laugh made me want to walk all the way to Bentham and crawl into that deep, deep bathtub with Devan.

"Make me a list of not-boring things to do if I ever see you yawning."

Now I was the one who was laughing. "I'll do that. But right now, I have to go deal with a house full of people."

"You do that. Call me when you can. I'll see you soon."

☙❧

Annie stoked the kitchen fire and made the soaking-wet footmen stand in front of it. I handed around the rest of my father's five hundred dollars in tips for all the borrowed servants. They'd worked hard, and I didn't want his blackmail money. Since my whole existence had been paid for with it, I had some thinking to do about my life.

Annie handed food around, packed in the lidded glass containers she used to store leftovers. "I fed everybody else while you gentlemen were gone. There's no sense in you sitting in your wet clothes to eat, but there's also not any sense in you going hungry because you were out searching for that poor girl. Mrs. Bakker will make sure the containers get back to me. How are you getting home?"

"Mrs. Bakker lent us two of her cars." Matthew said. "I can drive, and so can Doyle. We'll get everybody home."

The Bakkers must be wealthy indeed if they owned more than one car—more than two!—but I already knew that by the herd of servants they employed. I would once have winced at the thought of someone so rich knowing that we couldn't waste money on replacing everyday glassware, but I had come to the end of caring about such things.

Annie shooed the servants out the door, then she took Mother and Dr. Masters by the hands. "Come. You two are staggering on your feet. I had the guest rooms made ready in case anybody was too tipsy to go home, so I've got a bed for you, Dr. Masters. And, Madam, your bed is turned down for you, as always."

Dr. Masters didn't think twice. "Thank you so much. I wasn't looking forward to the drive."

Annie ushered them up the back stairs, calling over her shoulder, "The kitchen's clean except for the teacups. I'll be back down to finish them up."

"Don't be silly, Annie," I said. "I'll do them. Go to bed. After the week you've had, I hope you sleep until noon."

❦

Leontine and I washed the teacups in our evening gowns, then we went back to the library. I couldn't stop staring at its windowless walls and its thirty-two bookshelves, each of them eight shelves high.

I was haunted by the number thirty-two, and not because I would turn thirty-two on my next birthday. I had encountered the number recently, and it had been someplace significant. Where was it?

When it came to me, I took the stairs two at a time to get to my bedroom. Under my bed was my mother's book. It had helped me find her, but maybe it held more information than I'd realized—more information than even she realized.

I had a theory.

I opened the book to the table of contents. Yes, I had remembered correctly. My mother's book consisted of thirty-two poems, all of them marked with pencil lines and cryptic markings.

Each of those poems were in Emily Dickinson's favorite rhythmic scheme. Common meter—eight syllables in the first line, six syllables in the second line, eight syllables in the third line, and so on, all in iambic pentameter. Other poets might cheat those metrical requirements, but not my mother.

Also, her poems all consisted of two quatrains, making them eight lines long, and all of father's bookshelves were eight shelves tall.

And how had he hidden the photos I found? They were tucked into the first eight books on the first shelf I searched, the first six books on the second shelf, and the first eight books on the third. Each of those books corresponded to a syllable in one of Mother's poems. Each shelf of books corresponded to a poem's eight lines. And each of the thirty-two bookshelves corresponded to one of her thirty-two poems. No wonder he had tried to destroy the whole print run of her book. It was the key to his personal filing system. If anybody else ever got their hands on a copy, they might have decoded it.

Maybe Mother had seen how important one particular copy of her book was to him, even if she hadn't understood why. Maybe that's why her book was the object she chose to throw off Rockfall Bluff on a day when she was very, very angry with him. Maybe that's why, moments later, he had slapped her to the ground.

Had Dr. Jamison brutalized Marjorie in the same way? I felt the absence of Marjorie in my chest, a phantom pain that would be there until she was found.

I turned to the first poem in my mother's book. I saw again the marks on the page, the ones that I had thought she'd made, but no. They were Father's notes to himself. The marks were cryptic, it was true, but they were the key to the blackmail material he'd hidden in the library. I knew it.

Perhaps the letters in the margins were initials of his victims. Perhaps the underlined syllables corresponded to the most incriminating photos. Perhaps other marks stood for places and times.

Given unfettered access to his books, a deep understanding of the poems of Emily Dickinson, and my lifelong knowledge of the ways my parents thought—and I had all those things—I could have figured it out.

What I didn't have was time.

CHAPTER 29

Leontine, who knew her Dickinson, understood my father's code instantly. "He was using her book like a library would use a classification system. Like the Dewey Decimal system." She scaled the nearest rolling staircase in her peau de soie heels. It was so tall that her head disappeared into the darkness above the highest shelves. "That's because he couldn't use a publicly available system to organize his blackmail material. He had to invent his own."

I thought about how my father would have operated as a blackmailer. He was an exceedingly dramatic man. "He could have just hidden it all in files in the basement, but keeping some of it out here in the open suited him. He could invite a victim over, pull a book off the shelf, and show a piece of evidence that established his dominance. It would have been like dropping a bomb. And then, because he had a mean streak, he could throw a party later, fill the room full of his victims, and enjoy the stink of terror while he sipped his wine."

She peered down from above. "You say that there's a ton of other stuff in the basement?"

"Yeah. So if somebody threw a tantrum like Mrs. Jamison's and managed to destroy some of his incriminating evidence, there was always more where it came from."

I grabbed my father's wooden pointer, still leaning on a bookshelf near the head of the banquet table. "Can't you just see him using this thing to point at a book holding evidence that could send the poor soul in front of him to jail? Or get them fired? Or end their marriage?"

I held it up as high as I could and pointed at the first eight books on one of the very top shelves, chanting out an iambic rhythm. "Duh-DAH duh-DAH duh-DAH duh-DAH." Moving the pointer to the second row, I tapped on the first six. "Duh-DAH duh-DAH duh-DAH. If you open those books, you'll find things that people wanted to hide. I guarantee it."

I pushed Leontine's ladder into place to make it easy for her to check. She did, and she found exactly the kind of things we'd expected.

She found arrest reports. Bankruptcy paperwork. Birth certificates for children who lived far away from their straying fathers. That night, I learned that our mayor had done jail time in another state for assault. And I learned that Chief D'Amato had a history of looking the other way if somebody offered him enough cash.

I couldn't figure out the significance of everything we found, but one old newspaper clipping included a photo that was a shocker. The image showed dozens of smiling faces. The people wearing those smiles were standing in Bentham-on-Hudson's riverside park dressed in their best clothes, as if they'd just left church. Behind them, though, was a row of masked hooded people in white. One of them carried the red-and-white flag of the KKK. A banner held aloft by two of the people wearing their Sunday best read, "ANNUAL PICNIC OF THE KU KLUX KLAN."

There, in the front row, was Marjorie's genial father and his dimples, just like hers. Standing next to him was a young woman with her dark eyes. There was no dark-eyed child with them, so at least they hadn't brought their daughter to this thing.

My father hadn't bothered to save the part of the page that showed the date—I suppose everybody concerned knew when the picnic had happened—but my guess was 1920 or shortly after, based on the cars parked in the background. I would have been in elementary school. Leontine would have been younger. Marjorie would have been about the same age as Leontine.

The newspaper had reported the event as it would have covered any social gathering in those days, because in some ways it had been just another social gathering in the 1920s. The Klan had lost a lot of ground in the Northeast in the years since, and social pressure had led many of its members to throw a veil over that part of their past.

But as much as they might want to pretend the meeting hadn't happened, it had.

There had been a brass band beside a platform set up for dancing. There had been political speeches, souvenirs, refreshments. A minister had baptized babies outfitted in tiny white robes and hoods. I recognized the minister's name, because he had preached at a local church until I was in high school. After the sun went down, the attendees had stood under the light of a burning cross, fifteen feet tall.

I studied the photo of the attendees, and there they all were. Behind Mr. and Mrs. Steed, my dinner guests were looking back at me. I might not have recognized their faces otherwise, as the photo was at least twenty years old, but they had signaled their guilt by fleeing my father's library. There, on the left, were Chancellor and Mrs. Hampstead. They were many pounds lighter and minus the gray hair and sagging jowls, but it was them. She was cradling a baby who must have been the son preparing to graduate from Bentham College within a month. A young Professor and Mrs. Schmidt stood next to them, his arm curled protectively around her pregnant body. Dean Jamison and his wife, even younger than the others, stood on the right side of the photo, near Professor Hanssen and the wife who had left him. In 1920-something, they all looked very happy about their membership in a fraternal organization centered on hatred.

The Klan had lost the grip it had held on the nation in the 1920s, but I'd heard rumors of a resurgence. There were assuredly people across the country who still held the KKK's views, but in 1942 New York, acknowledging this past would have been exceedingly socially awkward. Fortunately for the former Klanspeople among us, human beings are very good at sweeping social awkwardness under the rug, when they want to.

I showed it to Leontine, perched on the top step of her rolling staircase. "This is too much, E. I can't believe any of it's true. But it is."

I wasn't wearing my watch, because social convention said that ladies didn't worry about time while at a party, but I knew it was late. "We should go to bed and come back to this tomorrow. It's going to take some time to get the full picture of what my father did, and D'Amato's crooked, so we can't go to him with our suspicions. We need to figure out a safe place to take our evidence."

"No, I'm not ready for bed. I just want to read this stuff and try to understand what it all means."

I was a little relieved to hear her say that, because my curiosity had me in a stranglehold, too. I wanted to know…what? I guess I wanted to know everything.

I pulled a chair next to the bottom of Leontine's rolling ladder and settled myself below her, searching books and studying the evidence as I found it.

I'll admit that my mind wandered. How could it not, when I was sitting in the room where I learned the truth about my father…the truth about most of the people I knew?

Dr. Masters seemed to have escaped my father's evil. There had to be some people in the world that even he couldn't blackmail.

Leontine had stood her ground when the others fled. This showed that she was a true friend. I still considered Marjorie my friend, and I always would, but she believed that her parents' guilt had somehow spilled over onto her. I hoped she was wrong, as I wanted no part of my father's guilt. I prayed that Marjorie was safe somewhere.

John had left before the ruckus started. His face wasn't in the KKK photo, and his name wasn't in the Nazi article. I hadn't found anything yet that would embarrass him, and I hoped I wouldn't.

Devan had left at about the same time as the guilty parties, but he'd left to take Mrs. Jamison home. Besides, he was brand-new to Bentham. My father was dead before he moved to town. There was no reason to suspect Devan of wrongdoing, was there?

This took me to a question I couldn't answer. Dr. Bower had also moved to town after my father died, coming out of retirement to take one of the positions vacated by professors who had gone to war. Why did he leave the party with the others?

The word "war" bounced around in my head. I remembered the terrible scene after Professor Jamison's suicide. I remembered Dr. Bower's comforting presence as we knelt beside the carnage. He'd said he knew my father.

I knew him during the war, the last war. We served together.

I also remembered what he'd said later, when I asked him what they'd done in the military. He'd said he couldn't tell me, and I'd asked, "After all these years?"

I could hear his answer as clearly as if he'd been standing in front of me.

Yes, after all these years. Same enemy, y'know. You could almost say that it's the same war.

My thoughts turned to the shadowy men filling in for other professors who had gone to war. I couldn't believe that they were who they said they were. They had been sent to Bentham-on-Hudson to keep an eye on the real professors in fields like military science, physics, and chemistry, any of whom could be doing research on weapons that would be valuable to the Allies. Or to their enemies.

They had someone doing surveillance in the political science department, where the enemy could have planted fascists or communists to sway the minds of impressionable students. The last thing that a nation at war needed was a revolution from within.

I was pretty sure that they had also planted a spy in the mathematics department. Leontine had said the shadowy professors were very interested in Dr. Bower's work on number theory. But what if there were two spies. Dr. Bower, too, had come to campus since the war. Why hadn't I lumped him in with the quiet strangers I suspected of spying on the people of Bentham College?

I supposed it was that Dr. Bower's story held up under scrutiny. He was about the right age to be a retired professor. He had enough social skills to perform the role of a senior scholar with limited self-awareness. In short, he was a better actor than the others.

Also, he had won my confidence in an unexpected way. He had told me that he knew my father during the last war, and Father *had* worked for the military in England during those years. It wasn't that I was primed to trust someone who knew my untrustworthy father, but I was rational enough to accept a story that made logical sense. To my chagrin, I realized that I should have paid attention when my mother didn't recognize him, but my father had spent my whole life making it clear that he thought she was irrational. His dismissal of her intellect had rubbed off on me.

But the fact that my mother was confused about whether she remembered Dr. Bower wasn't proof that he didn't work with my father on wartime projects. And that is how I would have described her response to Dr. Bower's reminiscence—confused. The point was not that she didn't remember him. It was that she was hiding her lack of the memories Dr. Bower wanted her to have, because he was so very convincing. He remembered her favorite card game, he remembered her favorite recipes, and he had used those things to convince her that she should remember him, too.

How lucky it was for him that she was a recent mental patient who was vulnerable to accusations of instability. She would have been terrified to contradict him—a respected professor—and open herself to the possibility of being put away again.

But how did he get information that was only available to people who knew what my parents did during quiet evenings at home? It was very intimate information. I supposed spies had their sources, but how many people alive remembered what my mother had been like in her twenties? Now that my father was gone, perhaps nobody did. And yet Dr. Bower, whom she didn't remember, had hit the nail on the head.

I was sure now that my mother was not unstable. If she didn't remember this man, then they had never met, but his knowledge of euchre and Dorset apple pie made me think that he had known my father well. More to the point, he had known Father well enough to hear him brag about the lovely young woman he had wed. Of course my father had told his friends that his bride was a beauty, an excellent cook, and a fearsome euchre player. The man did love to brag.

Once I accepted that Dr. Bower's story of working with my father during wartime was true, it was possible to see what an excellent espionage team my father and Dr. Bower would have made. Father spoke Russian, French, German, and Italian. Dr. Bower was educated in an era when his doctorate would have required him to speak a similar assortment of languages, even as a math student. Two polyglots, one with advanced training in words and one with advanced training in numerical methods, would have been a fearsome team in creating and breaking codes.

Codemakers and codebreakers handled secrets. And secrets were the very air that a blackmailer breathed.

There was no possibility that Father had failed to steal the military secrets that passed through his hands. It was not in his nature to let valuable information slip away from him. And now we were at war with the same enemy. As Dr. Bower had said, you could almost say it was the same war.

The people at Bentham College might have thought Dr. Bower was doing them a favor by coming out of retirement to fill a vacancy during wartime, but I didn't think that was why he'd come to town. I was pretty sure he'd come for the military secrets my father stole. Why else was he ingratiating himself to Mother and me, pretending to be a family friend?

This thought took me someplace that I didn't want to go. Devan, too, had done Bentham College a favor by filling a vacant faculty position. It was just as possible that he had been sent to retrieve my father's stolen secrets.

I thought of the stacks of files in the basement below me, all filled with yellowed paper, hidden behind a secret door in my father's darkroom. People on both sides of the war would have paid my father handsomely for them, if he'd lived. He had been intelligent enough to foresee that the great war wasn't over just because an armistice had been signed. He had also been intelligent enough to know that he could sell those secrets to either the Allies or the Axis.

That left only two questions. Which side sent Dr. Bower to retrieve my father's secrets after he died? And did they also send Devan?

I knew the answer to the first question as soon as I'd asked it. All the Allies had to do was ask me, and I'd give them everything I had. Surely, their intelligence agents were good enough to know this about me. Besides, if I didn't, they could throw me in jail. This meant that Dr. Bower had been sent by the enemy, probably the Germans, since Father's secrets had been retained from the last war we'd had with them. And perhaps the Germans had sent Devan with him.

I started to tell all this to Leontine, but the sound of a creaking stair stopped the words in my throat. It was coming from behind the door to the basement corridor. Somebody had been hiding below us and now they were coming up the stairs.

I remembered Dr. Bower's coat on the floor of the entry hall closet. He didn't leave it behind because he was in a hurry to flee my house. His coat was still in my closet because he'd never left. He'd disappeared unnoticed into the basement during the furor after Mrs. Jamison's breakdown, and he'd been waiting there for us to go to bed.

Leontine and I had been silent for at least fifteen minutes. We were in a room with no windows and four tightly closed doors. No light could possibly escape. Dr. Bower had no way to know we were still there, and he was coming.

Leontine had heard the creaking step and was sitting frozen high above me. I handed my father's wooden pointer up to her and mouthed one word.

"Hide."

Without a sound, she took the pointer and crawled into the shadows at the top of the bookshelf where I stood. Even in a formfitting crimson gown, she made this maneuver look effortless.

If I'd had any doubts that Dr. Bower was collaborating with the enemy, they left me when the door from the basement corridor opened, and he came through it, gun first.

CHAPTER 30

"Dr. Ecker." Dr. Bower's voice was cool, precise, clinical. "You have something I want. You have a lot of things I want. I believe that some of them are in this room. The rest? Probably downstairs. I've been in your basement since your party broke up, and I found some valuable paperwork sitting right out in the open. Who knows what lies behind the various doors and walls?"

"Why should I give them to you? You're going to kill me either way. If I hold my tongue, you may never find them all."

He shifted his weight, widening his stance and adjusting his aim. My chest tightened as I saw that the slight movement of the gun's barrel pointed it directly at my heart.

"You are correct. You are a dead woman because I can't have you telling the authorities that I took the documents. I can't even have you telling them that there were documents here to take. But if you tell me where your father hid his secrets, nobody dies but you. If you refuse and I kill you for it, my orders are to make sure nobody gets them. To do that, I'll have to burn the house down with your mother in it. Along with that fussy housekeeper you're so obviously fond of."

Mother. And Annie.

And Leontine and Dr. Masters, too, but he didn't know about them.

I eyed the handgun pointed in my direction. Its metal was shiny in a way I found hypnotic, and the hole at its muzzle's center was the blackest black I'd ever seen. There would be no bullet coming out of it until I gave him the information he wanted or until he was sure that I never would.

This only gave me a little time, but it was time. All I wanted in that moment was more time. Was this how my father felt as his mind left, little by little, until he finally went with it?

"What will it be, Dr. Ecker?"

In theory, I was going to take the option that gave everyone else in the house a fighting chance. That's what they would have if I took him into the basement, leaving Leontine to emerge from hiding and get Annie, Mother, and Cynthia Masters out of the house.

I couldn't know whether showing this man my father's darkroom and the secret room within it would cause the deaths of soldiers or civilians, but I knew for sure that refusing to do so would doom four people who didn't have to die. The decision seemed obvious, but I was having trouble making my mouth form the words that would lead to my death. I suppose this is how we all spare ourselves from thinking about the end. We stall for time, and we imagine that this will always work.

I was startled out of this paralysis when salvation fell from above.

I don't know how I had expected Leontine to use the weapon I handed her. Maybe I thought she'd hurl my father's stick down at Dr. Bower like a spear, but Leontine was a better strategist than I was. She jammed the pointy end of my father's wooden stick behind the bookcase towering over Dr. Bower, using it like a lever to push the top of the case away from the wall.

Dr. Bower only had a moment to react. Instead of using it to shoot me, he looked up. That's when books began to fall off the leaning bookshelf, like the sky above him was raining bricks. One of the books knocked the gun out of his hand and another broke his glasses, but he wasn't the kind of man to lose easily. He dropped to his knees and regained the gun.

I braced myself for a bullet, but Leontine wasn't done. She crawled onto the teetering bookcase and stood to gain more leverage, her head and shoulders pressing against the ceiling as she wedged the pointer farther down. Precariously balanced on the teetering thing, she pushed hard against the wall. When the massive bookshelf and all its remaining books fell, she rode it down. Dr. Bower fired once before he was crushed, but the shot went wild.

Leontine lay still atop the wreckage. I threw myself in her direction, desperate to find a pulse.

She opened her eyes and sat up, dazed but okay. She was also fully conscious, because she said, "I think I just killed a man."

I knelt to help her crawl off the debris, and then I stayed on my knees, moving splintered boards and smashed books. Part of me was trying to save a man who might still be alive, and part of me just wanted to be sure he was dead.

The doors from the entry hall burst open. My mother stood

there in a filmy white negligée, brandishing a sterling silver letter opener. Dr. Masters was at her side, wearing a pair of Father's red plaid pajamas. She was armed with a brass lamp and its electric cord trailed behind her. Annie arrived unarmed in a flannel nightgown, looking like she wished she had her rolling pin.

"What on earth?" Mother asked.

It was then that I heard a groan which fully brought home the gruesome thing that Leontine and I had done. I was as guilty as she was. I'd sent her up to hide with a weapon. The fact that she'd made better use of it than I would have didn't absolve me. If Dr. Bower was alive, we couldn't let him suffer. We had to get the bookshelf off him.

The groan sounded again, but this time I realized that it didn't come from Dr. Bower, whose silence and stillness were ominous. The sound came from all around us. The wind was howling, but was that enough to make a stone house groan?

This time it was Leontine who said, "What on earth?"

We had been in the windowless library for hours. How bad was this storm, really?

I walked past Mother, Annie, and Dr. Masters and opened the front door. I couldn't see much, but I heard the most torrential rain of my life. I could feel the din of it in my bones.

And again the house gave a sickening groan.

If it hadn't been for a brilliant flash of lightning, I would never have seen what was coming for us.

The lightning lit everything, like the bursts of light from the flash apparatus my father used when he didn't care who saw him with a camera. It showed me the surge of water that was coming over Rockfall Bluff, turning my father's man-made waterfall into a wide, violent cataract. The water was so deep and swift that it carried trees.

"The ponds," I yelled into the wind. "Their dams have failed."

Of course they had failed. My father stole stones from them to build his water garden, and he never considered the consequences.

Father built his life on larceny. Thievery defined him. His craven approach to life had succeeded impressively, for a time, but now his crimes were going to wipe away everything he had ever created. And one of those things was me.

The ponds at Stenen Klif Manor were not limitless. This flood had to end. But would it end before we all drowned?

It seemed unlikely. The ponds were downstream from the reservoir that had provided the mansion's drinking water. The reservoir was fed by a natural stream that drained rainwater from the entire top of Rockfall Bluff. Rain had been falling onto that watershed all week, and it was still falling onto ground that was completely saturated.

The temporary Niagara would flow down onto our property for as long as the storm lasted. It would keep flowing until the last of the stormwater went over the bluff. And our house stood directly in its path. No wonder it was groaning. I had two questions as I watched liquid death come for us.

How deep would the water get? And would the house hold?

That tremendous lightning bolt was followed by many smaller ones that flickered in the night. Along with the almost-full moon and the incongruously welcoming glow of our porch lights, the lightning lit the surface of the floodwaters rippling toward the top porch step, right where our guests had stood in their finest formalwear. I slammed the front door shut, as if it could stop the flood.

Several feet deep, the water was already exerting tons of pressure against the aboveground portion of the basement's wall. I was no architect, but I suspected that those tons were the source of the groaning. If the basement walls—the building's very foundation—failed, then the house would come down around us.

Leontine and I think a lot alike, but our conclusions aren't always exactly the same. At the same time that I said, "We've got to get out of here," she said, "We should call for help." We were both right.

I was right that we needed to leave. Leontine was right that it would be foolhardy to go out into that watery hell without telling somebody where to find us.

I ran to the phone and lifted the receiver, desperate to hear Selma's voice. She was well-capable of repeating what I said to anybody who would listen, so the town would know our predicament within minutes. But no voice came.

The line was deadly silent. In my mind, I followed its course, down through the floor, through the basement, and out through the basement walls. While he waited in the basement, Dr. Bower had cut the phone line.

He'd left the electrical line alone, but the odds were low that we'd have lights much longer in the storm. Thinking of the public utilities reminded me of the gas. If the stonework supporting the house failed, the gas lines would fail with it.

"Out," I bellowed, running into the entry hall where Mother,

Annie, Leontine, and Dr. Masters watched water seep under the door. "Everybody out. We can't stay here."

We all looked at the pile of books and wreckage piled on top of a man who had been alive minutes before.

There was no motion, no sound from the wreckage burying the man we had called Dr. Bower. He might or might not still be alive beneath it. I stared at the pile of books and boards. Did we have time to see whether he could be saved?

I thought of the gun he'd pointed at my chest. I thought of his calm statement that he was going to kill me, while inviting me to bargain for the lives of people I loved. I thought of his willingness to work for the enemy through two wars, selling out everyone around him.

It was a quick decision, because it had to be, but I made it, and I have never looked back. I would not let these people die trying to save that man.

"Leave him. We have to go."

Everything lit by the porch lights—the tent being tattered by the wind, the driveway beyond, and the head of the path leading downriver to Bentham-on-Hudson—was being quickly inundated by fast-moving water of indeterminate depth. If we waded into it, we risked being swept off our feet, either pinned to the house by the current or swept over the edge of the bluff. Upriver from the house, though, the land sloped slightly upward. We had to flee in that direction.

We couldn't get to that higher ground from the front door, but we had a chance if we went out the veranda door. I slung an arm around Mother and dragged her in that direction, and the others followed.

As I'd hoped, the cliffside path where Father had chased Mother all those months before wasn't flooded yet. The hulking bulk of the house was holding back the water, shunting all overflow around its downriver side. There was a good chance we could walk the Precipice Path to higher ground if we managed not to slip over the edge. Instinctively, we formed a single file line—me, Mother, Annie, Dr. Masters, and Leontine—with each of us holding on to the one in front of us with one hand while grasping the veranda railing with the other.

Have I mentioned the wind? Each step we took brought the risk of slipping off the bluff or being carried over the edge by the incessant gale. The pounding raindrops were a misery, making it nearly impossible to see or breathe, but it was the wind and the slick clay path that could kill us in an instant.

Rounding the corner of the house into the unseen was terrifying, but we found that the path's upward tilt kept it from holding water. More importantly, it angled away from the edge. We slipped, we fell, we picked each other up, but we climbed above the floodwaters, foot by foot.

In the boggy meadow where my father had struck my mother to the ground, our horror story took a detour through farce. Leontine and I still wore evening gowns, although we'd shaken off our high heels before we ever stepped off the veranda. Mother, Annie, and Dr. Masters were also barefoot, and they were dressed for bed. We all might as well have been naked, for all the good our flimsy clothing did. In the bog, we added mud to our indignities.

The mud sucked at our feet. When we fell, it covered us. When one of us sank down to the knees, the others squatted in

the mud to pull her out. The mud covered us, the rain washed it
off, and the process began again.

When we reached the far side of the bog, I judged that we
were high enough above the floodwaters to ride out the storm.
But where? I knew that the Meadow Path would take us to the
ruins of Stenen Klif Manor, but what then? Even if our way
wasn't blocked by the overflowing ponds, we would still be miles
from town, or even the nearest house. And who knew whether
parts of the path were flooded or washed out? The trees shading
the path looked like shelter, but a lightning strike would kill
us as surely as a fall from a cliff. We conferred and decided to
huddle a safe distance from the trees to wait out the storm.

Mother hid her face in my shoulder and said, "E, I'm so
afraid something will happen to you."

Leontine took my hand, the one that wasn't holding
Mother close. Dr. Masters—I should really remember to call
her Cynthia after all we went through together—took Mother's
hand, and Annie took hers. We waited, listening to the rushing
floodwaters and to the tree limbs banging together in the wind.
We felt the sting of a million cold raindrops. Below us, some
of my house's windows still glowed, but the light might as well
have been on Mars, for all the good it did us.

I should have realized that the warmly lit windows were a
bad thing. After we'd been huddled at the edge of the bog for
a timeless time, I heard a groaning like the one that we'd heard
from inside the house, but much louder. The water had been
pressing against the basement without ceasing, and that kind
of pressure can't go on forever with no effect.

When the basement wall gave way, it torqued the gas lines

attached to it. They quickly failed, too, filling the basement with natural gas. An electrical line must have suffered the same fate and had the audacity to spark. This sequence of events has to be true, because there is no other way to explain away the fireball that I saw rise out of my house, shooting up through the tower. The explosion blew out the windows of the cupola and flames shot out like Fourth of July fireworks. Those poor bats.

If anybody in town cared about us, they could look up at the conflagration and know that we were in danger.

Did they care? I didn't know.

Would they send us help?

Possibly, unless they had their own disasters to attend. And even if they sent help, how would anybody find us?

CHAPTER 31

We huddled on the rim of high ground surrounding the bog, but away from the trees, which were swaying in the gale. I didn't know what else to do.

The only thing I could do was think, and my mind took me to some terrible places. Were those Devan's footprints on the Garden Path? I remembered that he was trying to discourage me from going up there at the very instant I found them.

Was Devan also the person who had been watching my house from the cove? He knew a lot about boats, and he'd told me that he had access to Chancellor Hempstead's boat launch.

Was he working with Dr. Bower to do surveillance on my house, one spy on the water and one on the hillside?

And then there was the worst thought of all—was he seducing me to gain access to my father's stolen war secrets? Part of me hoped we were never rescued, because then I would never have to find out that this was true.

We heard great limbs thudding to the ground, reminding us that our best option was to hunker down and let ourselves be rained on for hours, hoping that things would change when the sun came up. Was this a reasonable hope? I wondered, but hope is a sturdy thing.

Mostly we waited in silent misery, but from time to time, Mother would say something like, "That silver evening gown is truly spectacular on you, E. I like the way it reflects the electrical storm, despite the fact that it's simply plastered with mud."

Leontine would answer with something like, "I designed it especially for electrical storms. Do you like the way the lightning highlights the sequins and spangles on my dress?"

And then we would all laugh and laugh, as if anything about our situation was funny.

I had forgotten that there was one more pond up top, far from the pools surrounding the ruins. It was far, even, from the reservoir. We knew exactly when that last pond failed, because of the stench.

It was designed for a practical purpose, so it took a great deal of pressure to rupture it, far more than it had taken to destroy the decorative pools. The dam holding back the waste generated by the old mansion's coal gasification plant held fast for a long time, but the storm had every intention of washing away all remnants of human habitation on Rockfall Bluff. Why would it spare the most disgusting one?

The released sludge smelled like melted coal and used motor oil, with a top note of mineral spirits. The odor pervaded everything. I think it was the odor that finally pushed me to despair.

The flood and the flaming gas leak had surely destroyed

everything my mother, Annie, and I owned. Our clothes, the glittering stained-glass windows, Annie's apron collection, the ornate wooden furniture, my childhood toys, the paintings, the rugs. The books—oh, God, the books.

I'd known in my head that all these things were gone when I saw the fireball go up. But I felt it in my heart when I smelled black, noxious waste rolling over Rockfall Bluff and enveloping the terraced water garden. From there, it would sweep through the vegetable garden and into what was left of the house. Everything would be coated in floating, stinking gunk, including Dr. Bower's body. Maybe the part of the house that wasn't flooded was still burning, and the coal waste would feed the flames.

The life I had known was over.

We'd done our best to choose a strategic location to wait out the storm, but we had failed. We should have been farther from the trees, far enough that we couldn't hear their groans as the wind battered them. We were close enough to hear one fateful tree's roots tear out of the ground. Once they were free, it plummeted toward us. The trunk missed us, but the five of were tangled in its wet, leafy crown.

"Is anybody hurt?" I yelled above the storm's din.

I could feel all of them moving, but it was an eternity before anybody spoke.

"I'm still here," my mother said, and I heard the leaves rustle as she stood.

Cynthia and Annie stood up beside her, saying. "Me, too."

I groped in panic through the leaves and branches. "Leontine?"

"I'm here." Her voice was strong and vital, but I could tell something was wrong. "There's something on my foot and something else across my chest. Heavy branches, I think. I can breathe okay, and I can wiggle my toes, so I don't think anything's broken, but I'm completely pinned down.

I groped through the leaves and found her leg, still wrapped in the silk of her ruined dress. I followed it down to her foot. "Is this the one?"

"Yes."

The limb pinning it was stout. There was no breaking it and there was no lifting it. "We need to dig under her foot to get her free. Can the rest of you do that? I need to check the one that's on her chest."

A day before, I could have never imagined my mother with her perfect manicure clawing at the dirt with both hands. And yet there she was, grunting—even cursing under her breath— between words of reassurance for Leontine. For all of us.

"I'll free her foot. There's only room for one person down here. The rest of you work on her chest. All will be well, dear. We'll have you up and around in no time."

In her way, my mother was heroic, and she always had been. My father had spent my entire lifetime hiding her light from me. And from everybody else.

Cynthia, Annie, and I set about the bigger task of digging a hole under Leontine's back, so that she could slither out from under that massive branch.

Then Leontine said, "There's another problem. My head is down in a hole or a hollow or something. It's filling up with water."

Cynthia immediately crawled through the network of tree branches toward Leontine's voice. "I've got her head in my lap. She's all right for now. I'll dig under her neck and shoulders so the water can drain down there, away from her face. That will buy some time while you three focus on getting her out from under this thing."

Leontine still had it in her to laugh. "I guess breathing is the important part."

I don't know how long we worked before I saw the light moving through the trees. I couldn't imagine what it was—A ghost? A will-o'-the-wisp? Ball lightning? St. Elmo's fire?—but I also couldn't imagine that a human being was wielding that light. Where could anybody have come from?

When I heard my name on the wind, I was ready to say that there was a ghost out there. Then the ghost used all my names. Well, all but Emily.

First, I heard "E! Can you hear me? Please." Then the voice cried out, "Estella! Dr. Ecker!"

I could barely hear the words, but I knew who was saying them. It was Devan calling out for me.

I rose to my knees to go to him, but I remembered Dr. Bower, probably dead now, lying on my library floor. I was certain that he had been a German spy using the cover story of filling an empty professorship at Bentham College. It was possible that Devan, too, had been sent by the enemy to get my father's war secrets.

Was Devan, whom I might possibly love, the man he said he was?

I remembered his lecture in my class. He had taught my research, showing no expertise of his own. Anybody could have given the same talk by simply reading my paper. He wasn't teaching classes of his own yet, so who could say whether his claim to be a Shakespearean scholar was true? I had seen no evidence that he possessed any qualifications whatsoever for his job (which should have been my job).

All I knew about Devan was what he had told me. Well, I knew from experience that he could sail a boat and drive a car and pack a picnic, and I knew that he truly knew how to kiss a woman, but that was about it.

Could I trust Devan? He might be no better than Dr. Bower, who had very nearly shot me. He could be standing out there holding a flashlight in one hand and a gun in the other.

Cynthia whispered in my ear. "I'm not sure we can keep her head above water much longer. It's rising fast."

If Devan was a fraud, he was a very good one. I remembered his kindness when I asked him to help me rescue my mother. I remembered that he let me do it my way, sending me off in his car instead of insisting on being in charge. I remembered his patience in teaching me to sail.

My father had been a con man through and through, but he never could have faked kindness, thoughtfulness, or patience.

Devan's voice cut through the rain again, louder this time. "E! Are you out there?"

The other four heard him, too. My mother tried to stand, but I pulled her back down.

I spoke quietly. "He's only calling my name. He doesn't know for sure I'm here. He has no way to know that the rest of you are here, and he might be dangerous. I'll go first. If I think we can trust him, I'll bring him here to help Leontine."

My mother was saying, "But what about you? No, E!" as I tried to stand.

I put my hand over her mouth. "Let me do this." And she let me go.

I had to stagger a few feet before I stepped into the beam of Devan's flashlight. He ran to throw his arms around me, repeating, "I didn't know where you were. I didn't know where you were."

He did not sound like a German spy who would trade my life for my father's secrets.

"I'm here. But Leontine's trapped, and she needs help. We're trying, but we're running out of time." I pulled him toward the downed tree.

"Leontine's here?"

"Leontine, my mother, Annie, and Cynthia Masters."

We crawled through the crown of the tree and found that Mother had freed Leontine's foot. Cynthia still had Leontine's face above water, and Annie had scratched out a cavity beneath her. Devan and I were able to lift the limb on her chest enough for the others to pull her free.

"Can you stand?" I asked Leontine.

She said, "Yes, I'm fine," but she was tottering.

"If it's okay, I'll carry you," Devan said. "It's way past time to get you all out of the storm."

This sounded great to me, but I didn't know how he planned to do it.

"How did you even get here?" I asked.

Leontine quit pretending she was perfectly fine and let him scoop her off her feet.

"Let's move," he said, striding down the Meadow Path into the woods. The trees terrified me, but we'd already had one land on us. I was ready to gamble.

"After the weather got so bad," Devan said, "I tried to call you, but Selma couldn't get the call to go through. I drove as far as I could but there was water all around your house. There I was, sitting in my car trying to figure out what to do, when I saw a big flash of fire."

"We saw it, too," Annie said. "My goodness, what a sight."

"At first, I thought I was watching you all die. Well, E, Annie, and Mrs. Ecker, at least. I didn't know anybody else was there. Then I thought, 'E's too smart to stay in that death trap. They're all too smart.' With the flood on two sides of the house and the cliff on the other, there was only one direction you could go."

"But how could you get here?" Cynthia asked. "We're completely cut off by the water."

"Not quite. E told me about Stenen Klif Manor's old driveway. I drove as far down it as I could—"

"I told you it was washed out pretty bad."

"But I was able to walk from there to one of the bridle paths that steered clear of the ponds. It took me around to this side of your house."

Something wasn't right about this statement.

"But I only took you on one bridle path. It doesn't do that."

He shifted his arms to get a more comfortable grip on Leontine. "I…um…may have explored those paths pretty thoroughly."

"This week? When it's been raining every day?"

"Um…ever since I moved to town."

I stopped in my tracks.

He stopped, too. Even in the dark, I could see him casting furtive glances at the others, as if there were things that he couldn't say in front of them.

"Were those your footprints? Was that you in the boat? Were you working with him?"

"It was Dr. Bower in the boat. I was sent to watch him. He was working for the Germans, and I was supposed to keep him from doing any more damage. He was not my friend. Nor yours."

If Devan had come to keep Dr. Bower from getting my father's secrets, then he must be working for the Allies. He had been using the bridle paths and carriage roads to keep tabs on a German spy watching me from a boat on the Hudson while he looked for a chance to get in my house. I supposed Dr. Bower was also watching to see who came and went. Any number of people could have wanted to get access to the war secrets my father had stolen.

"You already knew about the driveway before I told you. The entrance is overgrown. You'd never have been able to find it in the dark unless you'd been there before."

"Yes. Absolutely. But can we talk about this later? My apartment is tiny, but it has a working roof. I've got a fireplace and a bathtub to get you ladies warm again. I'd really like to get you out of the rain."

CHAPTER 32

D awn was breaking when we reached Devan's apartment, where we swapped our sodden evening gowns and night-clothes for Devan's entire wardrobe of pajamas. Then we used every tea leaf and coffee ground in his house, while he used his phone to get information that he dribbled out to us as it came in.

"Marjorie is safe. For some reason, she was hiding from the people looking for her. Once they gave up, she went home."

I knew why she was hiding. I hoped I'd be able to talk her out of the idea that her parents' shame was hers.

"Mrs. Jamison, on the other hand, has gone missing. I don't understand it. I took her home in my car. I watched her unlock the door and let herself in. But Selma, who is spreading way more gossip than she should, says that the Jamisons' next-door neighbor got worried this morning when she didn't answer the phone. The neighbor found Mrs. Jamison's front door unlocked and nobody home. There were wet footprints all over the first floor. There was a damp dining room chair next to her sewing basket, like she sat down in her wet evening dress to sew. The footprints led to the back door, which she also left unlocked."

That's what you do when you're not coming back.

Nobody ever found her body in the river, weighted down by rocks sewn into her coat pockets, but that's where I think she is.

⊗

John opened his house to Mother and Annie, and Cynthia went back to her own house. He offered a place to me, but that just wouldn't…it wouldn't have been comfortable.

Devan offered to let me stay with him, too. I no longer cared what anyone in Bentham-on-Hudson, outside of my family and friends, thought of me, but there was someplace else I wanted to go. "Leontine says she has a bed for me. She'll need help while her bruises heal, and we have things to talk about."

Leontine's car had been destroyed in the flood, so Devan drove us to her house and helped her limp to her sofa.

"Don't go yet," she said. "E, can you look in my mother's closet and pick out some clothes for Annie? My things will fit your mother better, although they'll be a little bit short. Pick out some clothes for yourself. And shoes. Take shoes for everybody. Maybe they'll fit well enough for now."

I bagged some clothes and shoes for Devan to take back to town, then we lingered by his car, enjoying the sunshine. "Leontine needs me for at least a day or two," I said. "I'll use that time to think about what's next."

"Can I be part of what's next?"

His arms were around me and I couldn't remember the last time I'd felt so warm. As he bent to kiss me, I said, "Oh, you are certainly what's next."

❦

Leontine's vegetable garden, unlike mine, was not drowned in water and coal gunk. She kept telling me to stop feeding her, and I kept cutting lettuce and pulling radishes. We ate the spring vegetables greedily, as if they brought warm sunlight right into our bodies. Bite by bite, crunchy salads and warm toast pushed the memories of that dark night away.

"So," Leontine said, munching on a broiled asparagus spear. "We know who killed Helena Frederick. What are we going to do about it?"

"Our evidence is gone, and it wasn't especially strong," I said. "We weren't sure that was Dean Jamison in the photo with her, and it's gone anyway. My father's dead, so he can't tell us. Even Helena's button is gone."

"There were the things Mrs. Jamison said in front of witnesses."

"Most of it didn't make sense to anybody but me. I'm the only person who knows what I said to her husband, and even so, there's a logical leap between what I said and the idea that he killed himself out of guilt over killing Helena. Nothing she said was even close to a confession."

Leontine's sense of justice was offended, and she wasn't wrong. "But the stitches in Helena's coat pockets still exist. You saw them."

"Helena could have sewn up her own pockets. Dean Jamison

could have done it. Hell. Maybe my father did it and helped dispose of the body, so that he could blackmail them."

Dignified Leontine actually snorted. "Could your father sew a stitch? Could any man who had been married since he was young, like Dean Jamison? I would swear on a stack of Bibles that Helena couldn't. When anybody at their house lost a button, Mrs. Frederick paid my mother to sew it back on. Rich people don't do anything for themselves. Mrs. Frederick wouldn't have taught Helena to sew, and you said the stitches were neat and tight."

"Tiny, even, neat, and tight."

"It had to be Mrs. Jamison. Even my mother respected her work. I'll tell D'Amato that."

"D'Amato is a crook. My father was blackmailing him over it. He'll only use our testimony to charge Mrs. Jamison if it suits him. More likely, he'll ignore it, because we don't have proof, because we're women, and because one of us isn't white."

"We have to try. Promise me."

I promised, but I knew what he would say.

Men in uniforms started sifting through the wreckage of my house as soon as the floodwaters receded. On the third day after the flood, I left Leontine napping while Devan took Mother and me to watch. When I saw the soldiers' faces, I recognized them as the silent men who had been pretending to be professors while they watched the rest of us for signs of treachery.

"You told them how to get into the secret vault in my father's darkroom?"

"Yes, and they've already opened it. It didn't even leak. We'll be able to get everything he hid there. They're picking through the rest of the house to see what else they might find."

My mother watched the men scavenging through her ruined possessions. "Knowing my husband, you'll find scandalous things hidden in his sock drawer."

My father's sock drawer was probably floating down the Hudson, and Mother knew it.

"If the Army finds any salvageable personal items, we will of course return them to you."

With the word "we," he claimed his place in the armed service that had sent him and his fellow fake professors to get my father's secrets or destroy them. I supposed they had also been watching me to see whether I was as traitorous as my father. Instead, they had found that Dr. Bower was the traitor, and that he was trying to get to my father's secrets before they did.

Now the Army was going to take Devan away from me.

"I want nothing from that house," my mother said.

"Oh, Mother. Your book. The last undamaged copy is gone. Hardly any of the poems in the copy I gave D'Amato were readable, even if we could get him to give it back." I should have thought before I blurted it out, but I didn't.

Even if she'd kept the manuscript after she had the book printed, it would have been in the house, so it was gone, too. Her poems, irreplaceable, were floating down the Hudson with my father's sock drawer.

"Oh, there's another copy."

"I thought Father destroyed all but the marked-up one he

used for his library system, which you saved for me, and the one that you threw over the cliff to spite him."

"There's another. Cynthia has it." She turned a calculating look at me. "I wrote it for her."

The poem about a love that reached across an ocean... I was right that it was about an American, but I was wrong about which American. I tried to remember whether any of my mother's poems had ever used the words "he" or "him." I was pretty sure that none of them did. My father wasn't the only person who had used my mother's poems as a code.

"Cynthia is very lucky," I said. "You're both lucky."

CHAPTER 33

I washed the mud of Bentham-on-Hudson off my feet as soon as humanly possible, and I see no reason to ever return. I see no harm in leaving my father's grave unvisited.

The grave of Helena Frederick is a different matter.

As expected, D'Amato laughed at Leontine and me and our silly, girlish idea that a few stitches in black thread could solve a murder. We went straight from the police station to Helena's parents, who didn't think we were silly at all. They listened. They believed us when we said that we were sure that Dean Jamison had killed their daughter and that his wife had helped him cover it up. They said that it gave them some peace to have a story that explained their loss, even if they could never prove it was true. Sometimes, faith is enough. The Jamisons' guilty consciences, in their view, had brought their daughter a kind of poetic justice, which is better than no justice at all.

Devan, who will revert to his real name when we win this war, is necessarily vague about his work for the Army, but it brings him in and out of Lower Manhattan at random intervals.

He let it be known to his superiors that he could recommend somebody who spoke several languages and was a cracker-jack typist. I now work in Lower Manhattan on projects that require me, too, to be vague about what I do. I have spent the war working my way up through a series of civilian jobs that are increasingly interesting, even fascinating. It turns out that, as my father's checkered career showed, armies in a worldwide war need people who can communicate complex ideas in many languages, doing so in code when necessary. I feel useful, and this is more important to me than I could have imagined.

I can walk to work from my apartment, a shabby place that occupies the ground floor of a house older than my mother. A violinist lives on the second floor, practicing at all hours of the day and night. Two of my colleagues share the third-floor apartment, spirited and intelligent women who keep me company when Devan is away. A painter lives on the top floor, where the roof leaks but the light is perfect. None of them gives Devan a second glance when he comes to visit a single woman for days on end. And for nights on end. They have more interesting things to do than worry about how we live our lives.

Mother sold the ruined house, the land under it, the grounds of Stenen Klif Manor, and the surrounding woodlands—all of Rockfall Bluff—within days of the disaster. The proceeds will support her and Annie, comfortably but not lavishly, for the rest of their lives, and I am at peace with this use of Father's dirty money. They now live on an Upper East Side block where the modest but tasteful homes are just right for people who used to be rich. Their relationship treads an ever-blurrier line between employment and friendship. Annie will always make the tea, because she does it better, but Mother has baked me some more-than-acceptable biscuits, and I have actually seen her with a broom in her hand.

John is the new owner of Rockfall Bluff. His offer to Mother was most generous, which she took as a chivalrous gesture. I see it more as an act of repentance, or perhaps a strategic move to hide his guilt, as settling my affairs in Bentham-on-Hudson uncovered certain irregularities. All evidence suggests that, although my father believed himself to be the ultimate con man, he was being fleeced by John for decades. I have reason to believe that Oscar Glenby helped John bilk my father and that John sent him to tell me that my paintings were worthless. It was in their interest for me to keep the collection intact until they could figure out how to cheat me of its value, but the watery end of Rockfall House and its art collection put a stop to that plan.

In short, I suspect that John's desperate desire to marry me was less about my irresistible animal appeal and more about his desire to take the rest of what I had. And about his fear of being found out.

I do believe that Mother dodged a bullet. If she hadn't had Cynthia, John might have been able to convince her to marry him, allowing him to cover his theft forever. And probably to cover some other things, since I hear that he is seen regularly around the city in the company of extraordinarily good-looking men.

Instead of marrying Mother or me, John married Marjorie. They have recently moved into a palatial new home on the grounds of Stenen Klif Manor. He had the ruins bulldozed, leaving just a few scenic stones in the garden, at the same time he bulldozed the remains of our house. I hear that, on warm days, the smell of coal gasification waste still wafts through Bentham-on-Hudson. This is a problem that John and Marjorie cannot solve with money.

I tell myself falsehoods when I think of Marjorie. I tell myself that she may be happy with John. How do I know that she isn't?

I know. She can't possibly be.

John is wealthy and handsome, but those things don't matter so much when you're alone in the house with the man you chose. I grew up believing John to be a kind man, but now I know that his kindness covered the fact that he was stealing my family blind. I see no reason for a man like John to go out of his way to be kind to Marjorie. There's nothing in it for him.

What I do see is that Marjorie is punishing herself, not for her parents' wrongs but for her own. The day that Dean Jamison died is engraved on my brain. The sights…the sounds… They will never leave me.

The first thing I heard was a long piercing scream. After that, there was a short brittle one. And after that, I heard pandemonium as many people leaned out their windows and cried out in shock. One of them was Marjorie yelling, "Dean Jamison! Oh, God, he jumped. Somebody help him!"

On the night of the storm, Marjorie looked at the shameful picture of her parents and gave a scream that I had heard before—short, lost, hopeless. Brittle.

I know how long it takes to run down the tower stairs at Hawke Hall, because I used to do it several times in a workday. If she left the tower room the instant that Professor Jamison went over the railing, she would have been descending while someone else gave the long, piercing scream. She could have made her short, brittle scream as she ran. If that sequence of events is correct, then Marjorie had time to get downstairs before she raised her window sash and called for help. I cannot know for certain, but it is not impossible that she pushed Dr. Jamison and then hurried to add her voice to the pandemonium.

If I were inclined to speak to Chief D'Amato about this, he would laugh in my face, as surely as he had laughed at Leontine and me about the stitches in Helena Frederick's pockets. But I am not so inclined. Mrs. Jamison is missing, and I believe she is dead. Dean Jamison is certainly dead, having paid for what I believe he did to Helena and Marjorie and who knows how many other women. I've decided that I don't need to know whether he died by his own hand or by Marjorie's.

Marjorie doesn't answer my letters, but I still write. If the time comes when she no longer wants to be the social queen of a town full of people she doesn't even like, she will need a friend to help engineer an escape from her wealthy, controlling husband. My mother didn't have anyone to help her, but I can do it for Marjorie.

I also have decided that I don't need to know why Annie stopped being able to find wild mushrooms that I know were there. I saw them in the woods with my own eyes.

I certainly don't need to know why she cooked her last mushroom harvest on the day she saw my father beat my mother. She told me that she had chicken in mushroom sauce waiting on the stove when he got home, just before his fatal collapse, but there were no leftovers in the refrigerator when I arrived. The chicken—and, more importantly, the mushrooms—were gone, despite the fact that she'd had no way to know that Mother wasn't coming home. She would have been cooking for the three of them, so why wasn't there any left?

I have a notion that she cooked up something dangerous, then had second thoughts about feeding it to him. I can imagine him striding into the kitchen and dipping a hunk of bread into the mushroom sauce before Annie was able to stop him. If I wished, I could also imagine him collapsing into a babbling heap as Annie realizes that my mother's location is locked up inside of his head. But I refuse to do that. I don't like to think of Annie in that kind of pain.

I have not looked up the symptoms of the poisonous mushrooms of the Hudson Valley, because I don't want to be seen with those books. I certainly don't want to make Leontine complicit by asking her to get them for me.

Thus, I choose to overlook Annie's changed relationship with wild mushrooms, just as I overlook the fact that her chronology of my father's last healthy day has always been hard to nail down.

As for me, my days are full of stimulating work. My nights, when Devan is away, are consumed with my writing. I followed Mother's advice and finished my novel. Its manuscript survived the flood because I left it in my Hawke Hall office. Other than a ruined evening gown, its accompanying undergarments, a jeweled barrette, a pair of platinum earrings, and a black lace jabot, that manuscript was my only possession to survive the night of Mother's party. I finished it in a white-hot heat, and it quickly found an agent and then a publisher whose interest was just as white-hot.

Unhappy People in Big Houses will be released this summer. My publisher is comparing it to *Rebecca* and *Jane Eyre*. My agent is talking to Hollywood. He has dreams of selling it to Alfred Hitchcock.

I live on my paycheck from the Army, and I plan to squirrel away my book income as insurance against…against what? Against becoming my mother, I suppose. Devan has asked me to marry him, and I want this very much. We both want children. But I never intend to play the role of an unhappy princess trapped in a castle.

I want to be the captain of my destiny, just as Devan is the captain of his. I hope that we are able to sail a course that keeps us together for life, but I will never consent to helplessness. He seems to find the notion of an active partner invigorating.

Most Saturdays, I take the subway uptown and spend the morning with Mother and Annie. And usually Cynthia, who makes frequent trips to the city. I imagine that she will soon retire and move to be with my mother. Outside the family, Mother maintains the fiction that Cynthia sleeps in the guest room, and that is her right, but it seems to me a heavy burden to fit your life to the expectations of people you don't know and don't respect.

On Saturday afternoons, I take the bus from Mother's house to Harlem to visit Leontine. With the money from selling her mother's house, she bought a bookstore with a chic apartment upstairs. The street in front of her store is a wide, busy thoroughfare like the ones she remembers from her childhood.

She hosts evening salons for people who like to read books and argue about them. They are attended by—and this is no exaggeration—literary lions. My arrogant professors at Yale pale in comparison.

Leontine is the doyenne of an intellectual world that would have been an unattainable fantasy for my social-climbing father. I once bumped into Langston Hughes as he left her shop, and I was too starstruck to even say hello.

On sunny Saturday afternoons, Leontine and I sometimes walk to the Hudson, the same river that still flows past the town where we were so unhappy. Mostly we look ahead, planning things we want to do and places we want to see, but sometimes we think about Helena Frederick. Perhaps Helena knows that people remember her, and perhaps this helps her rest better.

Devan arrives this evening, so I have the joyous task of making things ready. I must throw open the old double-hung windows that let in breezes and the sound of my neighbor's violin. I must take in the sheets hanging on the line, so that I can spread them, clean and fresh, on my bed. I must rush to the market and buy whatever food that the war, my pocketbook, and my ration cards will allow. Whatever it is, Devan and I will cook our dinner together in my tiny kitchen, and it will taste like love.

The war is a shadow on our happiness. There is no denying it. The war is a shadow on everything, but it also reveals the contours of our lives in sharp relief. Nobody is guaranteed tomorrow, but today? Today, we can choose to be happy.

Reading Group Guide

1. E is refused the title and salary of professor, and even a better office, simply because she is a woman. How would you navigate a world that didn't see you as equal to your male colleagues, despite identical qualifications?

2. Was there a room in your house or a particular object that, when you were younger, your parents didn't let you see or touch? What was it like to enter that room or touch that object for the first time?

3. Although there was little E could've done to prevent her mother's disappearance, she still feels guilt for not being there. Are there things you feel guilty about that you couldn't have prevented and were not your fault? Why is this so often the case?

4. How do E's friends Leontine and Marjorie support her throughout the novel, and how does she support them in return?

5. E's father has a very lofty view of literature, which influences what he believes his daughter should read. Do you believe there are certain books that shouldn't be considered "literature"? How can books of a variety of genres benefit us at different points in our lives?

6. Describe Annie's relationship to E. E claims Annie was more a parent to her than her actual parents—why is this the case? What makes a good caretaker?

7. After Helena was reported missing, Leontine's mother sent Leontine away to keep her safe, thereby missing out on many years of their lives together. Do you think this was the right decision? What would you do to keep the ones you love safe?

8. When E's mother returns home, E gets a chance to connect with her for the first time in her life. How much do you understand about your parents, and is your current knowledge different from your understanding as a child? Are there aspects of your parents' lives or personalities that you still don't understand?

9. If you had a house with secret doors and compartments, how would you use them?

10. E has a fear of turning into her father. Do you think this fear is warranted? How can abuse trickle down through generations, even after the abuser is gone?

11. If you came across E's father's store of blackmail photographs, what would you do with them? Would you continue the blackmail operation? Tell the military about the secret Nazis? Burn all the photos?

12. How does the war affect the events of the novel? How did such a massive war influence the lives of the people living through it, even if they weren't directly involved?

A Conversation with the Author

What kinds of research went into writing this novel?

I went to great extremes to research this one. I moved to the Hudson Valley!

I want to emphasize that the fictional Bentham-on-Hudson isn't based on my new hometown of Nyack, except perhaps geographically. Nyack is also a charming town with a long history that sits on the west bank of the Hudson, framed by scenic cliffs, but E's hometown's geography is more extreme. The town is smaller and farther from Manhattan. The bluffs are higher. Bentham-on-Hudson is more isolated and insular, and the people aren't as warm and friendly as I'm finding my new neighbors to be.

I drove around the Hudson Valley on both sides of the river, soaking up the ambiance of many small towns, then I blended them together and layered on a dark, disturbing vibe for Bentham-on-Hudson. And then I read up on the history of the region and added a few dark details that are true. The organizations I mentioned in the book did have rallies in the area, and my descriptions are based on the historical record, including newspaper articles and photos.

As for Bentham College and E's academic career…well…I am a university professor, and I have a PhD in English. I know academia and academics pretty well, so I read up on higher education in E's time, then I made everything darker…much, much darker than it actually was, I hope.

Did you have a favorite scene to write?

I think it was the party scene, although the scene where E finds her mother was a close second, because Lily is such a strong character and such an iconic presence in E's life that she doesn't have to say a word to be the center of everything. The party scene, though—I knew it was going to be important from the moment I started thinking about *The Dark Library*. I wanted it to evoke the devastating entrance of Daphne du Maurier's nameless protagonist in *Rebecca* to her own party, while still being new and different and true to E's character. (Unlike du Maurier's character, we know her birth name. She just doesn't use it.)

And so I gave E the thrilling anticipation of those pre-party moments as she waits in her fabulous gown, knowing her guests are gathering while she has the conversation with her mother that she's wanted for her entire life. What is more, her mother reassures her that she can release her fear that she's like her father, because she isn't. And then she descends the stairs and all hell breaks loose, because she looks just like him, and he was a monster.

Did you have the entire mystery plot planned out from the beginning of the writing process, or did you figure it out as you wrote?

I always need to have the basic structure of a story in my head before I start, especially a mystery. If I don't know what my characters have done and what they do and don't know, then I can't make their actions and words characteristic of them. And without that, they're just chess pieces being moved around so that the plot comes out right in the end. Other people find that this process works differently for them, but this is the way it works for me.

What do you want readers to take away from E's story?

Be yourself.

Chase your dreams.

Don't be afraid to love people. Some will disappoint you, and you might have to let them go in order to stay true to yourself, but love is worth the risk.

What have you enjoyed reading recently?

I'm currently reading *Things Fall Apart* by Chinua Achebe. It's so beautifully written in such spare, poetic language, and it is immersing me in a place and a culture that is so far from my own. Travel in space and time while inhabiting the mind of someone who is not you is the best thing about reading.

Acknowledgments

I am very grateful to Charley Wrather, who helped me with describing E's exciting sailboat excursion. He deserves all of the credit for the things I got right and none of the blame for the things I didn't.

Rachel Broughten, Chris Aurelio, Amanda Evans, Tony Ain, Anne Hawkins, Anna Michels, Diane DiBiase, and Beth Deveny all gave me their consistently excellent notes, helping me to make E's story the best it could be.

I'm also grateful to the towns and countryside and people of the Hudson Valley simply for being. I've moved there, so I clearly love the place. While some of the events in *The Dark Library* are based on historical events, Bentham-on-Hudson and its people are wholly fictional. The only overlap between Bentham-on-Hudson and the real Hudson Valley is their physical beauty.

About the Author

© Nadia Lombardero

Mary Anna Evans holds a PhD in English and an MFA in creative writing, both of which came in particularly handy while writing the story of *The Dark Library* and its troubled professors. She is also the author of the Justine Byrne Historical Mysteries and the Faye Longchamp Archaeological Mysteries, which have received awards including the Oklahoma Book Award, the Benjamin Franklin Award, and a Will Rogers Medallion Awards Gold Medal. Her essays on science and the environment have appeared in publications including the *Atlantic*'s Technology Channel, *EarthLines*, and *Flyway*. She is a professor at the University of Oklahoma, where she teaches fiction and nonfiction writing. Her scholarly interests center on Agatha Christie's depiction of justice and gender. She is the co-editor of the *Bloomsbury Handbook to Agatha Christie*, which was an Edgar Award nominee, an Agatha Award finalist, a Macavity Award nominee, and an HRF Keating Award finalist.